A Second Legacy

Also by Joanna Trollope
in Large Print:

The Men and the Girls
Next of Kin

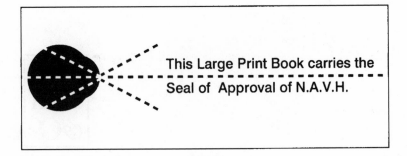

A Second Legacy

Joanna Trollope
writing as Caroline Harvey

G.K. Hall & Co. • Waterville, Maine

Published in 2002 by arrangement with Viking Penguin, a member of Penguin Putnam Inc.

G.K. Hall Large Print Core Series.

The text of this Large Print edition is unabridged.
Other aspects of the book may vary from the original edition.

Set in 16 pt. Plantin by Minnie B. Raven.

Printed in the United States on permanent paper.

ISBN: 0-7838-9742-1

Contents

Alexia

Chapter One

September 1965

"Oh, don't you mind *me*," the woman in the train said with heavy sarcasm. "You just carry on banging your case about." She twitched up the hem of her sunray pleated skirt and massaged a nyloned leg. "I always *did* bruise easy . . ."

"I lost my balance," Alexia said desperately. "The train lurched, that's all. And I did say sorry."

The woman sniffed. She dropped the hem of her skirt, and began instead, in a huffy sort of way, to rearrange her cardigan edges in dead parallel lines.

"No consideration —"

Alexia, already close to tears on account of having to leave Cornwall and return to hateful London, shouted, "I didn't bump you on *purpose!*"

"I never said —"

"No, but you implied it, you implied I'd done it deliberately. I didn't, of course I didn't, it's just that my case is heavy and I lost my balance, like I said!"

The woman said nothing, but merely watched

in offended silence, while Alexia manhandled her suitcase on to the luggage rack. Really, young girls these days, all the same, no manners, no nice feminine ways, no respect for their elders. She examined Alexia closely. Just as she'd expected — all backcombed hair and one of those dreadful fringes, and eye makeup like a giant panda and as for her skirt! She'd seen elastic bands wider than that skirt. Asking for trouble it was, wearing a skirt like that. She gave a tremendous sigh, to indicate to an invisible audience how forbearing she was being, sharing a railway carriage with a selfish dolly bird, and delved into her neat fawn plastic shopper for a barley sugar, and the *Daily Mirror*.

Alexia slumped in a corner seat as far away from her as possible and glared fiercely out of the window. The fierceness was necessary in order not to cry in front of a barley sugar–sucking stranger. It was always awful, leaving Cornwall and Bishopstow and the farm and Uncle James and Aunt Mary, but this time was the worst because all education was now finally over and with it the certainty of three long holidays a year. From now on, she'd probably only get to Cornwall for a fortnight a year. A fortnight! A small sniff escaped, try as she might to contain it.

The *Daily Mirror* crackled faintly. "There's no call to upset yourself," the woman said.

Alexia turned her face a little, keeping her head down so that her fringe provided a protective curtain.

"I hate leaving Cornwall, you see, I hate it. I hate going back to London."

The woman said, with the faintest hint of sympathy, "Got to go back to school then?"

"I left school at Christmas —"

"Oh yes."

"And then I did a secretarial course and now I've got to start a job —"

"That'll be nice."

"I don't think it will —"

The woman darted a glance at her. Some of the mascara had run and she looked more like a panda than ever. As an attempt at a diversion the woman said, "That Elizabeth Taylor's divorced Eddie Fisher if you please, and married Richard Burton just ten days later! It says so in the paper. Shocking, I call it. Give me Julie Andrews any day. I saw *Mary Poppins* four times last year, went with my sister. Lovely film."

"Yes," Alexia said politely. Privately she had thought *Mary Poppins* the acme of soppiness. Her own best film last year had been *Zorba the Greek* but there would be no point in saying that to the woman in the sunray skirt. She turned back to the window, to watch while the last of Cornwall gave way to the first of Devon or, in her view, where the romantic and free gave way to the tame and domestic.

She always wished she had been born in Cornwall. She had, in fact, been born in London, in a tall Georgian house in Culver Square, south of the river and close to St. Luke's, the great teaching hospital where her father was now a consultant. But her earliest memories weren't of Culver Square even if it was literally her birthplace; they were of Bishopstow, of lying in her

11

pram in the orchard under a branch of little red apples, of running across the wet sand of the wide beach nearby with slapping bare feet, of being allowed to sit up to table on a proper chair, stacked with a pile of cushions like the mattresses in *The Princess and the Pea.* When she had first gone to her senior school, Alexia had pretended that Cornwall was really her home and that she only came to London in term time for school, and her mother had discovered this and made her confess to her whole form and apologize to them for the lie. Even seven years later, Alexia still didn't think she'd told a real lie, in the sense of saying something that was deliberately untrue. She might have to spend more *time* in London, but time was nothing when her heart was in Cornwall.

"There's a picture of the Beatles here," the woman said, "I expect you like the Beatles."

"Not very much, I'm afraid —"

"I think they look like nice boys. Clean boys."

"They just don't make my kind of music —"

"Of course," the woman said, "of course to my mind nobody will ever hold a candle to Mario Lanza."

Alexia had no idea who Mario Lanza was. She said, trying to be friendly, "My Aunt Mary knows an awful lot about opera."

"Oh?"

"She's got heaps of opera LPs. She plays them while she does the farm accounts."

"Fancy that," the woman said. She looked across at Alexia. Such a pity to have red hair, even darkish red like that; always a mark of

12

temper, red hair. "You going to stay with friends in London then?"

"Oh no," Alexia said. "It's where my parents live."

"Do they? And your brothers and sisters?"

Alexia looked down again. "No. Just my parents. And me. That's all. That's all there is of my family."

At Paddington, Alexia hauled her suitcase down again and lugged it up the long platform to the Underground. It did not occur to her, even with a heavy case, to take a taxi. She had been brought up to believe that taxis were not only extravagant but also somehow immoral, and she had only ever been allowed in one once, when she had broken her leg playing lacrosse at school, and was encased in plaster.

It was a hot day for September, and the Underground was airless and grimy and crowded with people who regarded Alexia's suitcase with the same disapproval that the woman in the train had done. She bumped it with difficulty down the escalator to the Bakerloo Line, and then, once on the train, propped it up in the central space by the doors, where it fell over every time the train stopped. There was nothing for it but to stand beside it, wedging it with her legs, and endure it banging against her all the way to Waterloo, where she had to struggle with it from the Bakerloo Line to the Northern Line, going south. The case got heavier and heavier and Alexia got hotter and hotter, yet even as she emerged finally into the daylight with it, at Kennington Station, she felt resigned rather than furious. What else, after all, did she expect of getting back to London?

She certainly didn't expect anyone to be in at 17 Culver Square, and they weren't. Nobody was ever in, and Alexia couldn't remember, all her childhood, coming home to anyone except Edna, who lived in a council flat two streets away and cleaned the house and who had, until Alexia was fourteen, been there with a Marmite sandwich and a glass of milk when she got in from school. Alexia grew so used to Edna that she never asked herself if she actually liked her; she was just there, day in, day out, like a piece of furniture or the six o'clock news on the radio. Alexia didn't even know if Edna liked her either; all she knew was that Edna adored her mother. Everybody adored Alexia's mother. It seemed they always had. She'd been her father's favorite child, she was cherished by her two elder brothers, and by all accounts, she'd been hero-worshipped by everyone at school, and then in the war she had proved herself not just brave and resourceful, but compassionate too. Aunt Mary never tired of saying that she owed her sanity to Cara for what she had done for her during the war. "I know she may make the rest of us feel a bit inferior by comparison," Aunt Mary would say to Alexia, "but how can she help it, when she is such a wonderful person herself?" If Alexia had a pound, she sometimes thought, or even a shilling, for each time someone had said to her, "Your mother's a wonderful woman," she'd be a millionaire by now.

She'd only once rebelled. "Where's your

14

mother?" her father had said, when she was about fourteen — her father adored her mother too — and she had shouted, "I don't know! Why should I know? Out being wonderful somewhere, I expect!" He had been deeply shocked. He had explained very carefully to Alexia what a literal lifeline Cara was to so many people in Lambeth, with her crèche for the babies of working mothers, and her citizens' rights clinic and her chairing for the Friends of St. Luke's Hospital committee and her work for primary schools and youth groups and old people. "She is an extraordinary person," Stephen Langley said gravely to his daughter, "she simply never thinks about herself."

Alexia had gone up to her room at the top of the house after this, and had shut the door and lain down on her bed and put her face into her pillow. Then she had yelled into the muffling feathers, "She never thinks about me either!" Then she had cried for a bit, and chucked a few things around her room in temper, and that, really, had been that. Her father never spoke of it again and Alexia certainly didn't. What was the point of trying to confide in a person who clearly found you utterly, totally disappointing?

She put her latchkey into the lock and opened the front door. Silence. She heaved her case in and crashed it on the floor and then stripped off her skinny rib jersey which might be the last word in fashion, and just like the one Jean Shrimpton wore in magazine photographs, but it was also, that afternoon, the last word in overheating. Then, dressed only in her bra and skirt

15

and the white boots Uncle James had teased her about, she went down the steps at the end of the narrow hall to the kitchen.

The kitchen windows were shut, and several flies were banging noisily against the glass. Edna had also half drawn the curtains, horrible curtains which Alexia hated with black fish on them printed on a blue and white checked ground, so that the room was gloomier than ever. Cara didn't care about curtains. She didn't care about kitchens either. Some of Alexia's school friends' mothers were having new fitted kitchens put in with gleaming runs of matching cupboards and counters, all sheathed in Formica, but not Cara. Cara was perfectly happy with this awful kitchen out of the ark where nothing matched and there was holey linoleum on the floor, like in a school.

Edna had left a note on the table. It said, "Your fathers bringing 2 students to supper I've made a shepherds pie its in the larder your mother said for you to do the vegetables and theres some apples for baking no more milk for custard sorry Edna." There was no note from Cara. Alexia stood by the table, idly pinging a bra strap, and read the note again. She might be disappointing in terms of not being as brainy as her father or as socially committed as her mother, but heavens, they found her useful domestically. "She's rather a good cook," Alexia had heard Cara say once, to a friend, but she had said it in the tone she might have used to say, "She's rather a good toenail painter."

Alexia went across to the larder and opened the door. Edna's pie sat despondently on the slate

16

shelf, under a muslin dome. She always made shepherd's pies out of leftover cooked meat and the results were gray and tasteless. At least, Alexia thought, medical students were always so hungry they were grateful for anything, and at 17 Culver Square, anything was what they mostly got. She thought of the larder in Cornwall, the jars of jams and bottled fruits, the bunches of herbs and bay leaves, the hams, the baskets of eggs, the earthenware crock of butter, the strings of onions, the . . . Oh damn, Alexia thought, as a tear slid down her cheek and splashed on to her half-covered bosom, oh damn and blast, why does coming home have to be like this?

She toiled up the three flights of stairs to her bedroom. It was extremely hot up there under the roof, and stuffy, and it looked as if nobody had been into her room since she left it three weeks ago. It wasn't exactly dusty, it just looked tired as the air in it felt tired. She opened the sash window and the hot London afternoon barged in and brought noise with it, and the smell of petrol fumes and dust and the faint sweetish rotting smell from the dustbins that had been put out on the pavements of the square for collection.

Alexia sat down on her bed. Then she lay down and looked up at the ceiling. "I want *sea* air," she said to the ceiling. "I want sea air and the sound of the sea and my room at Bishopstow which my grandmother Alexandra had when she was my age — with flowers on the dressing table that Aunt Mary always puts out for me and cotton sheets, not beastly nylon ones just because they're easy to wash." She rolled over on her side and bumped into her childhood teddy bear who had been propped against the bedhead. She pulled him down into her arms and his fur rasped against her skin. "How do you bear it, bear? How do I bear it? Perhaps this job —" She stopped. Nobody could escape their dull lives via the kind of job Alexia had chose. She was ashamed of it already, ashamed before she'd even begun. She'd only insisted on it because she'd found it for herself and because it wasn't anything to do with medicine or hospitals or committees. She was going to work, as secretary and general dogsbody, for two women who had set up a tiny business making posh curtains for posh people, in their shared Chelsea house. They'd made a workroom out of the basement. One of them was called Amanda and the other was called Felicity. The Amanda one had dark sleek hair and wore black clothes all the time and sunglasses even indoors. She'd called Alexia "darling," but then she seemed to call everyone "darling." The Felicity one was blonde with a black velvet hair band and bubble pearl earrings. She was divorced. She said getting divorced was the best thing she'd ever done. The two of them were absolutely exactly the kind of people that Cara and Stephen Langley most despised, the kind they would call social parasites. When Alexia had told them that she'd be working for Amanda and Felicity, Cara had said, "I see." Nothing else, just "I see."

"It's just a start, just my first job —"

"I see."

"— to get a bit money —"

"I see."

"— and see if I like that kind of thing, if I like organizing, if . . . if I like —"

"I see."

Working for Amanda and Felicity would still mean living at home for the moment, because they would only be paying her seven pounds a week and she was sure she couldn't find a flat for much less than that, unless she went out to Acton or Ealing or somewhere even further away than Lambeth.

"Seven pounds?" Stephen said, "But with two A levels, it should be no problem for you to earn twice that. At a proper job. An intelligent job."

Cara said that as she would be earning, she should contribute two pounds a week towards food, and a pound towards gas and electricity.

"I'm not being mean, Alexia, but you have to learn what things cost, I don't want you just frittering it away down the King's Road."

"I hardly ever go down the King's Road."

"Don't split hairs, dear. You know what I mean. What will you save the rest for?"

"I don't know, I haven't decided."

But I did decide, Alexia thought, hugging her bear. I'm going to buy a car, a Mini, and I shall drive about in it in a chiffon scarf like Brigitte Bardot, and dark glasses . . .

Downstairs, the front door banged. Then there was an exclamation, a cross exclamation. Alexia sat up. She had left her case where she had crashed it, blocking the hall just inside the front door and whoever it was had just fallen over it.

"Alexia!"

"Coming, Mum," Alexia called. She crawled off the bed and opened the nearest drawer, and pulled out the first garment that came to hand. It was an old Aertex school games shirt, off-white with "A LANGLEY" embroidered in chain stitch on the breast pocket. She tugged it over her head, and ran downstairs.

Cara was standing in the hall, reading something that had just been dropped through the letterbox. Despite the fact that she wasn't in the least interested in clothes, she looked remarkably young and arresting for someone of forty-three, with her cropped dark red hair, and her trousers under a big man's jersey.

"Hello, darling," she said, not looking up. "Are you brown?"

"Look and see."

Cara looked, briefly. "So you are. What an idiotic place to leave your suitcase." She bent forward and gave Alexia the lightest of kisses. "James and Mary well?"

"Very. Sent lots of love."

"Look," Cara said, holding out the leaflet she was reading. "It's monstrous. The council is proposing to put the elderly at the top of those terrible new tower blocks they've built. The elderly! I ask you. They say it's for security. Huh." Alexia neither took the leaflet nor glanced at it. Cara went on, "I've got to fly. I just looked in to see if you were back and you are. Supper at seven-thirty, okay? I've got a citizens' clinic at eight-fifteen."

"Which vegetables?" Alexia said tiredly. She leaned against the nearest wall.

"Oh," Cara said with irritation, "I don't know. Why should *I* know which vegetables?"

Chapter Two

Supper was ready by seven twenty-five. Alexia had grated some cheese on to the shepherd's pie to make it look less depressing, and had then gone round to the greengrocer and bought two pounds of carrots and some runner beans. She hesitated about the runner beans; the ones in the garden at Bishopstow had been crisp and bright green, but these looked exhausted and floppy, as if they'd traveled for days, which they probably had. However, the alternative green vegetable was cabbage, and somehow Alexia couldn't quite face cabbage as well as Edna's shepherd's pie. So she bought the beans, and a block of vanilla ice cream from the tobacconist next door to the greengrocer to have with the baked apples, and took everything home.

It took her quite a long time to get supper because the telephone never stopped ringing. Some of the calls were for her father, none were for her and all the rest were for her mother. At seven o'clock, she took the telephone off the hook, so that she could lay the kitchen table with five places, cook the vegetables, find some cider and beer (her parents almost never drank wine) and have time to tease and brush her hair back into place and reapply her chalky pink lipstick. Then she went into the sitting room to pretend to read yesterday's paper and look as if she wasn't waiting for anybody.

At seven-thirty exactly, Stephen Langley let himself in. He was a tall thin man with a kind, serious face, who loved his daughter with all the love that was left over from loving his wife and career, which wasn't much. He brought with him two of his current students. Alexia had learned long ago not to get excited about medical students, who were, on account of having to be students for so long, pretty retarded in her opinion and only interested in beer and horseplay. This evening's students, one dark, one fair, at least looked a bit better than the usual run, but they'd turn out just the same, she knew it.

Stephen stooped to kiss her.

"You do look well. Have you had a lovely time?"

"Lovely."

"Where's Mum?"

"I don't know. She said she'd be back by now. She said she'd got a meeting at eight-fifteen."

Stephen looked worried. "I know. She's terribly tired. I'm trying to persuade her to cut down on her evening commitments —" He suddenly remembered something. "Alexia, this is John Mallory and Martin Angus."

"Hello," said John Mallory and Martin Angus, and grinned.

Alexia got up from the sofa. "Would you like some beer?"

There was the sound of a key in the lock. Stephen looked immediately relieved and went out into the hall.

"My mother," Alexia said in explanation.

Cara came into the sitting room with sparkling eyes, looking anything but tired. John Mallory and Martin Angus brightened at the sight of her.

"Hello, boys. Hello, darling. Supper ready? I'm in a tearing rush. What a day. Come along and let's eat. It's a dreaded Edna pie, I fear, but Alexia wasn't home in time to do anything more interesting. Did you bring us any goodies from Cornwall?"

Alexia said, "Last time I brought some clotted cream back Dad wouldn't let us eat it because of his new theories about fat clogging up the arteries —"

John and Martin laughed, and looked at Stephen in a familiar sort of way. Stephen said, "I'll be proved right, you know," and Cara said, "Of course you will, darling," and led everybody down to the kitchen.

Alexia sat beside John Mallory at supper. He was very tall and bony, with a thin, eager face and a shock of unruly dark hair. He ate with the careless ravenousness of a dog, and was really only interested in talking to Stephen about the secondary circulation of the heart. Alexia listened for a bit and said things like, "More carrots?" and "Could you pass the water?" but he didn't so much ignore her, as seem not to be aware that she was there at all.

Martin Angus sat opposite to her, and devoted himself to Cara. Cara told him a series of extremely funny anecdotes she'd heard at her weekly visit to the old Lambeth Laundry and Slipper Baths, which was where she picked up all her know-how about grassroots problems in the borough. Once she said, "Now, Alexia, tell us what you did in Cornwall," but the telephone had rung and by the time Cara got back to the table, she'd forgotten about Cornwall. While she was speaking on the phone, Martin Angus said to Alexia, "Are you going in for medicine too?"

He sounded polite rather than interested.

Alexia gave her stock response. "I'm not clever enough."

"I don't believe that —"

"And I expect I'm not really interested enough."

"Ah," he said. He put in a mouthful of pie. He didn't eat quite so doggishly as John Mallory, and he was better-looking, and more coordinated, with thick fair hair brushed straight back from his forehead, without a parting. "I like the cheese on this. It's a bit different."

"I was trying to cheer it up a bit —"

"Do you like cooking, then?"

"I like cooking for people who are interested in what they're eating," Alexia said priggishly, thinking of Cornwall.

"I see," said Martin Angus, and looked down at his plate as if he were trying to hide a smile.

"Maddening," Cara said, coming back to the table, "I'm losing one of my best helpers at the crèche because her husband thinks it's demeaning for her to look after other people's children, and he wants her to work in a supermarket where she'll be given a uniform —"

Alexia got up and began to clear the plates away. Neither of the young men made any move to help her. She got the baked apples out of the oven, and turned the ice cream block out of its cardboard sleeve onto a plate, and put both in front of Cara with a pile of dessert bowls. Cara said, "Ice cream! What a brilliant idea," and began to cut the block into slices.

Alexia said, "The Americans do it. They have hot pie and ice cream. It's called pie à la mode."

"Where did you discover that?"

"I read it in a magazine"

"Oh. A magazine —"

"But if there is a defective pulmonary function —" John Mallory began again to Stephen.

"I don't know what Lambeth would do without its public laundry," Cara said to Martin. "It's like an air raid shelter during the war, a refuge from everything threatening outside. People love it. It's where they can have a jolly good moan, and a laugh."

"Another apple?" Alexia said to John Mallory.

He looked at his bowl, as if amazed to find the first apple gone.

"Well . . . yes . . . I mean, yes please, I mean —"

She dolloped out more pie for him. What on earth could Mrs. Mallory be like? Was she, could she be, actually *proud* of producing this halfwit? She stared at Martin across the table.

"Another apple?"

He stared right back.

"No, thank you," he said.

At ten past eight, Cara whirled out of the house, Stephen and John and Martin went up to Stephen's first floor study, and Alexia began on the washing up. At a quarter past eight, the kitchen door opened, and Martin came back into the room and said, "I say. I'm sorry."

Alexia had turned on Radio Luxembourg very loudly, to wash up to, so she had to cross the kitchen to turn it off before she could say "What?"

He said, "I'm sorry, we all just walked out and left you to clear up. I've come back to help."

"Gosh," Alexia said.

"Unless, of course, you'd rather be alone —"

"No, I wouldn't." She nodded towards the old Rayburn on whose rail hung several tea towels with "Glass Cloth — Irish Linen" woven into their borders. "You can dry."

She went back to the sink and began to splash about in the soapy water. She was very astonished, and couldn't think of anything to say. After a while, during which Martin dried several spoons and forks with the exaggerated care of someone unaccustomed to drying up at all, he said, "Can I ask you something?"

"Of course."

He came and leaned against the draining board so that he could see at least her profile.

"Why are you so passive?" he said.

She went pink. "Passive?"

"Yes. Passive. I mean, why do you do all the cooking and clearing up and never interrupt and let them do all the talking? You see, you don't *look* passive, you look quite confident, but then you don't behave confidently. Am I being very rude?"

"I don't know. Do you mean you think I'm feeble?"

"Not exactly feeble. I don't think you're a drip, if that's what you mean. I just can't see why you're like this, when they are so positive. I can't think why you put up with it."

Alexia had never had a conversation like this with anyone in her life before, not even with Uncle James and Aunt Mary, who loved her and knew something of her predicament. She said, stammering a little, "I . . . I don't quite know what else to do —"

"Just break out —"

"But you can't break out just because you're anti something. That's childish. You have to be pro something else. Don't you?"

"True," Martin said. He was still looking at her, and drying up very slowly, polishing the ugly Woolworth tumblers until they shone. Edna always left them to drain upside down on the plate rack, so that they were usually slightly smeary. Alexia looked at Martin's handiwork approvingly.

"You've made those look nice."

"Don't you want to go a bit wild?"

"I'm full of all kinds of wants, but I don't quite know what they all are — I just feel terribly restless."

Martin went over to the Rayburn and hung the damp tea towels back on the rail. He said abruptly, "Can I see the family portraits?"

"Portraits?"

"Yes. Your father said you had some. From your mother's side. We were talking genetics and he said yours and your mother's hair had come down in an almost unbroken line for five generations and you could see it in these portraits."

Alexia dried her hands on the roller towel that hung on the back of the larder door. She had misjudged this particular student. Martin Angus was not, it seemed, only interested in rugger and pranks and internal organs. She said, "I'll show you. They're in the dining room."

The dining room at Culver Square was never used for dining, except at Christmas, but only for meetings. It was at the back of the house, looking out onto the forlorn space that passed for a garden, and it contained the huge red mahogany table Stephen had inherited from his father, a dozen miscellaneous chairs, a hideous prewar sideboard, and the two portraits. Alexia was used to the portraits, but Martin gasped.

"They're amazing!"

They were huge portraits, full length, painted in the late 1840s of Alexia's great-great-grandmother, Charlotte, and her second husband, Alexander Bewick. Charlotte, who did, indeed, have the same dark red hair as Cara and Alexia, was dressed in an elaborate cream silk dress and ropes and ropes of pearls, with a halo of thick furs around her shoulders. Alexander, who was dark and dashing, wore some kind of exotic costume, a tunic and breeches and glossy boots, and a marvelous deep red and blue turban embroidered in gold.

"His clothes are Afghan," Alexia said. "That's where they met, in Afghanistan. They had a scandalous affair because she was married to someone else at the time. They're a sort of family legend."

Martin went up to the portraits and looked at

them very carefully for a very long time. Then he looked at Alexia.

"You're very like her."

Alexia blushed again. "I'm not —"

"Yes, you are. Put you in clothes of a hundred years ago and you'd look like that."

"She was tremendously brave and daring. She had a sort of Afghan slave and she was a wonderful horsewoman."

"How do you know you wouldn't be like that if you had the chance?"

"Oh, don't be silly," Alexia said, suddenly cross, "I'm just ordinary."

"You don't know that," Martin said, "you just think that because you haven't tried being anything else." He stooped forward and lifted out a photograph which had been tucked into the bottom left-hand corner of Charlotte's frame. He held it out.

"Where's that?"

The photograph showed a romantic, castlelike house, with towers and turrets and bits of battlement, set on the shore of a lake with mountains rising behind it.

"That's Castle Bewick. It's where the portraits used to hang."

"Where is it? Is it yours?"

"It's in Scotland. It belongs to my Uncle James who farms in Cornwall, but he lets it out to a boys' school."

"So it's full of iron beds and smelly socks and blackboards. What a pity. Have you ever been there?"

"No. When the school took it over, Uncle

James had the portraits sent down here, because they were to be my mother's anyway. They are supposed to go down through the female line. The other family portrait, the one of my grandmother, my mother's mother, is in Cornwall, at Bishopstow, at my Uncle James's house. It's much more famous because it's a Michael Swinton."

"A Swinton!" Martin said. "You've got a Swinton!"

"He was my grandfather," Alexia said. "I never really knew him. He died when I was three."

"Good Lord," Martin said. He looked at Alexia with new interest. "Michael Swinton's granddaughter. Is your grandmother still alive?"

Alexia looked away. Her grandmother, her funny, fierce, loving, crippled grandmother, Alexandra, had died when she was fourteen. It had been a huge loss, not least because her grandmother had been the one person to understand what it was like, as a child, to feel you had failed your parents.

"I was so like you," she had said to Alexia, "so like. Solitary and shy, stuck in that great Scottish house and no better at making friends than you are, with great-grandmother Iskandara telling me I'd failed the family at every turn." She had gripped Alexia's arm. "But you mustn't give up. You mustn't. You'll be like me too in that it will all come to you if you don't let them bully you. You do what you want to do. We can't all be child stars, you know, and if you want my opinion, it's better to wait for your happiness."

31

Alexia shook her head. "No. She died five years ago. She —"

"She what?"

"She was my friend."

Martin let a little silence fall, as if out of respect, and then he said, in a slightly hearty voice, "And I suppose you've got lucky Cornish cousins who'll inherit the castle."

Alexia didn't like the look in his eye. "I haven't got any Cornish cousins. Uncle James never had any children and he's going to leave Castle Bewick to the Scottish National Trust when the school has finished with it, because it's very special and rare and absolutely everything in it was designed by the same architect, even down to the keyholes."

Martin went back to the portrait of Charlotte and slipped the photograph back into her frame.

"Never mind," he said, "it must be nice all the same to know it's there."

When Martin and John Mallory had gone, Alexia went upstairs and ran herself a bath. She was suddenly extremely tired, with the journey and the cooking and clearing up and, above all, the strain of being back where she felt she neither belonged, nor was approved of. She climbed into the soothing water, and lay swishing it over herself with a face flannel, and thought about the day, and Bishopstow, and her job that was starting on Monday, and then she thought, with a queer sensation of interested pleasure, about Martin Angus. He had talked to her so differently from the way people usually talked to her, as if she was an individual and not just an example of a type, and he had looked at her speculatively, as one might look at a tumbledown cottage and think what a delightful place it could be made with enough time and trouble. He was odd, in a way, she thought, but nice odd, attractive odd. All her adolescence, she'd been prone to having crushes on boys, mostly on brothers of school friends, but she hadn't yet met a boy who interested her, intrigued her. She sat up and began to wash. Martin Angus must be put out of her mind. When he said good night, he hadn't uttered a single syllable that would make her think she'd ever see him again.

She climbed out of the bath, and dried herself, then she put on her nightie and her quilted dressing gown and tied her hair back in a ponytail and went downstairs to say good-night to her parents. They were drinking tea, as they usually did, in the sitting room, with the tea tray balanced on piles of *British Medical Journals* which seemed, apart from the newspapers and campaign leaflets from the CND, to be the only printed paper that ever entered 17 Culver Square.

Stephen and Cara were sitting side by side on the sofa, under the harsh center ceiling light, Cara with her feet tucked up, leaning against her husband. They looked up when Alexia came in, and Cara patted the sofa arm beside her. Alexia perched obediently on it.

"You seemed to get on well with young Angus," Stephen said.

"He wasn't as medical studentish as most of them —"

"He's the ablest I've had in, oh, ten years. Formidable."

"I thought John Mallory looked the one," Alexia said. "He was the one who couldn't think about anything except lungs all supper."

Stephen yawned. "He's tremendously dedicated, never stops working, but he isn't really gifted in the same way that Martin is. Martin seems to have an instinct for medicine, it's the only way I can describe it. Often, in the wards, I'm amazed at his ability to diagnose."

Cara said sleepily, "Apparently his mother is a Labour councillor for some borough in North London. Camden, I think. She's deep into the women's liberation movement."

Stephen kissed her forehead. "Sounds right up your street."

Alexia looked at them both. They seemed quite content and at peace leaning against one another in easy companionship.

"I think I'll go to bed," she said.

They didn't look at her.

"Night, darling," Cara said, dropping her head on Stephen's shoulder. "Sleep well."

Chapter Three

On the following Monday morning Alexia dressed herself in her newly washed skinny ribbed jersey, her black mini-skirt, her black and white wide belt with the big perspex buckle, and her white boots. Then she brushed down her fringe, backcombed the rest of her hair into a smooth-surfaced bob, put on all her makeup (though not her false eyelashes) and set off for the tube station and her first morning's work in Chelsea.

It was a pretty day, with a high pale blue sky and that sharp edge to the air that heralds the beginning of autumn. Walking along, Alexia hoped very much that she looked like a full-fledged girl-with-a-job, and not just a very recent school girl. Several of her best friends from school had gone on to university, but although Alexia's A-level grades had been good enough for a university place somewhere, she had not in the least wanted to go. She had been afraid that university would be just like school, only a boarding school this time, with a room in a women's hall of residence somewhere like Reading or Leicester. Her refusal even to think about going to university had been yet another reason for Cara and Stephen to feel very disappointed in her. Cara also made her feel guilty.

"Most girls of my generation didn't even get a chance to go to university, you know." Alexia did know, all too well. After all, she'd been told about it, regularly, all her life.

"I couldn't go, of course," Cara went on, "not at your age, because of the war. And when I did get a place after the war, to study medicine at St. Bartolph's where Daddy was, of course I had to give it up almost at once, because I became pregnant. With you."

The implied reproach hung heavily in the air. Alexia had felt both awful and angry; guilty at being the cause of her clever mother's not gaining a longed-for qualification, furious at being blamed for something for which she was utterly blameless. She'd said, as she so often found herself helplessly saying to Cara, "Sorry. Sorry. Sorry —" but she hadn't given in.

She took the Northern Line back up to Charing Cross and then changed to the District Line for Sloane Square. Whatever her feelings about the job, and the prospect of Amanda and Felicity, she couldn't help being slightly excited at the thought of getting out at Sloane Square and walking down the King's Road, and then back up it again in the evening. All the tourist posters said "Come to Swinging London!" and things were supposed to swing particularly wildly in the King's Road, where the original Chelsea girl had been born, the girl Alexia hoped she looked like. Quite what happened when you got into the swing of the King's Road, Alexia wasn't sure, but then she'd had no practice since there was precious little to swing about in Lambeth.

She had to walk miles and miles down the King's Road, almost to the turning to Battersea Bridge, because Amanda and Felicity lived somewhere called Danvers Street. From the far end of Danvers Street you could see the river and the bridge, but their house was at the northern end, a tiny house like a town cottage, painted pink with Spanish style wrought iron grilles over the downstairs windows, and a toy balcony to match above, too small for anyone to stand on.

Alexia rang the doorbell. It was ages and ages before anybody came, and when Felicity did at last open the door she said, "Oh my God, I'd clean forgotten you were coming."

Alexia opened her mouth to say politely, "Shall I go away then?" but found herself saying quite firmly instead, "You distinctly said to come today. You said to come on this Monday, at nine-thirty, so I have."

Felicity looked rather startled. She was wearing a grubby white broderie anglaise dressing gown, and last night's makeup was still smudged round her eyes. She said, "Oh well, I expect you're right. You'd better come in. 'Scuse the mess, we had a bit of a binge last night."

Alexia followed her into the tiny hall which had a black carpet and smelled of cigarette smoke. All the doors were shut except the end one which led into a very smart, very disordered galley kitchen in which a disheveled-looking man in a blue silk dressing gown was groaning and trying to make coffee.

"This is Ludo," Felicity said. She waved a hand

at Alexia. "Ludo, this is — what was your name? Alice?"

"No. Alexia," Alexia said.

Ludo squinted at her. He looked glamorous and depraved and his dark hair was very long. He said, "Can you make coffee?"

"Yes."

"Well, could you then? My hands are shaking and every time I look down, I think I'm going to be sick."

Alexia opened her mouth to say she wasn't there to make coffee, and then shut it again because it struck her that perhaps the dogsbody part of this job meant precisely doing things like making coffee. If so, being at work was going to be very like being at home.

"Angel," Felicity said. "You get stuck in here, and I'll go and wake Amanda. Ludo, you're not to pounce on her while I'm upstairs."

Ludo groaned again. "Have a heart. I couldn't pounce on a kitten, the way I'm feeling. Particularly not a kitten actually. Alice, make the coffee in that glass thing would you —"

"My name is Alexia."

"That's what I said. I suppose you wouldn't go out and buy me some more cigarettes, would you?"

"If you gave me the money, I might."

Ludo pulled his empty dressing gown pockets inside out and made a face. "See?"

"No cigarettes then," Alexia said. She picked up the Cona coffee machine. It was full of cold coffee and the top part was clogged with old grounds. The last person who had picked it up

38

had had marmalade on their hands, or golden syrup, or honey. The whole kitchen as far as Alexia could see, was in a similar condition, piled with dirty plates and glasses, everything sticky and lightly dusted with cigarette ash. She said, "Why don't you go and dress and when you come back, there'll be coffee."

"How bossy you are," Ludo said. "They said they'd employed a secretary bird but they never said she was a bossy bird, too."

He trailed out of the kitchen. From upstairs came several crashes and thumps and the sound of bath water running. Feeling oddly elated, Alexia tied the least revolting tea towel round her waist and turned the hot tap on full blast into the cluttered sink.

It was three-quarters of an hour before anyone reappeared, and by the time they did, the washing up was done and Alexia was sweeping the floor. Amanda, dressed in her usual black, surveyed the kitchen through her sunglasses and said, "Aren't you utter heaven."

Alexia said slightly sarcastically, "I can type too, you know." She was astounded at her own courage. "There's coffee in the Cona thing."

"Bliss," said Amanda. "Do not, on my advice, ever have Algerian wine and Algerian hash and, as far as I can remember, Algerian men all in one evening. I want to *die.*"

Alexia said nothing. She swept all the rubbish off the floor into a dustpan and held it out. "Where's the dustbin?"

Amanda flapped a hand towards the back door. "Out there. What utterly dinky boots. Fe-

licity said you were going to be a complete treasure and I can see you are. Have you seen *Dr.*
Zhivago because I think you have a *distinct* look
of Julie Christie. Distinct. I suppose you haven't
got a cigarette?"

"No," Alexia said. She took the dustpan out
into a minute dank courtyard where two over-
flowing dustbins kept company with a rusty
white wrought iron table and two wobbly
matching chairs. When she came back into
the kitchen, Amanda and Felicity — now dressed
in a very short red skirt with braces, and white
lace tights — were leaning against the kitchen
counter clutching mugs of coffee and saying,
"Isn't she divine?" to one another.

"I don't mind doing it very occasionally,"
Alexia said, "but I didn't think you'd employed
me to be a maid."

"Are you offended, angel?"

"No, not particularly but —"

"We *are* naughty. We really won't do it again.
Or often, to be strictly truthful."

Amanda heaved herself upright. Her black
trousers, Alexia could see to her amazement,
were made of leather. She said, "Now take off
that martyred face, treasure child, and come
down to the basement. I'm going to show you
wonderful things. I am going to show you —" she
leaned forward and prodded Alexia, "how to
make a curtain!"

"But I didn't come for that," Alexia said, "I
don't want to know how to make curtains —"

"Yes, you do," Amanda said, suddenly
sounding much more brisk. "Of course you do.

40

Who knows, it may one day prove an absolute lifesaver to you that you know how to make a decent curtain."

It was one of the most peculiar days Alexia had ever spent and one of the most peculiar things about it was that she rather liked it. The basement workshop was dark and smelled of damp, but it was full of rolls and bales of interesting stuffs and, as the day wore on, a steady stream of Amanda and Felicity's friends who all came in for coffee and a cigarette and, very occasionally, for curtains. She was given a chair and a small rickety table in one corner, and a white telephone. Every time the telephone rang, she had to pick it up and say "Chelsea Curtains. Good morning," and then usually the person at the other end said, "Oh come off it, Amanda darling, I know it's only you and I have the most amazing piece of gossip to tell you —"

The filing system consisted of a wobbling stack of old shoeboxes from extremely expensive shops, with Italian labels on the ends, absolutely crammed with invoices and receipts and catalogs and torn envelopes with measurements or telephone numbers scribbled on them. There seemed to be no basic list of customers or suppliers, let alone any kind of bookkeeping system.

"Do you have an accountant?" Alexia asked Felicity.

Felicity rolled her eyes. "Don't talk about him. We thought he was going to be sweet but he's an absolute ogre. The last time he rang we had to pretend to be Irish daily helps who didn't know where we were."

Despite the chaos and the chatter however, Alexia observed that Amanda and Felicity were astonishingly steadily working. At the huge central cutting-out table, and the industrial sewing machine that stood below the only window, they measured and cut and sewed away, keeping up a stream of nonsense to their friends and calling out to Alexia things like, "Look in the Kurt Geiger box with the bust corner, would you, treasure, for Marcia Linton's bedroom measurements?" and "Angel, do ring the Sanderson warehouse and see what time they close. The number's on the wall behind you in green crayon."

Amanda was also as good as her word. During the slight lull that passed for lunchtime — Alexia was sent out to buy salami sandwiches and a bottle of rosé wine — Amanda said, "Over here, my duck. Curtain lesson number one," and set Alexia down beside her at the edge of the cutting table.

"Now," she said, drawing on a piece of scrap paper. "Rule number one. Always line curtains for a proper hang and whenever possible have them floor length."

Alexia stared. At Culver Square, the curtains were all unlined and all windowsill length. Amanda said, as if reading her mind, "Most English curtains are still in postwar mode, darling. That is the point of Felicity and me, you see, we are pioneers of proper curtaining. I shall teach you about headings and interlinings and locked-in linings, and if you are very good and display even a hint of promise, I shall show you how to make pelmets and introduce you to buckram and bump and pinch pleats and gimp. Today however, we shall start with the mitered corner. Are you paying utter and complete attention?"

At five-thirty, dazed but strangely exhilarated, Alexia emerged from the Danvers Street basement like a mole coming up into spring sunshine. She was exhausted and grubby, and she couldn't imagine why she didn't feel depressed, but she certainly didn't. She walked up the King's Road very slowly, savoring what felt like — no doubt about it — a sense of achievement. She must be mad. What on earth had she achieved except a dozen very mundane telephone calls, seven hours of paper shuffling, two practice mitered corners on scraps of old curtain lining and about two thousand cups of coffee and the subsequent washing up? It couldn't possibly be, could it, that she'd do anything for anybody as long as they called her "angel" and "treasure"? Of course not. Amanda and Felicity were the sort of people who said "angel" and "treasure" to everybody, even dustmen and ticket collectors; it was a sort of shorthand for them, to save them from having to remember anybody's names. So what was it? Why did she feel pleased and curiously satisfied and why, despite being so tired, was she looking forward to tomorrow and already planning how she would tell Amanda and Felicity that she needed a filing cabinet and index card boxes and a proper invoice book and a typewriter? She sat in the Tube and wriggled her toes in their white boots and remembered how one of Felicity's endless friends — a tiny, black-haired friend in a equally tiny, bright yellow PVC suit — had said that she simply had to go to a shop called Biba in Kensington Church Street, where she could buy amazing dresses for a pound and sometimes seventeen and six. She thought she would like some amazing dresses, just as she thought she would like to get Amanda and Felicity a bit organized. She also thought, slowly climbing the Underground steps up to the Kennington Park Road, that she had just spent a day which had had, for all its bizarre differences, something in common with days in Cornwall; she had not for one moment felt impelled to apologize for herself to anybody.

She dawdled home. She imagined that when she got in, she'd probably find another Edna note and doubtless some gloomy piece of fish on a plate in the larder for supper, but she didn't really care. Tomorrow, she'd be out of the house soon after eight-thirty and . . .

Someone was sitting on the steps of number 17. Very occasionally people did sit there; the odd tramp, or children from other houses in the square using the steps to play jacks on. But this someone was a man, a young man with thick fair hair who stood up as Alexia approached.

"Hello," said Martin Angus.

She said, in amazement, "What are you doing here?"

"I've come to see you. If that's all right."

"But medical students never have any free time —"

"Oh, they get about two hours a week. This is one of my two hours. Do you mind?"

"What?"

"My coming to see you?"

"No. No, of course not. I'm just a bit surprised."

He smiled and held out his hand for the latchkey. "Can I come in then?"

He unlocked the door, and stood aside to let her go in. The house was, of course, empty and silent, but inspection of the larder revealed that Edna had not left fish but sausages instead, in a fat, pale pile.

"Ugh," Alexia said, and shut the larder door on them. "I hate London sausages. All grease and bread."

"Don't eat them then," Martin said.

She turned and looked at him. He was smiling again, and she noticed that although his hair was so fair, his eyelashes were dark and his eyes were blue and full of life.

"What?"

"Do stop saying what to me. I said, don't eat the sausages. Your mother can cook them for her and your father. Any fool can cook sausages. And then you can come out with me and eat Italian. Please."

She gazed at him. Then a huge smile broke out and spread until her whole face was illumined like a lamp.

"I'd . . . I'd *love* to . . . but they're expecting me."

"Don't you think it's time they learned not to? Or do you intend to play Cinderella all your life?"

Alexia hesitated, still shining with smiles. "And . . . and . . . after today and everything, I'm so dirty —"

He sighed, a big sigh of mock exasperation.

"Well, go and get clean then, though you look perfectly all right to me. While you're gone, I shall go and talk to your great-great-grandmother. Don't be long."

He took her, in his tiny battered car, almost back the way she had come that day, to a trattoria off the Fulham Road. Before they left, he dictated a note for her to leave on the kitchen table. It said, "Dear Mum and Dad. Gone out to supper with Martin Angus. Back by midnight. Sausages for your supper in the larder. Alexia." Alexia had wanted to put "Love from Alexia" but Martin said, "Don't. They need a bit of training. Start as you mean to go on."

The trattoria had pink cotton tablecloths and rush-seated chairs and huge blown-up photographs of Positano and Capri and Rapallo all round the walls. The ceiling was draped with fishing nets, and in the hammocks this made were clusters of big exotic shells and the green glass balls from lobster pots and bunches of plastic grapes. On every table was a Chianti bottle in its pale straw overcoat, acting as a candlestick. It was very full and very noisy and, to Alexia's mind, very wonderful.

It was also rather wonderful to be with Martin. He seemed to know exactly what he was doing, ordering wine (wine!) telling her which pasta she ought to choose off the huge menu the size of a sandwich board, and speaking some Italian. He asked her all about her day and when she tried to brush it aside, he said, "No, no, I'm interested."

So she told him. She told him about the glamour and the squalor and Ludo the lover, and the shoeboxes and the salami sandwiches and learning to miter the corner of a curtain. Then she said, rather shyly, twirling her fork round and round in her pile of spaghetti, "I really like it."

"Well, why shouldn't you?"

"I suppose because it didn't require much intellect —"

"Why should it?"

She looked up at him. He was holding a glass of wine in one hand and smiling at her.

"You *have* been brought up daft, Miss Alexia Langley, and no mistake. Why do you despise practical skills?"

"I don't, but —"

"Do you despise your Uncle James, the farmer?"

"No, of course I don't, I think he's wonderful, but —"

"Mummy and Daddy think if you don't either fling yourself into social work or do something intellectual you might as well throw yourself away into the wastepaper basket of history?"

Alexia began to laugh, nodding and laughing. "Something like that. I mean, I thought you'd think like them too, because of being about to be a doctor."

Martin stopped smiling. "Well, you'd be wrong."

"But Dad says you're brilliant."

"Dad's brilliant himself. That's why I stick to him like paint. He's probably one of the most brilliant people in his field in western Europe. Don't get me wrong, I love medicine. I'm fascinated by it, really fascinated. But when I'm your father's age, I don't intend to be patrolling the wards of St. Luke's with people like me trailing behind me."

Alexia stopped chewing. "What do you intend then?"

"I intend to have a brass plate up in Harley Street. I want to be very good at what I do and very famous for it and rich because I am both good and famous."

Alexia let out a breath. "Wow."

"And I'll tell you something else," Martin said. He leaned forward and fixed her with his bright, smiling blue gaze. "I shan't ever make the mistake of despising anybody because they don't do what I do. If someone does their job well, whether they're queen or a curtain maker, they'll get my support. And I mean, if you'll let me, Alexia, to start with you."

Chapter Four

"What d'you mean, a typewriter?" Amanda said.

"We ought to have one. It means all your invoices and estimates will look more businesslike. Just a little portable one."

"But, darling, I've bought you a filing cabinet for heaven's sake —"

"I can't type," Alexia said patiently, "on a filing cabinet."

"But you've got delicious neat writing —"

"It doesn't matter how delicious or neat my handwriting is, it's only *writing*. It looks amateur. It looks as if you and Felicity are only running a hobby, not a business."

"Heavens!" Amanda said. "Do you know, I think that's what we thought we were running, treasure. That is, until you came along."

She went upstairs to the kitchen, where Felicity was having her daily quarrel with Ludo, and Alexia could clearly hear her say, "Too amazing but that child wants a typewriter now. A typewriter! It'll be board meetings next, and she'll want her own secretary and when we have hangovers, we'll have to get notes from the doctor. Priceless."

She wasn't really cross, you could tell. She was laughing and she even sounded pleased. Well,

Alexia thought, looking round the Danvers Street basement, she jolly well ought to sound pleased. There wasn't a shoebox to be seen and in their place was a gray filing cabinet and two long gray index card boxes and a huge cork pinboard covered in Alexia's lists.

"Too sweet," Felicity said. "You really like lists, don't you?"

"Don't be ashamed of efficiency," Martin had said to her. "Don't let anyone sneer or tease you out of being proud to be efficient."

In a mere month, Chelsea Curtains not only looked different, it was different. It wasn't just a matter of Alexia Hoovering the basement every evening before she went home, and organizing the contents of the shoeboxes, but of organizing her employers too.

"Look, if you said she could have the dining room curtains by Wednesday the seventeenth, then she's got to *have* them by Wednesday the seventeenth —"

"Honestly, angel, it couldn't matter less. She's gone to France for a fortnight and she's probably forgotten all about them, she's so hopeless —"

"It doesn't *matter* where she's gone or how hopeless she is. She's got to get back from France and find those curtains hanging in her dining room. And it's no good charging her less because she's a friend and useless with money and then slapping huge amounts on to Lady Fanshawe's bill because she's stinking rich and you loathe her."

"But, darling, Lady F.'ll never know. I mean, they'll never meet, they move in completely different circles, they'll never see each other's curtains in a million years —"

"Felicity, that's not the *point*. The thing is, you've got to work out what your markup is, according to how much time curtains take you on account of how complicated they are, and *stick* to it. You can't just pull figures out of the air and say, oh well, that'll do."

"Heavens, you're so businesslike, angel, it's quite frightening. I thought you were just a dear little harmless schoolgirl who couldn't say boo to a goose, but you aren't a bit. You're like a really scary headmistress. Where did you *learn* all this, for heaven's sake? I never learnt anything at school except two poems I've forgotten and how to tell lies with a straight face."

"I didn't learn it anywhere," Alexia said. "It's just common sense. Everybody's got common sense."

"Not me," said Felicity, "I wouldn't be seen dead with it," but she kept sewing.

Alexia made them order tiny woven labels which said "Chelsea Curtains" and the telephone number, to stitch inside each curtain. She found a firm which would supply huge polythene bags for the finished curtains to travel about in, and telephoned all the likely women's magazines for the cost of advertisements. She learned that Amanda was in love with a married man who had no intention of leaving his wife for her, and that Ludo was only one of a series of men who passed through Felicity's hands like beads on a necklace. She also learned where to shop and what to buy and was introduced to avocado

51

pears, and Mary Quant tights with daisies patterned on them, and the films of Roman Polanski. She was, although almost too busy to stop and think about it, very happy for the first time in her life except for those precious holidays in Cornwall.

There were, of course, other reasons for being happy. The chief of these was Martin Angus. A month after her first strange and successful day at Chelsea Curtains, she could not only say to herself with perfect truth that she was rather a good secretary and dogsbody, but also that she had a boyfriend. A real, live boyfriend. At least . . . she had a friend who took her out to supper and to Ronnie Scott's Jazz Club and to the Café des Artistes and for walks in Regent's Park and Richmond Park and held her hand and who was a boy. But he didn't kiss her. Or at least he did, but only on her cheek, or her forehead and once her nose. On the nose occasion she had thought with hope and rising excitement that her mouth must inevitably come next, but it hadn't. It was very puzzling and it cast a small blight — no, be honest, she told herself, quite a *big* blight — over the first four weeks in her entire life when she could say she had a boyfriend.

In consequence she spent a lot of time in front of the mirror trying to discover why Martin didn't kiss her. True enough, for five days out of that first month, she had a spot and nobody could ever bear to kiss anyone with anything as repulsive as a spot glowing away there on their chin. But apart from the spot, she looked quite clean, she thought, and she brushed her teeth with Pearl Drops constantly and rubbed Morny's Pink Lilac ice-stick behind her ears and on her wrists. Cara seemed so pleased with Alexia for acquiring Martin as a boy-friend that Alexia almost came to the point of saying to her mother, "Why don't you think he ever tries to kiss me?", but the constraint between them was of such long standing that she could never quite bring herself to do it.

In the end, much to her own amazement, the person she told was Amanda. She just blurted it out one day, while they were going through the outstanding orders.

"Martin hasn't kissed —"

"Who hasn't?"

"Martin."

Amanda said, "Is that the very appealing tall fair arrangement that comes to pick you up once in a while and calls Felicity Mrs. Treadgold?"

"Yes."

"Too delicious."

"But he hasn't *kissed* me! We've been going out for four weeks and three days and he hasn't kissed me —"

"Well, kiss him then."

"Heavens, I couldn't, I mean, it'd look so . . . so . . ."

"Darling Alexia, this is 1965, not 1865. If you want to be kissed, start it off."

"Suppose I put him off?"

Amanda was so amazed, she lowered her sun-glasses for a fraction of a second.

"Are you sure you weren't brought up in a *nunnery?*"

"Quite sure."

"Then stop being so prissy and miss-ish and generally sickening. You boss Felicity and me up hill and down dale from morn till dewy eve, and then tell me you are too much of a simpering virgin to ask for a kiss when you want one. In my view, you don't deserve a kiss, if that's your attitude. You deserve a smacked bottom."

"I can't help being a virgin," Alexia said defensively.

Amanda gave a huge sigh. "Darling, I truly don't know who *else* you can blame, do you?" and went back to the order book.

Alexia thought about this conversation all afternoon. It was perfectly plain that Amanda and Felicity didn't think twice about letting their hair down, just as several school friends of Alexia's hadn't thought even once about letting theirs down either, but Alexia had always supposed that they were just different. What was easy for one person to do was agonizingly difficult for another, and that's all there was to it. The fact that you were a teenager in London in 1965 and therefore the envy of the world because of free love and the youth cult and everything being so groovy and swinging, meant absolutely nothing if you didn't happen to have a naturally groovy and swinging personality. You couldn't be like Marianne Faithfull just because you wished you were. You were as you were made, and if you were uncertain of your sex appeal, as Alexia was, then you had to wait for a bit of help and encouragement. But Amanda had suggested that waiting for help and encouragement was (a) wet and (b) wouldn't get you any further. "If you want a kiss," she'd said, "ask for it." Well, Alexia thought, I could try, couldn't I, and the worst he could do would be to turn me down, and if I'm prepared for the worst, I won't be too devastated when it happens. Will I? She went to Amanda and Felicity's amazing black and mirrored bathroom, and looked at herself for a long, long time. If I were Martin, she wondered, why wouldn't I want to kiss me? Or perhaps I would, in theory, but I'm put off because I *do* look like a simpering virgin? And then Amanda came in and said, "*There* you are. I thought it's where you might be. Now, I've two things to tell you, darling. One is that the answer lies in what's inside your head not outside it, and the other is that I'd like the use of my own bathroom please, so would you kindly get the hell out of it?"

Two days later, greatly daring, Alexia asked Martin to supper. Cara and Stephen would be out, first at a concert given in aid of a fund for a new intensive care unit for premature babies at St. Luke's, and then having supper with friends, so the coast would be clear until at least eleven-thirty.

There was very little to be done about the kitchen in terms of improving its ambience, but Martin was, after all, familiar with its dingy awfulness. Alexia laid the table with a piece of red-checked gingham she had once bought to make a shirt out of, and wedged two candles in the necks of a couple of beer bottles. Beer bottles unquestionably did not have the cachet of wine bottles, but there were no wine bottles to be had in 17

Culver Square. When she had finished she hoped that with the candles lit and the overhead light off, the room would resemble a romantic French bistro rather than a shabby south London kitchen that hadn't had a lick of paint since 1952.

Martin was very punctual. He wore a tweed jacket and corduroy trousers and Chelsea boots, and he carried a bottle of wine and a paper sheaf of pink gladioli. He held them out to her.

"For you."

She said, "I've never been given flowers before," and instantly regretted it as being naive.

He just said, "Well now you have," and followed her down the hall to the kitchen. He looked around approvingly. "I like the candles. And there's a wonderful smell."

"It's coq au vin. I've never cooked it before, but it seems all right."

She unwrapped the stiff pink flowers and put them, one by one, into a tall jug. Somehow, having Martin at home wasn't quite as easy as having Martin in a trattoria or a park or a jazz club. She said, "You'll find a corkscrew over there. In the drawer under the sink."

He went across the kitchen with the wine bottle in his hand and began to rummage among the spoons and can openers and fish slices for a corkscrew. With his back to her he said, "Alexia —"

"Yes?"

"Are your parents well and truly out? I mean, they're not going to burst in on us out of the blue?"

She could feel the color rising up her face and neck.

"Oh no, they've gone to the concert and then to supper with the Wilkses and that always takes forever because Mum's trying to convert Mr. Wilks to the need for an equal opportunities commission because he's a civil servant, you see, and —"

"Alexia," Martin said.

She stopped and waited, holding the jug of gladioli. He came over to the table with the opened wine in his hand and poured some of it into two glasses.

"I wanted time to talk to you, you see. To talk to you properly."

"Oh yes —"

"About us."

She swallowed again, and nodded violently. Martin picked up one of the glasses of wine and held it out to her, saying seriously, "I expect you think I'm either mad or a bastard."

Her voice came out as a squeak.

"What —"

"You're so pretty and so sweet and so accomplished, and we've had such a good time together, and I expect you're wondering if there's something the matter with me because I haven't tried to kiss you."

The color rushed into her face. "Oh no! I mean . . . I haven't . . . I mean, I thought you probably didn't . . ."

He looked very grave. "I owe you an explanation."

She gazed at him. He pulled a chair out from

57

the kitchen table, and motioned her to sit in it, then he went round to the other side of the table, and sat down opposite to her.

"Alexia, I've got something to confess to you —"

He's in love with someone else, she thought, or he's married, or he's had some awful illness and he can't . . .

"When I was eighteen," Martin Angus said, "I met a girl called Susie. She was a friend of my sister's and we really fell for each other. It was the first time I'd fallen for anyone and it was pretty serious. I expect you know what I'm talking about, I expect you know about first love as well as I do."

Alexia took a deep breath. "No, actually —"

He didn't seem to hear her. He went on, "We had everything in common, same background, same ambitions. I have to tell you all this because I want to be completely honest with you, completely. Do you understand?"

"Yes," Alexia said. She found she was almost holding her breath.

"Well, we were together for five years. And then . . ." He glanced down at the red checked tablecloth. "The long and the short of it was that just over a year ago, she chucked me, for a bloke who's going to inherit his father's company, Jaguar XJ6, house in Sunningdale, holidays in Majorca, you name it —"

"Oh Martin —" Alexia's voice was full of sympathy, and she put a hand out to him across the table.

He took it in his. "You're very sweet."

58

"Oh no, no, I'm just so sorry, it must have been so awful for you —"

"It was." He picked her hand up and turned it over and kissed the palm, folding the fingers down afterwards as if to keep the kiss in place. "Then, when I met you and I could feel . . . could feel that I was . . . well, you can see how I'd be a bit cautious, perhaps, can't you, you can see that I'd want to be pretty sure I wasn't going through the ice again?"

"Of course," she said fervently. She was so sorry for him she felt quite faint. "I'm so sorry, Martin, so sorry —"

He smiled. "Don't you be sorry! You've done nothing but good."

"But I'm sorry for you —"

"And I'm sorry to have behaved like an idiot. You must have thought I was barmy."

"Oh no," she said. "Oh no, I didn't, I just thought it must be me."

"Of course it isn't you."

She looked down.

"Look at me," he said.

For some reason, she couldn't. He got up, and leaned across the table and put his hand under her chin and lifted her face.

"Look at me," he said again, very softly, and then he said, "Aren't you lovely, aren't you lovely through and through?" and then he bent his head and kissed her on the mouth.

Much later, full of coq au vin and wine and kisses, Martin had said to her, "Are you on the pill?"

59

She was rather startled. Lulled by the intimacy of the evening, comforted by the unquestionable proof that she wasn't, after all, violently unattractive, she had been in a happy daze of romantic pleasure. She said, "No, I'm not —"

"Surely your father —"

"He doesn't approve of it. He says it hasn't been tested sufficiently yet and the side effects are still too —"

"Alexia, are you always, always going to do everything your parents tell you to do, and parrot their opinions, as if you were a kid of seven?"

"Of course not, but —"

He slid his arm round her again, and buried his face in the soft skin where her neck rose out of the little black and white checked shift she had so proudly bought from Biba the week before, a shift costing twenty-two and six. He put his mouth against her neck, and then she felt his tongue.

"D'you like that?"

"Yes —"

He moved his head round to her throat, and at the same time put up his hand to the buttons that fastened her dress in front, little round black buttons like berries . . .

"And that?"

She gave a little gasp, "Yes!"

"Of course you do. Sex isn't for the future, it's for now, Alexia, now." He drew away from her a little and looked down at her. "Don't worry," he said. "Don't worry. I'll take care of everything. I'll look after you."

Chapter Five

Easter 1966

Lyddy sat in the kitchen at Bishopstow, cleaning the silver. At seventy-eight, with sixty-three years of service to the house and family behind her, she reckoned she could now do just the jobs that pleased her and cleaning the silver pleased her a good deal. She liked it because all the pieces had a memory for her, like the heavy Victorian spoons and forks which had been used by everyone in the family since Emily Talbot had acquired them as a bride in the late 1840s, or the coffee pot that had been a wedding present to Alexandra and Michael Swinton in 1907, and, of course, the christening mugs, James's and Alex's (Alex, who had been killed in the war and for whom Alexia had been named) and Cara's.

Despite her age, there were still distinct traces in Lyddy's pink face of the girl who had come to be Alexandra's lady's maid, all those years ago. The shadow that had fallen across her features when Alexandra died after almost twenty years in a wheelchair had never quite lifted again, but Lyddy, though a warm-hearted and loyal woman, was not sentimental. Whatever the agony of loss, life had to go on; which, in her case, was life at Bishopstow, the house, the farm, the clotted cream business, and above all, the family, however much it might change and fragment and disperse. Having never had a family of her own, the Bishopstow family had become Lyddy's.

She took out an old toothbrush in order to work silver polish — she despised the new impregnated wadding — into the grooves running round the base of Cara's christening mug. Cara had never taken her mug to London, indeed she had hardly taken any personal possessions to London, in 1946 or subsequently, just a suitcase of clothes and some books and her love for Stephen and their future together. Lyddy pursed her lips. She had a deep affection for Cara, and an abiding admiration — the pluck that child had shown during the war! — but you couldn't say Cara had been a good mother. Perhaps she'd have been different if she'd had sons; Alexandra, after all, Lyddy's beloved Alexandra, had been much better with James and Alex than she'd ever been with Cara. Except when she was here, Lyddy thought, she'd never considered that poor little Alexia'd had much of a childhood.

She began to rub the mug briskly with a soft yellow cloth, and became aware that the familiar nagging anxiety about Alexia was beginning to seep back into her mind. She gave herself a mental shake. It's nonsense, she told herself sternly, the child's not gone from this house for two hours on her way back to London with that young man of hers, and you're worrying again. But Alexia *was* a worry, and she was, too, so like her grandmother at the same age — so like, in fact, that Lyddy couldn't feel very sensible about her, try as she might. She had in her, Lyddy was sure of it, Alexandra's practicality and warmth of heart, but she didn't seem to have Alexandra's accompanying sturdy independence. What worried Lyddy most of all about Alexia was how much she needed to be loved. It makes you vulnerable, Lyddy thought, no doubt about it. You're an easy victim if you want to be loved that much.

The door to the yard at the back of the house opened, and a small figure in dungarees came in and dumped a basket of bantam eggs in front of Lyddy.

"Look at that! Laying their little heads off —"

June Reeves had arrived at Bishopstow during the war as a land girl, and had simply never gone away again. In Lyddy's eyes she was as much part of the family as if she'd been born into it.

"I'm glad to see you," Lyddy said, "I was sitting here having my usual worry —"

"About Alexia?"

"About Alexia."

June pulled out a kitchen chair and sat down beside Lyddy, propping her elbows on the table and her chin in her hands.

"What did you make of that young man?"

"I dunno —"

Lyddy shot her a glance. "Yes you do."

"Alexia seems happy enough —"

"Oh, she's happy all right," Lyddy said, picking up one of the dining room candlesticks. "She's so grateful to have someone want to marry her, she's as happy as a lark. But —"

"But?"

"He asked a lot of questions, that young man. He wanted to know the exact acreage of the farm and how many nephews and nieces James and Mary had besides Alexia, and who the old Langley grandparents favored."

"Don't you think he's fond of Alexia?"

Lyddy pursed her lips again. "I thought he was fond all right, but he was interested in a lot more besides Alexia herself."

"Me too," June said, "I mean, I thought the same. Did you talk to her?"

Lyddy hesitated. She'd gone upstairs one evening to turn down the beds, as was her habit of over half a century, and found Alexia in the bedroom she always had, the bedroom that had been given to Alexandra when she first came to Bishopstow. It had hardly changed in sixty years, even though the flowered chintz of the curtains had now lost its glaze, and had rotted here and there in little strips where it caught the sun, and the carpet had worn in patches, like well-used paths through a meadow. Alexia loved that room, she had loved it even when she was tiny. Cara, on the other hand, had always refused to sleep in it, saying it was too fussy and feminine, too crowded with Edwardian knickknacks and overstuffed Victorian furniture. When Lyddy had gone in that evening, Alexia had been sitting in the window seat, gazing out at a clear spring sunset across the estuary. She said at once, "Lydd, d'you like him? D'you like Martin?"

"He has lovely manners," Lyddy said with perfect truth. "And he's nice looking and clever. More than that, I can't tell in three days."

Alexia turned away from the window.

"He's made such a difference to me, Lyddy, he's made me believe I can do so much more than I ever thought I could."

"I see he's teaching you to drive —"

"No, no, not that. Not just driving. Much more important things. You know what it's like in this family, with everyone being such strong characters and there being so much to live up to, and here's just me with my funny little job and no real talent and — oh, Lyddy, you understand why he means so much to me, don't you?"

"Yes, dear," Lyddy said.

"Mum and Dad are really pleased we're getting married. Mum says it'll be the making of me —"

"Does she? You'll barely be twenty, you know."

Alexia laughed. "Twenty's *ancient!*"

Lyddy had taken a deep breath. In all her years at Bishopstow, she had never pushed her own opinion, unless it had been asked for. But now, asked for or not, she felt bound to deliver it.

"For most of us," she said to Alexia, "marriage is the biggest decision we ever take in our lives, and so it's got to be a decision we put our minds to as well as our hearts."

Alexia looked at her. She looked at her for a long time very seriously, and then she said, "I have."

"I did try," Lyddy said now to June. "But she's sure. Sure as sure, she said."

She got up, a little stiffly, and fetched a big lacquered tray on which to put the silver to take it back where it belonged.

"What do they think?" June said, "James and Mary? They dote on that child after all." She stood up too, to help Lyddy load the tray.

"I don't know what they think," Lyddy said, "but I should think they've got their opinions. Mary doesn't miss a thing, for all she's so quiet."

Mary Langley had been engaged to Cara's brother, Alex, and when he was killed she had had a nervous breakdown, and Cara had made a mercy dash to London to rescue her from a bombed-out house. That episode had become a family legend, just as Charlotte and Alexander Bewick's Afghan love affair had become a legend. After the war, Cara had helped to get Mary into Cambridge, because Mary was scholarly, but it had only lasted a year, and poor Mary had had to come home to Cornwall in the bitter winter of 1947, unable to cope with life on her own and desperately disappointed in herself. There, waiting for her, she had found the patient James, Alex's older brother, a man designed by nature to mend broken things and make them flourish. It was a great grief to her that she never had a baby, a grief she tried to assuage by devoting herself to the child of her brother Stephen, and her sister-in-law Cara. It was plain to everyone that Mary saw Alexia as much more than a niece.

"There's few people who notice as much as Mary," June said, picking up the laden tray and indicating that Lyddy should open the kitchen door. "She'd know if someone'd got heart as well as brain. And Martin Angus —"

"Yes?" Lyddy said.

"Well, he has plenty of *brain*," June said tartly, and bore the tray out of the kitchen and into the hall.

In late May, James Swinton packed his wife Mary, Lyddy and June into his cumbersome ten-year-old Rover and drove them to London for Alexia's wedding. Alexia had wanted to be married in the little grey stone church at Bishopstow, where her mother and her grandmother and James and Mary had been married, but she had been overruled by both Cara and Martin. Cara had persuaded her that it was hypocritical to be married in a church when you were not a practicing Christian and also that a Cornish wedding would be terribly difficult to organize from London. Martin had simply said that none of his friends would come so far, and that he wanted his friends to be there. So Alexia was to be married, not in the white full-skirted, floor-length wedding dress in the little old church of her childhood, as she had imagined, but in a short cream suit with a tiny matching pillbox hat, in the registry office in Lambeth.

The Bishopstow Rover made a stately progress to London at fifty-five miles an hour. The conversation inside it was only sporadic, partly because the four occupants knew each other so well there was no need to speak for politeness's sake, and partly because a slight misgiving in the heart of each one of them was very preoccupying.

"I can't put my finger exactly on what troubles me," James had said to his wife several times.

"After all, it's perfectly reasonable for a man marrying a girl to be interested in what she's worth, and I couldn't actually fault anything in young Angus's manner to me or to Alexia, but I just have this *feeling* —"

"I know," Mary said, "I know exactly. I feel just the same. I have no evidence but my instincts are ringing warning bells. I also feel we mustn't talk about it any more, in case we talk something into happening that wouldn't happen otherwise."

As the car approached London, they all began to look out of the windows with distaste.

"It's only Alexia," Lyddy said, glaring accusingly at a passing factory, and speaking for all of them, "that'd get me to leave Cornwall for *this*."

Seventeen Culver Square had never had so much attention. Edna had been persuaded to bring her sister Freda and clean the whole house. They had started at the top, and taken a week to complain and clean their way down to the bottom. The piles of *British Medical Journal*s had been banished to the shed in the garden; Cara had employed a window cleaner, and an out-of-work man from a basement flat further down the Square to repaint the front door and then, to everyone's amazement, Amanda and Felicity had turned up in a taxi, all the way from Chelsea, laden with wonderful flowers they had bought that morning in Covent Garden market and a wedding present for Alexia. The present was a sewing machine.

Cara stared at it. "A *sewing* machine —"

Alexia was thrilled. "But it's lovely, it's a really

lovely one, it's Swiss, oh they're so generous because these cost at least fifty pounds —"

"But why should you want a sewing machine?"

"To make curtains on, and clothes. All sorts of
things."

"If you ask me," Cara said, "they'd have done
better to give you the money."

When Lyddy and June arrived at Culver
Square, they admired the sewing machine.

"It's the only practical present she's got, poor
mite. Who wants three Ali Baba baskets and
seven French iron casseroles too heavy to lift?"

Cara laughed and put her arm round Lyddy,
"Darling Lydd. You never change do you? No
newfangled nonsense for you of any kind. But
I'm sorry about the sewing machine, not least because it puts Alexia under an obligation to those
two, and none of us want that. I was talking to
Martin about it only the other day, and we just
wish she'd give up that absurd job. She's paid
eight pounds a week — they've just given her a
pay rise of a pound — for doing things you
wouldn't ask a girl in a typing pool to do. I just
hope that once she's married she'll see sense."

Lyddy gave a tiny snort, "I hope that young
man's not going to bully her."

"Of course he won't. He adores her, but like
the rest of us, he can't bear to see her throwing
herself away on trivia."

"Where is he?"

"At St. Luke's, working. You know how hard
they all work, but he's particularly dedicated. Stephen and I think the world of him." She gave
Lyddy a squeeze and laughed. "You can't bear

seeing your baby married, can you? You and James and Mary, you're as bad as each other. To you, Alexia will always be six and needing a bumped knee kissed better, won't she?"

The night before the wedding, there was a small family dinner in the dining room, under the lofty gaze of beautiful Charlotte and Alexander Bewick. Alexia had put some of Amanda and Felicity's flowers — a bowl of early yellow roses — in the center of the table, and had insisted that she, and not Edna should do the cooking. She looked pretty and pale, with just the right bridal air of excited apprehension, and she wore, wound high round her throat like a choker, the pearls that Alexandra had given Cara on the day war broke out, September 3, 1939, the day Cara was eighteen. The pearls were Cara's wedding present to Alexia.

Martin was late. Nobody seemed in the least worried by this and Stephen knew exactly what he was doing.

"I left him in charge of the last round on men's surgical this evening. It shouldn't have taken long, but something will have cropped up. It always does."

When he finally arrived, when the others were halfway through eating Alexia's excellent crown roast of lamb, he was full of apology.

"I'm so desperately sorry, truly I am." He caught Stephen's eye. "I'll tell you the details later, but it isn't really table talk, as I'm sure you understand." He bent over Alexia and kissed her. "I'm so sorry, my darling, it's so awful for you, this foretaste of what being married to a doctor's like, even if you didn't know already —"

She smiled up at him. "That's all right. I quite understand."

"You're sweet. You're not only sweet, but," his eyes strayed to the plateful June was putting down in the empty place laid ready for him, "you're a brilliant cook and I'm a lucky fellow." He sat down and picked up his wineglass and his blue, full-of-life eyes traveled round the family. "Let's drink to Alexia," he said, loudly. "Let's drink to lovely Alexia, and to my incredible luck."

Later that evening, Alexia lay wakefully in her top floor bedroom. It had been such a happy evening, and when Martin had left, he had held her for a moment with particular intensity and said, his face only inches from hers, "Tomorrow you'll be mine, d'you realize that? *Mine!*" It had been a powerfully erotic moment, much more erotic than most of the actual lovemaking that Martin had introduced her to nine months ago. When it came to sex, Alexia wasn't sure if she was doing it quite right because it never seemed to be quite as thrilling each time, as she hoped and thought it would be. Probably when she was married and relaxed, she would be better at it.

Married! She rolled on her side and looked at her suit, hanging on the wardrobe door, and her hat in its shroud of tissue paper, and her new cream shoes neatly side by side on the floor. Married. Mrs. Angus. Alexia Angus. She held her left hand up in the dim light and twisted the little half hoop of diamonds and sapphires that to-

71

morrow would be paired to a wedding ring. It was terrifying to think of, and absolutely wonderful too. Tomorrow, Alexia told herself, is when life *begins*.

She sat up. It was no good. She would have to go down to the kitchen and make herself a drink, and come back up and remake her bed and start going to sleep all over again, otherwise she'd have bags under her eyes for the great day when her real life would start. She got out of bed, and padded softly down the stairs in bare feet, past all the closed doors behind which everybody slept, all the poor people who didn't have a new, lovely life beginning in the morning, Lyddy and June, Uncle James and Aunt Mary, her parents.

Someone had left the light on in the kitchen because Alexia could see a bar of yellow light under the door. She crept down the steps towards it, and put her hand out for the familiar knob, and stopped. There were people in the kitchen, and they were talking. She held her breath. The people in the kitchen were her mother and her Uncle James.

"What I don't understand," Cara was saying, "is your reasons. I mean, whether one chooses to give presents or not to anyone at any time is of course a purely personal decision, but there are a few occasions like Christmas and christenings and weddings, when it looks . . . well, odd not to give a present. Alexia hasn't said anything to me, she wouldn't, but she must have noticed that you and Mary haven't given her anything —"

"Yet."

"Well, why not yet?"

"Cara," James said, "don't you think that any discussion of presents from Mary and me to Alexia should be between Mary and me and Alexia?"

"But I'm so puzzled. I know you adore her, so I can't see —"

"That's exactly why we aren't giving her anything yet. Because we love her. We want to wait and see."

Cara's voice grew angry and Alexia shrank back against the dark wall outside the closed door. "Wait and see what?"

"If she's happy," James said calmly.

"What *do* you mean?"

There was a sound of a chair being scraped back as if James was standing up. Alexia tensed herself to run.

"What I mean," James said, "my dear but obstinate sister, is that Mary and I see what we see, rather than what we want to see. Whatever we choose to give to Alexia will be for *her*, and only for her husband too if he makes her happy."

"You're ridiculous," Cara said. She sounded furious.

"I'm nothing of the sort," James said. He sounded quite unruffled. "I'm a canny old farmer and a loving old uncle, and I'm also a tired old fellow who's driven up from Cornwall, so I'm now going to bed."

His voice came nearer the door and Alexia took a step away from it.

"Don't you like Martin Angus?" Cara demanded.

Right behind the door, James's voice said, "I've told you. I'm not expressing any opinion. I'm just going to wait and see," and then he turned the handle of the door, and Alexia fled away back up the stairs to her room, before he caught her.

She flung herself across her rumpled bed, and buried her face in the pillow. Uncle James! Uncle James of all people, to doubt Martin, to doubt her choice, to withhold a present! It was like a betrayal, like finding that somebody on whose loyalty you had utterly relied, had failed you. She raised her head. Her teddy bear watched her steadily with his round glass eyes. "It doesn't matter," she said to him, "it doesn't matter, does it? Tomorrow I'll have Martin, I'll have Martin to be my very own, to share everything with. I can tell him about Uncle James, I can talk to him, he'll listen to me. From tomorrow, I won't ever be lonely again, will I? Not ever. Tomorrow —" she reached out and pulled the bear to her so that their noses were touching. "Tomorrow, Teddy, is my wedding day."

Chapter Six

Alexia and Martin moved into a minute flat in a shabby early Victorian house not far from the Tate Gallery. Martin had been determined not to live south of the river and Alexia had been determined to live happily wherever he chose. The flat consisted of a single room with a cupboard off it that passed for a kitchen, and a tiny bathroom with no outside window. The rent was two pounds ten shillings a week, electricity and gas extra. Alexia, bent upon being an excellent wife, estimated carefully that she could then spend a further three pounds a week on food, and still have two pounds and ten shillings left out of her wages for bills and clothes. Martin, who had an allowance from his father, ran his car, bought any extras they might like, such as the odd bottle of wine or a trip to the cinema and said he was saving the rest so that, when he was qualified, they would have a deposit to put down on a flat of their own. He showed Alexia the building society pass book into which these weekly savings would go, and she felt that they were behaving responsibly.

She was very eager to make the flat charming. During the frequent evenings that Martin was working, she painted the main room; three walls pale olive green and the fourth deep olive green.

On her wedding present sewing machine, she made her first real curtains, out of a William Morris–designed fabric that Amanda let her have for two shillings a yard. She made cushion covers for the cushions she piled on their bed in the daytime to make it look like a sofa, and a table-cloth to disguise the state of their table. She bought butcher's hooks to hang from a bar in her tiny kitchen, and hold her pans and jugs, and made curtains to hide the crude shelves that took the place of kitchen cupboards. She found, rather as she found working for Amanda and Felicity, that doing these domestic things gave her a sense of achievement. They also gave her something to do while Martin was working.

She had always known what it would be like to be married to a doctor, and she had told herself that she was quite prepared for the long, long hours that medical students and young interns had to devote to their hospitals. After all, how else could they learn what could only be learned by experience? But what she found she was not at all prepared for was Martin's preoccupation with St. Luke's. He came home, it seemed, as if his mind was still in another world, and as if he could hardly remember that Alexia was supposed now to be the most important thing in his life. He would kiss her, but not with real attention, when he came in and he would talk to her, but again not as if he were really focusing on her. She told herself he was terribly tired. He worked such long hours — now for another consultant, not Stephen — and the work was so intense, so of course he was tired. Alexia tried very hard not to remind herself that before they were married, he had never seemed too tired either to take her out or to concentrate upon her as if she really interested him.

She continued to work for Chelsea Curtains, which had now grown so much as a business that it was employing an extra curtain maker, a girl called Tamsin who smoked French cigarettes and wore tiny tunic dresses that fastened up the front with enormous zips. Ludo the lover had been replaced by a political zealot called Hank, who made Felicity go with him on protest marches against the war in Vietnam, and came down to the workroom to harangue everybody about the Rhodesian question or read to them out of the works of Mao Tse-tung.

"Darling, he's too utterly boring," Amanda said, but Felicity didn't care. "Not in bed," she said.

Oddly enough, it was at work that Alexia felt she was more in touch with life than in the flat, even though she was now a married woman, with a husband and a wedding ring. If it wasn't for the basement at Danvers Street, with its slightly raffish clientele, and its endless chatter about everything from Soviet spacecraft landing on the moon through the rise and rise of the miniskirt to the latest films and songs, Alexia sometimes felt that she might have been quite as lonely as she'd been before she was married. There was a new Beatles song, called "Eleanor Rigby," about a lonely spinster, which everybody sang, all the time — that is when they weren't singing "Born Free" — and for some reason, Alexia couldn't bear to hear it. She couldn't think why, because she was the very reverse of a solitary old spinster herself — wasn't she? — but whenever she heard the song on the radio in the flat, she stopped whatever she was doing, at once, to turn it off.

In October, Alexia missed a period. She was immediately apprehensive. Unknown to Martin, she had stopped taking the pill when they were married out of an ill-defined anxiety about the pill's effect on any children they might have, and had been to a family planning clinic which had fitted her with a diaphragm — a horrible device, she thought — and several large white unromantic tubes of spermicidal cream.

Martin had said even before they were married that he didn't want even to think about children.

"Not until I'm qualified. How would we manage financially? I'm afraid it's out of the question."

Alexia had agreed. Of course she must support him for these final two years through all his biggest examinations and then, equally of course, she would stop work and have a baby. That was what happened. They would move into a bigger flat, preferably with a garden to put a pram in, and there wouldn't be any more decisions to take about her life because, once she had married and had a baby, everything would have decided itself.

But now this plan looked as if it wouldn't even get off the ground. Alexia decided to wait and to tell nobody, not even Martin. It crossed her mind to tell Amanda and Felicity, but they would probably just say well darling, if you don't want to have a baby, you don't have to have it in this day and age, and she didn't want anyone even to suggest that. So she waited anxiously, for another month, and then, with a mixture of elation and fear, went back to her family planning clinic.

"Mrs. Angus," the doctor said to her, smiling, "Mrs. Angus, I'm delighted to tell you that you are pregnant."

Alexia swallowed. Her throat felt dry.

"Am I?"

"Definitely."

"But —"

"But what?"

"Well, it's a bit awkward because my husband isn't quite qualified yet and we need what I earn —"

The doctor's smile faded a little. "I'm sure you'll find a way of coping, Mrs. Angus. You're a healthy young woman and, may I tell you, extremely fortunate to have conceived with such ease."

Alexia went out into the street. She was sure the sun had been out when she went into the clinic but now the sky was muffled with clouds, quite grey, just as the street and everybody walking along it seemed. Alexia leant against the railings outside the clinic. She was pregnant, finally irreversibly pregnant, which was not what she wanted to be because Martin didn't want it yet. How was she going to tell him? And what had happened to her, to them, that she should be afraid to tell Martin, her husband, her best friend, that she was pregnant because she had stopped taking the pill because she had an instinctive fear of it? She suddenly thought of Lyddy, of Aunt Mary, and a babyish longing to be with them, to be at Bishopstow safe and sound, swept over her and tears rose thick in her throat. Well, it was no good. She couldn't go running to anyone, certainly not to Cara, she'd simply have to confront Martin, tell him what she'd done and tell him, that in June 1967, he would become a father.

She walked tiredly home from the clinic through the Warwick Way market, and bought some chicken legs to casserole for supper, and a brown paper bag of spinach and a small bunch of bananas which she thought she could sprinkle with butter and brown sugar and lemon juice, and grill, for pudding. Whatever she cooked had to be capable of either sitting in the oven for hours, or being grilled at the last minute, because she never knew when Martin would be in for supper or, indeed, if he would be in at all.

She carried everything home and, weary though she was, conscientiously made the casserole and put it in a low oven, scrubbed two potatoes to bake and put the spinach to soak clean in a bowl of cold water. Then, suddenly unable even to stand up for fatigue, she lay down on the bed, and fell into a deep and instant sleep.

When she woke, it was quite dark. Disorientated by having slept in the afternoon, she lay for a while wondering where she was and what was happening. Then she remembered with a lurch of misery. She was pregnant and had yet to confront Martin with the news.

She rolled off the bed and felt her way to the nearest light switch. Her watch said eight-forty! The casserole would be ruined. She flew to the oven and took out the dish. It was far from perfect. There was no time to bake the potatoes, she'd have to peel and boil them for mashing, which she would do at once, now, so that they could be cooking while she brushed her hair and washed the sleep from her face and straightened the bed and laid the table and put the lamp on, so that when Martin came in everything would be welcoming and pretty and . . .

She froze. There was, unmistakably, the sound of a key in the lock. The door opened.

"Hello," Martin said. He wasn't smiling. He stared at her, at her rumpled clothes and wild hair and stunned sleepy face, and then he threw his keys on the table. He didn't even attempt to come into the kitchen alcove to kiss her.

"I went to sleep," Alexia said, "by mistake. I . . . I'm afraid supper isn't quite ready —"

"I'm not hungry," Martin said. He went into the bathroom and Alexia could hear him washing vigorously, splashing his face noisily with running water from the tap. She put down the potato peeler, and began to hurry round the room, plumping cushions, turning the overhead light off and the lamp on.

Martin came out of the bathroom.

"Can we talk?"

"Of course," Alexia said. Her voice sounded polite and obedient. She put up her hands to smooth her hair a bit, and then tugged at her jersey.

"Come and sit down," Martin said.

An anxiety — quite a different anxiety from the one she had lived with for the last month — began to form in a cold pool in the pit of Alexia's stomach. She sat down on the edge of their bed, with her knees together, and leaned forward, clasping them, to stop herself from shaking. Martin sat opposite, in their only armchair. He looked as exhausted as she felt, and his eyes had a bright glitter in them, like that of a fever.

"Alexia —"

"Yes?"

He looked up at her and took a deep breath. "Alexia, I'm afraid it isn't any good. It's never been any good, and I can't go on pretending."

Her mouth was suddenly so dry that when she opened it to say that she didn't understand him, no words would come.

"I don't want to hurt you," Martin said. "You must believe that. I really don't. I never did. I never meant —" He stopped.

Alexia whispered, "You . . . you never meant what?"

Martin looked down at the floor. He began to twist his fingers together so hard that Alexia could see the bones pressing whitely through the flesh. It seemed an age that they sat there in silence, Martin staring at the shabby carpet, and Alexia staring at his twisting, grinding, miserable hands.

At last he said, with visible difficulty, "Alexia, I never meant to see Susie again."

"What?"

He raised his head and looked at her. She saw

the wretchedness in his eyes deepen as it reflected the horror in her own.

"I never meant to see Susie again. Not ever. For one thing, I'd found you, and for another, she'd given me the push in a pretty humiliating way. When we got engaged, when you took me down to Bishopstow, I remember thinking, 'What a relief, now I'm free of Susie for ever, now I've got Alexia and a real future.'"

"And?" Alexia said, her voice unnaturally high.

Martin said flatly, "She rang me. She saw our engagement announcement in the paper and she rang the hospital to say . . . to say —"

"To say what?"

Martin twisted sideways in the chair so that Alexia could hardly see his face.

"To say that she had something terribly important to tell me, and that we had to meet."

Alexia said stonily, "So you did."

"Yes."

"Why? For God's sake, Martin, *why?* You were engaged to *me!*"

Martin turned still further so that his face was almost buried in the chair back, and his voice was muffled.

"I . . . I don't know. I suppose she . . . she'd been so important to me once and I sort of felt I couldn't just slap her down now. She sounded as if she was in such trouble —"

"Turn round!" Alexia shouted suddenly. "Turn round and look at me!"

Slowly, slowly Martin straightened in the chair.

"And what happened?"

"She . . . she said she'd made an awful mistake,

leaving me. She said it broke her heart to open the newspaper and find our announcement."

"I see."

"I never meant to!" Martin cried. "I just meant to pat her shoulder kindly and say goodbye —"

Light dawned slowly in Alexia's brain, cold, horrible, unwelcome light. She gaped at him.

"You were engaged to me and going to bed with me and you went to bed with *Susie?*"

He said pathetically, "I only meant it to be once —"

Alexia slipped from the bed to the floor, and crouched there, like a wounded animal. I mustn't cry, she thought, I mustn't, nor must I beg or plead. I must simply accept that this has happened, that it happened before we were married, and that he has confessed and then I must do my utter best to forgive him.

"Martin —"

"Yes?"

"All this happened before the wedding?"

He said nothing. Alexia made a huge effort and sat back on her heels, pushing her hair out of her eyes.

"Let me put that more clearly. You had another little fling with Susie before we were married, and it's been lying on your conscience and now, at last, after all these months, you can't bear the burden any more, so you've told me?"

There was another long pause, and then Martin said, "No."

"No!"

"Once . . . once I'd started seeing her again, I couldn't stop. I tried to, believe me, I tried to, all the time I tried to —"

"Not very hard!" Alexia screamed.

He looked deeply hurt. "Oh yes I did. I tried harder than you'll ever know. Because of you."

She stared at him. Hysteria rose in her throat in thick, wild bubbles.

"Because of *me?* Hah!"

"I love you," Martin said, "I still do. But Susie's something else, a sort of —"

Alexia slapped her hands over her ears.

"Don't tell me!"

"I didn't want it to be this way, I never thought it could be such a bloody mess —"

Alexia looked at him in disgust. She took her hands away from her head.

"Don't keep whining!"

He said huffily, "I'm trying . . . I'm trying to say I'm sorry."

"It's no good being sorry! It's useless being sorry! The only thing that's any good is giving up Susie —"

He looked down again.

"I can't."

"You can't? Why can't you?"

"Susie's pregnant."

In a flat, hard voice that seemed to come from miles away, Alexia said, "Is she?"

"Yes. Six months. She's got no one to support her and her family are furious and she hasn't any money —"

"So?"

"I've been giving her money, you see —"

"What money?"

"Money from my building society account —"

"But that was *our* money! For *our* flat!"

He put his chin up. "Well, it's gone now."

Alexia stood up, so that she could look down on him.

"You are absolutely despicable."

He shrugged. "Of course I'm not *proud* of what I've done. And I'm bloody scared of the future. Bang go all dreams of Harley Street —"

"To which I looked like the passport?"

"Yes."

"But you," her voice took on an edge of sarcasm, "can't do without Susie."

"No, I can't."

"So?"

"I want a divorce, Alexia."

The room seemed to rock and sway a little, as if the walls were bulging and buckling.

She whispered, "A divorce?"

"Yes. Yes, please."

Something suddenly snapped in her. She looked down at him sitting in the armchair as if he was a stranger and not only a stranger but a mad stranger.

"Get out."

"What?"

"Get out," Alexia said. "This is my flat that I pay for and I don't want you in it, not for another second. You're a cheat and a liar and a swindler and an adulterer and a con man and I wish I'd never set eyes on you." Her voice rose and she shouted, "And you're also the most utter and complete fool in the entire world!"

He got up and stood staring angrily at her, so that for a second she thought he might hit her.

Then, without another word, he pushed past her and not even picking up his keys from the table, fled out of the flat slamming the door behind him.

When he had gone, Alexia scraped the chicken casserole into the waste bucket, and put the potatoes back in the vegetable basket. Then she turned out all the lights and lay down, still dressed, on the bed and stared into the darkness. She felt as if her feelings were under a kind of anaesthetic, as if, in a moment, she would remember her dreams of happy marriage, of being loved for ever, of being understood and appreciated, and then the real, dreadful pain would begin. But at this moment she felt nothing, she felt, quite simply, frozen.

Then she remembered. She gave a little gasp and her hands crept down her body to lie on her flat stomach. She was pregnant, newly pregnant. I'm twenty, she thought, I've been married for seven months and my husband has left me, and I'm pregnant. She turned over, until her face was buried in the cushions she had so carefully, hopefully covered, and cried and cried as if her heart would break.

Chapter Seven

"I don't know what to do," Cara said, "I simply don't know what to do."

Alexia said nothing. They were sitting opposite each other in the bleak room at Culver Square and Cara had her head in her hands.

"We've never had a divorce in the family before, in fact the family has always been renowned for its happy marriages —"

Alexia interrupted, with superhuman self-control, "Perhaps nobody in the family has ever been abandoned by their husband of seven months before."

Cara whispered, "Oh, I'm sorry, I'm sorry, I didn't mean that, I'm just so shocked —"

"Me too," Alexia said.

Cara looked across the returned piles of *British Medical Journal*s at her daughter. Alexia appeared to be about fourteen, shrunk to the size of a child with her face as thin and pale as a new moon and her eyes, by contrast, the size of headlamps. Headlamps with dark, bruised circles under them. Something in Alexia's face stirred a memory in Cara, a memory she usually preferred to keep buried, of her own betrayal, long ago in the spring of 1942, when a man she believed herself to be engaged to had turned out to have been married to someone else for months. That man was now her brother-in-law, Stephen's elder brother Alan. Alan had grown stout and prosperous and hearty over the years and hardly a trace of the young Alan remained, but one of the reasons Cara chose never to think of that part of her past was that he had, as a young man, thrilled her. Physically, Alan Langley had made her briefly feel — she shook herself resolutely. He had almost seduced her and then he had betrayed her. Martin Angus had succeeded in seducing her daughter, and then he too had betrayed her. The spirit and accepted morality of 1942 and 1966 might be worlds apart but human behavior didn't seem to have changed a scrap.

She put out a hand to Alexia. Alexia took it briefly, gave it a little embarrassed squeeze, and let it go.

"It isn't that I don't sympathize," Cara said, "I feel terribly for you, I swear I do, it's just that it's so much to cope with all at once. We believed in Martin, Daddy and I, we were so sure he . . . he —"

"Would be the making of me?"

"Yes."

"Well, you were wrong. And for other reasons, I was wrong."

Cara said tentatively, with none of her usual certainty of manner, "Do you still love him?"

Alexia's eyes filled with tears. "I don't know. I hate him in a way but I can't bear him to be with Susie, to want to be with Susie —"

"I'm sorry," Cara said, "I'm so sorry. I shouldn't have asked. I suppose I just hoped you were in a fury with him so there wasn't room for love."

Alexia got up and went over to the window. Outside in the square, a little autumn wind was blowing rubbish about and a bored au pair girl was sulking on a wooden seat while a little boy near her stirred a puddle with a stick. He was perhaps two. In under three years she, Alexia, would have someone of about two stirring puddles with sticks.

She said, without turning round, "He doesn't know I'm going to have a baby."

"But he must!"

"No, he mustn't. Babies ought to be conceived in love and this one was only conceived in love on my side, so it's not his business. He thought I was on the pill, but I stopped taking it because I was scared."

"But he must provide for you and the baby!"

Alexia turned round.

"No he mustn't. I'll do that."

"But you can't!"

"I can. The flat's dirt cheap, and later, when the baby's born, I'll take it to work in a basket."

"No," Cara said. She got up and smoothed her habitual man's jersey down over her neat trousers. She seemed to have pulled herself together and to be, once more, efficient public-spirited Cara, the Lambeth tower of strength. "No, you can't do that. You must come home. We'll look after you until the baby is born, and then we'll find someone local to look after it until it's old enough to join the crèche, and you can at last train for something worthwhile. I promise you,

Alexia, that we'll back you up. This horrible episode need in no way spoil either your chances or your life. We can make the room next to yours into a nursery and you can join these marvellous new prenatal classes at St. Luke's where they teach you how to breathe properly so as to relax yourself."

"No, thank you," Alexia said.

Cara came towards her. She put an arm a little awkwardly round Alexia's shoulders.

"Darling, I do understand. I'm so stupid, I'm going far too fast for you. You just run down slowly and give up your job and the flat when you feel ready."

Alexia moved away a little, out of Cara's embrace.

"I know you mean well, Mum, but I don't want to do any of those things."

The old familiar look of exasperation crept back into Cara's face. "I see. So what do you propose to do?"

Alexia said, "I shall go on living in the flat and working in Chelsea until the spring. And then I shall go down to Cornwall. I'm going to ask Uncle James and Aunt Mary if the baby can be born at Bishopstow."

Cara gave a little shout, something between a cry and a laugh. "I might have known it! I might have guessed! Life throws you the first problem you have ever known, and you go scuttling back to Bishopstow, like a child to a nursery!"

Alexia held on to the nearest armchair back in order neither to faint nor to lose her temper.

"That isn't the reason I'm going back."

"Isn't it? Isn't it? Then what, pray, might your reasons be?"

"I'm not telling you."

"You're not *telling* me?"

"No," Alexia said, "I'm not telling you because there isn't a hope in hell of your even beginning to understand."

Alexia went slowly, sadly home to her flat. Cara had wanted her to stay and see her father, but Alexia had come to the end of all her energy, emotional as well as physical, and had insisted on leaving. Despite their sharp words, Cara had attempted to kiss her as they said goodbye, and they had bumped cheekbones together in a way that had only made Alexia remember poignantly how easy it was to kiss Lyddy, and how easy it always had been.

She had, when she got home, a letter to write. Two, in fact. The first one she had told Cara she would write that evening, and begged Cara not to telephone Bishopstow until it had had a chance to arrive there. It was a very difficult letter, and she had to write it several times, and even when it was finished, it didn't satisfy her because it seemed bald and childish. But if she really let her feelings go, on paper, the letter would be unsendable.

Dear Aunt Mary and Uncle James,

I'm afraid I have some bad news for you, which will be difficult to explain so please forgive me if this letter isn't very well written.

Martin has left me. He was in love with someone else before he met me and he never stopped seeing her and now he has gone back to her. She is having his baby.

I am having a baby too, next June. Martin doesn't know about this and I don't want him to. He thought I was on the pill, so he won't think of pregnancy.

I am all right. I can keep going here this winter and I have a nice doctor. What I would like to ask you is whether I could come down to Bishopstow next May, so that when the baby is born, it can be born there.

Please say if this is inconvenient.

> With love from
> Alexia

P.S. I have told Mum today. She is very upset and wants me to go back to Culver Square but I can't do that. I expect she will ring you.

The second letter was easy. Alexia wrote it straight off.

Dear Martin:

I have packed up all your clothes and books and will take them to the main reception desk at St. Luke's Hospital for you to collect. You will find my wedding and engagement rings in an envelope in the pocket of your gray jacket.

Please don't get in touch. I am all right and am managing very well. Everything is finished.

Alexia

Then she put both letters into their respective envelopes — Martin's was addressed to St. Luke's — and went down into the autumn dusk to put them in the letter box on the Embankment.

Amanda and Felicity, mercifully, asked very few questions. Their own lives had been so riven with dramas, that Alexia's small tragedy was nothing uncommon to them. It never crossed their minds that Alexia should stop working for them.

"Honestly, angel, you know we'd rather strangle you than let you go, so we'll find a way. Hang the baby in a bag from the ceiling or something. Do you feel sick?"

"Only when I think of brown bread or bananas and only first thing and last thing."

"Poor sweet. And do you simply crave lumps of coal in the middle of the night?"

"Not so far —"

"Well, just say the word when you do and you shall have your very own scuttleful. That bloody man."

"All men," Felicity said, "are bloody. At least Alexia's discovered that at twenty so she has no illusions. Have you, angel?"

But Alexia couldn't bear mention of Martin, not even a jokey one. It reminded her anew, every time, that Martin hadn't just taken himself away, but he had taken her new belief in herself, the fledgling self-confidence that he had given her. When he went away, he had left her with exactly what she had had before — her same old lonely, clearly unexciting, domestically competent self. True, she had stood up to Cara, but that too was nothing new. She had, after all, stood up to Cara over the matter of university.

Felicity and Amanda wanted her to work shorter hours, but she said she didn't want to.

"I don't mind getting tired, it makes me sleep better, and honestly, I'd rather be busy."

"Then we'll put your wages up. You shall have nine pounds a week and as much coal as you can eat when you start craving it."

"But that's two pay rises in a year!"

"Suppose you're worth it?"

Alexia blushed.

"Honestly, darling," Amanda said, "sometimes I could smack you."

In the evenings, Alexia walked very slowly up the King's Road on her way home, usually pausing at the Safeway supermarket to buy something for her solitary supper. Try as she might not to feel sorry for herself, she couldn't help noticing how many couples there were, men and girls shopping together or walking together hand in hand. And if people weren't in couples, most of them looked, to her, as if they had left the other half of a couple at home waiting for them, and they didn't have to turn the key on to an empty room which would look exactly as it had looked, and been left, in the morning.

"But I chose this," Alexia said to herself, over and over, "I could have gone back to Culver Square, but I chose to live alone, so I can't complain. Well, I can, but I shouldn't."

Every evening, when she turned the last corner into her street, she had to take a deep breath and square her shoulders. The street was almost always empty, even though it was so close to the busy Embankment, because the houses in it were almost all condemned, and were occupied by elderly tenants clinging on to the ends of their leases who never went out after dark. But one evening, there was someone standing on the steps of the house where Alexia lived, a male someone in an overcoat. With a lurch of panic, Alexia thought it might be Martin, and stopped walking.

The man had seen her. He raised his arm in a wave, and came down the steps, and hurried down the pavement towards her.

"Alexia, Alexia, my dear child. Alexia —"

It was Uncle James. He came straight up to her and enveloped her in a hug that seemed to bring all Cornwall with it. To her shame, Alexia burst into tears.

"I'm so sorry, really I am, I shouldn't cry, I'm fine, but it's so lovely to see you, it's so —"

"Sh," said James, patting and soothing. "There, there. Sh."

Sniffing and laughing, she detached herself from his comforting tweed embrace and led him up to the flat. He looked round it. It struck him that it was about the size of the scullery at Bishopstow, the smaller scullery where the hen buckets lived and the vegetable baskets, and the gumboots.

"Is this all of it?"

"Oh yes," Alexia said. "And I promise you it's a lot for two pounds ten a week. Three pounds in the new year. Do you like it?"

James looked again very carefully. He couldn't but notice the effort she had made. He said gruffly, "You've made it very pretty."

"It's better for one than two," she said bravely.

He regarded her. "You're too thin."

She took off her coat and stood sideways. "No, I'm not. Look. I look as if I've swallowed an enormous egg."

"A tiny egg," he said. He suddenly wished Mary had come with him. He thought he was going to cry.

"It's so lovely to see you," Alexia said, coming to help him off with his coat. "You're super to come."

"We've been so worried —"

"I'm all right, you know."

"You can't be," James said fiercely. "You're still only a child yourself, you can't possibly be. I want to murder that young man."

"Please don't talk about it," Alexia said quickly. She went into the kitchen cupboard and he could hear her filling the kettle. "I don't mean to be rude but I don't seem able to talk about him yet without screaming or bursting into tears. Would you like some cinnamon toast?"

James sat down in the armchair where Martin had sat when he announced he was leaving.

"I should love it. I'm famished. I came up on

the train and the very sight of a British Rail sandwich made me want to weep. I've booked myself into Brown's Hotel — don't smile, Alexia, it's where I *always* stay, I've stayed there since 1946 — and I'm going to take you out to dinner and feed you up."

Alexia spread slices of bread on the grill pan, and turned the grill up high. Then she came and crouched on the corner of the bed, close to James.

"I'd adore that, I really would. How is Aunt Mary?"

"Better."

"Better? Was she ill, what was the matter, what happened —"

James patted her hand. "She had a little relapse, poor girl, when she heard about you. You know how she is. Ever since the war. But she's so much better and sent as much love to you as I could carry."

"I'm so sorry, I never meant —"

"Of course you didn't," James said. "You wrote the simplest letter you could. Much better not to telephone."

"I haven't got a telephone," Alexia said. She leaned forward. "Uncle James —"

"Don't you think, at your advanced age, we could drop the uncle?"

"I'll try. Uncle James, I mean James, could I ask you something before we go out to dinner because it would set my mind at rest?"

"Ask away. Anything you like."

"Could I," Alexia said, spooning tea, "I mean, will it be all right to come to Bishopstow for the baby?"

James got up and came to stand behind her.

"I tell you, my dear, you'd break our hearts if you tried to have it anywhere else."

Alexia turned round and looked straight at him. "Thank you," she said. "Thank you more than I can say." Handing him the teapot and two mugs, she added, "Well, there's nothing left to worry about now."

He gave a little bark of laughter.

"Nothing to worry about? My dear child, the worries are only just beginning. That's what I'm here for, that's why I've come up to London." He put the pot and mugs carefully down on the table. "Mind you, none of the immediate ones are things we can't do something about. Get you out of here for a start, and into a decent flat, stop you working —"

"Dear Uncle James," Alexia said. "Really dear. But no thank you. I don't want that. I don't want money and I don't want to stop working."

James looked baffled. "But you can't want to go on living here. And your mother says your job is menial and ill paid and —"

"Mum doesn't like the sort of people I work for. She thinks they're social parasites. But they've been really kind to me and I've come to like them. They aren't like us, and they are pretty sociable, but they're rather brave in their way and they never whine. And I like the job, I really do. I'm good at it."

James grunted. "Where is it?"

"In the basement of a little pink house in Danvers Street. In Chelsea. They're called Amanda and Felicity."

"And the money?"

"I'm managing," Alexia said.

"But —"

"Listen," Alexia said firmly, in a voice that suddenly reminded James very much of his mother, "I'm managing. I really am. And after the baby, I'll manage again. You'll see."

After a night tossing and turning in his comfortable bed in Brown's Hotel and longing for his Cornish pillows, James ate a solitary breakfast, telephoned Mary, and then ordered a taxi to take him to Danvers Street. He had not told Alexia he was going to Danvers Street, and had in fact only decided to when, after a very happy dinner the night before, she had said she would be late for work the next day as she had a checkup doctor's appointment first.

There was, James was relieved to see, only one pink house in Danvers Street. Amanda opened the door, expecting him to be a delivery man with three bales of buff lining and a dozen boxes of heading tape.

"Heavens," said Amanda, lowering her dark glasses for a fraction of a second, "what *have* we done to deserve someone like you?"

James, immediately charmed, began to laugh. "I'm Alexia's uncle."

Amanda gave a little squeal and leaned forward and kissed him. "In that case, come in and stay for ever. *You* are Alexia's absolutely perfect Uncle James! Felicity, Felicity! Come quickly and see what I've got! So sorry, do come in and I'll drag her out of bed. She's got a new man and she's running him in and it always takes a lot of concentration."

She led him, still laughing, up a narrow black-carpeted stair to the first-floor sitting room whose curtains were half drawn. It was filled with extraordinary black and white furniture, and there was a huge plant, almost a tree, in one corner with a stuffed parrot hanging upside down in it and a bat pinned on the top.

"Now, sit down and don't move an inch until I come back with Felicity. I'm sure you want to talk about Alexia —"

"— yes, I do, it's why I've come —"

"— and so do we, like mad, and we must do it quickly by ten o'clock before she comes because she'd go mad if she thought we were conspiring and she's so frighteningly punctual."

She was gone for five minutes. While she was gone, he looked at the bat and the parrot and the op-art fabrics and the lamps on the floor, and thought that however peculiar, Danvers Street was a much better advertisement for a house in London than Culver Square. Culver Square reminded him of Cara. He'd had a very difficult conversation with Cara. Poor old girl, trying to reconcile herself to the fact that she and Stephen had seriously misjudged Martin Angus on top of trying to come to terms with the fact that her only child was about to be virtually an unmarried mother.

"The worst thing," Cara had said on the telephone, "is that she won't let me help her. She just won't. I think she'd rather have help from anybody in the world but me. Oh James, what have I done wrong?"

"Well," Felicity said, coming into the room wearing a pale pink trouser suit and pale pink boots. "What an utter treat."

James got up. They were quite mad, these girls, but he couldn't help rather liking them. They made him somehow feel a bit younger and — well, to be honest, they made him feel a bit *frisky*. He winked at Felicity.

Amanda came in with a tray of coffee.

"I'm afraid it'll be disgusting. We can't make coffee without Alexia. She bosses us into a cocked hat, you should see her, sergeant majors having nothing on Alexia, but she gets things done all right and she gets us to get things done."

James accepted a fuchsia pink mug of coffee covered with black spots.

"I've rather come seeking advice. I don't know if you've seen where she lives —"

"She simply refuses to let us come," Felicity said. "But of course we've been. We just prowled about. It's awful. All those houses are scheduled for demolition and I bet there isn't room to swing a cat."

"There isn't. I've offered her a better flat —"

"Which," said Amanda, making a face at her coffee, "she turned down."

"Yes."

"And I expect you told her she shouldn't be working, especially not for two idiots who chain her in a sopping basement, and she said she liked it."

"Yes."

"We've been thinking," Amanda said.

Felicity looked amazed. *"Have* we?"

"Yes, darling. I do the thinking and you do the other thing and then I tell you what I've thought."

"Brilliant," said Felicity. "Super."

James leaned towards Amanda.

"What have you been thinking?"

"This," she said. She put her coffee mug down and adjusted her glasses and went on, "I thought at first that I'd find a very rich kind man for Alexia who'd marry her and adopt the baby and hey presto, happy ending. Then I thought, no, that won't do because Alexia'll just lean on him and collapse back into being a feeble little heap. *Then* I thought, looking at her the last few weeks since that unutterable shit sugared off, I thought hey baby, you quite *like* a challenge, don't you? That's what all this independence is about, all this no, I don't want any money, and no, I don't want a nice flat and no, I don't want you to be sorry for me. Isn't it?"

"All very fine and good," James said, also abandoning his coffee, "but she can't do it alone. She can't look after a tiny baby and work enough hours to keep it and her. She *needs* help. How do we get her to take it?"

"By stealth and cunning," Amanda said.

"What *do* you mean?"

"Dear Uncle James, all I can do is give you the theme and then you'll have to write the plot."

James raised his eyes to the ceiling in mock despair.

"I give up —"

"Oh don't do that, angel," Felicity said, "not

just when Amanda's coming to the boil."

"Well, then."

"Well," said Amanda, "you've got to think of giving her some help that's got strings attached. A loan she's got to repay, for example, or a task she's got to perform for you in return for renting her a flat. Make it as difficult as you can for her. Think of something to give her, dear Cornish Uncle James, that has millions of conditions or, even better, something that's a *real* challenge. It's not her tiny mind that needs stretching, or her tiny capabilities, it's her tiny courage."

James looked doubtful. "But are you sure — I mean, would that be kind?"

Felicity opened her eyes as wide as blue saucers.

"It would be the utterly kindest thing you could do."

Chapter Eight

Whether because of her letter to him or not, Martin Angus didn't attempt to get in touch with Alexia for the whole winter. Escorted by Felicity, who was an expert in these matters, Alexia went to see a solicitor, and petitioned for a divorce, citing Martin's adultery with Susie Connolly. She learned that Martin and Susie were living together at an address in North London, in Islington, an area Alexia hardly knew, and she also learned that Martin had left St. Luke's and transferred to St. Bartolph's, the hospital where her father had trained. She was given all these facts, quite impersonally, by the solicitor and received them as impassively as she was able to. It was only afterwards, alone in her flat, that her imagination went helplessly to work on Susie Connolly, picturing her and Martin together in their Islington flat and their — still agony to think of — passionate relationship.

"I don't suppose," she said one day to Felicity, after one of these depressing legal visits, "that anyone will ever feel so strongly about me that they'd actually leave someone else for me. I'm not that sort of person."

Felicity was unsympathetic. "Well, angel, you'd simply hate it if they did because then they'd become a whacking great responsibility that was all your fault."

Felicity, following the principle established in the conversation with James, had offered to lend Alexia the money to pay for a solicitor on condition that if the money wasn't repaid within two years, Alexia must return her wedding present sewing machine.

"Of course I wouldn't take the machine," Felicity said to Amanda, "I only want her to think I will. She's such a fool, giving back her rings. They'd have paid for the solicitor. It's *such* a mistake to have honorable principles, it gets you nowhere."

Nowhere was where Alexia privately felt she was getting, all those long cold months. She went dutifully to work, and conscientiously for prenatal checkups, and tried to remember that if she didn't look after herself properly (which was hard to do because there didn't seem much point to it) the baby would suffer. She steeled herself for Christmas in Culver Square, and found herself genuinely distressed to see how her parents — her father in particular — had aged in the last few months.

Stephen was very tender with her. He didn't say much, but his glance frequently rested gently on her and he was very solicitous. It made Alexia want to cry. It was easier, in fact, to cope with Cara, whose briskness and frequent bouts of exasperation resulted in making Alexia feel cross. She decided, by Boxing Day, that she would rather feel cross than be pitied, and so, despite Stephen and Cara's protestations, she took herself back to the flat, and lay in bed, rolled up in her quilt, rereading *Jane Eyre* while the dark December day faded into night.

The spring, though more cheerful in weather terms, brought few developments. Alexia was awarded her decree nisi, which seemed to her a most discouraging document since, while it freed her from being married to Martin (and she was still not at all sure she wished to be free) it didn't free her enough to marry anyone else (and she couldn't, at the moment, imagine that anyone else would ever want her). She grew suddenly much rounder, and had to make smocks to accommodate her bulge, and sit much further away from tables and her typewriter. Chelsea Curtains won its first big contract to supply curtains for ten bedrooms in a Mayfair hotel and Amanda announced to Alexia that they would, of course, have to find a temporary replacement for the three months that Alexia would be away in Cornwall having her baby.

"We've got to plan ahead, darling. I'm sure you see that. I hope you are too. What are you going to do about your flat?"

"I was going to give it up and find another when I come back to London."

Amanda looked at her in such a way that Alexia could feel the penetration of her look even through the black glass.

"Treasure child, you must think this *through*. Suppose we take on someone to replace you who turns out to be perfectly adequate and so we can't just sack her when you come waltzing back?

And suppose you can't find another flat so cheaply? You can't just use people as hammocks, darling, to flop into when you can't be bothered to think for yourself any more, you've got to *plan*."

"I felt a complete beast," Amanda said to Felicity later. "Complete and utter. She looked *stricken*. But we've got to do it for her own good, we've got to keep putting little boots in. I only wish I knew what dear old Uncle J. was planning to do. If anything."

Alexia was indeed very shaken by this conversation. She realized that she had been just drifting along thinking that she would have this baby and then life would bumble on the other side of it, much the same as it always had, except that there would be a baby too, rather like a dog or a kitten. She spent a sleepless night. She suddenly saw that the baby wasn't just a little hiccup in her life but was instead both a dead end in one area and a huge new start in another. Whatever life was like after the baby, it would be — this was now perfectly clear — utterly different. She would be busier and more tired, and — this was quite a frightening thought — she wouldn't be free any more. She couldn't even go out to buy a loaf and a newspaper for five minutes without taking the baby too. If Amanda and Felicity didn't take her back (and they well might not, and she had no right to complain because they had been wonderful to her and really had had no obligation to be wonderful, being only employers), she would have to find another job

108

where she could take a baby, or a job well paid enough to allow her to employ a nanny, and she wasn't qualified enough at anything to get a well-paid job. She felt suddenly full of fear and equally full of self-disgust at being so childish and pathetic and just assuming life would somehow turn out all right.

As the first glimmer of dawn began to filter through the curtains, Alexia was still awake. Sleep was now clearly out of the question. She got up and brushed her hair and teeth, and put the kettle on; then she sat down on an upright chair, her hands around her bump, and waited for the water to boil. She might have made some terrible mistakes, she told herself, and being her, she would probably make a whole lot more, but she wasn't going to give in, all the same. She would think of a plan, a way of living, she would get through somehow, but she wasn't — she straightened her back a little and gave the bump a reassuring pat — she wasn't going to waste all the distance she had travelled so far on the road to independence, by going back to Culver Square.

Bishopstow had never looked so welcoming to Alexia as it did that late May day. The sky above it was like an illustration in a children's picture book, pale clear blue, dotted with fat white clouds, and the fields stretching away around the house were bright with soft green growth. There were lambs, and two litters of piglets and a new brood of ducklings, no bigger than eggs and furry with first feathers, brown and yellow like floating bumble bees.

In her bedroom there was a vase of white lilac in the hearth, and the last of the tiny frilly wild daffodils in a green glass jug by her bed. Everything else was blessedly, chokingly familiar — the thick, worn faded carpet, the huge well-polished pieces of Victorian furniture, the pile of pillows on her bed in much darned, perfectly ironed linen pillowcases, embroidered with all those nostalgic initials of the past — ET for Emily Talbot, AS for Alexandra Swinton, even an IA for Iskandara Abbott, Alexia's strange and crippled great-grandmother whose life had been quite ruined by being the great Charlotte's only child.

There was also something new. Above the bed hung a picture, a smallish picture that Alexia couldn't ever remember seeing before, in a heavy Victorian frame. It was a charcoal drawing of a most arresting young woman, done in a free, almost impressionistic style.

"It's Charlotte," Mary said, "I thought you'd like to have her. Your grandfather drew it. It's been hanging in our bedroom and I thought it ought to come to you now. I thought —" She turned her thin, kind, worried face to Alexia, "I thought it might comfort you to feel that she found great happiness at very much your age. *Great* happiness —" She stopped.

Alexia couldn't speak. Dear Aunt Mary, racked by her own nervous instability, yet so sweet and imaginative and never self-absorbed. No wonder Uncle James — no, James — loved her. She put her arms round her aunt.

"Thank you. Thank you so, so much."

Mary kissed her cheek. "I'd have been so unhappy if you hadn't come here, for your baby. You can't imagine what it means — no, enough of that. I must pull myself together and you must go down to the kitchen and see Lyddy who is bursting to boss you about, and then you must go and find James. He wants to see you specially." She gave Alexia a smiling glance. "He has something to tell you."

After she had seen Lyddy, and been told that she was too thin and too pale and that it was downright indecent to wear a miniskirt if you were pregnant, even under a smock, and had found June and admired the piglets and been told that she, June, had delivered two Bishopstow village babies during the war because of her expertise with pigs, Alexia went in search of her uncle. He was, June said, in the dairy office, which was a euphemism for the dilapidated shed in which James did the slightly haphazard administration of his highly successful clotted cream business, posting neat little quarter- and half-pound tins all over the British Isles. He was an excellent farmer, but he was no businessman. Mary kept the accounts with absolute precision and made secret sorties to the dairy office, when James was out, to clear up the muddles he had made.

He was standing in the office, frowning over a batch of invoices, when Alexia appeared.

"Look at you," he said proudly, giving her a hug.

"Lyddy thinks I need fattening up."

"Lyddy just thinks nobody can look after

themselves without her supervision."

Alexia leaned against the ancient kneehole desk whose fourth foot was a brick. "Aunt — I mean, Mary — said you had something to tell me."

"I have," James said. He put the invoices down. "Let's go down and have a squint at the sea, and I'll tell you there."

He took her arm, and led her out into the late spring afternoon, past the dairy and the yard where the milking parlor was, and through the rose garden that Emily and Richard Talbot had designed and planted over a century before, to the little iron gate that led to the fields which hid the sea. Alexia remembered that when she was little, she had been told that she must never, ever, go through that gate until she had learned to swim.

"I used to call this the swimming gate —"

"I remember. Doesn't seem so long ago to me, either."

They walked companionably up the gentle green slope and stopped, by silent and mutual consent, when they came in sight of the sea. It was full of movement in the light wind, sparkling and shimmering, with the currents making great shining arcs in the water as it ran away to the open sea.

"I never get tired of it," James said.

"Nor me —"

"You breathe it. Breathe it right in. Give that baby a gulp of proper air."

Alexia said, "I'd love to live by the sea. By water anyway."

James shot her a glance. "Would you? Not in London?"

"Oh no. I think I've probably got to live in London for a bit for work, but I don't want to live there for ever."

James sat down on the short turf by the dunes, and patted the grass beside him.

"Come and sit yourself." He took his pipe out of his pocket and began on the soothing familiar routine, packing and tamping the tobacco, lighting it with an ancient Zippo lighter an American had given him in the war, puff, suck, puff, suck. "Alexia, what are you going to do, after the baby?"

She began to tear up tiny handfuls of grass. "I very much hope Amanda and Felicity will have me back. I know you've never met them, and Mum doesn't like them, but they've been wonderful to me. If they can't give me a job because my replacement turns out to be fine, then I'll have to find something similar, quite a casual sort of place that won't mind a baby. And I'll have to find another flat. I've given up mine and taken all my stuff to Culver Square."

"Will that be easy?" James said, squinting at her.

She looked at him. "No."

"And if you can't find a job and you can't find a flat?"

"I thought I'd try and get a job in a school. Undermatron or something. I could live in, you see, and it would be quite jolly for the baby."

"What about going back to Culver Square and letting them help you and training for something?"

"No, thank you," Alexia said. "You've been talking to Mum."

James gave her a little grin. "Only testing."

Alexia pushed her fringe off her face. "To be honest, I've got quite scared thinking of the future, but it seems to me that the only way to stop being scared is not to do the easy thing and give up, but just keep going on."

James looked at her approvingly. He puffed on his pipe in silence for a while, and then he said, "I've got something for you."

"Something for *me?*"

"But you may not like it."

She was very excited. "I like everything you and Mary have ever given me —"

"But this is different —"

"Tell me, tell me —"

"Then listen," James said. "Listen very carefully." He took his pipe out of his mouth and fixed his gaze on her. "Last Christmas I wrote to Castle Bewick School, reminding them that a new ten-year lease would begin in September, and that I should then be reviewing the rent. I had a letter back, after several weeks, from the headmaster, saying that the school was in some financial difficulties and that any increase in rent would be out of the question." He paused. Alexia's eyes were fixed on his face. "I replied that I was afraid that I couldn't continue to lease him the house at a rate fixed in 1956. There was another pause and then, rather ironically, on April Fool's Day, I received a letter saying that he was giving up the lease and closing the school and intended vacating the premises by August 31."

James stopped again and maddeningly began to puff on his pipe. Alexia, leaning forward, could hardly contain her impatience.

"So," James said at last, "what am I left with? I'm left with a huge great house and thousands of acres of land of which only a few hundred are farmable as I farm here, on a loch in Scotland, where I neither live nor wish to live. So —"

"So?" She was on her knees and could scarcely breathe for expectancy.

"So," said James almost casually, "I'm going to give it to you. It's a delayed wedding present."

She fell over sideways on to the grass. "Give it to me, give Castle Bewick to *me?*"

"Yes. Would you like it?"

"Why me? I mean, of course . . . I mean, what about the others . . . I . . . I . . . but what would I do with a castle?"

"That's up to you. I'm giving you this for you to make something of. I may divide Bishopstow up for Alan's children, I may not. I haven't decided. But they don't need anything yet, and you do, and I've got Castle Bewick to give to you, so I'm giving it. If, of course, you want it."

She screamed. "Of course I want it! Oh darling, generous, heavenly James, of course I want it!" She stopped. "But how do I live in it?"

He looked at her. "I don't know."

"But —"

"Alexia, I'm not even discussing it. I'm giving you the house and the land and such contents as remain. I shall also give you your train ticket to Glasgow and a few hundred pounds to tide you over. Then you're on your own."

She gazed at him, her face alight.

"I could start another school, or sell some

land, or learn to farm —"

He put his hands over his ears. "I don't want to know," he said. "For your sake. For your dear sake. Don't ask for advice, don't tell me things. Just take that great barrack, my very dear Alexia, and make a future of it."

Chapter Nine

Charlotte Emily Angus was born in her great-grandmother Alexandra's bedroom on a pouring wet June morning. She weighed seven pounds and one ounce, had dark blue eyes and a pale red fuzz of hair.

"Like a baby orangutan," James said, peering at her.

Alexia lay exhausted and elated on a draw sheet over thick layers of faintly crackling newspaper — the result of a tiny victory by Lyddy over the local midwife, who thought newspaper was old-fashioned. But the doctor who delivered tiny Charlotte, a new young general practitioner with a surgery and dispensary in Bishopstow village, backed Lyddy, to the midwife's indignation. He was very gentle with Alexia. "Clever girl," he said at intervals. "Well done. Just a few more pushes, long and slow. That's right. *Clever* girl."

She felt clever. She lay there with the baby snuffling slightly in the crook of her arm, and watched the summer rain sliding down the window, and heard, in a detached and comfortable way, the sounds of Lyddy and Mary and the midwife doing whatever they were doing, around the room, and felt supremely, wonderfully clever. It was an unbelievable feeling, a feeling of rapturous achievement and satisfaction. She looked down at the tiny, oblivious crumpled face beside her.

"I'm not me any more, you know," she told the baby. "I'm us." She turned slightly so that she could look straight at her daughter. "And although you will be christened Charlotte, so that you can be Charlotte when you are old enough, while you are little, I shall call you Carly. Hello, Carly."

The telephone rang and rang. Calls from Cara and Stephen, from Felicity and Amanda, from the old Langley grandparents at Langley Dene, from Alexia's Uncle Alan who also sent her an extravagant bouquet of pink roses in a basket woven with pink ribbon.

"Rather typical of him," Mary said, apologetically, putting the basket down in the hearth, "very well meaning and much too much."

She turned towards the bed with a doubtful look, and Alexia wondered if she was about to say something else, but all she said was, "Is she feeding properly?"

Alexia nodded. "Beautifully. We're both frightfully good at it."

"You seem to me to be frightfully good at this whole thing."

There was a tiny pause and then Alexia said, "I can't make a career out of it, though, can I?"

Mary stooped and kissed her, and kissed Carly, lying rolled up in her shawl like a little knitted prawn, and went downstairs to her study, the tiny room off the hall where she did her meticulous accounts. James was in there, frowning over a bank statement.

"I nearly told her," Mary said. "It was on the tip of my tongue to tell her, but then I didn't."

"About Stephen?"

"Yes, about Stephen. I've got such mixed feelings."

James put the bank statement down. "Me too."

"I mean, I know Martin Angus is Carly's father and therefore has a right to know of her existence, but I can't help feeling he forfeited that right by leaving Alexia as he did and never trying to get in touch with her, even if she did tell him not to. And I also feel that Stephen had no business to tell Martin about Carly without consulting Alexia. He said he didn't want to upset her, but I think he should have waited until she was strong enough to decide for herself. I think it's *her* decision, not his. The trouble is, doctors get so stuffed with impersonal ethics, they stop thinking about the human side, the individual human side."

James put his arm around his wife. "Why did you nearly tell Alexia just now?"

"Because I feel she ought to know that Martin knows. Stephen said he didn't react at all, and when Stephen told him about Alexia inheriting Bewick, all he said was 'So she will be really all right then,' and sounded relieved. I don't *think* he'll be a nuisance, but you can't tell, can you?"

"And if you tell Alexia that he knows," James said, pulling his pipe out of his pocket with his free hand, "then she'll feel haunted by the possibility of his coming to find her."

"Exactly."

"So it's a temporarily quiet mind for now,

119

versus a possibly valuable but unpleasant piece of knowledge for the future?"

Mary's brow puckered into a frown. "Yes. Yes, that's it exactly. And then there's this." She leaned forward and picked up a long white envelope with a London postmark.

"What's that?"

"It's her decree absolute. It was due this week. I don't want to take it up to her. Carly's only two days old. I don't want to remind Alexia at the moment of all the wretchedness of the last year. I want her just to lie there for a little and revel in being safe and happy in having achieved a baby."

James leaned sideways and kissed Mary's forehead. "I don't just think you're kind," he said, "I think you're right."

Mary bent her head so that her face lay against his shoulder. "I hope I am. I so hope I am. But you can only decide to do what seems best to do at any given moment. Can't you?"

The next day, Alexia was allowed to get up and sit in a chair by the window, holding Carly in her arms.

"That's where your grandmother sat," Lyddy said, "holding your mother. And James and your uncle Alex. She wouldn't have babies in the bed in the big bedroom, the one she and Mr. Swinton shared, the one James and Mary have now. She said she'd have her babies in her own bed, thank you. This little madam," she bent over Carly, "is going to be her spitting image. Carroty hair and all."

"Not like Charlotte?"

120

"Not to judge by the pictures. You're the one who looks like the pictures of Charlotte." Lyddy paused, folding her hands over the starched blue checked apron she had worn about the house all Alexia's life. "What about her father? Does she look like him?"

Alexia drew Carly closer. "I don't know. I'm not thinking about it. She's mine, not his. He doesn't know about her and he's not going to."

"I see."

"People don't *have* to have fathers. Think of all those children in history whose fathers were killed in battles or died of the plague. They had to manage. Carly will too."

Lyddy sat down opposite Alexia and regarded her. She looked, Lyddy thought, different since the baby, less girlish, less waiflike, more grown up.

"And you?"

Alexia looked back at her.

"I don't know about me. For the moment, Carly's enough for me. And . . . and Scotland —"

"What are you going to do about Scotland?"

"I don't know," Alexia said, but her voice didn't sound frightened, it simply sounded rather cross. "I know you mean well, darling Lyddy, but will you please stop asking questions, because when I say I don't know, I mean it." She stopped and took a deep breath. "I haven't got the faintest idea about what to do with Castle Bewick, and that, for the moment, is that."

Chapter Ten

October 1967

The train journey to Scotland started at the station at Bodmin Road and ended half a lifetime later, it seemed to Alexia, at Glasgow Central. James and Mary had escorted her to the station, with Carly in a straw Moses basket which Lyddy had lined with quilted pink spotted cotton, two suitcases, her sewing machine and a bulging canvas bag containing Carly's necessities. There was also a small hamper packed with food and drink, owing to Lyddy's belief that nothing nourishing to eat was to be found east of the River Tamar.

"I don't know," James said, surveying their possessions. "Taking a baby about is like sending a Victorian bride to India. I never saw so much kit for someone not two feet long."

To Alexia's amazement, the parting wasn't tearful. She thought later, as the train rumbled its interminable way northwards, that she was probably so stunned at the size of the adventure ahead of her, that she was in a state of shock. She had half expected James to relent at the last minute — or Mary to persuade him to relent — and offer her some ideas, or someone, at least, to turn to. But he had offered her nothing. He had simply said, "You'll find all the deeds and documents you need waiting at what is now *your* solicitor's office in Glasgow, and you may find, at Bewick, some descendants of Elsie MacPherson who was my grandparents' housekeeper." That was all. Mary looked very much as if she longed to say more but had been strictly forbidden to.

Carly liked the train. She had been, for these first four months of life, an amenable baby, her bright dark blue eyes following people about with evident interest. Now Alexia put her on the train seat beside her, and she lay contentedly, pleased by the rhythm of the train, and the flickering patterns of light and shade cast by passing buildings and trees. Nobody attempted to join them until after Cheltenham, so Alexia could feed Carly in peace, a gauze nappy draped modestly over her shoulder. After Cheltenham, a family got in, three children, and an exhausted and harassed-looking mother, with whom Alexia shared the contents of the hamper. It seemed symbolic to do so, as if she was taking nothing of Cornwall to Scotland with her, except James and Mary's faith in her, and her baby.

"This is so peculiar," Alexia kept thinking. "This is the strangest thing that has ever happened to me. I'm sitting in a train with my baby chugging off into the utter unknown and I can't believe it's happening. Perhaps it isn't, perhaps it's a dream." She looked down at Carly, sucking determinedly, her minute feet rigid with ecstasy and effort. "You're not a dream, are you, bundle? You're the most real thing that's ever happened to me though I couldn't possibly imagine that before you came. Perhaps Scotland will be the same. Perhaps the same miracle will happen when I see Bewick as did when I saw you, and I'll know just what to do with it, just as I seemed to know what to do with you."

It was dark when she reached Glasgow, and she was very tired. To her relief there were porters on the platform, with barrows, and one of these, who smiled a lot and whose conversation she found absolutely incomprehensible, piled all her luggage up and set off with it at a great pace, leaving her to struggle behind him with Carly in her basket. He took her to a taxi rank.

"The Hibernian Hotel," Alexia said.

The porter smiled at her expectantly. He said something else, still smiling. It was like being addressed in a foreign tongue. A sudden hot panic of not knowing what to do descended upon Alexia. How much should she give him? And what about the taxi, only the second taxi she could remember getting into in her life.

She held out two shillings. The porter stopped smiling. She lost her head and held out five, and the porter seized the half crowns from her hand and fled, trundling his barrow before him like a plough. The taxi driver looked at her. He sucked his teeth. "A fool and his money are soon parted," he said, and he sounded scornful.

Wearily, Alexia loaded her bags and her baby into the taxi. It was by now quite dark and impossible to gain any impression of Glasgow except that the street names looked distinctly

124

Scottish and the streets themselves were much emptier than they would have been in London at eight o'clock at night. The taxi stopped outside a vast and not particularly welcoming-looking building.

"Here y'are," the taxi driver said. He made no attempt to help her out. She looked nervously at the meter in his cab. How much should she add for a tip? He seemed to read her mind. "Fifteen percent is customary," he said. She fumbled in her purse and dropped some coins in the gutter by mistake. Carly began to cry and the first drops of rain started to fall. The omens, Alexia felt with a sinking heart, were poor.

They were not much better inside the hotel. It was huge and heavy, painted dirty cream with acres of red Turkish carpet. The clerk at the reception desk looked at Carly as if Alexia had attempted to bring a piglet into the hotel, and had to explain to her, with ill-disguised contempt, how to fill in her registration form. Then there was the long trail up to her room, too high for its width, with no pictures and no charm and a single window covered by thin gloomy green curtains which would have disgraced even Culver Square. The porter who brought up her bags clearly required another tip and was not at all gracious about being given a shilling, and when she asked if she might have some sandwiches sent up by room service, he said, with some satisfaction, that room service had ceased for the night some ten minutes ago.

"And the dining room?"

"The dining room is open until nine," he said,

and then, with a grin, "but you can't take the bairn in there."

Carly's whimpers now turned into real screams. The porter shouted, "Well, good night to ye!" and slammed the door behind him. Alexia hurried over to the Moses basket and picked up the furious baby, holding her against her shoulder and trying to soothe her. "There, there, don't cry, don't be sad. You're just tired like me. I'm gong to bathe you and feed you and tuck you up and when you wake in the morning, you'll feel as good as new."

She carried the screaming Carly into the bathroom — bleak and functional like a school bathroom, with a cork floor and curtainless windows and ran a bath for her in the wash basin. Carly roared and kicked and hurt herself against the taps, galvanizing herself into a paroxysm of rage with her tiny face screwed up into a furious yelling red ball. It was terribly difficult to wash and dry her in her temper, and then to get her into her nappy and her nightie and roll her in her shawl ready to be fed. Only when Alexia had finally settled with her in a hideous armchair covered in fawn cut moquette which scratched as if she was sitting on sandpaper, did Carly finally subside.

The minute supper was over, however, Carly began again. Alexia tried putting her to bed, but that was no good, and then walking round the room with her, but that was no good either and a man came and knocked loudly at the door and told Alexia that his wife in the next room was suffering from a migraine and Carly was definitely contributing to the agony.

Alexia was in despair. What could she do? Carly was overtired, just as she was overtired herself and unless she could somehow be persuaded to sleep, they were both in for a terrible night, exacerbated by the woman next door with a migraine.

"You must take the child away," the man said. "It isn't right, you know, to bring a child to a hotel like this. It isn't considerate."

"What do you expect me to do?" Alexia shouted. "Sleep in the street?"

The man looked offended. "I am only thinking of my wife. You must simply take the child where my wife cannot hear it."

All right, Alexia thought in a rage, I will. I'll walk Carly through this whole horrible unwelcoming hotel and wake everyone up and spoil people's dinners and see if I care. She rolled the baby up firmly in her shawl, picked up her room key, and stepped out into the corridor. Then she walked down it to the great Victorian stairwell, Carly's wails floating behind her, and began to descend to the foyer. Carly hesitated. Above her, glittering and sparkling, hung an enormous chandelier like a waterfall. It was very strange and wonderful. Carly stopped crying.

Relieved, Alexia decided she couldn't go back to her room until the baby was asleep. She went through the foyer and found herself in a bar, dark and smelling of alcohol, and was shooed out by a bartender. She went back across the foyer and met double glass doors lined with pleated net, and a wooden notice on a stand which said in gold letters, "DINING ROOM CLOSED." She turned and made for the back of the foyer, where there was a lounge area, dotted with armchairs in rigid groups and people drinking coffee and whispering to one another.

A waiter approached Alexia. He was clearly some kind of senior waiter because he wore a black coat, not a white one, and an air of officiousness.

"I'm afraid you mayn't bring a child here. This area is for hotel residents."

"I am a hotel resident," Alexia said, "and so is my daughter."

"I'm afraid no children under twelve are allowed in the lounge."

"Nor are they allowed in the dining room, I'm told, nor may I stay in my bedroom because of the woman next door who has a headache, nor may I have any food from room service because they've all gone home. I tell you," said Alexia, her voice rising in temper, "I'm never coming near this appalling hotel ever again in the whole of my life and I jolly well hope you shortly go out of business."

The waiter looked as if she had hit him. There was complete silence all around, and all the faces in the lounge turned in horrified curiosity in Alexia's direction. Then Alexia noticed two things. One was that someone, somewhere was laughing, and the second was that Carly had fallen asleep. She looked around for the person who was laughing. The waiter said, "Perhaps you would like me to call the manager so that he can impress upon you more forcibly than I seem able to do —"

"Oh shut up," Alexia said.

Someone was coming towards her. It was the someone who had been laughing, a tall broad-shouldered man, perhaps in his thirties, in a tweed jacket with thick dark brown hair and hazel eyes which were, at the moment, crinkled up with amusement.

"What a display," he said to Alexia. His voice had a distinct Scottish accent. "What an admirable display. What can I do for you? What can I make this minion do for you?"

Alexia said, "I'd like a ham sandwich and a pot of coffee and a banana, please. Brought here."

The man turned to the waiter. "You heard the lady."

The waiter hesitated.

"Hurry," the man said. "Ten minutes, at the outside." The waiter hurried off, muttering, and the man turned back to Alexia. "I'm afraid you'll regret the coffee and you may well regret the sandwich. No one can make coffee north of the border."

"I don't mind," Alexia said, "and thank you so much."

The man gave a little bow. "My pleasure. You have made my evening. I'd have happily made your sandwich myself after such a superb performance," and then he bowed again and went across the foyer and out through the vast swing doors into the darkness beyond.

Alexia sat down in the nearest unoccupied armchair, thankfully resting the unconscious Carly across her knees. There was a middle-aged couple next to her, and she waited for them to tell her that they didn't like seeing a baby in the public rooms of a hotel, but instead the woman leaned across and said, in a charming American accent, "Oh my dear, you do have my sympathy."

Alexia smiled at her. "I don't know what I'd have done if I hadn't been rescued."

The woman said, "Well, as a matter of fact, if that gentleman hadn't spoken up for you, I was going to. Wasn't I, Herman?"

Her husband nodded, his eyes resting fondly on Carly. "Herman will tell you," the woman said, "that we've just about had it to here," she laid her hand against her throat, "with Scottish hotels. Nobody's looked at them since the Day of Creation and they are simply disgraceful. And the food! My dear, the food is simply terrible. Right now, I'd cheerfully *kill* for a mere hamburger."

At this moment the waiter reappeared, looking much ruffled, and bearing a tray with a coffee pot, a cup and saucer, a small milk jug and two white plates. On one lay, quite unadorned, the most basic of ham sandwiches. On the other was an unripe banana.

"Thank you," Alexia said.

The waiter said nothing. She looked up at him, but he had turned away. Then they all, Alexia and the Americans, looked at the banana and the sandwich.

"Isn't it insane?" the American woman said. "Isn't it just insane? There are all these beautiful castles to see and all this wonderful landscape and the lochs and the deer and these adorable men in their kilts and all this *history* and yet there is nowhere, just *nowhere*, civilized to stay?"

In the morning, it was raining. Alexia drew aside the meager green curtains, and then the dingy net ones behind them, and peered out. What she saw was not encouraging. A big square lay before her lined with buildings blackened with the grime of age, around which traffic was swirling on the rain-slicked roads. The people on the pavements appeared to have dressed to complement the buildings and the leaden sky, and were mostly half obscured under black umbrellas.

"Oh heavens," Alexia thought, her heart sinking, "oh heavens, where have I come?"

She turned back to the Moses basket. Carly, having woken several times in the night, was now tranquilly asleep, oblivious of the grim Scottish day awaiting her. She had to be woken, washed, dressed, and fed, and then somehow Alexia had to find breakfast for herself — she was starving hungry by now — and then they both had to sally forth into the rain to find Mr. McReadie, Solicitor, of Sauchiehall Street.

Mr. McReadie's offices had not been touched, it appeared, since the turn of the century. The vast mahogany doors had insets of frosted glass lettered in gold, and the only decoration beyond the basic furnishings of huge Victorian desks and chairs, were dusty palms standing gloomily here and there in brass pots. Such daylight as there was struggled to reach the rooms through discol-

131

ored net curtains. Alexia, suddenly conscious that her London-short skirt made her appear virtually naked in such surroundings, waited for Mr. McReadie to appear in a frock coat and with mutton chop whiskers.

He almost did. He had a heavy moustache and wore a waistcoat across which hung the golden chain of a pocket watch. His eyes bulged at the sight of Carly, and even more so at Alexia's skirt, but he managed to usher them, with stiff-necked courtesy, into a great dreary room where a small coal fire burned reluctantly and gave out eye-watering fumes. He motioned Alexia to a heavy chair, its seat upholstered in red leather, and then vanished to the safety of the far side of his immense desk, where he sat down and put his elbows on the desk, placed the tips of his fingers together, and surveyed Alexia over the top of them.

He made her very nervous. He said, "How old are you, Mrs. Angus?"

"Twenty-one."

There was a tiny disapproving pause.

"And you are fully aware that your uncle, James Swinton, has made over to you, in unconditional possession, the dwelling house known as Castle Bewick, and, in addition, five and a half thousand acres of land of which merely one hundred and thirty acres by the loch is suitable for soft farming, and the remainder only for sheep and the running of deer?"

Alexia swallowed. He was managing to make her inheritance sound like a prison sentence. "I am."

"And are you aware that the said dwelling house has been used as an educational establishment for the past twenty-one years and, though structurally reasonably sound, it is not in a good state of repair within?"

"No, I wasn't, but I'm sure —"

"And do you," Mr. McReadie went on inexorably, "have any experience of any kind in managing either a house or land of this size?"

Alexia went scarlet. "No, I don't, but I can learn —"

Mr. McReadie laid his hands flat upon the desk.

"In my view, Mrs. Angus, your uncle Mr. James Swinton, has taken leave of his senses. What is a slip of a girl like you, with a child to care for, to make of a great gloomy place like that which has been neglected for years, and land which hasn't brought in any income since your great-grandfather died in 1920?"

Alexia thought she might be going to cry. She simply must not, not in front of Mr. McReadie. She said, desperate to make conversation, "Did you know my great-grandfather?"

Mr. McReadie permitted himself a ghost of a smile.

"Despite present appearances, Mrs. Angus, I was but a child of ten in 1920. But my father knew your great-grandfather. He always said that James Abbott knew more about sheep than any man west of Loch Lomond."

"Perhaps," Alexia said, lifting her chin a fraction, "I'll turn out to have some Abbott blood in me."

Mr. McReadie looked as if he doubted it.

"I feel bound, Mrs. Angus, to offer you some advice."

She leaned forward, immediately grateful. At last, someone would help, someone would offer at least a guideline . . .

"My advice is that you should sell the estate, lock, stock, and barrel, and invest the proceeds to give yourself at least a reasonable unearned income. In my estimation, the house and land should attract offers of around thirty-five thousand pounds which at present interest rates should give you —"

"No!" shouted Alexia. They glared at each other.

"I beg your pardon, Mrs. Angus, but it is my duty to advise you that any alternative course can only lead straight to —"

"No," Alexia said again, more quietly. "No. I'm not going to give up before I've even tried. I'm simply not going to. It may be that in a year or five or ten I have to come to you and confess that you were right, but I'm not going to do that before I've even had a go. I'm just *not*."

Mr. McReadie gave her a hard look.

"I *see*."

"Well, would you, in my position?"

Mr. McReadie's gaze slid rapidly over Alexia's clothes and grew startled.

"Mrs. Angus, we are hardly in any way comparable —"

"I shall go out to Castle Bewick and have a look at it, Mr. McReadie, and then in a month or so, I'll come —" She stopped, and then obeying some impulse she hardly understood, she said, "In a month, perhaps you will be good enough to come out and see me, and we can discuss what conclusions I've come to?"

He said stiffly, "As you wish."

"I do wish."

"I have, Mrs. Angus, done my best by your family over the years as did my father before me, but sometimes I feel there cannot be a solicitor in Glasgow so sorely tried as I have been. Your uncle neglects his property for twenty years and then proposes this ridiculous scheme. I offer the soundest advice available and have it rejected out of hand. I tell you, Mrs. Angus, it is very, very hard to bear."

There was something about his long Scottish face and lugubrious moustache that made Alexia feel sorry for him rather than furious. She said, "Couldn't you regard this, as I'm trying to, as a kind of adventure?"

"An adventure!" He sounded deeply shocked.

"Yes. A bit of a gamble, a chance to do something a bit different, a bit exciting. Can't you think, even for a moment, d'you know, I think I'll help her however mad she seems?"

Mr. McReadie gazed at Alexia for a long, long time. Then he rose and came round his desk and looked down at Carly who lay plucking at the sides of her Moses basket with tiny hands.

"Mrs. Angus, I have to confess to you that I prefer the adventures in my life confined to the pages of John Buchan and Robert Louis Stevenson, but for all that, I'll not stand in your way. We'll sign the papers now, if you please, and I will forward to you the small amount of cash your uncle instructed I should give you, and on this day month, I shall present myself at Castle Bewick to hear your . . . your decision."

He reached out and struck a huge brass bell button on his desk. At once, a secretary appeared, a neat and spinsterish secretary in a long tweed skirt and a toning blouse and cardigan.

"You rang, Mr. McReadie."

"I did, Miss Barclay. I'd be obliged if you would bring me the file for Castle Bewick."

"At once, Mr. McReadie."

When the door closed, Mr. McReadie turned back to Alexia.

"Mrs. Angus, when you reach Castle Bewick, you will not find it entirely empty. I gather one of the masters declined to leave with the school, having become attached to the area, and the cook, a Mrs. MacGregor, wished it to be made known to you that her mother had worked for your family in the past. I trust," said Mr. McReadie, giving Alexia a tiny glimmer of a smile, "I trust, Mrs. Angus, that you will find the natives are friendly." He paused and then he said, "And I'd advise you to acquire yourself a wedding ring."

"But I'm divorced!"

He gave her a hard stare.

"Times move only slowly in the Highlands, Mrs. Angus. As you will find."

Chapter Eleven

The road from Arrochar station snaked round the head of a loch and then began to climb up into the misty hills beyond it to the west. Alexia sat in the back of the taxi, holding Carly on her knee, and wearing the embarrassingly new, cheap wedding ring she had bought that morning from a disapproving Glasgow jeweler, and looked at the landscape with awe and apprehension. Her previous notions of what Scotland was going to look like were hazy, based largely upon the faded photograph of Castle Bewick in the dining room at Culver Square, and a crude reproduction of Landseer's *Stag at Bay* which had hung in the art room at school, and been much ridiculed. What she was looking at, out of the taxi windows, didn't look much like either. The road, a narrow one, seemed to be climbing up a kind of pass between immense, rearing ocher hillsides, scattered with grey boulders and patches of heather. There was, apart from the odd racing burn foaming its way down the hillsides, neither movement nor sign of life. Alexia held Carly very tightly. It all looked terribly empty.

The road climbed up and up. The driver, who had said nothing since leaving Arrochar station when he had remarked that there was a fair bit of

137

rain due by evening, suddenly slowed the car by a small loch of still black water and said, "Rest and be thankful."

"What?"

"It's the top o' the pass. It's called Rest and Be Thankful."

Alexia looked about her. There seemed little to be thankful for. The hillsides looked as impenetrable as walls and the heavy grey sky shut the pass in, like a lid on a box. She thought that she had never been anywhere that seemed so absolutely, utterly alien. She also thought, with a rising throb of panic, that she must not, on any account, revert to her childhood habit of thinking of Bishopstow every time the going got rough.

"You'll find it a sad old place," the taxi driver said.

Alexia said, a little tartly, "I'm not expecting otherwise."

"I'd not take a wee bairn there myself —"

"Where I go," Alexia said, "she goes."

"Awful damp. And cold, bitter cold."

She said nothing. She was becoming exasperated by this Scottish game of goading her to give up and go home to where — they clearly thought — she belonged, south of the border. She turned her head to look out of the window once more. The pass was widening out, the hills moving aside to let in other hills, a mountaintop or two, and even close to the road, the occasional whitewashed cottage with smoke straggling from its chimney. The valley floor grew broad, and fir trees appeared and then suddenly Alexia gave a little gasp — water came into view, a stretch of shining silvery water and beyond it the inky hills of the photograph in Culver Square.

"The loch!"

"Aye," the diver said. He swung the car suddenly left off the road, down a narrow lane between rough stone walls, sprouting ferns. The trees that arched overhead were soft trees, deciduous trees, some now golden and red, and the harsh Highland landscape was as suddenly gone as if it had never been. The lane plunged steeply down towards a cluster of whitewashed cottages on the loch shore — the tiny village of Bewick, Alexia supposed — and then, just as it turned right to hug the water and the pebbly beach strewn with black and golden seaweed, the taxi turned sharp left, and drove between two high wrought iron gateposts on which were black shields with gilded initials intertwined — CB and AB: Charlotte Bewick and Alexander Bewick.

Alexia sat up, her heart beating high. She lifted Carly against her shoulder so that she too could see the place she was coming to. The drive ran beside a little river splashing down to the loch, a romantic little river full of pools and baby waterfalls, over which trees dropped in graceful arches. The drive rose a little towards the wooded hillside, away from the loch, crossed a stone bridge, turned back towards the loch — and then Alexia saw it.

"Stop!" she cried to the driver. "Stop! Oh, please stop!"

"As ye wish," he said.

She scrambled out, clutching Carly. Through the straggling larches that bordered the drive on the lochside, she could see a gently sloping field which had obviously done duty as a football pitch for twenty years, since two broken goalposts lurched drunkenly among the thistles. But beyond the field, outlined against the gleaming water beyond, stood the house, familiar from the photograph, but unfamiliar too because of the beauty of its position and its tangible charm. It was built of pink sandstone under a brownish-pink tiled roof, and its roofline was a fantastic dancing silhouette of towers and turrets and stretches of crenellation and wrought iron finials, delicate as black lace. The walls were huge and high, but full of windows, windows facing in every direction so as not to miss one millimeter of the astounding views visible from every one of them. It was a most mad and magical house. It was the least sensible-looking house Alexia had ever seen, and her heart went out to it.

"Look," she said to Carly, pointing. "Look at that! Look at *our* house!"

But Carly had seen a squirrel in a tree and would look at nothing else.

The taxi stopped finally outside the front door. It was immense, made of oak and studded like the door of a medieval fortress, and it was framed in an enormous stone arch with Charlotte and Alexander's initials carved into the peak.

"There y'are then," the taxi driver said. He would quite have liked Alexia to break down at this point, when she saw how dirty the windows were, how overgrown the drive, how peeling the paintwork, because it would have made a satisfactory story to tell his wife at home in Tarbet, but she didn't. She simply got out of the taxi, holding her baby, waited for him to unload her luggage, paid him with what he considered a fair but hardly generous tip and turned away. There was nothing for him to do but to get back into his cab and drive off.

Alexia left her luggage in a pile on the weedy gravel and approached the great door. Mr. McReadie had given her a key, a ludicrous key like a prop for a pantomime, huge and curly, but before she used it, she pulled the long iron bell pull that hung by the door, beside four empty screw holes that had presumably once held the plate that said "CASTLE BEWICK SCHOOL." Deep inside the house, a bell clanged like something in a film about Count Dracula. Carly, hungry and tired and sensing Alexia's apprehension, began to whimper.

Alexia counted to twenty, slowly. Then she rang again and began to count once more, but before she reached eight, there was the sound of hurrying footsteps, and then of a key turning, and one half of the great door groaned inwards. Alexia half expected to see an aged crone appear, robed in black, with a crooked, beckoning finger, but instead there was a plump woman, perhaps in late middle age, who, although she wasn't smiling, looked neither sinister nor unwelcoming.

"Mrs. Angus."

"Yes —"

"I'm Elsie MacGregor."

"Yes, Mr. McReadie told me you might —"

It was much colder inside the house than out.

When Elsie MacGregor had closed the door, it was also almost dark. Alexia could just make out a vaulted stone ceiling and a great flight of stone stairs and stone archways and stone doorways, and a strong unmistakable smell of school.

"I've lit a fire for you," Elsie said. "In the snug Mr. Preston used. He was headmaster here."

"My luggage —"

"Hughie'll see to that."

"Hughie?"

"Hughie's my son. We're the only two left here now, apart from Mr. Burton. Mr. McReadie said you would see Hughie and me right."

"Did he?"

"Oh yes," Elsie said. "He did. Quite certainly. Follow me."

Alexia followed her up the stone stairs to a towering hall, like the chancel of a cathedral, from which more stairs led up, twisting away into the gloom of the upper floors.

"In here," Elsie said. She pushed at a door, and led Alexia and Carly into a charming room, a square panelled room with a leaping fire and wide windows looking down to the loch. "We always used to call this the Mermaid Room," Elsie said. "It was Mr. Preston who called it the snug."

"Why mermaid?"

"Look up," Elsie said, "and look round you."

Alexia looked up. Above her hung a tarnished silver chandelier. When she peered more closely she saw the branched arms were fashioned like mermaids, their fishy tails towards the center, and their graceful human arms holding up the brackets for the candles.

"And here," Else said, pointing to the fireplace. "And here," indicating the door.

Above the fire was a panel of carved, golden wood, a panel of mermaids holding torches. There were more mermaids, stone ones, holding up the chimneypiece, and more twined round the latches of the windows and wreathed about the finger-plate and the handle of the door. Only the keyhole cover was not a mermaid; it was a shell.

"It's lovely, it's absolutely lovely, it must go back to being the Mermaid Room at once —"

"No hurry," Elsie said. She came forward and held out her arms. "You'll be weary," she said. "It'll be a shock, coming here. Give me the child, I'll see to the child, I'm used to children. You sit yourself down and get your breath and I'll send Hughie to bring in your things."

Alexia clutched Carly. "She isn't used to anyone but me —"

Elsie said, "Then she'd better learn, hadn't she? How are you going to run a great place like this if you've always a bairn in your arms?"

The door opened softly. A man's voice, an English voice, kind and polite, said, "Am I disturbing you?"

Alexia sat up with a jerk. She had fallen into a half-doze by the fire, sitting in the shabby brown leather armchair that Elsie said, with a sniff, the school had been so good as to leave behind. She turned round.

A young man was standing in the doorway, smiling shyly. He had a sweet face, and a thatch of brown hair, and he was dressed in a younger version of the comforting sort of clothes that Uncle James always wore, tweed and corduroy and well-polished leather.

"Do come in," Alexia said. She put her hand apprehensively to her hair, and to her face where her mascara was bound to have smudged while she slept. "Please . . . please come in —"

"You must be Mrs. Angus —"

"I'm Alexia. Alexia Angus."

The young man came forward, still smiling, and perched on the leather-topped club fender (its brass supports were, Alexia noticed, yet more mermaids, acting as caryatids) by the fire.

"My name's Peter Burton. I used to teach at the school. I taught games, and English and French to the younger ones."

"Did you? Is it rude to ask why you are still here?"

"I couldn't bear to go way. I'd fallen in love with the place, with the house, and the landscape, and the local people. I've been keeping going doing a bit of work for your neighbor, but I rather hoped that when you came —" He stopped. Alexia saw his color had risen. He went on, very diffidently, "I don't of course know what you plan to do with the castle, but I'd be terribly grateful . . . if . . . if . . . you'd think of some way I might be useful. Nothing much, you understand, I'm not at all ambitious, but I just do so want to be able to stay." He shot her a glance. "It's awfully presumptuous of me to talk to you like this, especially when you've just had a long journey and must be feeling very strange, but I felt I ought to explain why I'm still here, and . . . and

. . . what I hope for —" He broke off again and got up and went over to the window. "I'm so sorry. I shouldn't have bounced this on you. Elsie said I wasn't to say a word until you'd had some time but . . . I couldn't help myself."

Alexia said slowly, "I'm afraid I can't help you just now, either."

He spun round. "Of course, how stupid of me. You've probably got other people —"

"No, I haven't," she said, interrupting, "I haven't got any anything. No plans, no people. I've just got a baby and two suitcases and enough money to keep going for a few weeks. I got here an hour ago after a very difficult few days with everybody making it abundantly plain that I wasn't welcome in Scotland and that I was barking mad even to think of taking on such a house. I don't know what I think, and I don't know what I'm going to do. I don't even know, unlike you, that I want to stay, even though my first sight of the house nearly knocked the breath out of me."

Peter Burton came back to the fender, and sat on it, leaning towards her.

"I'm a tactless oaf. I'm so sorry. Really I am. Forget everything I said, just wipe the slate clean, and tell me what I can do to help you."

She regarded him. His expression was almost childish in its regretfulness and its eagerness to make amends.

"Are you living in the house?"

He blushed again. "I wanted to, but Elsie said it wouldn't be right, so I've got a room in her cottage for now."

"I don't see why you shouldn't have a room here. After all, it's a big house for Carly and me to rattle around in at night alone. I couldn't pay you anything just now, but if you can keep yourself —"

His face lit up, "Oh, I wouldn't cost you anything! I'd pay for my keep, I promise, but to have a room back here —" He swallowed. "Perhaps you ought to think about it. I've behaved so badly. I mustn't bounce you into something just because I want it. I'm perfectly comfortable with Elsie, and I'm working part of every day —"

"For my neighbor?"

"Yes."

"Who is my neighbor?"

"Duncan McGill," Peter said. "His land meets yours at the head of the loch, and then runs down the far side, in the direction of Craigmuir. I've been helping a bit with his new forestry schemes, and he has ideas for a fish farm —"

"A what?"

"A fish farm. For salmon —"

Alexia stared at him. The foreignness of the place and the life she had come to struck her like a cold blade slipped down her back. She shivered.

"Perhaps," Peter said gently, as if reading her mind, "perhaps I could help . . . introduce you to Bewick? Explain things, you know. I felt so strange myself when I came up here, so I know what it must seem like to you and now I can't imagine being anywhere else."

She smiled at him.

"How old are you?"

He smiled back. "Twenty-six."

"I won't be that for five years."

He said, "I came here when I was twenty-one too. Straight from university. I came because my father wanted me to go into the city and learn to be a stockbroker and I wanted to be an architect but he wouldn't pay for my training. I just ran away as a kind of compromise. Rather pathetic really."

Alexia hesitated. "I've got too much past even at twenty-one, to tell you in a single sentence."

"There's heaps of time," he said. He rose and held out a hand. "There's so much time up here, it's one of the lovely things about it. Come on, I'll take you down to the kitchen. Elsie said I was to show you the way. She's made some leek soup, she said, and she thought the baby might need feeding."

Alexia looked up and smiled, and took Peter's outstretched hand. It was, she thought, the first really friendly hand she had seen in a long and lonely time.

Chapter Twelve

In the night, Alexia woke because it was so quiet. It was utterly quiet, with a queer complete silence that was as far removed from the traffic of London or the sea and wind of Bishopstow, as if she had been on another planet. She sat up in bed, peering into the gloom. Carly's Moses basket was where Elsie had placed it, on an ottoman at the foot of Alexia's bed, and its inmate was as quiet as the night. Alexia crawled to the end of the bed and put a hand on the sleeping baby; Carly was warm and still and breathing with the evenness of deep, tranquil sleep.

Alexia pulled the quilt off the bed and wrapped it round her and tiptoed to the window. The quilt was old-fashioned, heavy and plump with feathers and covered in faded taffeta. It perfectly matched everything else in the room in age — the brass bedstead, the washstand with its china jug and bowl, the faded splendor of the curtains, the just discernible wreaths of flowers in the threadbare carpet.

"I've put you in the Seahorse Room," Elsie had said. "It's not the grandest, but it's one the school hardly touched, with the matron just using it as a place to do mending with the view down the loch being so grand."

Alexia had got into bed, and lain clutching the hot water bottle Elsie had provided, and, before she turned out the light, she had looked at the stained and discolored ceiling from which hung a tiny, silvery chandelier formed of arching seahorses. They were somehow very comforting because they looked so merry prancing in a circle above her in their carefree way.

Now, in the darkness of the night, she couldn't see them. Nor, putting her hand on the window latch, could she see the seahorse that formed it, though she could feel him. She peered out. There was no moon, but the loch gave off a pewter glow, and the mountains opposite stood up blackly against the night sky, like a wall between her and the outside world. She thought how strange it was that she, who had been alarmed by so much in her short life, should not feel particularly frightened on realizing that she and Carly were alone in this enormous house, and that beyond this engaging room with its dancing seahorses, spread a maze of echoing empty passages and stairs and rooms with nothing living in them but mice. She really did not feel frightened; excited, yes, but not frightened. Perhaps it was that the whole situation was just too mad to be frightening; was it really just some great joke to be left penniless in a fairy castle in 1967 when the rest of the world — the London world she had left behind — was buying silver paper suits from Biba for three pounds; and singing Sandie Shaw's "Puppet on a String"?

In the morning, there was a gleam of sunshine,

pale autumn sunshine that rose above the mist on the loch and made the landscape look even more fairylike than it had seemed to Alexia in the middle of the night. She came carefully downstairs, carrying Carly — she was anxious still about dropping her on the harsh stone stairs — and found Elsie already in the kitchen. The kitchen was terrible, a nightmare of old-fashioned inconvenience and institutional bleakness, but the door of the old range was open to let out the warmth, and one end of the huge scrubbed table had been laid with a blue cloth, and on it stood a plate of oatcakes and a jar of honey and an empty bowl.

"Porridge," Elsie said firmly. She brought over a black pot.

"I don't eat porridge —"

"You do *here*," Elsie said, spooning. "Have you fed the bairn?"

"Yes."

"Then give her to me while you eat."

Alexia took a reluctant spoonful. It was delicious, creamy yet faintly salt. Elsie watched her.

"Don't eat porridge indeed —"

"I meant I usen't to eat porridge. In England."

"Ah. *England.*" Elsie put Carly against her shoulder and began to rock her. "And what are your plans for today, Mrs. Angus?"

"Alexia."

"That'd no' be respectful."

Alexia sighed. "I've got to think about money, and I've got to look round the house."

"There's nearly three months' wages owing to Hughie and me, since the school left —"

"That's as may be," Alexia said, heartened by the porridge, "but I didn't ask you to stay. I didn't know you were even here to ask."

"Mr. McReadie —"

"I didn't know of Mr. McReadie's existence either. I'm sure you and Hughie have done a marvelous job, and I can't imagine what my arrival yesterday would have been like without you, and I shall certainly reward you for that, but I am not responsible for the past and I haven't decided about the future." She stopped, amazed at herself.

"I've always worked at the castle," Elsie said. "And my mother before me, Elsie MacPherson that was. She —"

"Kept house for my great-grandparents."

"That she did."

"Look," Alexia said, buttering an oatcake. "Look, Elsie. If I can come up with a future for myself in this house, and if we find we suit one another, then, and only then, will we come to some permanent arrangement. Until then, I shall pay you, and Hughie, by the week, starting from yesterday."

There was a silence. Elsie walked across the kitchen to a door leading to one of the nameless sculleries, and walked back again.

"And if Hughie and I can't wait until such time as you make up your mind?"

Alexia looked up at her. "Then you'd better start looking for something else."

They regarded each other for some moments, and then Elsie turned her face and kissed the top of Carly's head.

"I'll be getting on with the washing then," she said.

After breakfast, Elsie took Carly away and tucked her up in a huge old pram, like a vintage Rolls-Royce, that she produced from what had once been the stable block. It was dark blue, with panelled sides outlined faintly in gold, and it was balanced on huge, high wheels with solid tires.

"Where on earth did that come from?"

"Hughie cleaned it up for the baby. I've no doubt it was your grandmother's."

There was something wonderful in that idea. Alexia put her hand on the cracked stiffened folds of the pram hood and bent to look at Carly's face underneath. Carly's little face lying exactly where Alexandra's little face had lain ninety years before. It seemed very natural.

"Sleep well," Alexia said to her daughter.

Carly blinked and gave a tiny yawn.

"Babies always sleep well here in the west," Elsie said. "I'm taking her down to the lawn below the house, on the lochside. My mother said it was where your grandmother used to bowl her hoop."

"I'm going to look at the house," Alexia said.

Elsie gave a little snort. "Don't go expecting too much —"

In the cathedrallike hall, a curious creature was waiting, a little stooped creature with a boy's face, dressed in dark trousers, and an immense jersey that had been knitted for someone much larger.

"Are you Hughie?"

"Aye."

"Thank you for cleaning the pram for Carly."

"No trouble."

"Are you going to show me the house?"

"Aye."

He came forward a step or two. He was, she saw with surprise, about her own age. He said, "You'll no' like it, you know," and went past her up some steps to open a door into a huge dim room, the size of a church. Alexia followed him. The room smelled stale and dusty, and as Hughie ran down the length of it folding back the barred shutters, she saw that it had probably once been a drawing room and, more recently, a school assembly hall. The walls were of panelled plaster and very dirty, and in some of the panels, hanging in tatters from battens, were the remains of pieces of corn-colored silk damask. At one end of the room was a wooden dais, and a simple lectern, and behind them, a huge piece of board which had been nailed across the wall, a piece of board irregularly studded with rusty drawing pins.

"They'd prayers in here," Hughie said, "and concerts. And the school play."

Alexia went to the windows, a long line of them in a shallow bay that jutted out from the walls of the house to make the most of the marvelous views, up the loch, down the loch, across the loch to the mountains and the sky. Down below, Carly's pram was parked under a huge, glowing maple tree, a flat stone wedged beneath one wheel.

"I suppose this was once the drawing room —"

"Aye," Hughie said. He pointed towards the opposite end of the room to that occupied by the dais, where an immense stone fireplace, carved with roses and lilies, yawned sadly round its empty grate. "That's where the paintings hung."

"The paintings?"

"The lord and the lady," Hughie said. "They were there when I was a wee lad. She'd on furs and diamonds, and he'd a sword."

"They're in my mother's house in London," Alexia said, staring at the great faded spaces either side of the fireplace, "but of course they should be here. After all, they lived here —"

"Aye," Hughie said. He watched her. "You've the lady's face."

"Oh no —"

He gave a smirk. "But no' her clothes!"

Alexia blushed. Her clothes, her southern, London clothes, suddenly seemed absurd here, too short, too flimsy, too towny. She said quickly, "Let me see the rest."

He led her out of the drawing room along a stone gallery above the hall to the drawing room. It again was enormous, and still seemed to hold the unlovely smell of thousands of school meals, but it too had windows looking out to that irresistible water, those magnificent hills. The walls of the dining room were panelled in mahogany, scuffed and neglected, and in two corners of the uncarpeted floor lay mousetraps, newly primed with yellow cubes of cheese.

After the dining room, the tour of the house descended from the depressing to the desperate. Toiling behind Hughie, Alexia went through room after room, desecrated by their last occupants and reeking of cold and damp. Grim bedrooms that had clearly been dormitories gave way to grimmer bathrooms and doorless lavatories where taps dripped in the chilly quiet and green mold edged the window frames. The school had left behind only its most disagreeable relics — a few iron bedsteads with broken and rusty springs, rows and rows of menacing coat hooks and splintering lockers, boarded-up fireplaces and north-facing windows, torn canvas blinds in black and dark blue, crumbling linoleum, chipped paint, drifts of broken shoelaces, and crumpled pieces of paper — and the smell. The smell was everywhere, the smell of children who had been neither perfectly clean nor perfectly fed nor adequately warm. It was the smell, Alexia decided, of the unmistakably second-rate.

After two hours, she was worn out both in body and spirit. Hughie had proved a tactful companion, merely opening doors onto yet another dismal apartment without comment, before leading her on down more dark passages or echoing stairs, and he finally showed her back into the Mermaid Room with an air of unspoken sympathy. In the Mermaid Room, not only fire waited, but also Peter Burton, who leaped to his feet as Alexia came in. She was startled to realize how very pleased she was to see him.

"I really don't want to butt in," he said anxiously, "but I was worried — so was Elsie — that you might need cheering up."

Alexia climbed over the club fender, and sat down, so that she was almost sitting in the fire. She said wearily, "It's awful. I'd no idea it would be so bad."

"I expect a good clean —"

"No," she said. "No. It's more than that. It needs heating and drying out properly, and I should think the roof needs mending, and then every inch needs removing and decorating. I —" she stopped and then she said, "I don't know how anyone begins on that."

"Oh, bit by bit —"

She looked sideways at him. "Only if you know what it's all *for.*"

"Yes."

"And I don't. I haven't a single clue. I can't live here, plainly, I can't rattle about in this room and my bedroom, and trek a mile and a half to the kitchen for meals. Can I?"

Peter said nothing. He sat down beside her on the fender, and after a long silence, he said, "Did Hughie take you up to the turret?"

"I don't know," Alexia said tiredly. "I can't remember. We kept going up and down and round and round and I really couldn't tell you where we'd been. It all became a blur. I think I'm going down to get Carly. I need a consolation —"

"Would you just come up to the turret first?"

She looked at him. "Why?"

"I slept there. I slept in the highest room in the house. There's something up there I'd like you to see."

"All right," she said uncertainly. She stood up, pulling down her jersey and the hem of her skirt. "As long as it's quick. I haven't got the energy for anything that isn't quick."

"I promise," he said, and held out his hand again.

He led her quickly back out into the hall, and up the short flight of stairs to the gallery, and then along its whole length to an archway leading to more stairs, twisting stairs winding round a central column of stone.

"I can't remember this —"

She followed him as he began to climb. The stairs had been built on a medieval pattern, turning round inside a tower without any kind of handrail and with narrow windows, like arrow slits, every eight feet or so, giving tantalizing glimpses of lawn, or loch, or hill, or sky. Just as Alexia opened her mouth to say she must pause for breath, Peter said, "Well done, you've made it, we're here," and opened a narrow door at the head of the stairs.

"The turret room," he said. His voice was shy and proud, wanting her admiration.

She said, "Heavens!" And then she simply stared.

The door through which they had come was set in a curved solid wall in which there was a small iron grate. The curve of the walls enclosed them like two shallow arms, and, at the far side of the little room, melted to form windows, windows so high that being up there was to be above everything, above the trees and the tumbled pinkish-brown roofs of the house, above the wheeling gulls.

"It was always terribly cold up here," Peter said. "I used to lug up endless buckets of coal. But it was worth it, don't you think?"

Alexia nodded.

"Come here," he said. "This is what I want to

show you. This is what I brought you up here for."

He was by the window, stooping a little, his forefinger resting against the glass.

"Look."

She bent to peer. There, in a corner of the window-pane, were two tiny letters scratched unevenly in the glass: AA.

"Elsie said your grandmother did that. This was her refuge, when she was a girl. Could that be right. She was called Alexandra Abbott, wasn't she?"

Alexia put out a finger and traced the letters.

"And you are AA too, you see," Peter said. "Aren't you? Alexia Angus. I . . . I don't want to bully you into anything but I thought you ought to see. That's all — AA meets AA."

In the afternoon, Alexia put Carly back into her majestic pram and took her for a walk down by the loch. There was a rough road along the shore, a private road, that ran south, Elsie said, for two miles until the Castle Bewick estate ended, and north, towards the head of the loch, until it met the land of Duncan McGill. Duncan McGill had already made his presence felt. A load of logs, with his compliments, had been delivered to the castle that morning, and also a great hunk of venison wrapped in a cloth sack. Alexia had never eaten venison in her life.

"How very kind of him —"

"Duncan McGill is not a kind man," Elsie said. "He's a fair man, but he's not kind. He's not of the opinion that you'll stay."

"Really!"

158

"His keeper's lad said to Hughie —"

"I don't really want to know, Elsie."

Elsie sniffed. "Then I'll be larding the meat."

"Thank you."

"And you'll be airing the bairn."

"Yes," said Alexia, "but that was my idea. From now on, whatever I do round here is my idea. Is that clear?"

She pushed Carly for a mile down the lochside. It was as ravishingly lovely as her morning tour of the house had been the reverse. High above her, the great purple hillsides swooped down, and as they descended, they softened and mellowed until at the level of the water, they had become soft fields bounded by stone walls and divided by clear brown streams tufted with ferns. To her right the pebbly beach was completely empty of everything except wreaths and garlands of seaweed, sloping down to the waters of the loch which lapped back and forth as the tide came slowly in.

It was a deeply soothing walk. Alexia decided that the one thing she would not do on it was even attempt to make up her mind about anything; she would, instead, simply walk and look, and dream about nothing in particular, pushing her baby and reveling in the soft air and the tranquillity of the place.

"After all," she said to Carly, "we could do worse than just follow Mr. McReadie's advice and sell the whole thing. Couldn't we?"

When she got back to the house, she took Carly up to the Mermaid Room, and laid her on a rug in front of the fire so that she could kick and wriggle. After a while, she lay down beside Carly, her face at the same level as the baby's, and thought how strange it was to feel at once so at peace in this lovely place and so haunted by having to decide what to do about it. It was a real, jarring shock when the telephone rang.

"Darling," Cara said.

"Mum!"

"We were so worried. We were expecting you to ring last night, when you arrived —"

"I just forgot, I'm sorry —"

"Are you all right? Is it habitable? Are you coping?"

"Yes," Alexia said.

"Just yes?"

"Yes," Alexia said.

"Just yes?"

"Yes." Alexia said again. She was filled with a sudden reluctance to give anything away.

"Are you warm enough?"

"Someone's given me some logs —"

"And is there anyone in the house? James thought —"

"There's Elsie."

"Who's Elsie?"

"Her mother worked for Grandmamma."

"Alexia," Cara said, her voice growing warm with persuasiveness, "Alexia, when you're settled a little, you must give some thought as to what you are going to do."

"Do?"

"Yes. Don't be stupid. You can't just camp there like some mindless hippy. Daddy and I —"

"Yes?" Alexia said sharply.

"We've been giving a lot of thought to this —"

"Have you?"

"A huge great house like that has to be some sort of institution, doesn't it? And if it isn't a school again, we wondered what you would think of the idea of a nursing home —"

Alexia shouted, "A nursing home!"

"Don't shout. It's a perfectly practical suggestion. I mentioned it to James and he said —"

"I don't want to hear."

"Please, Alexia —"

"Listen," Alexia said, furiously, "just listen for once, will you? I'm sick and tired of being told what to do, of having instructions issued thinly disguised as suggestions. I'm sick and tired of being treated like a half-witted child and I'm sickest and tiredest of all of hearing the assumption in everyone's voices that I won't be able to cope because I am, basically, so utterly hopeless. Well," her voice rose, "I'll show you. This is my house, however dilapidated, and my land, and most of all, my life! Will you kindly just leave me alone to get on with all three of them and find some other poor mutt to boss about."

There was a dead silence at the other end. Then Cara said stiffly, "I'm sure I never meant to offend you, but you really have to admit that you have never yet shown one atom of aptitude for managing your own affairs —"

Alexia gave a little squeal and banged the telephone down. On the rug, not liking the atmosphere, Carly rolled her gingery little head towards her mother and began to whimper. Alexia knelt down by her.

"Sorry, baby, sorry, really sorry. Do you think I'll make you as absolutely hopping mad one day as she makes me?"

She scooped Carly up and held her so that her soft head was against her neck.

"You know, the only way to shut them all up and confound them is to think of a plan. That's what we've got to do, Carly Angus. We've got to come up with a scheme, we've got to. We've got to think of a way to make use of this house, to . . . to civilize it —" She stopped. She took a breath. Somewhere, quite unbidden, a clear, delightful American voice spoke in her memory. "Isn't it insane?" the voice said. "Isn't it just insane? That there's nowhere, just *nowhere*, civilized to stay in Scotland?"

Chapter Thirteen

Peter Burton volunteered to go to Arrochar station and collect Mr. McReadie. Alexia accepted at once. She had allowed Peter to come back to the castle, and occupy the great paneled bedroom which had been used by the former headmaster and his wife, and in return, Peter seemed only too eager to be of use. He was of use. He would go shopping in Craigmuir; he would mind Carly; he would help Alexia deal with the slightly suspicious villagers in Bewick; and he would run errands. As he was the only person around with a car — an elderly Morris Minor estate car with half-timbered sides — this was just as well.

In his absence at Arrochar, Alexia dressed very carefully for Mr. McReadie. She had been shopping in Craigmuir and had bought a length of heathery Harris tweed which she had made into a knee-length skirt, and a matching polo-necked jersey of irreproachable modesty. She brushed her hair smoothly, without backcombing it, and tied it back with a piece of Black Watch tartan ribbon. She took off all jewelry except her watch and changed her shoes for some sturdy brown lace-ups that Peter Burton had helped her to buy with much giggling. The final result, she decided, surveying herself in the moony, speckled glass of the Seahorse Room, would have made Amanda and Felicity rock with laughter, but it was just the thing for Mr. McReadie.

She took as much trouble with the appearance of the Mermaid Room as she had with herself. With Peter and Hughie's help, various peculiar pieces of furniture had been salvaged from attics and outhouses, as well as rugs and a lamp or two, and the wonderful find of a huge untouched roll of deep green linen union patterned with cream and golden lilies which Alexia had made into curtains and cushion covers. These curtains had been the turning point in Elsie's opinion of Alexia. The sight of Alexia's deftness and ingenuity — old sheets had been used for lining and old curtain tape unpicked from decaying velvet curtains found in a lumber room — had aroused Elsie's real respect. When the curtains were up — hung by Peter — Elsie could not restrain herself.

"You're no fool, Mrs. Angus," she had said to Alexia, and then she had blushed deeply at hearing herself utter what was for her such unbridled praise.

Alexia had laughed. "You're just like Lyddy. She never thinks I can do a thing for myself either. Well, I'll surprise her as much as I intend to surprise you."

But the person she was really looking forward to surprising was Mr. McReadie. A month ago Mr. McReadie had seen a forlorn child he regarded as too young and silly to fend for herself in the smallest degree. What he would find now, Alexia intended, would be someone quite unrecognizable from that forlorn child. He would walk into the Mermaid Room and find comfort and charm and a fire and a very competent person with appropriate clothes and a firm and decided manner — and a *plan*.

Mr. McReadie was too discreet a professional to ask Peter Burton a single question about Alexia on the journey from the station. Instead, he talked about the weather, and the scenery and a report in the *Glasgow Herald* that morning that a woman in America had caught a blue shark weighing over four hundred pounds.

"As a fisherman myself," Mr. McReadie said, "that seems to me highly improbable. A woman indeed!"

Peter drove Mr. McReadie up to the front door of the castle where Hughie, on instructions from Alexia, was waiting to open the car door. Mr. McReadie was agreeably surprised.

"Good morning, Hughie."

"Good morning, sir."

The front door was opened from the inside. There stood Elsie.

"Good morning, Mrs. MacGregor."

"Mrs. Angus is expecting you, sir. In the Mermaid Room."

Mr. McReadie peered at Elsie. Her face was perfectly serious.

"Is she indeed."

"I'll take you up, sir. I hope you had a comfortable journey."

"Tolerable," said Mr. McReadie. None of this was what he had been expecting. He wondered, just briefly, if he were being made fun of. He allowed Elsie to help him off with his coat and scarf and hat and gloves and then, grasping his black case, he set off up the stone stairs behind her. The stairs were as gaunt as they had ever been, but it struck Mr. McReadie that they had recently been scrubbed and that the air, so recently scented with rubber and small boy, smelled of wood smoke and polish. He sniffed appreciatively.

Elsie opened the door to the Mermaid Room.

"Mr. McReadie, Mrs. Angus."

Mr. McReadie blinked. The sun was not out, but the room he was looking into seemed as full of warmth and light as if it had been. He blinked again. The huge windows let in water-reflected light from the loch, and a fire was leaping with flames and there appeared to be lamps with golden shades and white and golden lilies and rich rugs and cushions and . . .

"Good morning, Mr. McReadie," Alexia said. "It's so good of you to make the journey out here."

He stared at her. For a moment, he told Mrs. McReadie late that night over a simple supper of smoked haddock poached in milk with boiled potatoes, he'd simply not recognized Mrs. Angus. In a month, in four short weeks, she seemed to have turned from a girl to a . . . well a . . .

"Woman?"

"Yes," Mr. McReadie said, slowly shaking his head at the memory. "Yes. That was what it was. She's become a woman."

Alexia led him to the brown armchair by the fire where she had sat herself the first day she had arrived. He wasn't quite sure what he had expected, but he certainly hadn't prepared himself to be so competently dealt with, nor for Alexia's appearance.

He said stiffly, "You look well, Mrs. Angus."

She smiled at him. "D'you think so?"

He looked away. For the second time in five minutes he had a feeling he was being teased. He said, in a stately way, "The air of the West Highlands is generally considered to be most relaxing."

"I've found it good for thinking in, too," Alexia said. She settled herself on the leather top of the club fender, and leaned forward. "I've made a lot of progress since we met in Sauchiehall Street."

"So I see," said Mr. McReadie, pulling himself together.

"A lot."

He waited. It suddenly struck him that he was about to hear some harebrained scheme that would immediately require him to knock it on the head. It was his duty, after all, as the family solicitor with responsibility for the property in Scotland . . .

"I've decided what to do," Alexia said, interrupting his thoughts.

He eyed her suspiciously. "You have?"

"Yes," she said. Her eyes were very bright but not even Mr. McReadie could honestly have said that she seemed overexcited. On the contrary, she appeared full of self-control.

"What I want to do," Alexia said, "is to turn this house into a hotel."

Mr. McReadie nearly leapt from his seat.

"A hotel!"

167

"Yes," Alexia said, "a hotel. A new kind of hotel. A hotel which is as comfortable and charming and warm as staying in someone's country house."

"But who would come to such a hotel?"

"Americans. Londoners. People from cities all over the world who want to look at Scottish scenery and walk in it, and who want to fish and relax, and eat Scottish food." Alexia leaned forward again. "My hotel will have really good food, you see. Interesting food."

Mr. McReadie, who had never seen interesting food in his life, looked absolutely astounded. The whole idea seemed to him both preposterous and faintly immoral. A *comfortable* Highland hotel? Warm? Charming? He said, in a voice slightly strangled by his feelings, "And how do you propose to finance such a scheme, may I ask?"

"By selling the land."

"Selling the land? Selling the land without the house? Leaving such a house as this without the land to support it?"

"The house, when it's a hotel, will support itself."

"I know of nobody who's done such a thing!"

"Well," Alexia said, smiling, "soon you'll know me."

Mr. McReadie got up from his chair and began to pace agitatedly about the room.

"I consider the scheme foolhardy, Mrs. Angus."

"Certainly, it's a gamble —"

"Have you consulted your uncle? Your parents?"

"No."

"Can it possibly be wise to proceed with such a risky undertaking without experienced consultation?"

Alexia's chin went up.

"Oh, I shall talk to hoteliers, Mr. McReadie, and caterers and wholesalers. I'm not a fool. But I don't need to talk to my family."

"You are a most headstrong young woman."

"Yes."

"My professional opinion runs entirely against your proposal."

Alexia got up.

"I'm so sorry, Mr. McReadie, but I can't help that. If you really feel you are quite unable to help me, then I will simply, however reluctantly, have to find another solicitor."

The room swam round Mr. McReadie. He cast his eyes upwards and thought he saw a circle of mermaids dancing on the ceiling. He wondered if he were going to have one of his dizzy turns.

"Mr. McReadie," Alexia said, taking him steadyingly by the arm, "I'd so much rather you acted for me. You know this house, you know the area, you know Scottish law. I'm not proposing anything so very mad you know, and if it doesn't work, I'll still have the capital asset of the house."

He allowed her to lead him back to the armchair and settle him in it.

"What is it," he said weakly, "you would like me to do?"

"I'd like you, please, to find a buyer for five thousand acres of land."

"Five thousand acres of land —"

"Yes, please."

"D'you not think, Mrs. Angus, that to start with five —"

"No," said Alexia. "I need so much money. I need to put in central heating and bathrooms and a professional kitchen, and redecorate inside and out and furnish it and rescue the garden and hire staff —"

There was a knock at the door.

"Come in," Alexia said.

"I've just brought a dram in," Elsie said, "for Mr. McReadie."

She came across the room towards him, and put, on a small table at his elbow, a little silver tray bearing a glass and a jug of water and a decanter of whisky.

"It's a cold day," Alexia said. "And you've had a long journey —," Elsie added.

Mr. McReadie looked from one to the other and then he looked, with undisguised longing, at the whisky decanter. For the third time that morning he felt, unaccountably, that he was being made gentle fun of. He also felt something else, something that he couldn't remember feeling often in over forty years of legal practice; that he had, in the simplest way, been outmaneuvered.

"In the ordinary course of events," said Mr. McReadie, stretching out a trembling hand to the decanter, "I never take a dram before the evening. But I do not feel today is ordinary. I feel that today is, through no fault of my own, an exception."

It was only five days later that he telephoned

Alexia. He disliked the telephone as being an un-necessarily hurried way of communicating, but even Mr. McReadie found himself astounded by the ease with which he achieved Alexia's request.

She took the call in the kitchen, where she and Peter were poring over the first plans they had drawn up for the conversion of the castle.

"Mrs. Angus?"

"Yes —"

"Mrs. Angus, I have good news for you."

"You do?"

"I believe I have found a purchaser for the land. Or rather, a purchaser for the land has found me."

"How did anybody know about it?" Alexia demanded.

"Local gossip, I should imagine. The person in question is your neighbor, Duncan McGill."

Alexia gasped.

"Duncan McGill! But I've never met him! I've been here almost five weeks, and he hasn't been near me! He's sent things, logs and game and so forth, but he hasn't come to call or anything —"

"He would like to call now," Mr. McReadie said. "He would like to have a meeting to discuss the purchase of the land."

"Heavens —"

"It is a meeting at which I should be present, Mrs. Angus."

"Oh, of course —"

"I shall leave you to consider the matter. You should reflect that you will be almost sur-rounded by Mr. McGill's land if you accede. You should reflect upon the effect on the value of your own property if you —"

"Mr. McReadie," Alexia said hurriedly, "thank you so much. Thank you. I'll think it all over and ring you back."

She put the telephone down. Peter, at the table, and Elsie, peeling vegetables at the vast old stone sink, turned expectantly towards her.

"Duncan McGill wants to buy the land! I don't even know him!"

Elsie said, "I thought he'd have a try. He's a shrewd business man, they say, a hard bargainer."

Alexia sat down abruptly in one of the kitchen chairs. Her cheeks were burning.

"Well, he's certainly got no manners. The nerve! I come to live here as a total stranger, and he never comes to call and then coolly proposes to buy my land!"

"He did send you the wood and the venison —"

"It's easy to do that! You just give someone orders! What costs you is actually to take trouble yourself with someone. Honestly, he's only got to drive three miles —"

"He's been away a lot," Peter said defensively. "He's got businesses all over the place —"

Alexia turned on him. "Why are you sticking up for him?"

Peter colored a little, "He's —" He stopped.

"He's what? Rude? Yes. Arrogant? Probably —"

"No," Peter said carefully, "he's different. Tough certainly, but fair. He just doesn't behave quite like other people."

"Clearly."

Peter bent over the plans again, laying his surveyor's rule carefully along the line of a new bedroom corridor proposed for the second floor. "You ought to think about it, Alexia. I really think you ought. He's a local man, he loves this place, he looks after his own land beautifully, people like working for him. A stranger somewhere like this would be such a risk."

Alexia said, "I'm a stranger."

They both looked at her.

"Yes."

She got up. "I'm going out into the garden to get Carly in," she said.

The air outside was cold, certainly, but it still had that soft quality that Alexia was beginning to recognize as Highland air. Carly lay tucked up in her magnificent pram in a sheltered corner of the lawn by a stout holly hedge, with only her tiny sleeping face visible under the blankets and bonnet. Alexia bent over her. It seemed silly to wake her, selfish really, just because she, Alexia, would like the comfort of a cuddle. She straightened up again and took a breath and set off down the rough grass to the water's edge.

The loch itself never failed to soothe her. She loved it in all its moods, placid or turbulent, and she loved the life that the sea tides gave it, washing it up and down the pebbly shores, over the weed and the rocks and the black clusters of mussels. She found a dry rock above the water's edge and sat down on it, pulling up her knees and wrapping her arms around them. If she loved the loch, she knew too that she now loved the castle and the hills and mountains. Five short weeks and it was true love. Sometimes, as now, it hardly seemed to her possible that the Alexia Langley of two years ago could have become the Alexia Angus of today. I haven't got much to show for it on the outside, she thought, but there's so much change on the inside, so much.

She was slightly ashamed of her outburst in the kitchen against Duncan McGill. She was determined to make a hotel of Castle Bewick, it was her dream and her purpose, and she had to sell the land to achieve that, and clearly it was sensible to sell it to someone who knew it and loved it, and would look after it. If she was honest with herself, she hadn't anything against Duncan McGill except that he hadn't come rushing round with flowers and chocolates, but as he was a crusty old bachelor by all accounts, it wasn't really at all reasonable to have expected him to. Was it? She gave herself a little shake and turned to look at the castle which looked kindly back at her with all its many windows.

"I love you," she said aloud to it, "And I love Carly, and my freedom and my future. And I like Peter and Elsie and Hughie. I just wish —" She stopped. It was weeks, even months, since she had thought of Martin, and she wasn't, she told herself firmly, going to start now. "I just wish that in the midst of everything, of all these plans and excitement, I didn't feel a bit lonely." She got up and stretched. "Though I don't know why I shouldn't mind," she added to a seagull regarding her from an adjacent rock. "After all, I've always been lonely. I ought to be used to it." The seagull didn't look as if it cared, one way or another, and its indifference was somehow a comfort. "I've just got to get on with things and then perhaps something lovely will happen when I'm not looking. And the first step in getting on is to go back to the house and pick up the telephone and bravely ask to speak to Duncan McGill."

Chapter Fourteen

Two days later, the weather changed. The kind late autumn days gave way to wild weather with raging winds and squalls of rain sweeping up the loch, and obliterating the view. The trees in the garden bent under the onslaught and groaned and creaked in the wind, and Carly had her morning rest in one of the sculleries, with the window open for her to avail herself of the fresh air without which Elsie plainly thought she would perish.

Despite all previous reports of its structural soundness, the house itself was transformed by the weather. From being Alexia's magic castle full of promise it turned into a leaky old ship in a storm, with water pouring through cracks in the roof gullies and window frames and spouting from broken gutters and drainpipes. A foggy miasma of moisture rose from the stone floors, and the walls in the stairways passages felt as damp as dungeons. It was almost impossible to keep anything dry or warm, and the rain-darkened skies made it necessary to have the lights on all day; that is, until the house's old generator coughed and wheezed and died, and had to be expensively revived by the local engineer summoned by Peter all the way from Oban.

Alexia's spirits sank with the weather. They

were in no way helped by letters from Bishopstow, loving, encouraging letters to be sure, full
of praise for Alexia's plans and spirit of enterprise, but also full of the autumn comforts
of Cornwall. Those letters from Bishopstow ex-
uded cosiness. By contrast, Bewick was about as
cosy as a ruin. In fact, toiling round it putting
buckets and bowls under the worst leaks, and
trying to find a warm dry corner where Carly
could sleep or kick without becoming instantly
covered in mold, Alexia thought that a ruin
would actually be preferable to a house in an appalling state of repair because at least a ruin
wasn't even pretending it could shelter people.
Bewick, which had looked so solid, now felt as
frail as a sieve. It also felt, by the minute, a bigger
and more expensive challenge than she had ever
imagined possible.

"Wouldn't it be cheaper," she said in despair to
Peter, "just to build a hotel from scratch?"

"You mustn't give up," he said, drawing on.
"You mustn't let a little weather affect you."

"A *little* weather!"

"Yes," he said. He looked at her with sympathy.
"I do understand, you know. I do see how frightening it looks. But you can't give up before
you've begun."

"Isn't that the very time to give up?"

"Think of your grandmother."

"I can't."

"Well, think that tomorrow you have to see
Duncan McGill, although I suppose you could
always tell him you've changed your mind and
you want to sell him everything and go back to

177

London. Couldn't you?"

She gazed at him. Dear Peter. Dear, steady, good-tempered capable Peter, quietly giving up so much of his own life to help her realize a dream that he understood.

"Why are you so good to me?"

His gaze faltered, just a little.

"You know why. I love it here."

"Peter —"

"Yes?"

"If . . . if I gave up, you'd understand why, wouldn't you? You wouldn't be angry?"

His voice wasn't quite steady. He said, "I wouldn't ever . . . be angry with you. I wouldn't —" He stopped. She had an impulse to go round the table and put her arms around him but some other impulse held her back. She just gently said, "Thank you," and then she went out of the room because she was suddenly afraid of what might happen next.

Duncan McGill was absolutely punctual the next morning; Alexia, out of an instinctive perversity, was not. She heard his car stop on the gravel, and she heard the front door being opened to admit him, but she remained deliberately in the Seahorse Room for several minutes afterwards.

She dressed as she had dressed for Mr. McReadie. If anything, she pulled her hair back tighter, to make herself look older and less vulnerable. Duncan McGill didn't know how old she was after all, he didn't know anything about her except that she was called Mrs. Angus and that she had something to sell which he wanted to buy. Being a crusty old bachelor, he probably wouldn't even look at her properly at all.

She counted slowly to a hundred. It wasn't rude to be a little late — Mr. McReadie was, after all, there to welcome him — and in any case, by all accounts and appearances, Duncan McGill was quite a specialist in rudeness himself. Then she gave herself a last look in the glass, frowned, and went slowly downstairs to the Mermaid Room, past the buckets in which drips from various leaks were ringing out in a gloomy sympathy.

She paused outside the Mermaid Room. She could hear their voices, male Scottish voices. She put her chin up, just a little. "This is my house," she told herself, "my house and my land and I am over twenty-one and nobody can make me do anything I don't want to do with either."

She opened the door. There, with his back to the fire, stood the familiar figure of Mr. McReadie, long face, moustache, decent dark suit, and there, with his back to her, stood Duncan McGill, tall and broad shouldered and, to her surprise, brown haired rather than grey.

"Ah," said Mr. McReadie, catching sight of her in the doorway, "Mrs. Angus. Mrs. Angus, allow me to present to you Mr. Duncan McGill."

Duncan McGill turned round. Alexia gave a little gasp.

"But you're the man in the hotel!"

There was an awkward little pause. Duncan McGill had his hand out, but he wasn't smiling and he certainly wasn't laughing as he had laughed that night in the Hibernian Hotel.

"I beg your pardon —"

"You rescued me," Alexia said impulsively, forgetting that she was trying to appear older and businesslike, "you made the waiter bring me a sandwich. Don't you remember? I was the girl with the baby —" She paused. It was disconcerting to find yourself babbling away to someone, hoping for a response they clearly weren't going to give.

Duncan McGill said, "Certainly I remember. I had no idea, of course, that I was helping Mrs. Angus of Castle Bewick."

"Would it have made a difference?"

"Not then," he said. His voice was cold. "Not until I heard of her plans to turn this house into . . . into a *hotel*."

Mr. McReadie looked flustered. "Mrs. Angus, Mr. McGill, I beg you. We must conduct this meeting in a proper —"

Alexia ignored him. She marched up to Duncan McGill and glared up at him.

"What do you mean?"

"I mean what I say. I mean that I was happy to help anyone being maltreated by the Hibernian Hotel, but that my happiness would have been clouded had I known that the person I was helping cherished plans for the destruction of the lochside."

Mr. McReadie tried again. "Mr. McGill, might I suggest —"

"Destruction?" Alexia shouted. "Destruction? What do you mean? I am going to *rescue* this house. I am going to give it a new life!"

180

"It's the wrong life."

"*Wrong?*"

"You're a newcomer here," Duncan McGill said. "You don't understand the ways of a place like this. If you import rich tourists here, they will literally pollute life here, they will destroy the balance of man and nature, they will urbanize —"

"Please stop," Alexia said. She was shaking with rage. This awful man, this domineering, humorless, patronizing man was filling her with a fury so intense that she was literally trembling. "I see no point in continuing this meeting. There can be no possible arrangement with someone —"

"I beg you to be calm, Mrs. Angus," Mr. McReadie said, laying a hand on her arm, "and, Mr. McGill, I beg *you* to confine yourself to the matter that concerns us, the matter that is the reason for our meeting."

Alexia twitched herself free and went across the room to sit in the brown armchair. She sat very upright with her knees pressed together and her hands in her lap. She took a deep breath.

"There will be no meeting. Mr. McGill is the last person on earth I'd think of selling an inch of ground to."

"In that case," said Duncan McGill, "I shall block your application to the local planning authority to turn this house into a hotel."

She turned on him. "But if you buy the land, you give me the means to turn the house into a hotel!"

"But I will safeguard the land. I will be saving what I can."

"The hotel will give local people jobs!"

181

"So will my forestry schemes and my fish farms, dignified jobs on the land, traditional jobs, natural to Scotland and to Scotland's resources. What does it do for a man's self-respect to open door and carry trays for tourists?"

"What nonsense!"

Duncan McGill opened his mouth as if to reply as angrily as she had spoken, but then seemed to think better of it, because all he said was, "My offer still stands, Mrs. Angus."

She turned to Mr. McReadie.

"What offer?"

"Mr. McGill has offered fifteen pounds an acre, Mrs. Angus, which I am obliged to advise you is a far better price than you would see on the open market, the current price of high land being at present —"

"It still wouldn't be enough to turn this place into a palace," Duncan said to Alexia, cutting across Mr. McReadie. His expression had changed and his voice was gentler.

"I can try —"

He said nothing. She rushed on, "You don't know anything about my plans. You don't know the kind of hotel I have in mind because what I have in mind just doesn't exist in Scotland at the moment. You haven't taken the trouble to meet me or welcome me or anything. You don't know anything about me."

He said quietly, "I do know that you are very young."

Temper began to rise in her again. She turned her head away.

"Mr. McReadie, if you would be so good as to

show Mr. McGill out —"

"There's no need, thank you, I can find my own way."

Alexia remembered something. With her face still averted, she said stiffly, "Thank you for the presents of the wood and the venison. It was very thoughtful of you."

"But it would have been more thoughtful, you think, if I had come in person?"

"I never said that!"

"Mrs. Angus, you did not need to. I am not a fool."

Then he gave her a little bow, just the kind of little bow he had given her that night in the Hibernian Hotel when he had appeared to be a gallant, romantic stranger rather than an over-bearing and contemptuous neighbor, and left the room.

Much later that day, when she had bathed and fed Carly, and tucked her up for the night, Alexia went down to the kitchen in search of warmth and supper, and found Peter already there. One end of the table was laid, on the blue cloth, and Peter had turned off the harsh overhead light and was sitting poring over the plans as usual by the light of a little cluster of candles stuck in old beer bottles. The fire door of the range was open for warmth, casting a rosy glow. The sight of the room, warm and welcoming, with Peter quietly absorbed at the heart of it, was the most soothing spectacle possible for Alexia's jagged feelings.

She had been out, all afternoon, on the hill. She hadn't gone out with any particular purpose beyond that of getting too tired to think, and had simply climbed and scrambled until the fading light had sent her home. It had given her quite a shock, sliding down the last wet, rough slopes in the dusk towards the house, to realize how much she now thought of it as home, and how infinitely hospitable it looked in the gloaming, its fretted black outline solid against the darkening gleam of the loch, with here and there the odd golden-lit window glowing like a beacon.

Peter didn't look up as she came in. He simply said, "Elsie made us a stew."

Alexia came forward into the warmth. She stooped to look at what Peter was doing. He was drawing, with infinite care, an impression of how the entrance stairs and hall would look if carpeted and properly lit and decorated.

"What are those?"

"Pikes and bayonets and things. They have them in Craigmuir Castle arranged in patterns and they look wonderful."

"A bit menacing —"

"We don't want this place to look soft. It's got to be romantic, but Scottish romantic, not soppy romantic."

Alexia sat down opposite Peter. He looked up at her at last.

"You look worn out."

"It was an awful interview —"

"Yes. I rather gathered that."

"If I don't sell him the land, he'll obstruct planning permission, and if I do sell him the land, he'll do everything to make things difficult for me. He doesn't think local people ought to work here, he thinks it's undignified for them to. He thinks I'm young and silly and that I don't know what I'm doing. And even if the deal goes through, it will only bring in seventy-five thousand pounds and Mr. McReadie says the roof will cost two thirds of that."

"Well?" Peter said.

"Well what?"

"Are you going to give up and go home?"

Alexia leaned forward. "No. This *is* home."

"So?"

"I've just got to start small. I've got to get the house into good shape, and open it up, bit by bit. It's not so exciting, but it's what's turning out to be practical."

Peter got up and went over to open the oven door of the range and take out a covered casserole.

"I thought you wanted to give up this morning."

Alexia got up too.

"I suppose Mr. McGill served one useful purpose at least. He made me absolutely determined to stay."

Peter put the casserole down carefully on a rush mat.

"Alexia —"

"Yes?"

"You said . . . you said 'I must just start small.' Could it . . . could it be 'we'?"

"We?"

He blushed. 'I just mean . . . I hope so . . . I mean, I'd so love it if you would let me help you. After all, I do know something about architecture

185

and surveying and I could probably save you some money. I'll work for nothing but my keep until the place is going but . . . may I?"

He looked up at her. His sweet open face was full of pleading.

Alexia said slowly, "I'm awful, I've just taken you for granted."

"No, no you haven't, I mean, I've wanted you to, I've wanted to be here, helping. The thing is — I don't quite know how to put it, but the thing is that I adore it here as you know but I also . . . I also just want to be where you are."

There was a pause. They looked at each other. Alexia put out a hand to him and he seized it and held it in both his.

"Peter —"

"Yes?"

"Peter, I'm so grateful, I'm more grateful than you can imagine. You've been kinder to me than anyone, but —"

"You've not been divorced a year. Is that it?"

Alexia struggled to be truthful.

"Partly that, of course."

"And we've only known each other for five weeks."

"Partly that too. But mostly I . . . I just don't know about love at the moment —"

Peter lifted her hand and kissed it.

"I won't mention it again, I promise. Not for . . . well, not for ages anyway. But when I walked into the Mermaid Room and saw you sitting in the chair and you'd obviously been asleep and you looked —"

Alexia gently removed her hand. "Sh —"

"I know," he said, "I'm sorry, I really am. And I'll shut up now. Promise. But can I stay and help you?"

Alexia smiled and lifted the lid of the casserole.

"Smell that! I'm ravenous. Of course you can stay. I don't really know what I'd do if you didn't."

In the morning there was a hand-delivered letter from Duncan McGill.

"I much regret," he wrote, "that our meeting yesterday was dominated by, at least on my part, such an unconstructive display of personal opinion. I remain opposed to your scheme for the reasons I hope I made quite plain yesterday — I was, after all, born here — but for all that, I will make no public obstruction to your plans if you will sell your land to me rather than to an outsider."

Alexia held the letter out to Peter.

"Is that victory or defeat?"

"Victory, I think. Victory with provisos."

"What a weird man." She turned to Elsie who was hanging Carly's diapers along the bars of an immense old-fashioned ceiling airer before hauling it aloft. "How old is he?"

"He'll be thirty-four this Hogmanay. I remember his being born. Blizzards and a drift over the pass six feet high and poor Mrs. McGill in labor for the first time at the age of forty-three. It was Mary McPhee delivered him. The winter of 1933."

"He seems much older somehow —"

"Comes of living on your own," Elsie said.

187

"Why didn't he marry then? He's —" Alexia stopped and went pink. She had been about to say, "He's terribly attractive," but recovered herself and said instead, "I mean, he's obviously rich."

"He wanted Fiona Murray from Lochgilphead, but she wouldn't have him and as far as I know, he hasn't tried another."

"I wonder why —"

"Mrs. Angus," Elsie said, turning round. "You listen to me. Duncan McGill's a queer fellow and you'll not get to the bottom of him and you'll be a fool to try."

Alexia grinned. "You sound just like Lyddy —"

"And I'll tell you another thing," Elsie said. "Thinking about Duncan McGill isn't going to put a roof on this house or food in our bellies. Is it?"

"No, Elsie." She stood up and stretched. "Today is the first day of our new beginning, so I'd better go get on with it."

Chapter Fifteen

September 1968

In the August edition of *Scottish Country Life*, a small advertisement appeared. It showed a drawing of a turreted house, and below the drawing was printed "Castle Bewick. Country House Hotel. Open from September 1st. Brochure and rates on application. This is a hotel with a difference."

"The trouble is," Alexia said, "that the difference is that the owner has never done anything like this before in her life."

Nor, she reflected, had she ever worked so hard or believed she could work so hard. The winter had been a torment, bitterly cold and raging with wind, not only freezing them all to the marrow but also frequently delaying the workmen who had the daunting task of repairing the castle's huge and fanciful roof. At the same time that half the roof was off, it seemed the kitchen was completely dismembered, all the floors were ripped up for new central heating pipes and great channels were gouged in the walls for rewiring. The mess and discomfort were indescribable. The sticky, clotting, choking dust of building work lay on everything they touched or trod on or ate. It

189

was bitterly cold and there were long periods when the only hot water to be had was boiled by Hughie and Peter on huge bonfires made out of rotten and discarded timbers from the house. They moved, Peter and Alexia and Carly, like grimy, shivering gypsies from corner to corner of the great, filthy, chaotic house, sustained by hot meals brought up by Elsie, and by the not very comforting thought that Alexia's investment in the house was now so enormous that she could not possibly retreat. The only way, however difficult, was forward and when her heart failed her, really and truly, she would toil up the stone spiral of stairs to the icy, beautiful little turret room and run her fingers over her grandmother's initials — her own initials — in the windowpane, for strength and comfort.

She was astounded to discover what she could do if she had to. Clearly, she and Peter couldn't rewire and replumb the house alone, but they could certainly learn from the workmen she hired to do so. In the course of nine months she became an adequate plasterer and welder, and discovered the enormous satisfaction of having warmth and light result from a successful bit of wiring up. She wasn't the only one. Hughie, near silent and apparently so ill coordinated, became such an expert plumber that the contractor Alexia had hired offered him a job. He had shaken his head. "I could no' live away from here."

He echoed Alexia's own feelings. There were days when she would have sold her soul cheerfully for a deep, hot bath, but there were never

190

days when she would have sold it to be anywhere else — not even, she realized with a stab of amazed delight, for Bishopstow. Bewick, demanding, cold, comfortless and beloved, had gradually obliterated even Bishopstow.

By early summer, most of the workmen had gone. The house stood solidly against the weather with its window frames newly painted, and an enormous Swiss boiler, like an entire ship's engine room, waiting for the day when it could be harnessed to hot water tanks and radiators all over the house. But that was all. Castle Bewick had been mended, but it stood as bare as a barn, and there wasn't a penny piece left of the seventy-five thousand pounds Duncan McGill had paid for the land.

There was nothing for it, Alexia decided, but to take out a mortgage. She brushed the building dust out of her hair and scrubbed the paint and filth out of her nails, and dug out some of her London clothes — so strange they looked, so fragile and frivolous to someone who had spent the winter in trousers and Wellington boots and as many cast-off jerseys as Peter could spare — and set off for Glasgow and the bank manager. It was like a journey to the moon after the seclusion of winter, but it was a successful journey. Alexia returned to Bewick with five thousand pounds.

"It's far from a fortune, but it'll do up the drawing room and the dining room and a few bedrooms and bathrooms. Thank heavens I can make curtains! Amanda always said I'd bless her for it one day."

"Amanda?"

191

"I used to work for her once, in London before . . . before I was married."

Peter flinched slightly. He had been as good as his word all winter, and never spoken openly of his feelings, but they were very plain, all the same. His patience, his encouragement, his steady support, his sweetness to Carly, his considerable skills and dedication were all, of course, part of his personality, but they were also part of something else. Alexia couldn't hide from the fact that you didn't work like this for someone with no reward unless you loved them. She was deeply, truly grateful to Peter for everything, but sometimes, when she saw him looking at her, or saw him suffer at something she said that was quick or careless, she wished that she had never allowed their arrangement to begin, and that she was paying him a salary. Seeing him flinch now, at the mere mention that she had once been married, made her vow that when the first guests came, a proportion of what they paid would go first, and straight, to Peter.

The first guests were a Mr. and Mrs. Farquhar. Mr. Farquhar telephoned from Stirling and said he would like to reserve a double room with bathroom for his wife and himself for two nights, and that they would require dinner on both nights, and that Mrs. Farquhar was allergic to house dust and to feather pillows.

Alexia was sick with apprehension. At least three times an hour, on the day of the Farquhars' arrival, she went into the Seahorse Room and anxiously checked and rechecked every detail.

Certainly the room was transformed out of all recognition from the room in which Alexia had spent her first night at Bewick, but equally certainly, she was bound to have forgotten something. She had made a special trip to Glasgow to buy a foam rubber pillow, but would Mrs. Farquhar prove allergic to the pretty cushions, stuffed with feathers, that sat in the comfortable armchairs by the window, both now upholstered and curtained in ivy-patterned chintz by Alexia's own hand? And would she object to the undeniably new smell of the deep cream carpet, or think the beds too hard or too soft or too high or too low? And were the lamps placed just right for her to read by as well as to see to powder her allergic nose? And would she hate rose geranium soap, and would the plumbing gurgle and did they really, any of them, have a hope in hell of pulling off this idiotic pantomime of being professional hoteliers when they were nothing but a bunch of amateurs, not even thinly disguised?

When she wasn't in the Seahorse Room and its new adjoining bathroom, Alexia was pacing round the dining room, worrying that the Farquhars would think it odd that they were the only people dining, or tweaking curtains in the drawing room, anxious about the great fire's tendency to smoke, or crawling up and down the new carpet on the entrance stairs, checking for specks of dust. It didn't matter how often she was reassured that it all looked perfect, that her idea of an informal welcome with just a visitors' book not a reception desk was brilliant, and that the Farquhars would turn out to be charming, she was determined otherwise, and when, punctually at six, the sound of wheels was heard upon the gravel, she was so wound up that it was all she could do not to scream.

Mr. and Mrs. Farquhar took a very long time getting out of their car, and when they finally emerged, turned out to be identically middle-aged, middle height and unsmiling. They both wore tweeds and Mrs. Farquhar carried a large crocodile handbag. Alexia went forward to greet them.

"Good afternoon. I'm Alexia Angus. We are so pleased to welcome you to Castle Bewick."

Was her voice shaking? Mrs. Farquhar looked at her as if she would have preferred her to be a hotel porter in uniform who would carry their cases.

Hughie appeared, shambling slightly as was his wont, from the stableyard. He wore his usual motley uniform of old corduroy and knitting, and in an illuminating flash, Alexia suddenly saw him through the Farquhars' eyes.

"Hughie will bring in your cases —"

"He will?"

Hughie went straight to the car boot and put his hand on the catch. Mr. Farquhar was upon him in a flash.

"Kindly do not interfere with my motor."

Hughie gaped. He looked at Alexia.

"He was only trying —"

"When I have personally unlocked the boot," Mr. Farquhar said, "he may carry in our luggage under my supervision."

Hughie looked mulish. There was a brief moment when Alexia thought he might just turn and run, so she fixed him with a compelling gaze. With dreadful precision, Mr. Farquhar drew on his driving gloves again, unlocked the boot and opened it very slowly. Two suitcases lay neatly within, shrouded in linen covers.

"You may lift them out."

Hughie seized the cases, and almost ran with them towards the house. Mrs. Farquhar gave a little cry, her first utterance.

"He's perfectly reliable," Alexia said, slightly desperately. "He's the son of my housekeeper, he was born here."

The news seemed only to add to Mrs. Farquhar's alarm. She took her husband's arm and leaned on it heavily as he guided her inside. Alexia led the way, hoping that the sight of the new grass-green carpet laid over the freshly scrubbed stone stairs with gleaming brass stair rods and huge stone jars of early autumn leaves and berries would elicit some delighted response. But Mr. and Mrs. Farquhar climbed the stairs behind her with as much apparent interest as if they were climbing the stairs of a public library.

At the top, Mr. Farquhar looked about him, not at the huge Victorian painting of a kilted Highlander that Alexia had found in a junk shop in Dunoon, nor at the wonderful brass hanging lamp Hughie had discovered in a sack in a potting shed, but for a reception desk. Alexia took a deep breath.

"This is a hotel with a difference, Mr. Farquhar. Our aim is to make you feel that you are staying in a country house with room service.

Our aim is to help you to relax and therefore we wish to be as informal as possible. If you would just be good enough to sign our visitors' book?"

He bent disapprovingly over the book. It was a new book and it was open at the first page. There was no hiding it. Without straightening up, his gaze traveled from the virgin page to Alexia. It was like being looked at by a very reproachful fish.

"I had no idea," Mr. Farquhar said, "that my wife and I were to be guinea pigs."

"They'll go after breakfast," Alexia said despairingly to Peter. "They'll go straight home and tell the whole of Stirling never to come near us and probably write to *Scottish Country Life* and warn the readers —"

"Dinner was good," Peter said encouragingly. "They ate most of dinner."

"But that won't be enough, will it? Not after Carly and the plumbing and being the first people ever to come?"

Mrs. Farquhar had proved allergic to almost everything, particularly babies. She had fancied there was a draft through their bedroom window (she appeared oblivious to the view), had pronounced having carpet in a bathroom unhygienic, and had then been outraged to meet a briskly crawling Carly coming down the corridor outside the Seahorse Room.

"A baby!"

"Yes, she's my baby. She was learning to walk beautifully until we put the carpets down, but now she likes them so much, she's reverted to crawling."

"A child! In a hotel!"

Alexia opened her mouth to say indignantly, "It's her home, Mrs. Farquhar," and shut it again. She must remember that guests, however ghastly, were always right. She began to say instead that she would keep Carly confined for the length of the Farquhars' visit, when there was a roar from the bathroom within the Seahorse Room.

"Donald!" screamed Mrs. Farquhar and scuttled inside, followed by Alexia with Carly in her arms.

"Hot water!" cried Mr. Farquhar "Hot! I might . . . I might have —"

Hysterical with apology, panic and fury, Alexia fled downstairs. Hughie had been the last person to check the plumbing in the Seahorse bathroom, Hughie . . . Still with Carly in her arms, she raced through the kitchen and out into the yard. Hughie was there, as instructed, chopping logs to fill the huge wicker baskets that Alexia had found to stand beside the drawing room and dining room fires.

"Hughie!"

He stopped chopping and turned. When he saw her expression, his own became immediately stubborn.

"Hughie, what the hell have you done? The lavatory in the Seahorse bathroom is gushing blazing hot water! Mr. Farquhar is furious and I don't blame him. How could you be such a fool and how many other bathrooms have you done it to and how do I know you haven't connected the Farquhars' bathroom to the cold water system instead?"

Hughie stared at her.

"I have na'."

"How do I know?"

"I'm telling ye."

"But if you've made one stupid mistake, why shouldn't you have made hundreds?"

He said nothing. She was still beside herself.

"Go and mend it! At once. Do you hear me? I'll have to move the Farquhars and of course the Thistle Room isn't ready yet because I wasn't expecting to have to use it. Go, Hughie, go on. *Move!*"

He went, but slowly. She followed him, a little unsteadily. Elsie met her at the kitchen door and took Carly from her. She had clearly heard every word.

"It never helps to shout, Mrs. Angus."

"He deserved it. I'm sorry, Elsie, he's your son but he's made a simply terrible cock-up on the very first vital occasion when he shouldn't have."

"And you think he isn't aware of that himself?"

"I don't know, Elsie, and at this moment, I hardly care. I have to move the Farquhars into the Thistle Room, and calm them, and I shall probably have to offer them a free stay and the whole thing will be an utter disaster because your —" She stopped herself just in time.

The Farquhars were surprisingly amenable about being moved. Mrs. Farquhar said she thought the windows of the Thistle Room fitted better. They went out for a walk down by the loch and when they returned, the drawing room fire was blazing, and decanters of whisky and sherry had been left beside it on a pretty rosewood table, and Mr. Farquhar was moved to say that he considered it quite pleasant. They ate their dinner without enthusiasm, but without distaste either, and retired to the Thistle Room with no further complaints or requests except that Mrs. Farquhar believed her pillow smelled of foam rubber, and that they wished to be brought first hot water with slices of lemon in it at seven-thirty and then Indian tea with milk at eight.

In the morning, they ate a substantial breakfast and Alexia waited for them to say that they were leaving. They didn't. Instead, they climbed into their car and, as Mr. Farquhar put it, motored to Craigmuir. They returned for Mrs. Farquhar to have an afternoon rest and then the day passed as the previous one had except that Mr. Farquhar asked for a second helping of blackberry tart.

"Will you congratulate the cook, Mrs. Angus?"

"Actually, it was me."

He gazed at her. He gazed at her for a very long time and then he said, "Well, well. You've at least a light hand with pastry."

In the morning, Alexia felt obliged to offer him a reduction on his bill in view of the lavatory episode. He seemed to think about this for a long time, rocking slightly on his heels. Mrs. Farquhar and Alexia watched him anxiously. Finally, he said, "No. Upon consideration, no. I realize two things, Mrs. Angus. One is that we all have to start somewhere, and the second is that you must be of an age with our daughter Mary, who is still being educated, at the University of St. Andrews. For these reasons, I shall pay the full amount but," he shot her a penetrating look, "you should know that for a pound less per person per night, Mrs. Farquhar and I might have stayed at the Argyll Arms in Craigmuir."

When they had gone, anticlimax rather than relief fell upon the house like a leaden hand. Alexia went into the Mermaid Room, which she was using as both office and living room, and calculated drearily that she had made a profit of exactly three pounds two shillings and fourpence. She then turned to the day's mail out of a sense of duty. As usual, it was mostly bills, and a few estimates for various projects, like rescuing the garden, that she couldn't, for the moment, even contemplate accepting. There was also a letter from Cara which she decided to read later when she was feeling stronger, and another letter, typed in a blue envelope with a North London postmark. Hoping that it might be the miracle of a second booking, she slit the envelope carefully open and drew out a single sheet of paper. It was not a booking. It was a letter — a letter from Martin.

Dear Alexia,
Forgive my typing the envelope of this letter but I thought that if you saw my handwriting, you might not even open it.
I expect you are surprised to hear from me, but then we go in for surprising each other, don't we? You are doubtless as surprised at my silence since our parting as I am by your silence on the subject of our daughter. Without your father, I shouldn't

even know of her existence.

However, that is not the purpose of this letter, which is in fact one of congratulations. I hear that you have been given Castle Bewick by your uncle. I am naturally pleased for you and for little Charlotte.

Yours,
Martin

It was an extraordinary letter. Alexia stared at it for a long time, both at what Martin had written, and at the address — Flat 4, 19 Northbourne Street. Then she picked it up and put it in her pocket. She would take it down to the lochside and think about it.

It was a cold day, but still, with pale grey clouds reflected in the dark grey water, and the only color the golden seaweed on the shore and the patches of heather in bloom on the slopes across the loch. Alexia walked slowly down the little pebbly beach and sat on her favorite rock. Then she took the letter out again and read it. "This is a letter of congratulations," Martin had written. "I am naturally very pleased for you and little Charlotte." The whole tone of the letter made Alexia deeply uneasy; indeed, the fact that Martin should have written at all, out of the blue, was disconcerting. What did he want? To say he knew about Carly? Or to imply that he knew about Carly and intended somehow to use that knowledge? And if he had some sinister purpose about Carly, did he also have one about the castle? He couldn't, Alexia told herself, he couldn't. They were divorced and he had been entirely indifferent to any kind of custody of or access to Carly. He couldn't touch her property, he couldn't — could he? She shivered a little. On the face of it, it was an absolutely innocent, if slightly snide, letter, but underneath Alexia was afraid it implied something quite different. He had written his address very clearly, almost as if to emphasize the difference between Flat 4, 19 Northbourne Street, and Castle Bewick, Argyllshire. Well, she was not to be intimidated, not any more, she wasn't the vulnerable, emotional child Martin Angus had married. She would ignore the letter and put it away somewhere safely, and hope, very much, that she could simply forget it.

There was a crunch of feet on the pebbles behind her. Alexia turned, thinking it might be Peter, coming to cheer her up over the Farquhars, and make her laugh about the hot water lavatory. It wasn't Peter, it was Hughie, dressed more neatly than usual, with a thick dark jacket over his clothes, and his deerstalker in his hand.

"Hughie!"

"Aye," he said.

He stopped about six feet away from her and stood there, quite motionless.

"Hughie," Alexia said, "I'm so glad you've come. I've been wanting to apologize to you, for losing my temper the day before yesterday. I really am sorry, but I got in a panic. I suppose it was because the Farquhars were my first guests and everything seemed to be going wrong. But

I'm sorry I shouted at you."

"That's fine," Hughie said. He dropped his gaze. "It's no matter now."

"I'm so glad —"

"I'm off, Mrs. Angus."

"What?"

He shuffled a bit. "I can't do work like this, Mrs. Angus. I liked restoring the castle but I can't fetch and carry. It's no' right."

"Not right? What do you mean?"

He spread his hands. "It's no' work to me. I need to work with my hands."

Alexia said wildly, "But what do you mean? D'you mean you're leaving Bewick?"

"Oh no. No, I couldna do that —"

"Then where are you going? What are you going to do?"

"I'm going to work at the new fish farm, Mrs. Angus. I'm going to work for Mr. McGill."

Chapter Sixteen

In a year at Bewick, Alexia had never been inside Inverbrae, Duncan McGill's great Victorian house which lay two miles up into the hills with wonderful views down the length of the loch. Though perfectly civil whenever they met in the village, and having kept his word that he would cause no public obstruction to her plans, Duncan McGill had exhibited no further signs of neighborliness. He had paid the money for the land promptly and in full — local rumor said that he had sold a business in Edinburgh to do so — and Alexia had observed, not without a pang, McGill sheep scattered over slopes which had been, until January, hers. She had also observed, down on the lochside, a low dark green building, like a huge windowless shed. It was apparently the beginnings of a fish farm, one of the first in Europe outside Scandinavia. It occurred to Alexia to complain bitterly about the erection of an industrial building in a beautiful place, and also to question why the local planning authority had been so wonderfully amenable to a powerful local landowner like Duncan McGill, but both Peter and Elsie were strongly of the opinion that she should hold her tongue.

"There's been three men in Bewick out of

work this winter," Elsie said, "and two of them married with children. Think what the fish farm means to them. And think what it would mean to turn Duncan McGill into an enemy, good and proper. You've a truce with him just now, but it's an uneasy one."

Inverbrae lay up a long drive that led directly off the lochside road. The drive began with huge stone gateposts crowned with crouching lions, and led steeply upwards between magnificent tree rhododendrons in which Duncan McGill's father had been a specialist. After what seemed an interminable time, the drive emerged from the tunnel of dark leaves, and Alexia found herself on an amazing platform of level ground with, on one side, the breathtaking view down to the loch and on the other, a great granite house, as forbidding as a fortress.

She hadn't telephoned to say she was coming. She hadn't even said anything to Peter or to Elsie — relations with Elsie were, in any case, a little strained just now with Hughie's defection — she had simply left a note on the kitchen table to say she would be out for an hour. They would think nothing of it. She was always going out just now, either on foot or in the car, to escape the restlessness induced by waiting for bookings to come that didn't come. Getting out of the car now, it struck her that Duncan McGill might be out himself.

She marched bravely across the gravel drive and pulled at the huge greenish iron bell that hung beside the front door. Nothing happened. She was reminded of her arrival at Castle

Bewick, and began to count. She had reached nineteen — she intended to ring again at twenty — when she heard footsteps inside the house coming, without hurry, towards the door. She rehearsed, quickly, what she would say.

"Good morning. I am Mrs. Angus from Castle Bewick. I wonder if I might see Mr. McGill for five minutes?"

The door opened, and there stood Duncan McGill himself. He wore tweed breeches with knee socks and heavy brogues and a polo-necked jersey and he looked both absolutely right and much taller than she had remembered.

"Mrs. Angus!"

"I'm sorry not to have telephoned," Alexia said with as much dignity as she could manage, "but I would be grateful if I could speak to you briefly on a matter of some importance."

There was a tiny silence, and then he said, "Come in." He led her across an echoing hall from whose walls various antlered heads peered down at her, and then into a warm, book-lined room, with windows looking down to the loch, and two springer spaniels who rose politely from the hearthrug as Alexia came in and stood wagging their feather tails.

"I hope you've no objection to dogs."

"No, no, I love them."

Duncan motioned her to a chair by the fire.

"You have come, I imagine, Mrs. Angus, because of Hughie MacGregor."

"Yes, I have," Alexia said in a rush, quite forgetting her attempt at dignity. "I think it's frankly despicable of you to put ideas into his head that working at the castle is beneath him. Hughie's not exactly simple but you know as well as I do that he isn't very strong-minded and can be persuaded —"

"I did not persuade him, Mrs. Angus."

"I don't believe you."

Duncan sat down opposite Alexia and fixed his gaze on her. His eyes were very clear hazel. He said calmly, "He walked up here to see me three nights ago. He didn't get here until well after nine. He simply asked me if I had any vacancies for work down at the fish farm."

Alexia burst out, "How convenient for you! Hughie just walks in and asks for a job, thereby proving to you most neatly that you were right all along and it's demeaning for a man to wait on other people!"

Duncan's gaze didn't waver.

"I tried to persuade him to go back to you. I pointed out that the castle was virtually his birthplace and had always been his livelihood and that he had an obligation to you."

She said sarcastically, "Did you indeed!"

"Yes, Mrs. Angus, I did. Hughie said nothing to me about feeling insulted, he just said it wasn't going to be his kind of work any more."

"But it is! There'll hardly be any suitcase carrying and who will do the fires and the odd jobs if Hughie goes! We had some difficult guests —" She stopped. Of all people, she wanted Duncan McGill to hear only of her successes.

"I heard," he said gently.

She shot a glance at him.

"What else did you hear?"

"That's of no consequence. I'm not a man for gossip."

"But you must be pleased —"

"Pleased about what, Mrs. Angus?"

She was quite thrown. She had been, as usual, too impulsive. She had been going to say, "Pleased that my hotel isn't an instant success and that one of my two staff wants to leave already." She said, a little unsteadily, "Hughie said he wanted to work more with his hands."

"Suppose we believe him?"

"But —"

Duncan leaned forward. If she hadn't known that he disliked and despised her, Alexia would have said that his voice was almost kind. "Mrs. Angus, as you say, Hughie is not strong-minded. A few weeks on the fish farm — it's hard, cold, monotonous work — and he may regret he ever left. And in the meantime, I shall send you Jimmie Blair."

"Jimmie Blair?"

"He's my keeper's son. He's to go to Perthshire in the new year as underkeeper on a big estate and he needs occupation."

"But why — ?"

"Why what?"

"Why," said Alexia, utterly bewildered, "should you help me?"

Duncan smiled for the first time. "Let's just say, shall we, Mrs. Angus, that the days in the Highlands when you made sure that your neighbor was also your enemy, are long gone."

There was a little silence, then Alexia said faintly, "Thank you."

Duncan stood up. "And now if you'll forgive me, I've an appointment with the hydroelectric board. They want to dam a loch up at the top of the glen. I've no real objection except that I used to swim and catch brown trout up there as a boy, but I can't let sentiment stand in the way of progress, I suppose." He walked across the room and opened the door. The dogs rose again too, in a polite signaling of dismissal.

"I shall send Jimmie to you this afternoon."

Alexia looked up at him. He wore an expression she simply couldn't fathom.

"Thank you, Mr. McGill."

He gave his now familiar little bow.

"My pleasure, Mrs. Angus."

Back at the castle, Elsie was waiting for her.

"I imagine you have been to see Mr. McGill."

Alexia was suddenly very weary. She dropped into a chair by the kitchen table and put her head in her hands.

"Yes, Elsie, I have. And I owe him an apology for thinking ill of him, and Hughie an apology for thinking ill of him and I'm sorry all round and tired out."

"You'd no right to suppose Hughie —"

"I know," Alexia said, interrupting, "I know, I know. I've just said so. Mr. McGill is sending Jimmie Blair down to fill Hughie's place."

Elsie, who was stirring something at the gleaming new catering sized cooker she affected to despise, spun round, a dripping wooden spoon still in her hand.

"I beg your pardon!"

"You heard me, Elsie. I'm actually very grateful

because I don't know who else would do the work."

Elsie said loudly, "If there were anybody to do the work for!"

Alexia stood up. It was too much. "I know there are no bookings," she said furiously to Elsie, "and I see that you are outraged that anyone should work here instead of Hughie, but may I remind you that it was Hughie's choice to leave, and that the hotel has been open precisely and *only* three weeks! I'm going to find Carly."

Elsie turned back to the stove. Alexia suddenly realized that it was soup that Elsie was stirring, and that she was violently hungry at the rich comforting smell of it. But not for anything, just now, would she ask Elsie for soup. She marched out of the kitchen, and attempted to bang the door behind her, forgetting that the smooth new swing mechanism she had installed to cope with hurrying waiters bearing laden trays to dozens of guests, wouldn't slam. It was most frustrating.

She went upstairs to the Mermaid Room. Peter was there, with the account books, and Carly was sitting on the floor with the Noah's ark animals that James and Mary had sent for her first birthday.

"Lo!" said Carly with enthusiasm at the sight of her, "Lo! Lo!"

"Hello darling," Alexia said, stooping to kiss her curly red head.

"You look worn out," Peter said, "I supposed I can guess where you've been?"

Alexia sat down in the brown chair, which now symbolized to her something like a comfortable pair of old slippers to be put on at the end of a long day.

"Yes. It was most peculiar. I'd almost say he was kind."

"I keep telling you he is."

Alexia gave a tired smile. "I know you do. And maybe you're right. He's sending me Jimmie Blair."

Peter's face brightened. He put down the books and went to kneel on the carpet by Carly. She offered him a giraffe.

"Thank you, Carly. Jimmie's a nice boy. He used to come down here, to the school, and play football with the boys."

"If he's going to be a keeper, I hope he won't think making up fires for nonexistent guests is beneath him."

Peter put the giraffe down with its mate and Carly, with a crow of pleasure, knocked them both over with a hippopotamus.

"He won't think anything beneath him that Duncan's told him to do. I'm glad Jimmie's coming. I can't bear to see you so tired and worried."

"Peter," Alexia said, suddenly close to tears, "why doesn't anybody come?"

He left Carly and her animals and came to kneel by the brown chair, gathering Alexia into his arms.

"They will come, Alexia. I promise you they will. Word will get about. It's such early days yet. Please don't cry, please don't. You've done so wonderfully and achieved so much, you simply mustn't give up just the minute you begin to get somewhere."

She said, sniffing, into his shoulder, "I'd never have done it without you."

He lifted her face and looked into it for a long, serious time and then he bent his head and kissed her. It was the first time for almost two years that a man had kissed her, and she did not draw away. A little later he said, "You know why I've worked like this, don't you?"

She looked away. "Yes."

"Don't get me wrong, I've loved doing it, I've been happier this winter than I've ever been, but —"

"Peter —"

"Yes?"

"Peter, I feel very guilty about you. I've felt guilty for a long time, having you here on such an unfair basis, unfair to you, that is, I wonder —" she paused and then she went on, "It would be such a help to me, as well as the right thing by you if you — if you would become my partner."

His face lit up.

"Your partner!"

"Yes."

He held her hard against him, laughing and delighted.

"Oh, Alexia, Alexia! Dream come true! Are you sure, are you absolutely, completely sure?"

She thought of his kindness, his steadiness, his competence, his reliability. She thought also of shared problems and burdens.

"Yes, I'm completely sure."

He took her face in his hands.

"Does this mean — ?"

"No," she said as gently as she could. "No, it

just means a business partner."

"Don't I mean anything to you?"

"Yes. You mean a great deal. You are one of the most important people in my life. But I think I'm just not ready to be in love again yet. I'm not ready to be committed."

"I see," he said. His face was still glowing. "Can I kiss you again?"

"Of course," she said. "Kissing partners —"

"No!" Carly shouted from the floor.

"Bossy little baggage," Peter said, affectionately. He took Alexia in his arms again and kissed her and this time, she found she was waiting politely for him to finish. It was a sweet kiss, but that was all. When Peter drew away, she said, "I'll go and ring Mr. McReadie and we'll have a day in Glasgow and fix it all up. He'll be delighted to see a man in the business and we might as well have a day out while nobody comes here!"

It was, perhaps inevitably, impossible to sleep that night. She had moved, in deference to all the expected guests, into a room on the second floor, smaller than the Seahorse Room, but its size was more than made up for by the fact that it had a little snug cupboard room off it for Carly, and the views, from so high up, were even more wonderful. It was a wild night, with a tugging, hurrying early autumn wind, and the old spruces against this wall of the house were creaking and groaning as if they were in pain.

Alexia had always found it difficult to lie in bed if she were awake. She got up now and rolled her quilt round her as was her habit, and padded over to the window, parting the curtains and kneeling down to gaze out. It was a moonlit night, and the moon, huge and brightly silver, was sailing calmly in and out between rags and tatters of cloud and casting lovely glittering patterns on the ruffled waters of the loch. The window faced not across the loch, but up towards its head, and while the village of Bewick lay huddled in darkness on the right-hand shore (it was two in the morning after all and decent folk should be asleep) there was, far away, a single steady yellow light in the darkness, high up on the hillside. Clearly, Duncan McGill couldn't sleep either, and was poring over his fish farm plans or the proposal from the hydroelectric board.

Had she, she wondered, done the right thing in proposing partnership to Peter? It had been such an impulse, an impulse born of a whole mixture of things, gratitude, anticlimax, fatigue, anxiety, loneliness, to name but a few. And what, quite literally, would she do without him always there, always good-tempered, always useful and resourceful? She had known him less than a year, but she felt she owed Peter Burton more than she had ever owed anyone, with the possible exception of Uncle James. He was so straight, Peter, he would never take advantage of her, he would never think she meant more by partnership than she did. And certainly, it was a vast relief to think there would be someone else to carry the burdens with her, someone else who was as practically involved in making a profit as she was.

Suddenly, the little yellow light in the far distance went out, and the only light left in the landscape was the moon. At the same moment, a thought came to Alexia, a thought so blindingly obvious that she almost cried aloud at the stupidity of not thinking of it before. She threw off the quilt, and found her dressing gown and slippers, and, after checking to see that Carly slept peacefully, went out into the passage.

It was cold out there, and not yet carpeted, so that it was a comfort to go down to the luxurious corridor outside the three finished bedrooms. Despite her worries, the sight of her achievement gave Alexia pleasure, the pale clean walls hung with pictures and pretty old plates, her faultless curtains, the charming old pieces of furniture that she and Peter had found or bought and that they and Hughie had glued and waxed and polished back to health.

The fire in the grate of the Mermaid Room had sunk to cold grey ashes. Alexia switched on the lamp at her desk and sat down, pulling towards her a sheet of the writing paper, embossed with a tiny engraving of the castle, that she had ordered in Glasgow with such pride and anticipation.

Dear Amanda,
   I have embarked on something very mad, and I need your help. As you will see from the letterhead, I have started a hotel in the house my uncle gave me, and everything is running now — but for no guests. I can't think where to turn to spread the word except to you. I never knew anyone who

knows as many people as you do.

This is a lovely place. I promise that anyone who comes will want to come back. This is a very clumsy letter but I hope you can forgive that.

With Love from,
Alexia

Chapter Seventeen

Christmas 1968

At Christmas, it snowed. Alexia stood at the window of the drawing room and looked out at the whirling white world outside, and half of her rejoiced to see it because it was the finishing touch to all the comforts she had prepared, and half of her was panic-stricken that the Rest and Be Thankful Pass would become blocked and consequently they would never get here.

Behind her the drawing room lay waiting for its first real Christmas in fifty years. Garlands of evergreens were swagged around the huge fireplace, and a nine-foot Norwegian spruce, donated by Duncan McGill, rose to the ceiling, hung with gold and silver fir cones and looped with curls of scarlet ribbon. The tree had arrived silently like all Duncan's presents, just appearing in the yard one day without comment.

Jimmie said, "Mr. McGill told me to get it brought down."

"Was there any message?"

"No, Mrs. Angus, no message."

She telephoned Inverbrae.

"I just wanted to thank you very much indeed

for the Christmas tree."

"You're most welcome."

"It was so kind of you to think of it, Mr. McGill."

He said laconically, "There's about eleven hundred more where that came from."

It was a beautiful tree, thick and dark. Jimmie cut off a few lower branches to get it into a pot, and with these and a lavish supply of holly and ivy, Alexia wove a wreath for the front door, and garlands for the chimneypieces in the guests' bedrooms, tied up with red ribbons and complemented by red candles. Four bedrooms were finished now and they would all be full, for five days. Amanda and Felicity were coming and they were bringing six friends with them. For the first time since the hotel was open, it was going to be full.

And now it was snowing. The snow was lying too, in soft even white cushions along the terrace balustrade, along branches and hedges, and in an even white blanket across the lawn. Only the loch resisted it, black and shining in the dizzy white landscape. Peter had gone over the pass to Arrochar to guide everyone back, because they had flown, most dashingly, to Glasgow, and were then hiring cars. Only Amanda and Felicity, Alexia thought affectionately, would think of flying, just as only they, when they came to stay, would do it so magnificently and bring six other people with them.

"Darling, we are such tycoons these days, you simply can't think," Felicity had said on the telephone. "We even have to turn people down and we've had to hire a workroom and we've got a staff of seven and we're so busy that I've hardly a second of the day to get into trouble. Too boring."

It would be more than just boring if they didn't get here; it would be a disaster. Once they were here, it didn't matter if they were snowed in for weeks, but they simply had to get here, they had to! The previous weeks, after the long slow autumn of no more than a handful of people, and mostly Farquharish people at that, tidy middle-aged Scots couples taking a little autumn motoring break, the preparations for Christmas had been the most optimistic time Alexia could remember. She had flung herself into the cooking and cleaning and decorating and the seemingly endless journeys to Glasgow for wine and fruit and vegetables with an energy that worried Peter.

"You'll wear yourself out."

"I won't, I won't, I love it! It's *for* something!"

She had to admit to a great thankfulness at having Peter as a partner. Not only had he borrowed enough money to do up the great panelled bedroom looking down the loch — they called it the Bewick Room — but his attitude was steadily, wonderfully optimistic.

"Look, I'm borrowing the money because I believe this will all work. I could borrow it simply for us to live off, but that would be shortsighted. I firmly believe that the hotel will take off very suddenly, and we must be ready to cope when it does. We worked out that we couldn't even break even on fewer than four bedrooms, so four bedrooms at least it has to be."

Secretly, Alexia was sick with pride over the Bewick Room. She had invented a four-poster bed for it, without any actual posts, by an ingenious system of curtains hung from curtain track screwed into the ceiling by Jimmie. Jimmie spoke very little, but he was very capable, and the finished effect of the bed was both professional and dramatic. With the bed and the panelling and the sofa before the fire, the Bewick Room was exactly what Alexia had hoped for, a mixture of great comfort and great charm. She arranged books and magazines in the window, and left a blue and white china bowl of fruit on the desk. She was in and out constantly, patting cushions, plumping up quilts, counting towels, rubbing invisible smears off mirrors and polished surfaces. It would be unbearably awful if all this happy excited attention to detail, not to mention the groaning larder, went to waste merely because of the weather.

Carly, who had been sitting on the floor, sucking two fingers and gazing yearningly at the Christmas tree which she had been forbidden to touch, suddenly unplugged her fingers and said, "Car!"

Alexia listened.

"I don't think so, darling."

Carly tipped herself sideways off her bottom and began to crawl at great speed towards the door.

"Car, car —"

Alexia caught up with her and swung her on to her feet.

"You must *walk* now, darling. You really must.

Do you want to crawl up the aisle on your wedding day?"

"Car!" Carly wailed, wriggling and kicking. "Coming, car coming!"

Even above her shrieks, Alexia could suddenly hear something, the faint triumphant sound of several motor horns, toot toot, toot toot, through the muffling snowy air.

"They're here! They've made it!"

Laughing with excitement, Alexia lifted Carly into her arms and ran out of the drawing room and across the hall to the stairs down to the front door. Jimmie was before her, reliable Jimmie in the near dark trousers and jersey and collar and tie he had appeared in that morning without being asked, and as the hooting horns approached the door, he switched on all the stair lights and opened both leaves of the door wide in welcome.

For a moment, Alexia thought she was going to cry, but only for a moment, because in the next second, almost before she reached the bottom of the stairs, Amanda and Felicity were out of the cars and in through the door and engulfing her and Carly in hugs and enthusiasm.

"Angel, too utterly thrilling, what a place! What a baby —"

"Darling, how lovely to see you and aren't you looking superior and clever and no wonder!"

"Oh," Alexia cried, kissing and laughing, "I'm so pleased to see you, you can't think —"

"We're pretty pleased to see you, baby doll. Look at this! Will you *look* at this staircase!"

Alexia stepped back a little, just to see them.

They had hardly changed except that Amanda had exchanged her dense black glasses for huge smoky ones through which her eyes were at least dimly visible. She wore a sharp black suit edged in black braid and under it a white silk shirt with mannish linked cuffs. She looked, to Alexia, deliciously, wonderfully urban and sophisticated. Felicity, her hair grown long and straight and cut with a fringe across her brow, wore velvet knickerbockers and a ruffled shirt under a huge paisley shawl. Amanda caught Alexia gazing.

"It's her *Viva Maria* look, darling."

"*Viva Maria*?"

"Yes, darling, you know, the film. Bardot and Moreau."

"I'm afraid I don't know —"

"How perfectly sweet. It's like the Sleeping Beauty, isn't it, Felicity? And I suppose marooned here in your northern fastness, you don't know about *Hair* or midiskirts or the assassination of Robert Kennedy either?"

"Don't tease —"

Amanda swung around. Out of the snow, other figures were emerging, uttering little cries of excitement and apprehension. Jimmie and Peter, quiet and efficient, were following them burdened with luggage.

"Now then, Alexia darling, you must meet your customers. This is Marsha, who thinks she can dance, and we don't disillusion her out of kindness, and this is Algy, who's terribly dull but we brought him otherwise nobody else would take any notice of him all Christmas, would they, darling? And this is Marco, who is in a panic at being away from Milan, but Felicity says she needs him just now, so there we are, and here's Oliver and Patty who are *married* to each other, God help us — and this is Victor."

Victor was older than everybody else, and graver, and was the only one dressed suitably for Scotland. He took Alexia's hand.

"I'm so pleased to meet you."

"I managed," Amanda said, "to borrow him from his wife." Her voice was slightly desperate and Alexia saw that when she looked at him, she looked at him with real longing.

Alexia, still carrying Carly who was by now crowing with excitement at all the people and the activity, climbed up three stairs above her guests.

"I can't tell you," she said, "how pleased I — Peter and I — are to have you all. I just hope that we will be able to give you as memorable a Christmas as you will clearly give us."

They all broke into cheers. The girl called Marsha, who was wearing black PVC thigh boots, began to sing and even Milanese Marco stopped looking apprehensive and managed an optimistic smile.

"Come up," Alexia said. "Come up and see what we've done. Come and see the castle!"

Felicity tucked her arm into Marco's. "Can't wait," she said. "And to have a lovely fight about bedrooms."

It was a wilder success than even Alexia could have hoped for. Enthusiasm for the concept of the hotel, for the house and landscape, for the quality of the food, for her skills in curtain making, for Carly, for snowball fights and carol singing and sledding dangerously down the wooded slopes directly behind the castle, seemed absolutely unbounded. It was also harder work than Alexia would have believed possible. With only herself and Peter and Elsie and Jimmie to look after eight guests to a professional standard, let alone Carly in addition, taxed them all to the utmost. She was determined that particularly Amanda's eagle eye should find no fault in either service or quality of food.

"She *does* like me and she *is* a friend but she won't recommend us unless she really thinks we are worth it. She isn't like Felicity who's really a bit slapdash. She's a perfectionist."

It was also tiring because their eight guests were paying guests, and so, although all relations were extremely friendly, they were there to be waited on. Alexia discovered that she had to keep a slight, formal distance, that it was expected of her, and that even courteous Victor would say — and be entitled to say — "May we have champagne brought to our room immediately?" when all four of them were flat out doing something else. It was also the first time the four of them had been truly tested working together as a team, and Alexia began to dread the New Year and Jimmie's departure for Perthshire. He was to be replaced by a tall, ungainly boy from the village called Dougie. Alexia hadn't much hope for Dougie.

"But I *must* have someone local, both because I believe in it, and because I daren't do otherwise with Duncan McGill's beady eye on me."

Christmas night was the climax of the whole visit. Before a blazing fire in the dining room, a long table was laid for eight, scarlet candles and trails of stunning dark greenery on a white cloth, silver and glass shining and sparkling. Elsie and Alexia had labored over dinner all afternoon, peeling sprouts down to button size, stuffing and basting and chopping and stirring, grating orange rind into the brandy butter and glazing the mince pies golden brown with yolk of egg. To serve dinner, they all dressed up, Peter in a dinner jacket his godmother had given him when he was twenty-one in the hope that he would lead a full London social life as she thought appropriate, and Alexia in a long narrow velvet dress she had made out of a pair of old green curtains, and wearing Alexandra's pearls. In the kitchen below, Elsie wore a paper hat and a sprig of mistletoe pinned to her apron, and Jimmie, who had silently taken over the washing up, had threaded a knot of scarlet ribbon into the waistcoat of his best suit.

It was after midnight before the revelers finally went to bed, and after one before the remains of their feasting were removed from the dining room. Alexia looked round the kitchen, at the three hollow-eyed faces.

"Go off now, all of you. You've been wonderful. Quite wonderful."

"But there's breakfast to lay —"

"We ought just to see to the drawing room —"

"I'll do it," Alexia said, "you've done enough. The fires can wait till the morning, Jimmie, and I'll bet they all want breakfast in their rooms to-

225

morrow. I'll tidy the drawing room."

"I'll help you," Peter said. His eyes, in his tired face, were still bright, and there was an edge to his voice, an edge of excitement.

They went up to the drawing room together. The cushions were dented and the fire was out, but otherwise the room looked almost orderly.

"I've got something for you," Peter said.

"Oh, Peter —"

He drew her to the sofa, and took a small battered dark red leather box out of his pocket.

"It was my mother's."

"Peter, I can't — you shouldn't — not something of your mother's."

"It isn't a ring," he said, "it's just pretty. And I want to give you something. Don't you see?"

He opened the box and held it out. Inside was a delicate little Victorian bow pendant of pearls and white enamel and tiny diamonds like stars.

"Oh, it's lovely!"

He lifted it out and fastened it round her neck, where it hung gracefully inside the loop of pearls.

"There."

"Peter, I love it, it's lovely but —"

"But what?"

She looked at him, truly troubled.

"Dear Peter, I don't want you to think you could . . . could *buy* anything with it. Do you see?"

He flushed. He looked almost angry.

"I'm not such a fool. Can't I even give you a present without being accused of an ulterior motive?"

"I didn't mean that."

"Well, it's what you implied. Why should you be the one who always dictates what happens in our relationship? I have as much right as you do, you know, I'm not just a puppet!"

"Peter, I know that, I never meant to insult you, I'm just always afraid of you thinking —"

"Yes!" he shouted suddenly. She put her finger to her lips, apprehensive that they might be heard by their guests.

"Yes! Afraid's the word! You're afraid of men, aren't you, and you're going to punish me for everything that just one man did to you, aren't you, keeping me dandling, as always dancing in front of me, driving me *mad* —" He lunged forward and caught her wrist. "Well, Alexia, I'll do what you say nine times out of ten, but this time is the tenth," and then he pinioned her in his arms, and crushed his mouth down on hers, forcing his tongue between her teeth.

It was over as suddenly as it had started. Peter flung her away from him, and with a strangled half-whispered cry of, "Oh God, I'm sorry, I'm sorry, I'm sorry," stumbled out of the room, leaving Alexia there with her hand pressed to her bruised mouth. She heard his footsteps running along the corridor, and then the muffled thump of the door that led to their living quarters closing and then silence. She was shaking, partly with alarm and surprise, but partly also at the frightened realization of how much, how dangerously much, she had stupidly taken for granted. She put her hand down to the pendant, then she unhooked it carefully and laid it back in its box. It was too pretty and innocent a thing to be the

227

cause of so much unhappy trouble.

Well, there was no more to be done tonight. They were all strung up and tired out, and there was still Boxing Day and the day after to be got through with unruffled appearances. Alexia got up and smoothed the cushions and swept the grate cleanly ready for Jimmie in the mornng, and opened the window an inch to let the Highland air blow out Oliver and Algy's cigar smoke. Then she turned out all the lights and went softly out into the corridor and up the stairs to her own room and her sleeping daughter.

The lamp by her bed was on — kind Elsie must have done that, and put the welcome hot water bottle in her bed — and in the pool of light it cast, she saw the little pile of Christmas cards that had arrived during the previous few days, and which she had simply been too busy to open. She thought she would open them now as a little final private Christmas celebration, blessedly alone for a few hours of quiet before another relentless day began.

She took off her velvet dress and hung it up, and laid her pearls away in their case. Then she put on her pajamas — how thankful she was that Amanda couldn't see her pajamas, thick shadow-striped brushed cotton men's pajamas bought in Craigmuir — and brushed her teeth and hair and climbed into bed. For a moment, she simply lay there, savoring the absolute bliss of being off her feet. Then she reached for the pile of cards, and slit the envelopes roughly with her thumbs, hearing in her memory as she did so, Lyddy's scolding voice from long ago, "It's an insult to the sender not to open a letter with care!"

The first card was from Cara and Stephen. It had a check for a hundred pounds in it and a message which brought a lump to her throat.

"We wish you the happiest of Christmases, darling Alexia. We realize that you must be left alone to establish your new life, but we would love to visit you in the spring. *At your invitation.* A kiss to little Carly. All love Mum and Dad."

Then there were cards from James and Mary, and from her other uncle Alan, and from Lyddy and from June. At the bottom of the pile there was a card addressed to Carly, a typed envelope . . .

Alexia drew it out. It was a pretty little card, a child's Christmas card, of a teddy bear in a wreath of holly astride a rocking horse. She opened it.

"To darling Charlotte," Martin had written inside, "A very happy second Christmas with lots of love from Daddy."

Chapter Eighteen

Spring 1969

"Look at that!" Peter shouted. He came racing through the swing door into the kitchen holding a heavy glossy magazine open in both hands. "Just take a look! It's better than we could possibly have hoped!"

He laid the magazine down on the kitchen table, where Alexia and Elsie were doing the monthly housekeeping accounts, pointing excitedly at a double page spread of a huge and glamorous photograph of Castle Bewick with, underneath it, the heading "Truly a hotel with a difference."

"It's brilliant," Peter said. "The pictures are amazing and she couldn't find anything wrong with it! She even concludes by urging readers to hurry up and book before we are so well known that nobody can get it!"

Alexia's eyes were sparkling.

"God bless Amanda! She said she'd send us the right journalist and she clearly did."

"And there's more," Peter said. He was almost out of breath. "I telephoned the magazine to thank them, and they said the piece was appearing in their sister magazine in the States —"

Elsie gave a little cry.

"And what'll you do for bedrooms if half America tries to come and stay?"

They turned to her.

"Four bedrooms and one more only half done —"

"No more money —"

"No more time —"

But it was mock horror, because they were laughing. They looked at the photographs of themselves, of the views, of the Bewick Room and the drawing room and then they looked out of the kitchen window at the clear optimistic April day with little white clouds chasing each other across a pale blue sky, and they simply laughed.

"I can't believe it," Alexia said, "I simply can't believe it, but do you know that seeing us reproduced there in glorious color suddenly, and for the first time, makes me feel that we are real? That we exist?"

"I'm going to find some champagne," Peter said. "For once, we're jolly well going to drink the profits."

Elsie looked at them both with the affectionate exasperation of a parent looking at two over-excited children.

"How about saving the champagne until the telephone rings?"

"Oh Elsie —"

"Spoilsport!"

"Now, listen to me," Elsie said. "You've worked like nobody I've —"

The telephone began to ring. They looked at each other, and helpless giggles overtook Alexia and Peter.

"I don't believe it —"

"I can't answer it, I can't!"

"Elsie, please, darling Elsie —"

Elsie, snorting with mock indignation and contempt, went over to the kitchen telephone.

"Castle Bewick Hotel. Good morning. Yes, madam. Yes, we are most certainly the hotel featured in this month's *Good Living*. Thank you, madam. This weekend, this coming weekend, a double room with bath? Would you hold the line one moment, madam, while I check our bookings? I'm sure you will understand how busy we are just now —"

Elsie took the receiver away from her ear, and held her hand over the mouthpiece, and hummed an inconsequential little Scottish air. From the table, Alexia and Peter watched her in delight and admiration. After a little while she replaced the receiver to her ear.

"Are you there, madam? I am so sorry to keep you but I have managed to find you a room — yes, with a view, *all* our rooms have views — for next weekend. May I take your name and telephone number? Thank you. We shall look forward to seeing you on Friday. Goodbye." She put the telephone down.

"You are superb, Elsie!"

She shrugged, and opened her mouth to say that it was nothing and that they might now go and find the champagne, when the telephone rang again.

The next few weeks were a time Alexia, happy and excited and full of an undirected gratitude, vowed that she would never forget. Her Glasgow bank manager was amenable about an increase in the mortgage, and with the money, she embarked on doubling both the number of operational bedrooms, and the staff. Elsie's niece, Mary, who had left school at Christmas was recruited as chambermaid, and soon it was necessary for her great friend Maggie, to join her. The amiable but slow Dougie, who had now at last got the hang of fire lighting and brass polishing, was augmented by a cheerful, quick young man called Gregor, from Craigmuir, who had to be accommodated in two hastily done-up rooms in the stableyard. Elsie ceased to do anything but cook, and now needed help in the kitchen in addition. Between them, Alexia and Peter tried to provide it while also keeping the books, going endlessly to Glasgow for supplies that were not to be found in Craigmuir ("An avocado pear!" the local greengrocer had exclaimed in horror to Alexia, as if she had suggested his selling something really sinful), ordering and looking after the wine, waiting in the dining room, welcoming guests and dealing with the endless daily problems that there seemed to be no way of avoiding.

In the garden, a father and son now worked, cycling up the loch from the direction of Strachur every day, and cycling back in the evening. They were laborious, conscientious, silent workers, moving slowly about the grounds with their secateurs and tanks of weedkiller, gradually restoring order to a garden that had last been properly laid out at the turn of the century by Alexandra's parents, and had been left to decay.

233

But even with them, and Dougie, and Gregor, and the two girls in the house to do the cleaning, there were not enough staff when the house was full. Alexia was determined to stick to her principles of using only local people — she had had to bend the rules a little for Gregor — but was wondering where on earth she could turn, since the village population was now almost wholly employed by Duncan McGill, when she had two unexpected visitors.

She was sitting in the office — no longer the Mermaid Room, which was now a bedroom, and to her mind the prettiest and most romantic bedroom of all — in what had been the old ground floor gun room, wrestling with the wholesaler's invoice (he had, she had learned to her cost, to be watched like a hawk) when a muffled knock came at the door.

She said impatiently, "Come in!"

It had become a house rule that neither she nor Peter was to be interrupted, except for the most dire of emergencies, between two-thirty and four in the afternoons, otherwise the paperwork simply mounted into a pile that threatened to overwhelm them completely.

The door opened, and two figures came in diffidently and stood just inside it, a tall thin one and a short stocky one, Jimmie Blair and Hughie MacGregor. Alexia stared at them. She had imagined Jimmie safely in Perthshire, where he had gone in January, and Hughie as usual, at the fish farm.

"Good heavens! What are you two doing here?"

Jimmie cleared his throat.

"We've come —" He stopped. He looked at Hughie who looked at the floor. "We come to ask —"

"What?"

Jimmie colored. "For our jobs back."

Alexia said in amazement, "You want to work here again?"

Hughie nodded, still staring at the floor. "Aye."

Jimmie blurted out, "I want to cook, Mrs. Angus, I want to be a chef."

"Jimmie!"

"I do," he said, his eyes were slightly desperate. "I thought it all the time I was here, but I didn't want to let down my father or Mr. McGill, but I can't help that now. It's all I want to do. I'll learn from Elsie, I'll do anything —" He stopped and blushed deeply again. "If you'll have me, Mrs. Angus."

Alexia looked at Hughie. "What about you, Hughie?"

"I don't like that Dougie doing my job."

"But you left your job!"

"Aye," Hughie said, "but like Jimmie says, I'd like it back, if you'll have me. And there's girls at the fish farm want jobs here. They said to tell you. Jeannie Blair, Jimmie's sister, says she'd look after the bairn for you, and Flora and Bridget would like to work with Mary and Maggie, and there's wee Charlie McPhee, he mayn't be tall but he's strong and he said to me to tell you —"

Alexia was almost laughing. It must have been the longest speech Hughie had ever made. "Stop," she said to him, "stop! We can't employ all of you, you know that, and before we start discussing anything seriously, would you kindly tell me why there's this sudden rush to work at the castle?"

They looked at each other again. Jimmie said, "I do want to be a chef, Mrs. Angus, it's not nonsense."

"I believe you, Jimmie, but there must be something else."

Jimmie looked at Hughie. Hughie took a deep breath and said in a rush, "Well, Mrs. Angus, we've been counting the cars coming in and out, and there's been German cars and suchlike and . . . and . . . well, the fact of the matter is that you've got a fine business here now, Mrs. Angus, haven't you?"

"I'll have to go to Inverbrae again," Alexia said to Peter. "I'll have to go and see Duncan McGill. Otherwise he'll just think we're poaching all his staff."

"I'll go if you like," Peter said.

"It's all right. I sort of feel I ought to —"

Peter looked at her. "Why? You don't like him."

"That's exactly why. I feel I have to be extra careful of him."

"I see," Peter said. He looked, she thought, older than he had at Christmas, thinner in the face. He had never mentioned the episode on Christmas night, and Alexia had silently returned the pendant to him with a little note explaining her reasons, to which neither of them referred. Their relationship had, all the same, not become badly strained simply because the business was booming and they were too busy to have time or energy for conversations that did not refer directly to the hotel. The closest they got to a personal discussion was when Alexia managed, after great difficulty, to persuade Peter to be the first to accept a salary check.

"I don't want it, we're partners, we should do everything equally and simultaneously."

"But this is my house, and you have put far more into something that isn't yours than I care to think of. I insist, Peter, I insist."

She found she was insisting quite a lot these days, and she knew that when she said that she should be the one to go and see Duncan McGill, it finally would be so.

"Okay," Peter said, shrugging. "You go to Inverbrae. Just try not to quarrel with him."

In contrast to her previous visit, her second was made on a day of perfect, clear summer weather, with seals basking on the rocks in the loch at low tide, and the water as blue as the sky above it. This time, Alexia telephoned to make an appointment, and drove up the long, steep drive through the dappled shade cast by the rhododendrons with the calm and certain feeling that it was for her to be the kind and gracious one this time because it was she who had the upper hand.

As she emerged on to the drive, she saw that Duncan McGill was on the apron of lawn to the left, above the wonderful view, with his spaniels. He came forward courteously as she stopped, and opened the car door for her.

"A fine day, Mrs. Angus."

"It is, indeed."

She got out. The air up here was like wine.

"Will you come in, or would you prefer to talk in the garden?"

"The garden, please." She was pleased at the quiet businesslike tone of her own voice. "I've come, Mr. McGill, because I felt I owed you an explanation."

"Ah," he said. He led her across the grass to the stone balustrade that bounded it before the land dropped steeply to the loch. She perched on the broad top of the balustrade and felt the sun and the light wind on her face.

"It's about the staff —"

"Yes," he said.

She watched him, waiting for his face to darken in anger.

"I was afraid you might think that I had enticed Hughie and Jeannie and Flora away from the fish farm and that I had persuaded Jimmie —"

He turned away. He said, very quietly, "No, Mrs. Angus. I didn't think that."

"Mr. McGill —"

He turned back. To her surprise and horror, his face was simply sad. He said, "I'm sorry, of course, particularly about Jimmie, for all the reasons you know of old, but I never thought you'd had a hand in changing any of their minds."

"You didn't."

"No."

"Did . . . did you try and stop them?"

"No."

"But it's against all your principles!"

He turned so that he was leaning on the balustrade close to her, and his gaze was turned directly upon her.

"I think I once mentioned the new dam to you and said I couldn't stop progress out of sentiment. I realize that the same is true, in a way, of your hotel. These people of our village, these young people whom I've known since they were babies — I can't stop them wanting to lead a different life from the one I feel is best for their true happiness. I —" His voice faltered a little but his gaze never wavered. "I can't dictate to them, and I shouldn't try. I have to hand it to you, Mrs. Angus, you've succeeded where I never believed you could, and with your success, you've brought a breath of new life up here, to the castle, to Bewick and . . . and to —" He stopped. For a wild, mad moment, Alexia thought he was moving towards her and that if he did she might well fling herself at him, but then he went on, "to my ideas. I thank you for that, Mrs. Angus." He held his hand out. "I thank you warmly."

She took his hand. She was very much afraid that her own was far from steady. She said almost in a whisper, "This wasn't at all what I was expecting."

He smiled. "You thought I'd rant and rave at you, didn't you?"

She nodded.

"I'm saving that for the hydroelectric board these days."

She slipped off the wall. She felt that she ought

to go, and at the same time that she very much didn't want to.

"It's . . . it's very good of you to take it like this."

"Not at all. Most ogres have a soft spot somewhere, if you can find it."

"I didn't think you were an ogre —"

He raised an ironic eyebrow. "Oh no?"

She colored.

"Only at first perhaps —"

She began to walk back towards her car with Duncan at her side, and the spaniels following politely. He held the car door open for her.

"I wish you every further success, Mrs. Angus. I wish you endless blue skies."

She nodded violently, finding that she couldn't speak, that there was a lump in her throat. She reversed the car clumsily while Duncan watched her, and lurched unevenly down the drive. He had been perfectly sweet to her, and he had made her feel awful somehow, remorseful and longing . . . and . . .

"Damn," Alexia thought, as tears she didn't want and couldn't explain, rose thickly in her throat and then spilled over so that she couldn't see to drive, "Damn, damn, what is happening, what is the matter with me?"

When she got back, she went straight to the office. Gregor, who had been in charge of the telephone all afternoon, had left a list of calls — two more bookings, which meant that the hotel was now almost entirely full for the next three weeks, a message from the wine merchant that the new consignment of Burgundy was ready for collection, a further message that the boiler engineer would be calling to do a routine service on Monday, and a London telephone number beside which Gregor had written, "This was from a doctor and his wife who particularly wished to speak to you before they make their booking!"

Alexia sighed. All requests like this never failed to remind her of Mrs. Farquhar and her foam rubber pillow, but as the hotel prided itself on its personal service, personal it must be. She picked up the telephone and dialed the number Gregor had left, making a mental note to remind him that he must always, without fail, take callers' names.

The telephone rang out three times on the far end, and was then picked up and a man's voice said, "Hello?"

Alexia froze.

"Martin —"

"Oh, Alexia. How nice of you to ring back."

"I'd no idea it was you —"

"No, I didn't mean you to have."

She had an impulse to put the telephone down.

"Don't hang up on me," Martin said, "I won't keep you a minute. Did you get my letter?"

"Yes —"

"And the Christmas card for Charlotte?"

"Yes —"

"Oh good. I hoped you had. I really must congratulate you, Alexia. I can't pick up a paper or a magazine these days without finding a glowing piece about your hotel. It sounds wonderful. I only wish I could afford to come and sample it."

She waited, breath held.

"Are you still there?"

"Yes."

"I really am pleased for you, Alexia. You must believe me. I know we parted badly, but I still feel a great interest in what happens to you."

"Thank you," Alexia said, her voice almost strangled by her feelings.

"In fact," Martin went on, his tone verging on the laughing, the self-deprecating, "I sometimes wonder if I did the right thing —"

Alexia gave a gasp and held the receiver away from her ear so that she couldn't hear him clearly.

"Alexia! Alexia!"

She brought the telephone gingerly back.

Martin said, "I thought you'd gone!"

"You mustn't talk to me like that —"

"Sorry," Martin said, "I'm really sorry. I suppose it was hearing your voice again made me —"

"Why have you rung?"

"Ah. Well, Alexia, the reason I've rung concerns the one thing we still have in common and always will."

He stopped. Alexia waited, sickened and afraid.

"We have little Charlotte in common, Alexia, don't we? I suppose she must be about two now. I often think about her. In fact, I think about her whenever I look at her little half brother who isn't, I'm afraid, getting half the chances that she has —"

"No!" Alexia shouted.

"What do you mean?"

"You're not to threaten me, hint things! Carly's mine!"

"Alexia, I have to remind you that I'm her father. I don't want to upset any happy little apple carts, I just want my son to know his sister."

Alexia screamed, "You're no father to her! You've no rights to her!"

"Oh, but you see I have," Martin said calmly, "I checked Charlotte's birth certificate last week and was delighted to see that I was registered as the father. I mean, I didn't expect anything else because I know you are a very honest woman, but I was pleased all the same. So I've been to see my solicitor."

Alexia's legs were beginning to shake under her, hopelessly uncontrollable.

"What?" she whispered.

"It's all perfectly straightforward it seems," Martin said with false cheerfulness. "I just have to apply to the courts for access to Charlotte and there we are, turn and turn about."

Alexia closed her eyes.

"It would so help if you'd cooperate," Martin went on. "My solicitor says the court will take a pretty dim view of the fact that you have never troubled to tell me of my own child's existence. I'm afraid that'll be seen as extremely unsympathetic behavior. But I'm sure we can get over that if you do everything you can to make things easy for me to see Charlotte now, don't you?"

Alexia said nothing, but only subsided in silence on to her desk chair.

"Look," Martin said, easily. "No need to make definite plans now. You just look at your diary while my court application waits to be heard. Then we'll talk again and sort out times and places. I could come up to Glasgow to meet her, no problem. Thanks so much for calling me back. And congratulations once more. Oh — and love to Charlotte of course, Daddy's special love."

Then he put the receiver down at his end and left her listening in horror to the threatening silence.

Chapter Nineteen

Alexia had scarcely been in Mr. McReadie's office since that wet October day almost two years ago when he had advised her so soberly to sell Castle Bewick and her land and to retreat to the south with the proceeds. At least this August day wasn't pouring with depressing rain, but it was overcast and still, and Alexia's heart was heavy with anxiety now, rather than just fluttering with apprehension.

Nothing, she thought, climbing the stairs to his office, had changed. She might have rescued a house and started a hotel, and her hair might be a fraction shorter and her skirt a fraction longer, but nothing had changed about Mr. McReadie's office in the smallest degree. Even Miss Barclay seemed to be wearing the same bow-tied blouse and the same expression of faintly offended disapproval.

"I have an appointment, Miss Barclay, at eleven."

Miss Barclay sniffed. She didn't need to be reminded of Mr. McReadie's engagements, thank you. She motioned Alexia to an unfriendly armchair covered in dark red leather.

"If you would take a seat, Mrs. Angus —"

Alexia sat down, pulling her skirt over her knees. She didn't bother to dress specially for Mr.

McReadie these days, since on his visits to Castle Bewick (and he seemed quite keen to come rather often now) he invariably found her dressed for guests anyhow, and so today she had simply put on, largely without thinking, the tweed midiskirt Amanda had sent her from London.

"This is all the rage in London," Amanda's accompanying note had said, "but I expect it will pass quite unnoticed in Scotland."

In front of Alexia was a table bearing a few magazines and newspapers, arranged with strict precision. They were all Scottish, and Alexia knew that at least two of them contained pieces about Castle Bewick. One was headed "A Scottish hotel to put others to shame." She had cut that out, and put it on the notice board in the office which she and Peter called "the Fan Board." It was almost unbearable that just when everything was going so beautifully, this sinister cloud should drift across her sunlit horizon.

A bell rang on Miss Barclay's desk. She rose and trotted across to an inner door that led to Mr. McReadie's office, and vanished inside. A moment later she reappeared.

"Mr. McReadie is ready to see you now, Mrs. Angus."

"Thank you, Miss Barclay."

Mr. McReadie was standing up behind his desk, and he was actually smiling.

"Mrs. Angus, this is a great pleasure."

"Oh, Mr. McReadie," Alexia said impulsively, "I only wish it was!"

His smile vanished at once, to be replaced by his customary unenthusiastic lawyer's expression.

"Mrs. Angus, I do trust —"

Alexia sat down in the chair she had sat in on her first visit.

"Don't worry, Mr. McReadie, it isn't the hotel. That's doing wonderfully, thank goodness. It's something more personal."

Mr. McReadie, who hated anything personal, immediately looked uncomfortable. He resumed the chair from which he had risen when Alexia came in, and put his elbows on his desk, and regarded her with grave apprehension over the top of them.

"I'm sorry to hear it, Mrs. Angus."

Alexia leaned forward. He might not want to hear what she had to tell him, but he'd got to. She had as yet told not another living soul and she was desperate for advice.

"You know, of course, Mr. McReadie, that I was divorced shortly before I came to Scotland."

He gave the tiniest nod.

"I divorced my husband, Martin Angus, on grounds of his adultery, and from the moment he left me, before Carly was born, I have not seen or spoken to him. I never told my husband of Carly's birth because I never wanted to hear of him again after the way he had treated me, and I didn't think he was in any way a fit, responsible person to be a father. But my fa— a member of my family, I mean, felt he should be told, and he was, although it was without either my knowledge or my consent."

She paused, because she could feel herself getting angry, and she knew by now that it was self-defeating to lose control in front of Mr.

247

McReadie. She took a deep, steadying breath.

"Last September, I received a letter from him, ostensibly congratulating me on being given Castle Bewick. I say ostensibly, because it was perfectly plain that he wrote in order to let me know he had noticed I had come into a substantial property. I ignored the letter, and told nobody. There was no further word until Christmas, when he sent Carly an affectionate card. This too I took no notice of. But then he telephoned, four days ago. I was out, and returned the call not knowing it was from him."

"And, Mrs. Angus?"

"He threatened me."

"Threatened you?"

"Yes, Mr. McReadie, he threatened me. At the beginning, he just said all kinds of horrible, falsely flattering things, but then he began on Carly. He said he'd checked her birth certificate and found that he was registered as her father and that he'd applied to the courts for access to see her! And then he began to insinuate that if I didn't give him every help, I'd be in terrible legal trouble myself —"

"Mrs. Angus!"

"Mr. McReadie, you don't know him."

Mr. McReadie got up, and came out from behind his desk and began to pace about his room.

"Mrs. Angus, I'm afraid the fact that your ex-husband has shown no interest in your daughter for two years in no way militates against his right to see her now, if he so chooses."

Alexia spun round in her chair.

"He can't, Mr. McReadie, he can't! He was utterly callous about her conception and arrival, he's shown no true loving interest in her of any kind, he just wants to use her as a pawn in some nasty game he's going to try on, and I absolutely am not going to let him anywhere near her!"

Mr. McReadie stopped by Alexia's chair and looked down at her.

"I'm afraid you cannot do that, Mrs. Angus."

"What d'you mean, I can't?"

"She's her father's daughter too, Mrs. Angus. In my opinion as a lawyer, I have to say also that you have no right whatsoever to keep a child hidden from its father."

Alexia looked down. Her hands, she discovered, were shaking so badly they were like leaping salmon. She gripped them together in her lap and closed her eyes. The sight of her violent distress seemed to soften something deep inside Mr. McReadie. He said, a little more gently, "But we'll not upset ourselves on that score yet, Mrs. Angus. If you'll only abide by my advice, there need be no disagreeable dramas."

Alexia looked up with a white face. "So?"

"Mrs. Angus, my previous point still stands. Until he shows himself, in a proven manner, unfit to be her father, he has a right to access."

"What d'you mean? You mean I have to let him try and kidnap her before the law will do anything?"

Mr. McReadie clicked his tongue. "We mustn't get melodramatic, Mrs. Angus. No proposal has, after all, yet been made, and if and when it is, then I shall be better placed to advise you what to do."

"And what do I do in the meantime? Sit at Bewick watching Carly like a hawk and having a heart attack every time the telephone rings?"

"I'd advise you to take a few people into your confidence. Elsie, Peter, Jeannie Blair. And then I believe you should carry on as normally as possible. It may well be that any threat you believed your ex-husband to have made, was idle —"

Alexia leaped up, her eyes blazing, "Mr. McReadie!" she shouted, "Mr. McReadie, why won't you take me seriously?"

When she got back to her car, Alexia was shaking like a leaf. Mr. McReadie had been quite unmoved at being shouted at, and had refused to budge from his imperturbable position that Martin had parental rights, and that nothing could be done until an overt threat was made. Alexia had shown Mr. McReadie Martin's letter and Christmas card, and the incoherent notes she had made after their telephone conversation, and Mr. McReadie had professed to find nothing menacing in any of them. In the end, she had flung out of his office in a storm of tears, watched with deep satisfaction by Miss Barclay from behind her ancient Remington.

Sitting sick and wretched behind the wheel, something prudent in Alexia's brain told her that she shouldn't drive home. She ought to go and find herself a cup of coffee, and something to eat, and not attempt to drive until she was calmer. But the prudent element was overwhelmed by a sudden violent need to be back at Bewick with Carly, who now appeared to her frighteningly vulnerable since the law, in the form of Mr. McReadie, had declared itself not remotely interested in helping her because it declared coldly that Martin, being Carly's biological father, had as much right to her as Alexia did.

She jabbed the key into the ignition and turned it and the engine roared to life. It was a slow difficult journey through the western edge of Glasgow and then up the pretty but winding road along Loch Lomond, but at least she now knew it like the back of her hand, and could safely allow her mind to think about Carly rather than about driving.

Yet it was hardly bearable to think about Carly. Mr. McReadie's apparent indifference had, in its own way, terrified her quite as much as Martin's telephone call. And how could she have been so stupid as not to confide in at least Peter and Elsie before she left? She supposed she had just idiotically hoped first, that if she never mentioned or thought about the problem of Martin, it would simply go away, and second, that Mr. McReadie would have some wonderful, instant legal solution that would prevent Martin from even crossing the border into Scotland.

Well, both hopes had been bitterly dashed. Mr. McReadie had said, to all intents and purposes, go home and wait for something awful to happen, and then maybe I'll see what I can do. Alexia drove faster and faster. She had to get home to Carly, she had to, she was the only person who knew what danger Carly was in, not just because of anything that Martin might do to her, but also and almost worse, because he didn't

251

really love her, he was just using her, and the thought of Carly being in the hands of anyone who didn't really love her made Alexia feel absolutely frantic.

The road up Loch Lomond was blessedly free of traffic. The view across the water was as lovely as ever, but Alexia hardly gave it a glance. She raced through Luss, and then, at Tarbet, swung the car left to hurl it round the head of Loch Long and up — oh thank God, thank God, nearly home — into the home stretch of hills and the Rest and Be Thankful Pass.

Toiling up the pass was a grindingly slow lorry, driving in the center of the narrow road and emitting clouds of black exhaust fumes that obscured the view past it. Almost screaming with impatience, Alexia crept behind it, gripping the steering wheel with white-knuckled hands. At the pass, the driver troubled to look in his mirror, saw her, and pulled over to the side so that she could shoot by, with a casual, smiling wave as if nobody in the world could possibly find anything to be in a hurry about.

She flew down the far side of the pass, seeing with relief the dark fringe of trees that signified the lochside. There was one last bend, where a track came out, a track which led up into the mountains which had once been hers, and were now Duncan's, and just as she approached the bend, far too fast, the elderly Land Rover that was driven by Duncan's keeper appeared in the track's entrance. Thinking it was turning into the road, and hadn't seen her, Alexia leaned on the horn, jammed her foot down on what she thought was the brake, missed it for the accelerator, and went spinning past the Land Rover into the boggy ground beside the road.

She was down at the far end of a long, dark tunnel. It was an echoing tunnel, and along its length she could hear whispering voices, voices that seemed to be getting louder and louder, bouncing off the walls of the tunnel until she wanted them to stop, but couldn't seem to speak to say so. Somebody was whimpering quite close to her, mewing like a distressed cat, and she wanted to tell them to be quiet. At least she was warm. She could feel how warm she was, all down one side and across her back. If she hadn't been down this tunnel, she would have said that someone was holding her.

Her eyelids moved. Someone said, "And the crying's a good sign."

"Aye —"

"I think it was only a bad bump. Thank God she went into soft ground. She's done more damage to the car than to herself."

"Aye."

"Find me some water, Donald, would you? And that old blanket from the back of the Land Rover —"

"It's awful mucky —"

"She's in no state to mind about muck."

She felt something wet and cool on her forehead and cheeks and against her mouth. Then a cover was tucked round her, a cover smelling strongly of — what was it? Sheep?

"I had to put the water in my whisky flask,"

one voice said apologetically. "It was all I had —"

"Won't do her any harm. Come on, Mrs. Angus, take a little of this."

Mrs. Angus? Who was calling her Mrs. Angus? She made a determined effort to move down the tunnel, and an even greater one to say something.

"Alexia," she said stupidly, clumsily.

"Wonderful," the closer voice said. "Wonderful! What did you say?"

She attempted, with great dignity to say clearly, "Call me Alexia," but she sounded as if she was drunk.

"Alexia," the voice said softly.

Her eyes flew open. There, inches above her face and apparently multiplied by three, was the face of Duncan McGill.

"You're quite safe," he said. "You came off the road and tipped your car on its side, but luckily Donald and I were coming down the hill and we got you out. I think you've banged your head but there's no real harm done."

She gazed at him while his three faces resolved themselves into one. Then her hand crept up to feel her head and encountered his shoulder. He was holding her. He was on the ground with her across his knees, in his arms, and he was holding her.

She said, "Sorry —"

He smiled down at her very close. "Sorry for what?"

"Stupid," she said, "stupid —"

"You were driving like the devil, I will say. Donald had just said, 'There's Mrs. Angus in an awful hurry' when you came whirling past us and ended up in the bog."

She tried to sit up, but he held her down.

"Don't move. Don't try to move."

She didn't really want to. What she wanted, more than anything, was to turn her face safely into the tweed of his jacket, and just go to sleep there, in the soft air, while he held her. But obviously she couldn't do that. She said, "Where's Donald?"

"Over there. Inspecting your car."

"Have I wrecked it?"

"Nothing a panel beater can't put right. Why were you driving like that? Was there an emergency?"

Memory flooded her. She struggled again to sit up.

"Carly! Oh, Carly!"

He was holding her more firmly now.

"What about Carly? Is she ill? Were you getting a doctor?"

"Oh no, no it isn't that, it's her father —"

"What about him?"

It was no good. She couldn't keep any tears back now, nor could she give any coherent explanation of what was the matter. Hardly able to speak for sobs, she blurted out, "He never cared about her, nor me, he never cared at all, he just wanted my connections and things and then he left us, and he didn't care and now he's coming to get her because he says the courts will give him authority as Carly's father and that I'll be punished because I've kept him from her, but he doesn't love her, you see, he doesn't love anyone

except himself, he just likes playing games and —
Oh my God, Duncan, I've got to get back, I've
got to, I've got —"

"So you shall," he said. "And I shall take you.
Don't worry, I shall take you."

No longer caring what she did or what Duncan
thought of her or whether Donald was watching,
she flung her arms round Duncan's neck,
pressing her wet face to his. He didn't push her
away. Instead he held her against him strongly,
one hand pressing her cheek to his. And then he
said — or for one marvelous moment, she
thought he said, "You're safe now, sweetheart.
Quite safe."

Chapter Twenty

They put her to bed. She protested about this but there was no resisting them, so she lay in bed, with Carly standing at her bedside, gazing at her.

"Bump Mummy," Carly said, anxiously, "Mummy bump. Poor bump. Poor Mummy —"

"I'm all right, darling. It's the poor car really."

"Bump car. Poor car bump. Poor Mummy car bump —"

Duncan McGill had sent Donald back to see to the car. He had also sent Doctor Trewin in to see her. Alexia felt light-headed at the memory of her return to Bewick supported by Duncan, discreetly to the kitchen door, to the sight of Carly peacefully, safely, sitting in her high chair eating tea, and Elsie and Jeannie and Gregor, and dear Peter coming forward, his face creased with anxiety to take her from Duncan. She had fallen against him, sobbing, she remembered that. She also remembered the journey down to the castle in the back of the Land Rover, still in Duncan's arms. He hadn't spoken another word to her, he had simply held her until they got to the house when he said gently, "You'll see. You'll find her safe and sound here. Come with me."

As he gave her into Peter's arms a little later, he merely remarked, "I'm afraid she came off the road a little way up the glen towards the pass. I think it's only shock and bruises," and then to her, "You take care of yourself, now, Mrs. Angus."

Peter had sat her down in the big chair by the kitchen table, and Elsie had made her tea and Carly had struggled and squeaked to be released because of the atmosphere of drama. Alexia could do nothing but cry, so they helped her up to her bedroom and put her gently to bed, leaving only Peter with her, and Carly, from whom she wouldn't be parted.

Slowly, uncertainly, she told Peter everything. She told him the whole story of her marriage and the pathetic attempt it had been both to have someone of her own, and to please her parents, of its ending and of her strange, lonely pregnancy, and of Amanda and Felicity's part in providing her with a future. She told him about all that Bishopstow had meant to her and then about Martin's silence over Carly, and then his letter and the Christmas card and his telephone call, and then about the visit to Mr. McReadie and the blind panic it had thrown her into and how she had driven so wildly and carelessly as a result.

"And you know the rest. Duncan and Donald found me. Actually, I think I crashed because they were coming out of the track up to Archadoon, and I thought they hadn't seen me and I mistook the accelerator for the brake —" She stopped and turned her head away from him on the pillow. "He was terribly kind."

"A good person to be rescued by," Peter said.

He reached forward and took Alexia's hand which lay on the quilt. "He won't gossip. Anyway, he has other fish to fry just now."

She turned her head back.

"What fish?"

"Oh," Peter said offhandedly, "his lady love of long ago is back; now Fiona Westcott, newly divorced with a handsome settlement and an avid interest in red deer, which, as you know, is one of his passions too."

Alexia closed her eyes. A slow, dull desolation began to spread through her like a tide of cold water.

"I think I'd like to sleep —"

"Of course. It's the best thing for you. I'll take Carly."

Her eyes flew open again, wide with panic.

"Keep her with you, Peter, all the time —"

He smiled. He stooped over the bed and kissed her forehead very gently. Then he lifted Carly into his arms.

"Don't worry about that. Don't give that another thought. We'll talk about that when you're less shaken, when you've had some sleep."

"But tonight," Alexia said, rearing up suddenly. "What about tonight? We're full, aren't we, and how will you manage if I —"

"Sh —" Peter said. With the hand not holding Carly, he pushed her back down on to the pillow. "Sh. We'll manage fine, just fine. You go to sleep."

Carly leaned down over her mother.

"Go to sleep!" she commanded in the voice Alexia had often used to her. "Go at once, at *once*, to sleep!"

In the next few days, it was Peter who quietly took command. It was Peter who suggested Alexia should tell her parents the whole story and ask her father to go and see Martin in person, Peter who took over without fuss her duties in the hotel, Peter who undertook to tell the rest of the staff about the care that must be taken in keeping a watch on Carly. Alexia, though not in bed, found that she was very shaky and tearful, and didn't seem able to concentrate. She sat in the office (usually with Carly playing on the floor or mountaineering over the furniture), shuffling paper about and achieving nothing. Doctor Trewin had told her to expect to feel like this for some time, but somehow his warning was no comfort. Nothing seemed to be much comfort, not even Carly's presence three feet from her, tunelessly singing "Rock a bye baby," which she loved because of the crashing cradle at the end; not even her father's steady reassurance from London that he would deal with whatever mad schemes Martin was dreaming up; not even the fact that she hadn't killed herself up there on the glen road, but only bruised her head and her nerves, and required the car to have a new bonnet panel and a new nearside wing.

Sometimes, sitting there fiddling about in the long, fruitless hours of convalescence, she went back in her mind, with a kind of hopeless longing, to those ten or fifteen minutes when she had been dreamily conscious of lying in Duncan McGill's arms. She was now sure he had never called her either by her Christian name or "sweetheart," that that was all part of the confusion of half knocking herself out, of the muddle she was in about Martin and Carly, of the scarcely acknowledged fantasies she seemed to have when she was with Duncan that he might be going to say or do something thrilling. If he *had* said "sweetheart" that day, then he'd surely only said it in the tender reassuring tone that people use for endearments when speaking to sick or frightened animals and children. After all, he'd reverted to "Mrs. Angus" fifteen minutes later, when he delivered her back to Bewick, and if he'd held her for a moment as you would hold someone who was very precious to you, well, that was simply the reaction of a kindhearted man with strong feelings and old-fashioned manners into whose arms you had flung yourself, wailing like a banshee and shrieking that your husband hadn't ever loved you and that now he was trying to steal your baby . . . Alexia always shut her eyes at this point, flooded with humiliation. Why hadn't she behaved with even an atom of the dignity Duncan always behaved with? She was sure that if Duncan was half concussed, he wouldn't come to, babbling rubbish, and chuck himself sobbing at his rescuer. He would behave in a way that didn't embarrass anybody, that didn't get him into the emotional hot water that Alexia seemed to find herself drowning in half the time.

Duncan had sent flowers. He had sent a bunch of copper-colored lilies from a florist in Glasgow, with a note politely wishing her a complete and speedy recovery. She could hardly bear it when the lilies began to die and to shed their lethal rusty pollen on the surface around their vase, and had to be thrown away. Their despatch seemed to signify, in a way she couldn't properly define, the end of a little private fairy tale, hopeless perhaps, but magical all the same, and when they were gone, it seemed to Alexia that everyone was taking particular, eager care to tell her that Duncan McGill was to be seen constantly on the road to Lochgilphead, where Fiona Westcott was converting her parents' old house to standards of comfort and luxury it had never known before.

"Your father rang," Peter said.

It was late, almost midnight, and they were sitting tiredly in the office for ten minutes before going to bed.

Alexia gave a little gasp. "Oh?"

"It was this afternoon. While you were asleep. He said he had been to Nineteen Northbourne Street, but that Flat Four was now unoccupied and the young couple who had lived there had been gone some weeks."

Alexia said nothing. She merely stared and waited.

"Martin isn't at St. Bartolph's any more, your father said," Peter said quietly. "He gave up there, in his first year as a junior intern. They seemed to think he was going into the pharmaceutical industry. He hadn't done well in his finals at all, your father said, contrary to everyone's expectations."

"So where is he now?"

"Nobody knows. But your father said not to worry, that he will keep looking. He also said to tell you that, in his opinion, it's all a very poor joke on Martin's part, that you shouldn't take it too seriously."

"I don't want anyone else to say that to me!" Alexia cried. "No one else knows, can possibly know, what it feels like to —"

"Sh," Peter said, coming to sit beside her. "Sh, sweetheart. It's all right, I understand, really I do."

Sweetheart! She turned and stared at him.

"Why did you call me that?"

He hesitated. He took one of her hands and laid it on his knee and smoothed the fingers. Then he said, "Will you listen to me for a moment? For a whole speech without interrupting?"

"Of course," she said.

He picked her hand up and gave it back to her.

"Alexia, you know that I'm in love with you, that I've been in love with you almost from setting eyes on you, and that I continue to be. I also know that although you are fond of me and grateful to me, you aren't in love with me in return, and I am not such an optimistic fool that I think I can see a return of my own feelings just because I so want to. I've tried very hard not to beg for love and I hope I've succeeded, and by the same token, I hope you'll acknowledge that I haven't tried to exploit you by doing things that demanded your gratitude."

He stopped and stood up. Alexia waited. He went over to the fireplace, and stood looking down at the empty summer grate for a moment, and then turned back to face her.

"As all feelings and relationships are organic

and thus have to grow and develop, I've come to see in the last few months that ours — or mine, to be more accurate — has got to a point where something has to be done. I can't go on in a kind of limbo, only having a brotherly business relationship with you, because I can't bear it and, as a result, I'm beginning to feel exploited. So I've come to a decision. It seems to me that I — we — can do one of two things. Either I leave and you buy me out of my share of the business or — and this is what *I* want, Alexia — we get married."

She stared at him.

"Married!"

"Yes," he said. He was astoundingly calm. "Married. We have every ingredient for a good marriage except the one of your being as much in love with me as I am with you. We are excellent friends, we have the same outlook, we work admirably together, we have ambitions, we both adore Carly, and Castle Bewick. We fit together, hand in glove. We don't fight, we like the same jokes, the same people, the same food. Lots of people who get married out of passion find there's nothing left after two years. We'd be the opposite, and who knows, you might get to love me, in time, as I would wish you to. And I'd be Carly's stepfather. I'd be here, with you, to protect her and help bring her up. If we were married."

Alexia wrenched her gaze from his face, and looked away from him into the dim room.

"And if I don't marry you, you'll go away?"

"Yes."

She said, falteringly, "I do love you —"

"But?"

"It's a cozy love," she said more strongly. "It's born of familiarity and reassurance and gratitude."

"Don't you think that that's what real grown-up married love is like?"

Abruptly, without intending to, Alexia thought of her parents. Cara and Stephen certainly were comfortable together, almost cozy, so much so that she had often as a teenager felt herself to be excluded from their charmed coupledom. But they had something more than just companionableness, something more electric, something that had contributed strongly to Alexia's childhood loneliness. They admired each other still, she now thought. They do! In their own odd way they aren't just self-sufficient, they still find each other exciting. She turned to face Peter.

"I think real grown-up married love is that — and something more."

His look of calm was gone, and had been replaced by one of sheer misery. She gripped her hands together. It was necessary to be both clear and honest without being brutal. She had to make it plain to him why she couldn't marry him without saying straight out that she couldn't marry anyone with such a tendency to emotional dependency as he had, that she couldn't, in the end, marry anyone out of pity.

"Are you in love with someone else?"

"Oh, Peter," Alexia cried, flinging her hands out, "who on earth is there to be in love with round here?"

"I wondered about Martin —"

"Martin!"

"Sometimes people go on being in love with someone who's been awful to them."

"Not this person."

"And there's Duncan —"

"I hardly know Duncan." Her chin went up.

"Alexia —"

"Yes?"

"Is . . . is the answer no?"

She got up and went across to him and put her hands on his shoulders.

"Yes, Peter. The answer is no."

He tried to laugh. "Am I that repulsive?"

She was determined not to react.

"You're a dear, but —"

He twitched himself out of her grasp.

"What the hell are you looking for, Alexia?" he shouted.

"I don't know. I truly, honestly, don't know."

"Suppose you never find it because you're so hopelessly, idiotically romantic?"

She shrugged. "Then I don't."

"When all the time you could have years of security and contentment and loving loyalty from me?"

"Even so."

"I wonder if you've really got a heart, whether you aren't so wrapped up in yourself that —"

She interrupted him. "Peter, I've got quite enough heart not to insult you by marrying you for the wrong reasons."

He looked at her for a long time. Then he nodded, and took one of her hands again and kissed it.

"You're a bit of a bully, you know," she said, smiling.

"A bully who's taking himself off —"

She swallowed hard, to restrain the involuntary gasp of shock.

"Where will you go?"

"Don't know. Back south maybe. Or perhaps I'll start a hotel the other side of Scotland."

"I never meant to drive you out —"

"But you are, to all intents and purposes, aren't you?"

She regarded him with sudden asperity. Her mind, so shaken by recent events that it had felt useless and soggy, suddenly seemed clear again.

"Don't forget, Peter, that it was you who begged me to let you stay. *And* proposed the terms on which you should do so. Don't forget that."

He shifted slightly. "It'll be forgetting you that'll be the problem. You and Carly."

She moved away towards her desk, feeling, inexplicably, a sudden relief, as if a burden was slipping from her shoulders. "I'll ring Mr. McReadie in the morning. We'll work out a deal with him."

"And then you'll run this all alone? No time off, no shared responsibility?"

"If I have to."

He followed her across the room and laid a hand on her arm, gripping it.

"Alexia, for God's sake, don't you *want* any personal happiness?"

"Of course I do!"

"Well, why don't you take it when it's staring you in the face?"

She disengaged her arm and stepped back a pace.

"I may be younger than you, Peter, but I know some things you still don't know. One, I know that you seldom find personal happiness if you look too hard for it, and two, that if you do look too hard for it, you mistake something else for it and the results are terrible."

"I see," he said, and then he leaned forward and kissed her cheek and went slowly out of the room, leaving her standing alone by the desk.

Chapter Twenty-one

October 1969

Alexia celebrated the second anniversary of her arrival at Castle Bewick alone. The hotel was full, as it had now been, except for the occasional night, since the early summer, and, leaving Gregor in charge downstairs, she retreated to the turret room with a glass of champagne. She did not actually feel very much like either drinking champagne, or celebrating, but it was plain that Elsie and Gregor and Hughie and Jimmie and all the rest of the staff — whose wages she raised slightly to mark the day — expected her to celebrate the day in some way, and it was equally plain that she must not allow them to see how forlorn she felt.

The turret room had become her refuge since Peter's departure. It was a little recompense she had made herself for the huge hole he had left in all their lives — and in the hotel's life — a hole she didn't really want to admit to. The week after his going, despite the fact that paying him his agreed sum had left her mortgaged up to half the castle's value, Alexia had ordered in her usual local decorator, and the carpet layer from Dunoon, and had set about turning the turret room into a secret and private retreat, a sanctuary that would become to her a companion in place of the companion she had lost. The money hardly mattered. She was amazed to discover how little she felt that the money — any money — mattered.

She did miss Peter; she couldn't hide it from herself. She was thankful to be free of the guilty burden of not loving him as he had wanted her to, but she had loved him, in her way, and she missed, quite simply, having someone to love. She also missed his usefulness. Gregor was quick and eager to learn, but he didn't have Peter's imagination and ideas. But, she told herself, settling herself into the turret room with some of the odd but dearly familiar pieces of furniture from the Mermaid Room, this had happened to her before, this finding herself alone, and, as she had done on previous occasions, she had to pick herself up and get on with it. At least now she had the hotel to get on with. And Carly. Since that horrible time in the summer, there had been nothing further to frighten her about Carly, only something to distress her because Carly missed Peter too.

"Peter coming?" she said, over and over. "Coming soon Peter?"

Alexia sat down thankfully in the dear old brown chair — she had rejected the idea of re-covering it in a pretty chintz to match the curtains as quite wrong — kicked off her shoes and took a sip of champagne.

"Here's to you," she said to the room.

Her grandmother had kept mice up here once,

she remembered, and dreamed of being famous, a painter perhaps or a musician. "And look at me," Alexandra had said, laughing. "Look at me! An old Cornish farmer!"

"And look at me," Alexia thought. "A hotelier." She said the word again, slowly, to see if it made her feel proud and full of achievement. "A hotelier." It didn't seem to.

She put her head back and closed her eyes. She would give herself ten minutes more, and then she must go down and resume her duties. She had had the idea, as the autumn began, of opening the dining room to nonresidents, to ensure that even in the winter, when bedroom bookings were bound to fall off a little, the hotel would never be as achingly, echoingly empty as it had been the winter before. In ten minutes' time, at ten-thirty, the eight o'clock dinner bookings would be paying their bills and departing, and she liked to be downstairs for that, to wish people goodnight, to remind them, yet again, that hers was a personal service.

She yawned, and felt about on the floor for her shoes. Gregor had said they had three tables of nonresidents tonight, so the dining room, big though it was, would be quite full. It looked lovely, full of people, the paneling reflecting the candle flames and the firelight, the whole room exuding welcome and well-being. She found her shoes and slipped them on. Then she went across to the old gilt-framed mirror above the tiny fireplace and peered at herself. She looked tired. She looked older than twenty-three. Well, she *was* tired and she *felt* older than twenty-three, she felt a hundred. She picked up the brush and comb she kept up here for just such a purpose, brushed her hair back and tied it smoothly again with its black velvet ribbon. Then she put on more lipstick, adjusted her pearls at the neck of the slim black dress she wore in the evenings, and had another look.

"Hello, hotelier," she said to her reflection, trying to make it laugh. But it only looked sadly back at her. "Hello, Alexia," it said.

The dining room was by now half empty. Most of the residents had gone into the drawing room to have coffee, and only ten or twelve people remained, with coffee cups and brandy glasses. Gregor, with Jeannie's help now that Carly was tucked up for the night, was unobtrusively waiting on them. He was an excellent waiter, deft, polite, and invisible. He came up as Alexia entered the dining room.

"Mr. McGill would like a word with you, Mrs. Angus."

"Mr. McGill!"

"He's had dinner here. He wanted to tell you how impressed they've been."

Gregor's face glowed with vicarious pride. The fish farm and the hotel were still local rivals as employers, and to have the owner of the fish farm capitulate so far as to admire the hotel was a victory indeed.

Alexia swallowed.

"Of course. I shall go straight over."

Gregor indicated Duncan's table, a table for two in a quiet corner underneath Alexia's favorite painting in the room, a painting of a little bare-foot girl in a ragged frock and a plaid, standing in a herd of geese and shading her eyes to see out of the picture. Alexia crossed the room between the tables with a determined smile.

"Mr. McGill. How nice to see you here."

He stood up immediately, holding his hand out to her. He wore a dark suit of beautiful cut, and a cream silk shirt, and a tie patterned with dark red paisley. He looked utterly, absolutely devastating.

"We wanted to offer you our warmest congratulations," Duncan said, smiling.

"You are very kind —"

"May I introduce Mrs. Westcott? Mrs. Westcott, Mrs. Angus, who runs this magnificent establishment."

"Oh call me Fiona, please."

Alexia turned, resolutely smiling. "Thank you. Mr. McGill always calls me Mrs. Angus."

"He's a stuffy old prig," Fiona Westcott said, laughing. She was a handsome woman in her thirties, who would one day be stout, with an open, friendly face. "You don't want to take any notice of that. You just firmly call him Duncan. Or wee Duncan, as my mother used to." She glanced at him, an easy, familiar, intimate glance.

"I'm Alexia anyway. And I'm so pleased you enjoyed dinner."

"My dear, it was delicious. Absolutely first rate. I haven't eaten crème brûlée like that in London and I've never eaten venison so succulent anywhere. And the atmosphere is lovely and so are your staff. I shall *live* in this dining room, I swear it. Duncan says it's your family home."

"Sort of. My grandmother grew up here."

"Such a brilliant idea, making it into a hotel."

"Thank you." She was still smiling but she wasn't sure she could keep it up much longer, not with Duncan standing there looking so absolutely wonderful and happy and fulfilled and gazing at her in that unbearable kindly way. She began to back away.

"If you'll forgive me —"

"Of course," Fiona Westcott said. "You must be rushed off your feet."

"Good night, then —"

"Good night, Alexia. And well done."

As she threaded her way back across the room, she heard Fiona Wescott's penetrating voice saying, "But she's only a *child*, poor little thing! No wonder she looks worn out."

Duncan's reply was uttered too low for her to hear, and in any case it was obliterated by Gregor's coming forward and saying, "Weren't they pleased, Mrs. Angus? Didn't they say it was excellent?"

"Yes, they did —"

"They're a handsome couple, aren't they, Mrs. Angus? Elsie says they're to be married soon."

The warm, glowing room swam a little. Alexia put her hand out to steady herself against the great sideboard that had been there since the early nineteenth century.

"Married?"

"Oh yes," Gregor said, "Elsie says it'll be a sensible match. And if they get a move on, Mr. McGill might even get himself an heir!"

Alexia spent a long, wakeful night. During the course of it she first decided to sell up the hotel and leave Bewick altogether, then to write to Peter and say she had made a mistake and she now knew that any love was better than no love at all and finally, at her most irrational at about three-thirty, to go up to Inverbrae in the morning and tell Duncan McGill that he couldn't marry Fiona Westcott because she, Alexia, wanted to marry him.

This last decision was so preposterous that it brought her to her senses. At least, she supposed wretchedly, turning on her pillow for the hundredth time, she was now being honest with herself, and confessing, at least privately, that she was in love with Duncan and had been for months and that was why, at bottom, she couldn't bear the thought of an intimate relationship with Peter. She was in love and, as she seemed fated to be, she could not in any way expect a happy ending. Duncan was looking the other way. Duncan was in love with someone else. Duncan — like Martin — had gone back to his first love. And I, thought Alexia, was Peter's first love, and I didn't want to be. Why do I always, always seem to want to be loved by people who don't love me, from my mother to my husband to . . . She gave herself a shake. Self-pity wasn't going to get her anywhere. Nor was all this morbid introspection. She had a hotel to run, she was jolly lucky to have a hotel to run, and by knowing for certain now that Duncan was going to marry Fiona Westcott, she could stop indulging in silly reminiscent daydreams, and get on with running Castle Bewick and bringing up Carly.

She liked the look of her morning face even less than she'd liked the look of her previous evening's one. She bathed vigorously and dressed in clean neat clothes and put on a great deal of makeup to hide the circles under her eyes, and pinned her hair up on top of her head so that she would look very adult and sophisticated and *nobody* could pityingly say "poor child" of her.

She went briskly through the morning routine, greeting guests, breakfast, bills, suggestions for occupations for remaining residents, the day's menus with Elsie, the day's bookings, half an hour with Carly. Then she asked for a cup of coffee to be brought to her in the office and gave orders that she was not to be disturbed until lunchtime.

Elsie brought the coffee. Alexia was most surprised. Elsie, now supreme cook, with Jimmie working under her, and Dougie to wash up, was more accustomed these days to be brought coffee than to bring it.

"Elsie! How kind —"

"Mrs. Angus, Mr. McGill's here. I've told him you're not to be disturbed but he insisted he'd only be a moment, so I said I'd ask you myself."

"What does he want?"

"I've no idea, Mrs. Angus. He looks pretty bothered. There's been some restlessness up at the fish farm after you raised the wages here, so I suppose he wants a word about that."

Alexia briefly put her hands over her face.

"I suppose I'd better see him —"

Elsie peered at her.

"You look all in, Mrs. Angus dear."

"I didn't sleep very well. There . . . there seems such a lot to do."

"I'll tell him to go away," Elsie said resolutely. "He can badger you another day, when you're feeling stronger."

Alexia shook her head. "Dear Elsie. Thank you, but I'll see him now. Get it over with —"

Duncan came into the office wearing a very different expression from the happy confidence of last night. He was dressed in his familiar garb of breeches and tweed jacket and his face was grave, even sad. Alexia braced herself.

"I'm so sorry to interrupt you —"

"You're not," she said shortly. It was close to unbearable having him there in the same room with her and, in every sense, knowing him to be so far from her. She motioned him curtly to a chair, and sat down opposite him, bolt upright, her hands together in her lap.

"Alexia —"

She put her chin up a little. "Well done," she said.

He flushed a little. He said, "I hardly need reminding that I'm old-fashioned and pompous —"

"Perhaps you would like to tell me your business?" She could not bring herself to utter his name. "I imagine there's trouble in the village again about who works where."

"No," he said.

"No?"

He looked straight at her. It was a look she

couldn't meet, so she averted her gaze a little and regarded the chimney piece sternly, and the drawings propped along it that Carly had done, red and blue and green and yellow, big and bright and — happy.

"Alexia — I've come because I was distressed last night."

"Distressed? You didn't look it, and you and Mrs. Westcott were kind enough to say you had enjoyed dinner."

"We did. It was first class. It wasn't that —" He stopped. He seemed to be struggling with something painful. Alexia was in such pain herself that it was almost a relief to her to see him suffer too. She wouldn't help him; she would simply wait, in silence.

"I was so shocked," Duncan went on, "I am so shocked at — you'll think this an awful impertinence, I know — at the sight of you. You look tired out, so thin. And more than that —" He paused again and then said in a low voice, "You don't look happy."

For an impulsive, fleeting moment, Alexia opened her mouth to say, "I'm not," but she closed it again and said, "Oh?" The "Oh?" sounded very cold.

"Please forgive me if I'm interfering where I've no business to," Duncan said, "I've no wish to intrude on private feelings, on feelings of loss —"

"Loss?"

"I know — we all know — that Peter left last month. And although there are ways in which nobody can repair that loss, I've come down this morning because I couldn't bear to see the exhaustion of extra administration taking its toll on you, on top . . . on top of any other —"

He broke off again. Even if she had wanted to speak, she couldn't possibly have uttered, being on the verge of a storm of tears. She simply set her teeth, and kept her eyes wide open, staring at Carly's pictures.

Duncan said, "I've just come to offer any practical help I can. I'm a good businessman, I might be of use to you, and what I wanted to say today was that if I could help ease the pressure on you in any way, I'd be glad to. More than . . . glad to. I just want you to call on me, if ever you should wish to."

He stood up. She couldn't move, but simply sat there, rigid with self-control.

"I'm so sorry," he said, "I'm a clumsy brute. No doubt I've made things worse in trying to make them better. Fiona always says —"

She made an abrupt gesture, to silence him and he took it as one of dismissal.

"Goodbye, Alexia," he said. "Please forgive me," and then the door opened and closed softly, and he was gone, and it was only after he had gone that she realized he had come, with a full and sympathetic heart, to commiserate with her for the loss of Peter Burton, with whom he was convinced she was in love.

Chapter Twenty-two

In the second week of November, it was announced that a major brewery, which gave a much coveted annual award for the best new hotel to open in the previous twelve months, had chosen, as the winner for 1969, Castle Bewick Hotel, Bewick, Argyllshire, proprietor and manager Mrs. Alexia Angus.

It was a complete surprise to her. The six judges appointed by the brewery had come separately and anonymously to Bewick during the summer and early autumn, and the chairman wrote a charming letter to Alexia saying that it was the first time, since the award had been instituted in 1960, that all six judges had been unanimous in their decision. He also said that there would be an award ceremony in London in December, and that Alexia was naturally invited to be the guest of honor. He also offered her accommodation at the brewery's flagship hotel.

She wrote back immediately accepting everything except the hotel because, she said, she would stay with her parents. She telephoned Cara and Stephen at once, and it was the first time in her life that she heard in her mother's voice a note of real respect, almost awe.

"Darling —"

"It's worth five thousand pounds, which of

course is very handy, but it's the status and the publicity that's the really valuable thing —"

"I'm so proud of you," Cara said. It was always easier for her to express enthusiasm on the telephone. "I'm amazed. Look at you — not twenty-four yet!"

"I'm still awfully in debt —"

"Does that matter?"

"Not really."

"Is . . . is that why you sound a bit downcast? Is that why you aren't as euphoric as I'd expect, because you're worried about money?"

"No," Alexia said, "I don't think so. I expect I just haven't taken it in quite yet. And I'm pretty tired. It's been quite a year."

"Oh Alexia," Cara said, and something in her voice made Alexia feel slightly shaky. "Oh what a lot you've achieved! And on your own too."

"Not quite," Alexia said, thinking of Peter.

"You're brave," Cara said. "That's what you are. Really brave."

Putting the receiver down, Alexia reflected that brave was the last thing she felt. Every letter of congratulation that came in — and there seemed to be hundreds — every bunch of flowers that arrived seemed to make her feel more unsteady and emotional rather than secure and confident as everyone else at Bewick clearly felt. Among the letters was a most touching one from Peter. It had come — typical Peter — by the first post after the award was announced.

My dear Alexia,
    I haven't words enough to congratulate

you sufficiently, nor to tell you how richly I think you deserve this. And before you ring and tell me that it's my achievement too and that I must accept half the glory, I'm telling you that I won't have it. I only did what I did for the reasons you know. I don't have your vision or courage or independence. You must step out to take the applause that is rightly yours.

I'm doing all right. To be honest, it's a bit like learning to walk again after an accident, but at least I'm doing what I want to do now and I'm joining a small firm of architects in Norwich.

God bless, Alexia, and may you achieve your heart's desire.

Peter

It wasn't a letter she could read with any composure. Nor was another letter, a card in this case, which had come with a second blazing bouquet of copper-colored lilies, any easier to read, if for entirely different reasons. Where had such lilies come from, for heaven's sake, in November? Their accompanying card was brief.

"My sincere admiration and warmest congratulations. Duncan."

Just "Duncan." Not "love from Duncan" or even "with best wishes from Duncan." But why should she expect anything else? Wasn't taking the trouble to send her that glamorous, extravagant hothouse bouquet enough? And why should he think of sending love when he didn't feel it? He was too honest a man for any kind of dissembling, that was why people so often thought him rude. He was, Alexia reflected, perhaps the most honest person, with the exception of Uncle James, that she had ever met.

The day after he had come to see her to console her for the loss of Peter, he had telephoned. He was very brief. He was ringing, he said, to apologize again for the clumsiness of his behavior, and to reiterate that she was to turn to him for any help of any kind in the future, should she need it. He had sounded quite brusque, even curt. Alexia had simply said, "Thank you. Thank you very much," and put the telephone down.

That had been that. She had longed to tell him that he was mistaken, that her love for Peter had never been more than sisterly, but with a gigantic effort, she prevented herself. What would be the point? He would think it very odd to receive such an intimate confession from her when she couldn't go on and justify telling him by revealing the reason. In any case, if he were going to marry Fiona Westcott, what did it matter whom he thought Alexia loved or didn't love? I shall get over it, she told herself, and I have to. I have to take a leaf out of Peter's book, and learn to walk again, by myself. Don't I?

In early December, Gregor drove Alexia and Carly to Glasgow airport for the journey south to London. Alexia wore the skirt Amanda had given her the year before, and a jacket she had had made in Craigmuir of smooth dark green cloth, cut like a kilt jacket with square silver buttons. Carly wore a new harebell blue Harris tweed overcoat with a velvet collar that matched her eyes. Alexia had wanted to go on the train.

"It's so extravagant, flying —"

"This is the time for a wee bit of extravagance," Elsie said. "You're to spoil yourself. In any case, I'm sure you'll find the brewery are paying."

They were. They were also, it appeared, paying for a long black limousine with a chauffeur in a uniform cap, who met them at London Airport, and drove them, with great pomp and circumstance, to Culver Square.

"Is this a taxi?" Carly asked reverently.

"A very grand kind of taxi."

"And will the flying plane wait? Will it wait for me?"

"Yes. It'll wait for you."

Carly put her thumb in her mouth, her eyes fixed on the extraordinary spectacle of London flashing past the limousine's windows, only taking it out once to say conversationally, "Loch gone. All gone."

Alexia's stomach was tightly knotted. She hadn't been inside 17 Culver Square since the Christmas when she was pregnant with Carly. Impossible now to think of a world without Carly, a world without Bewick, without . . . come on, she told herself sternly, none of that. Culver Square seemed to have shrunk slightly in three years, but it had also become smarter, with a scattering of tastefully brass-knobbed front doors painted scarlet and avocado green, on account of the professionals who were moving into the graceful Georgian houses.

Nobody had painted the door of number 17. It looked absolutely, exactly the same with, Alexia could have sworn it, the same number of milk bottles on the doorstep, and the same neglected, straggling spider plant in the sitting room window. But what was not the same was that Cara was at home, a slightly older Cara, with a grey hair or two in her dark red crop and an air, Alexia observed incredulously, almost of diffidence.

"Darling!" Cara exclaimed, putting her arms around Alexia. "Oh my clever darling —" She knelt to kiss Carly. "And Carly darling too."

Carly regarded her.

"No loch," Carly said.

"No, I'm afraid not —"

"But there was a flying plane."

"Was there? Was it exciting?"

Carly pointed a short tweed-clad arm straight into the air.

"Up there," she said. "It had lunch in it."

Cara began to laugh. "Did it, darling?"

"Carly's very keen on lunch —"

Cara lifted her granddaughter into her arms.

"I'm terribly afraid I'm going to cry, and you know that's against my principles." She looked at Alexia with unnaturally bright eyes. "Come in, you clever child, and let me have half an hour of you before the others come."

"The others?"

Cara kissed Carly's red head. "Oh, they're all coming, they all want to see you receive your award. James and Mary and Amanda and Felicity. You'd think they'd all invented you from the way they're going on."

Amanda and Felicity took her shopping.

"Too sweet, the way you look now, but quite honestly, darling, you do a tiny bit resemble the fair weather lady in a weather house, and you have to look utterly chic for your award."

"At Bewick, I *do* look utterly chic."

"Treasure child, we know. We saw you. But this is different. This is London and your chance to shine."

They took her to Jean Muir.

"I can't afford *that!*"

"Yes, you can —"

"I mustn't, I can't, that's a month's wages for Dougie —"

"Shut up," Amanda said.

They put her into a soft, high-waisted sleeveless dress of matt black silk jersey with a narrow skirt that fell to the floor. It didn't just fit her, it enhanced her.

"Shut your eyes and write the check. Hairdresser next."

Alexia's eyes widened in alarm.

"Hairdresser!"

"We're going to have your hair layered. And probably colored."

"Colored!" Alexia screeched.

"Lightened a bit at the ends. Layering's so new it's hardly been thought of. You wait. You'll look amazing."

She did. She looked in the mirror and there was a faun-like creature with airy tendrils of hair around her face and neck and enormous eyes.

"But I look so *young!*"

"Precisely. Think what a selling point. Sweet photographs flashed around the world of the child who runs the best new hotel in the British Isles."

"But I don't want to be a child —"

Amanda suddenly knelt down by her, all among the snippets of hair on the salon floor.

"Alexia kitten, what is it?"

Her voice, which was never kind, was kind now. Alexia bowed her head and couldn't speak.

"Oh sod it all," Amanda said, "is it bloody love?"

Alexia nodded violently. Amanda put a hand over hers.

"My kind of bloody love, darling? Loving someone to hell and back again who likes you but really loves someone else?"

More nodding.

"And you'd rather look like a woman for him, a strong capable woman with no heart, not a poor lovelorn waif?"

"Yes," Alexia whispered.

Amanda stood up.

"Well, to hell with him, angel child. These photographs are going to fill the papers, and, as a result, fill your hotel until you're so rich you can go and lie in the Caribbean sun for the rest of your life. Think about that, darling, focus on that. Why on earth do you suppose that I've devoted my life to making wretched *curtains?*"

The award ceremony took place in the ballroom of an enormous hotel in Park Lane. Under the great chandeliers thirty tables were spread for ten people each — "Oh my God," Alexia said, "three hundred people! Three hundred people watching!" — with pale pink cloths and pale pink carnations. All around the edges of the room, long wooden screens had been erected, and on them were pinned photographs, huge, brightly colored blown up photographs of Castle Bewick, of the loch, of the Mermaid Room, of Alexia at the top of the front stairs, of Jimmie gutting a salmon and Elsie making pastry, of Gregor opening wine and Hughie carrying a vast wicker herring basket of newly cut logs. It was enough, she thought, to make her feel violently homesick, on top of already feeling sick with nerves at the prospect of having to make a speech of thanks to three hundred people. Three hundred people in dinner jackets and long dresses who had, most of them, spent decades in the hotel industry and knew more about it than she had even begun to realize there was to know. Even the sight of Stephen and dear James in the elderly dinner jackets — dreadfully tight in James's case — they had had since they were young men, and Mary in a blue frock that looked as if it had escaped from a museum costume department, and Cara nearly in tears, and Amanda in black with a jet choker and Felicity in a mad frock covered with tassels, all of them smiling like mad and almost bursting with visible pride, could hardly steady her. When she was presented with her award, a silver-gilt pineapple ("the symbol of hospitality," said the brewery chairman helpfully) on a mahogany plinth, she could scarcely remember what she had been going to say.

For what felt like several minutes, she just stood there, with hot cheeks, while the thunder of clapping went on and on, wave after wave of it, punctuated by cheers. Then the chairman thundered on the table with his gavel.

"Ladies and gentlemen, please. A little silence, please. I'm well aware that this is a most popular award" — more clapping — "and more possibly the most popular award we have yet made" — more cheers — "but I must beg you, please, for the courtesy of a little silence for Mrs. Angus."

The silence fell. It seemed to echo. Alexia stood up. The lights in the ballroom dimmed and dimmed until only one strong light was left on her. She took a breath.

"Thank you," she said. She stopped. What was she going to say next? She'd worked it out, rehearsed it, what was it? She opened her mouth. Nothing came. Suddenly it didn't matter, it didn't matter that she couldn't deliver a cool, polished, professional speech. All that mattered was that these three hundred people who had come to pay tribute to her should know how grateful she was, how truly, humbly grateful. She flung her arms out, as if to embrace them all.

"Oh, thank you!" Alexia cried to the enormous room, "oh thank you, all of you, so much!"

Back at Culver Square, no one went to bed until almost three. Amanda and Felicity came back with them, and Stephen opened champagne, and then Amanda told them all about James's secret visit to them and the deep-laid plot about Bewick. It was all terribly happy. Alexia sat in the circle of James's arm, and simply basked. They were all so pleased with her, so proud of her, even Cara, it was the kind of occasion which only three short years ago she would gladly have sold her soul for.

When Amanda and Felicity had finally gone, and James and Mary had taken themselves off to bed, Alexia remained in the sitting room for a while with Cara and Stephen. The sitting room was so unchanged it almost made her want to laugh, the same ugly sofa and chairs, the same even uglier overhead light, the same piles of *British Medical Journal*s. She sat in one of the armchairs, and Cara and Stephen sat opposite to her, on the sofa together as they always used to, Cara with her feet tucked up, leaning on Stephen.

"I've decided something," Cara said suddenly.

"Have you?"

"Yes." She sat upright. "I'm going to send the portraits back to Bewick."

Alexia was truly startled.

"What!"

"It's where they belong. They'll be yours in due course anyway, and they ought to hang where they were meant to hang and where they will be properly admired, instead of being stuck away here with only committee meetings as an audience."

"Oh Mum," Alexia said, stretching her hands out. "It's lovely of you —"

Cara said, a little sharply, "Don't you think it's time I was a bit lovely?"

"Oh no, I mean, it's over, it doesn't matter now —"

"Would you like them? The portraits? Would you like them to come home?"

"Oh yes, more than anything —" Alexia leaned forward, "There's just one other thing —" She looked at her father. "I wonder — did you ever track Martin down?"

Stephen shook his head.

"Don't worry about that."

"I can't help —"

"Alexia," Stephen said gently, "I mean it. Don't worry. Martin is a gambler, we all know that to our cost, and he'll exploit someone for his own ends if he can. But he isn't wicked. He isn't to be feared."

"He frightened *me*," Alexia said. "I'd feel better if I knew where he was, what he was up to."

Stephen's serious face was very kind.

"All reports I have are that he's working in the Midlands now, for some small drug company. I'm afraid his letters and his call to you were just a try-on, a silly impetuous try-on. But they weren't a real threat; he isn't that kind of man. Try to forget it. Forget all about it. The time may come when he and Carly should meet, but not now. Now is your time, Alexia, your time for being happy and successful. And you are, darling, aren't you?"

She looked at him. She nodded determinedly.

"I'm certainly — lucky," she said.

In the morning, every paper had her picture, standing in the spotlight with her arms flung wide, in her slender black dress and her halo of feathery hair.

"My mummy," Carly said excitedly. "My mummy!"

"Yes, darling," Cara said, "your clever Mummy."

Carly picked up the nearest paper and held it against her chest possessively.

"Now get coat," she said commandingly to her grandmother. "Now get coat on and Carly go *home*."

Chapter Twenty-three

Going home would have been an anticlimax if the pressure of getting ready for Christmas hadn't greedily demanded all Alexia's energy and time, leaving little of either over for reflection. It was truly touching too, to see Carly's rapture at being back again, bringing home to Alexia how deep Bewick had dug itself into her affections, how much it represented to them both in terms of security and identity. It was dusk when they came home, and as the car turned on to the part of the drive from which she had first seen the house, she caught her breath, seeing anew the enchanting, eccentric outline of the castle, pierced with welcoming oblongs of golden light, dark against the dimly gleaming waters of the loch.

Christmas was very different from the hilarious Christmas of the year before, with Felicity and her Italian lover shrieking with glee as they tobogganed behind the house, and Amanda and Victor exotically, decadently, wanting champagne brought to their room at teatime. This Christmas, the hotel was larger and fuller, almost all the guests being Americans, for whom Alexia wished to make an exceptional effort, not least for the gratitude she felt to the anonymous American woman in the Hibernian Hotel who had planted the seed of this splendid idea in her mind in the first place. She intended that no guest who came to Castle Bewick for this award-winning Christmas should ever forget it.

For three weeks, she and the staff worked harder than they ever had, turning the castle into a Christmas fantasy of red and green and gold, with all the gaunt stonework softened with garlands of spruce and ivy, and the air fragrant with spicy smells coming from the kitchen and with the scent of the apple wood from a decayed orchard which Alexia had been saving to burn for a special occasion.

As with the year before a beautiful, thick, blue-green spruce appeared silently in the yard. No message. Nothing.

She telephoned Inverbrae to say thank you. The telephone was answered by Mrs. Buchan, Duncan's housekeeper.

"I'm afraid Mr. McGill isn't here, Mrs. Angus. He's in Glasgow."

"I just wanted to thank him so much for the tree —"

"Would you leave a message?"

She hesitated.

"When . . . when will he be back?"

"Not until Friday, Mrs. Angus. And then he's away to Lochgilphead."

"Yes. Of course." She swallowed. "Would you, Mrs. Buchan, simply leave a note that I rang and that I'm grateful for the lovely tree and that I'll be in touch soon to say so in person?"

"Certainly, Mrs. Angus."

She put the telephone down, and walked to the

window of the office and looked out. Carly was climbing the iron fence on the other side of the drive that divided the rough grass, where a few Highland cattle now grazed, from the mown lawn. Jeannie was trying to help her, Carly was squealing indignantly that she didn't want help.

"Do it self!" Alexia could hear her shrieking. "Do it self!"

So that was that, then. Duncan was naturally going to spend Christmas with Fiona Westcott, and by next Christmas either he would have gone to live at Lochgilphead or Fiona would have come to Bewick to be mistress of Inverbrae. And probably yet another handsome Christmas tree would courteously come — "Oh, I think it's a lovely idea," Fiona would say to her husband. "Of course you must go on with it! She's such a clever child" — and Alexia would have to telephone Inverbrae yet again and say thank you equally courteously. It could go on for years, couldn't it, this ritual exchange conducted with perfect manners while she, Alexia, slowly bled to death inside, from a broken heart.

Her vision blurred with tears. She shook herself firmly. Goodness how greedy she was, wanting Duncan as well as this place and her success and above all, that dear stout bundle out there on the fence, bursting with independence and character. She opened the window into the cold afternoon.

"If you are rude to Jeannie," Alexia called, "I shall come out there and spank your bottom."

Carly tried to turn at the sound of her voice and fell off the fence.

"Don't care!" Carly shouted defiantly stranded on her back like a fat beetle. "Don't care!"

Christmas Day, though inevitably quieter than the year before, was very happy. By unanimous request from the guests, Carly was invited into the drawing room at teatime so that they could watch her unwrap her presents. Alexia dressed her in a Black Watch tartan smock with a white piqué collar, and white socks and red bar shoes with buttoned straps. She looked delicious. She sat on the hearth rug while twenty pairs of eyes watched her open the doll's crib she had from Alexia, complete with bed clothes and occupant; a large, simple jigsaw of the Three Bears from Cara and Stephen; and from James and Mary a most realistic toy West Highland terrier on wheels. The terrier was a huge success.

"Dog," Carly said reverently. She put her arms round it. "Dog, oh dog —"

She wanted it put right beside her bed that night. She lay on her side with her thumb in her mouth, so she could see it.

"When you're bigger," Alexia said, "you can have a real dog. Of your own."

She stopped to kiss her. What a good day, what — thanks to those sweet-natured, warm-hearted guests of hers — a happy family day for two people like herself and Carly who weren't quite a family. There'd been nothing to spoil it, nothing, not even this year, a card from Martin to Carly. Stephen had been right. "Try to forget it," he'd said, "Martin isn't a wicked man. He isn't to be feared. Now is your time, darling Alexia, for being happy and successful."

To tell the truth, she had recently almost forgotten Martin. Perhaps, she told herself, softly closing Carly's bedroom door, forgetting was something that got better with practice.

After Christmas, as expected, there was a lull. There were, in fact, no bookings for the rest of January after the Hogmanay celebrations were finally over. Alexia, looking at her staff's gallant but exhausted faces, decided to close Castle Bewick for three weeks. Gregor would go home to Craigmuir, Hughie and Dougie would move into his quarters just to keep the boiler ticking over, and everyone else would have three weeks' paid holiday.

"You can't stay here alone with the bairn," Elsie said.

"I can, I'd like to. I did when I first came here, and if I've got Dougie and Hughie in the stableyard, I won't be alone anyway."

Elsie looked at her doubtfully. "I don't like it. Three weeks is a long time."

"Three weeks is nothing. I *need* three weeks solitary in any case. And it won't be three whole weeks anyway, because my parents are coming up to bring the portraits back."

"You'd ring, wouldn't you?" Elsie said. "You'd ring if you needed anything?"

"Of course I would. But I won't. Carly and I will be quite happy together, doing nothing much. I'm looking forward to it."

All the same it was queer in the castle when everyone had gone. The silence hung so heavily it almost made a noise and the quiet, untouched rooms and empty grates were eerie. There was a brief interlude when Cara and Stephen intrepidly made the long journey from London with a hired van, bringing Charlotte and Alexander back home, and they had a little ceremony in the drawing room while Hughie and Dougie rehung the portraits where they'd always hung, Charlotte to the left of the great fireplace, Alexander to the right, so that both were slightly turned towards one another. It was a happy little visit, but only short, because snow was forecast, heavy snow, and Stephen was anxious about getting his van out over the pass before it came.

"Look after yourself, darling," they said as they drove away. "Have a real rest now, no work at all that isn't strictly necessary. Just snowball fights and cuddles with Carly."

"I'll try —"

She looked up at the sky. It had that bosomy, feathery look that heralds snow. "Go quickly and safe journey. Ring me when you get to London."

"Of course," Cara said. "What a lovely few days."

They had been. Buoyed up by the memory of them and the new harmony that seemed to exist between her and her mother, Alexia determined to devote the whole day to Carly, and not even to enter the office where a full filing tray ominously waited for her.

They went together into the kitchen and messily made gingerbread men, and then Carly took her terrier for a walk all around the hotel corridors and rooms that she was usually forbidden to enter, and then Alexia took Carly down to the loch and they threw stones into the water and tried to make them skip along the surface. After lunch, they curled up together in an armchair in the office, by the fire, and Alexia read to Carly and then Carly read the same book, upside down, to her dog. Then they went out for another walk to see if the snow was coming, which it wasn't yet, and returned to the kitchen to eat hot buttered toast and the gingerbread men. After Carly's bath time and story time and tucking-up time, Alexia, full of a rare and sweet contentment, had a very long and leisurely bath and then went down to heat herself some soup which she intended to drink by the fire, out of a mug, before she gave herself a luxuriously early night.

Elsie had left a jug of her excellent carrot and orange soup in the refrigerator. The fridge was groaning with food. It made Alexia smile; it was so like Lyddy, this assumption that Alexia still needed a nanny. She poured a mugful of soup into a pan and carried it over to the stove to heat it. The telephone rang. She put the pan down on the kitchen table and went to answer it. It would be Cara, ringing from London to say that they were safely home.

"Hello?"

There was a tiny pause and then, "Hello," Martin said, "I'm here." His voice was level and polite.

Alexia clutched the telephone receiver.

"Here? Where here?"

"In Bewick," he said. "At the Bewick Inn. I arrived an hour ago."

She couldn't speak.

"Are you still there?"

"Yes —"

"I rather wanted to see Charlotte, you see. I couldn't help thinking of her, seeing your picture splashed across every paper I opened, and I felt a bit forlorn. I don't want to upset anything, I promise I don't. I just want to see Charlotte. I did think of simply turning up, out of the blue, but then I thought that was a bit unfair and might embarrass all your guests. Don't you think? Actually, I gather I needn't have bothered to be so delicate because they tell me here that the hotel's closed for a few weeks and that you're alone there with Charlotte —"

She felt for the nearest kitchen stool and pulled it towards her to sit down.

"That's ideal, really, isn't it?" Martin went on. "It means I can meet her in relaxed circumstances and you and I can talk about the future —"

She found her voice, or at least a voice of a kind, "The future?"

"Yes. My seeing something of her on a regular basis, perhaps having her to stay. That sort of thing."

She had begun to shake. What he was saying sounded perfectly reasonable, but the effect it was having on her wasn't reasonable at all. All the old feelings of terror and panic, of being somehow his victim, in his power, in a way which no one, not even the lawyer, could or would prevent, were rising up in her in a boiling tide.

"I thought I might come up now, if that's all

right. Just for an hour —"

"Carly's asleep!"

"Yes. I assumed that. But there's quite a lot for you and me to talk over, and then I can come back in the morning and see her. Shall I come straight up?"

She thought rapidly.

"Actually, I was just getting into a bath —"

"I see. Well, you have your bath and I'll be there in three-quarters of an hour. Okay? I'll look forward to it."

He put the telephone down. With an unsteady hand, Alexia put hers down too. Three-quarters of an hour and he'd be here. Martin, of all people, would be at Castle Bewick. She sprang off the stool. There was only one thing to do. Martin might be here, she couldn't stop him — but she and Carly wouldn't be.

Chapter Twenty-four

She drove to Inverbrae like a mad thing, a sleepy, bewildered Carly rolled up in a quilt on the back seat of the car. The snow was beginning to fall, soft casual flakes spinning lazily down out of the dark air, making visibility difficult. Behind her the castle lay locked and dark, waiting impenetrably for Martin.

Her route took her inevitably through the village, past the Bewick Inn, at which she daren't look in case she saw him coming out or, even worse, he saw her flying by. There was no traffic on this dark night, nothing on the loch road but the powdering of snow like sugar crystals, glittering in her headlamps and softly crunching beneath her tires. Her teeth were chattering. She'd been in such a hurry to get out of the house that she hadn't even put a coat on over the old jersey and trousers she'd put on after her bath. She hadn't thought of her appearance. She hadn't even brushed her hair.

It didn't strike her either until she swung off the road at the head of the loch and started up the steep drive in its tunnel of twisting branches and heavy leaves, that Duncan might not be at home. She hadn't even thought of telephoning him, she hadn't thought of anything except that he had said to her, three months before, that she must always appeal to him for help if she needed it. Now she did. She needed a haven and someone to turn to, and only as she crept up the drive did it occur to her with a cold fear that that someone might not be there to be turned to. And even, if he *was* there, that he might not be alone and that she would find herself helplessly having to include Fiona Westcott in her confessions. "Don't worry, dear," Fiona would say, "I think you're just terribly tired and you're exaggerating it all —"

She emerged at the top of the drive and saw with a thudding relief that there were lights on in Duncan's study, showing as lines of gold between the drawn curtains, and a welcoming, comforting light above the front door. She was here, she had made it, and if Fiona Westcott was one of the prices she had to pay for a place of refuge, well, so be it. She stopped the car, and got out to open the back door and get Carly out. Carly had remembered something.

"Dog!" Carly wailed, "Mummy get dog! Mummy go and get dog!"

"In a minute," Alexia said. "When you're in the warm."

"Now!" Carly insisted.

Alexia bore her to the front door of Inverbrae and rang the bell.

"Now!" Carly demanded again, but Alexia hardly heard her above the beating of her own heart.

She heard the inner door open, and then the heavy latch of the outer door being lifted.

"Now!" Carly wailed.

The door opened.

"Dear heaven," Duncan said, "Alexia! My — Alexia, what are you doing here, what's the matter —"

She stumbled forward. He caught her, and she felt Carly lifted out of her arms, and then the sudden warmth as the door closed on the snowy night. She said, in a rush, "I'm so sorry, I think I've panicked, I think I've been terribly stupid and hysterical, but you said to come if ever I needed help, you said —"

"Dog!" Carly interrupted in rapture, catching sight of Duncan's spaniels who were coming forward across the hall. Gently, Duncan stooped to set Carly on her feet, still trailing her quilt, and then he turned to Alexia.

"Tell me. Come into the warm and tell me."

The sight of his study was enough to break down all the remaining shreds of her self-control, particularly as there was, blessedly, no one else in it. The firelight and the lamplight reflecting off the books that lined the walls, the rumpled cushions and newspapers, the warmth, the security were all too sweet to be borne with composure. She was aware, as Duncan led her to sit down on one of the huge old sofas that flanked the fire, that she was shaking as if she had flu.

"Carly, where's Carly?"

"She's here," he said, "she's right here. She's with the dogs. Now tell me."

"I feel such a fool," Alexia said, "I think I've over reacted and been a complete idiot but I was so afraid —"

His arm was still around her. He said gravely,

"If the fear is real to you, then that's good enough for me."

She looked at him. His face was very close to hers.

"It . . . it's Martin." She darted a look at Carly, who had settled down on the hearth rug between the two spaniels and was cooing to them and playing with their ears. "She doesn't know about him, doesn't know he exists, and I know that's wrong, I know I should have told her; I know they should know each other but I couldn't bear —" she broke off, choking. Duncan's arm tightened around her. "He's here, Duncan. He rang an hour ago from the Bewick Inn. He said he was going to come straight up to the castle and that we had a lot to talk about and . . . I panicked. I just panicked. I thought he might take advantage of my being alone and just take her and I thought the safest place to hide was . . . was here. With you."

There was a small silence. During it Alexia became anxious that she had made a terrible mistake and that Duncan was going to chastise her, very kindly, for behaving like a fool, and she was preparing to seize Carly and rush back into the snow and just drive and drive, anywhere, any distance, to get away. When he spoke he said simply "You stay here."

"What?"

"You're worn out. You're too tired to cope with anything anymore. I'm going to get you and the little one pillows and blankets, and then I'm going to get you a dram —"

"I don't drink whisky —"

"You do tonight. You'll drink your whisky, and then you'll both settle down here by the fire with the dogs for company and I shall go down to the Bewick Inn and sort all this out."

She looked at him. She looked at him for a long, long time and then she gave a shuddering sigh and leaned forward and laid her head on his shoulder. He let it lie there for a few minutes and then he said in a voice which was not at all steady, "Come on, now. Let's get you both tucked up."

It was heaven to be there. Warmed by the fire and the whisky and a bowl of game soup, Alexia lay on the sofa and gazed with unspeakable gratitude at the scene before her, the two liver and white spaniels stretched out on the rug, Carly already fast asleep on the opposite sofa, and beyond her the lamp that Duncan had lit. "For comfort," he said, "so that you can see where you are when you wake. I don't want you to feel afraid." She didn't think she had ever felt less afraid in her life, lying there on Duncan's sofa, her cheek pillowed on an old beautifully ironed, much-mended linen pillowcase reminiscent of those at Bishopstow, guarded by his dogs and his solid great house. I must treasure this, she thought, I must treasure this as one of the loveliest times of my life.

Duncan had been gone half an hour. He'd said not to expect him back for ages, to sleep reassured that he'd tell her what had transpired in the morning. He had made her tell him the whole story of hers and Martin's marriage, of the circumstances of her pregnancy and Carly's birth, and then he had pulled on a greatcoat, and said he'd take the Land Rover for its four-wheeled drive grip in the snow, and he'd gone.

"You're so kind," she said. "You're too kind —"

It was the only moment when he'd shown anything but gentleness and understanding. He said, almost angrily, "I'm nothing of the sort," and then he went, and she heard the tires in the snow and the sound of the engine fading down the drive.

Now there was nothing to do but wait in this perfect heaven. It wasn't even anxious waiting, because of Duncan. Duncan had said he'd sort it out. He said don't think about it, just sleep, that's what you need to do, sleep. Go to sleep. Pulling up the covers around her chin, safe and happy, Alexia obediently closed her eyes and slept.

When she woke — she had no idea at what time — the fire was still quietly burning and the lamp was still on. She raised her head. The dogs didn't appear to have stirred and neither had Carly. Perhaps she had only been asleep for a little while, an hour or so. She thought that if that was the case, she ought to get up and put more wood on the fire before the cold of dead of night set in. She sat up. Where were the logs?

Then she saw him. He had pulled an armchair across the study door, and he was lying asleep in it, utterly relaxed, his arms along the chair arms and his face, his sleeping face, turned towards her and the firelight. Why was he there — and how long had he been there?

With infinite stealth, Alexia pushed back the covers and swung her feet to the floor. Then she stood up, very gingerly. She longed to go over to him but she didn't dare. Instead she crept across to the window to pull back the curtain just enough to see how dark it was, and if she could gauge any idea of the time. There was a table in the window, a round table covered with books and papers. Alexia sidled past it and moved the curtain an inch. Outside, gleaming weirdly in the first faint light of day coming over the eastern hills, was a thin even blanket of snow. It lay on the lawn outside, and on the drive, and on her car, parked as she had left it, just anyhow, in the middle of the gravel.

It might be seven, even seven-thirty. She had slept for nine hours then, the longest she had slept in months. She let the curtain fall back, and as she glanced idly at the table beside her, her gaze fell on something in the center of the table; in the midst of the muddle of newspapers and country magazines and books, was a photograph frame, an old-fashioned silver photograph frame, ornate and heavy. And in the frame was a photograph of herself, standing at the award ceremony in London with her arms flung out and her hair lit up like a halo. Alexia stared and stared at it. Then she lifted her head and stared at the sleeping figure in the armchair. She edged round the armchair so that her face was only inches from his. What did it mean? Why did he have her photograph?

His eyes opened. He smiled. He showed no surprise at finding her nose almost touching his.

"What are you doing here?" she whispered, so as not to wake Carly. "What are you here for?"

"Protecting you," he said, "I didn't want you to wake in the night and feel worried or afraid."

"What happened? What happened with Martin? Why didn't you wake me? Are you all right? Was he rude to you? Is it going to be all right? Why have you got my photograph?"

Duncan turned slightly in his chair so that he could cup her face in his hands.

"It's going to be fine," he said.

"Really, oh really? Oh Duncan —"

"He's a pathetic fellow, really, but there's no harm in him. He's failed himself, that's the trouble, and he's finding your success hard to face."

"But Carly? What about Carly?"

Duncan's hands tightened a little. She didn't want him ever to let go.

"We're all to meet. You, him, Carly and me."

"No!"

"Yes," Duncan said. "Yes. I'll be with you. Nothing can happen. But she has to know her father. She has to."

Slowly, Alexia nodded. "But you'll come? You'll stay with us? You promise?"

"I promise." A little shadow fell on his face, and he took his hands away.

"He asked me something painful too. I'm afraid, Alexia, that he asked about Peter Burton. He wanted to know — I don't quite know how to put this — he wanted to know if —"

"If what?"

Duncan said grimly, "If you had been going to marry him."

"No," Alexia said. A light was dawning in her mind, a beautiful bright, joyful light. "No. Peter asked me to but I refused because I didn't love him, so he went away. I couldn't love him because —"

"Because?"

She took a deep breath. "Because however hopeless it is, I was already in love with you."

"With me?"

"Yes," she said, "with you."

"Dear heaven," Duncan said, "dear bountiful heaven," and then he pulled her to him and kissed her roughly on the mouth.

She clung to him. Still kissing, she moved herself round the chair until he could lift her into his arms and hold her there, hard against him. After a little rapturous while, she struggled free.

"But what about Fiona?"

"What about Fiona?"

"You're going to marry her. Elsie said —"

He said incredulously, "Marry Fiona! What nonsense. I was never going to marry Fiona. I proposed to her when I was twenty and she very sensibly turned me down, and I've spent some time with her recently because we've our childhoods in common and it stopped me from sitting here alone gazing down the loch at Castle Bewick and eating my heart out."

"Oh Duncan —"

He pressed her against him again, his mouth moving down her neck to the warm skin inside the open collar of her shirt. His voice came to her, muffled by the kissing.

"You asked why I've got your photograph. I've

got it because I'm in love with you. Why have I stayed away from you? Because I loved you and I thought you loved someone else. Why do I send you stupid damn Christmas trees and lilies the color of your hair? Because I love you, I adore you, and I've done so since you turned on me at our first meeting at the castle and told me I didn't know the first thing about you, and I realized that knowing about you was all I wanted to do, then and forever. Why didn't I come out with all this two years ago? Because, as Fiona rightly says, I'm a dull old bachelor with stuffy old-fashioned ways who a girl like you, a beautiful, talented, adorable girl like you wouldn't give a second thought to."

"But I have, I have, I've thought about nothing else! Oh Duncan, I've longed and *longed* for you!"

He stopped kissing her neck and raised his head to look at her.

"You're a miracle to me, Alexia."

She shook her head. "No. No, it's the other way about —"

"What?" demanded a voice behind them, "what you doing?"

They turned. There, her ruffled head appearing over the sofa back, stood Carly, glaring at them.

Duncan said, laughing, "I'm kissing your mother. Do you want to join in?"

"Yes," Carly said decidedly. Her head bobbed out of sight and then reappeared as she scrambled off the sofa and came towards them, towing her quilt, "Carly do kissing too."

And then she held up her arms to him, and laughing still, Duncan bent down to scoop her up into the chair with them, and into his embrace.

Carly

Chapter One

June 1988

My twenty-first birthday, which should have been a perfect day, ended in a row. It was a colossal row, between my mother and me, and I know we said all sorts of things we should never have said and I also know we both regretted a lot of those things later. Don't get me wrong, I loved my mother, and she loved me. I loved her and I admired her, but at twenty-one, I just couldn't live with her any more.

I grew up in one of the most beautiful places on earth. At least I think so. It's called Bewick, and it's a village and a couple of big houses scattered along the shore of a sea loch in the Western Highlands of Scotland. My mother owns one of the big houses and my stepfather owns the other. My mother's house is called Castle Bewick and it's the most wonderful house I know. It's a magical house. It's got everything you would want if you were designing a castle for a fairy tale — towers, turrets, pinnacles, battlements, arches, and huge old doors with curly black hinges. Because of its outlandish appearance, and because it's got so many windows, it always looks to me as if it were only lightly poised there, on the edge of the loch, and might, one autumn evening, just cut its moorings and drift away into the mist on the water.

If it did, of course, it would take a lot of pretty surprised tourists with it, because my mother turned it into a hotel when she was only a year older than I am now. I think that's a pretty amazing thing to have done. She says she did it because she remembers herself at my age as being afraid of almost everything and everybody and only any good at washing up. My great-uncle James gave her the house when my father left her, and she was pregnant with me, and he said, "Here's Castle Bewick. Now get on with it." So she got on with it and started one of the first ever country house hotels, and now of course, it's very famous and people come from all over the world to stay there, and it's covered with awards and trophies and stars.

I lived there until I was three. My mother and I had a room high up on the second floor, and my bed was in a little kind of cupboard off her room. That room is now a single hotel room, and my cupboard is a bathroom, a dear little ingenious bathroom with everything you could wish for fitted into a tiny space, and a romantic slit window, like an arrow slit, looking up the loch. I don't really remember sleeping there very clearly, except for the Christmas night when I was given my stuffed dog on wheels by Uncle James and Aunt Mary. I remember that all right. I don't think I've ever been so pleased with any present in my whole life as I was with Dog on Wheels. I remember lying in my bed in the cupboard just gazing at him in adoration. I've still got him, actually. He looks very well for a dog of nearly nineteen even though he's lost an eye.

He's in my bedroom at Inverbrae. Inverbrae is my stepfather's house, and my mother and I went to live there after they got married. I must be one of the few people around who really likes their stepfather. He's pretty stuffy and old-fashioned about some things, but he's one of the kindest people I've ever met in an absolutely nonfussy way, and he's strictly fair. Although I used to make a bit of a song and dance about it when I was fourteen, I can't honestly say that, after my two half-brothers were born, he treated them and me any differently. In fact, I think he was a lot tougher on Jamie and Xan (he's Alexander really, but as my mother is Alexia, he had to have a nickname so that we weren't always getting mixed up) than he's ever been on me. He's also the only person who can really cope with my mother. Ma is such an odd mixture, partly a very professional, successful hotelier with an extremely strong will, and partly someone really vulnerable who can't bear it if people don't love her. I *do* love her. I just can't keep saying so.

Inverbrae isn't romantic like Castle Bewick. It's a big, solid Victorian house with square rooms and wide windows and too much red mahogany everywhere. Castle Bewick is light and feminine, and Inverbrae is heavy and masculine, but whereas you feel the castle might just drift off into the mist, you feel that Inverbrae will still be standing there in thousands of years' time. It's the safest-feeling house I've ever known. Ma ran away with me there once, on a wild January night, because she thought my father was coming to kidnap me, and Duncan, my stepfather, always says it was the night his life began. I don't remember much about it, except for the dogs, and being in a big chair with them both and not wanting Duncan to kiss me because he needed a shave.

He took over the business side of the hotel when they were married. He said my mother was quite orderly, but has no real feel for figures — she could only remember which the debit column was by reminding herself that it was the one nearest to the window. Of course, by marrying, they united their two estates, so there really is an enormous amount of land, and two big houses, for Jamie and Xan and me to inherit, and somehow I didn't like that. We didn't have a luxurious upbringing at all — Duncan would never have allowed it — but we didn't have to struggle either, and as I got older, I began to feel a bit stifled. This was one of the things I tried to explain to Ma and she took it all wrong and said furiously that she had worked, largely with her own hands, for twenty years to get what she had got. I knew she had. I was just trying to explain that I needed to feel I had earned my life, that I wasn't just being given it, but she wouldn't listen.

The day began so well. You never can really rely on weather in the Western Highlands — at least, you can only rely on rain — but my birthday dawned fair and calm and still, with the view down the loch sharp and clear. I woke very early. I got out of bed carefully, so as not to wake my current spaniel — Duncan has given me spaniels ever since I came to live at Inverbrae — who hates getting up with a passion, and I went over to the window and looked out and thought that I couldn't ever get tired of this view, not if I never saw another one. And yet I *wanted* to see other ones — I was eaten up by restlessness. That was another part of the quarrel.

Then I put on my jeans, and a new white T-shirt and an old gray jersey of Duncan's — Duncan is pretty big so all his jerseys are a very satisfactory forty-six-inch chest — and went downstairs to have a look at the world before anyone else got up and wanted to look at it too. It's funny how people don't understand about privacy, they think if you're alone you must be lonely, but I really like it, just as I like open spaces, and riding and driving too fast, and animals, and all the old people in Bewick, some of whom haven't even been as far as Glasgow in their whole lives, even though it's less than an hour away now, by car.

I went down to the kitchen. It's a lovely kitchen, warm and friendly, full of morning sun, and beautifully done up by Ma so that it's got everything you could want in it but doesn't look at all nineteen-eighties. She's brilliant at that, she's got a really good eye. All three cats were asleep in a row in front of the Aga and they didn't even open an eye when I nearly trod on them as I put the kettle on. Then I went down the long stone passage to the gun room, and let out Duncan's two spaniels, who are beautifully brought up sporting dogs and never try to lick your face or get on sofas or nick biscuits out of your hand like mine does.

The three of us went out into the garden. It was absolutely perfect. I went across the drive to the apron of lawn bounded by a balustrade that hangs, like a natural balcony, above the stupendous view, and I thought to myself that this was a very momentous day, because it marked the end of growing up and the beginning of being grown up. I leaned on the stone of the balustrade and looked down the shining length of water between the rearing hills, to Castle Bewick, with its pinkish walls and sparkling windows and turrets rising out of the trees that grow round it. Duncan, who is not an unburdening sort of man, once told me he used to spend literally hours gazing down the loch at Castle Bewick, and longing for Ma whom he mistakenly thought to be in love with someone else. They wasted two years like that. Two years! I shan't be like that but then I'm a generation later. If I want someone, I'll tell them straight out.

When I turned back to look at the house, the curtains in Ma and Duncan's bedroom had been drawn back, but all the others were still closed — Jamie's, Xan's (teenage boys sleep as if sleep were going to be rationed any minute), and the guest bedroom, where my grandparents were staying. My grandfather was knighted, when I was seventeen, for being such a distinguished physician, but I think he forgets, half the time, that he *is* Sir Stephen Langley. He looks like a heron now, very tall and thin and grey, with his hair slightly slipping backwards, and specs. He is deeply absent-minded. He calls me Cara all the time because that is my grandmother's name — he adores my grandmother with an adoration that is visible for all to see, like a halo — and I suppose Cara and Carly are pretty alike.

We are both Charlotte really of course. Charlotte, like Alexandra, is a family name. The best Charlotte of all was the first Charlotte, whose portrait hangs in the drawing room at Castle Bewick, and who kicked over the traces of being a respectable early Victorian girl and, as the new wife of an army officer, had a wild romantic affair with another man in Afghanistan, a man called Alexander Bewick, and he later married Charlotte, which is why we've got the castle at all. He's glamorous too but not to my mind as glamorous as she is. She was a hopeless housekeeper by all accounts and I don't think she was much of a mother — her only daughter was called Iskandara, poor thing, because that was the Afghan version of Alexandra, and she was born with a deformed leg and married beneath her, in her mother's eyes — but there's something about Charlotte's wild free spirit that I can't resist. I adore her portrait. When I look at it, I see somebody who really lived; she didn't merely exist in a dreary way, from day to day, just getting by. Unfortunately, I don't look like her. Ma does, more and more as she gets older, but I look like my great-grandmother Alexandra, carroty hair and too big a nose. I suppose I look a bit like Cara too, except her hair is dark red still, even though she's nearly seventy and it's natural because she'd be the last person on earth to think of dyeing it.

I like my grandmother. She and my mother

don't get on very well — they're perfectly polite to each other, but they simply aren't relaxed together. Ma is still convinced that Cara (I call her Cara because she asked me to so that when she was terribly old and all her contemporaries had fallen off their perches, there'd still be me left to call her by her Christian name) is disappointed in her or disapproves of her, and Cara who dresses like a tramp and is only interested in all her down-and-outs in Lambeth, just doesn't know how to handle her sophisticated-seeming daughter. Being a granddaughter makes it much easier. When I got into trouble as a teenager — I was *always* in trouble as a teenager, I ran away from boarding school twice in three years — Cara was very understanding. She said she'd been pretty wild as a teenager too, and that it had taken the Second World War to sober her up. The last thing I want is a war, and I don't much want to be sobered up, either.

As I was looking at the guest bedroom window, one of the curtains twitched aside and Cara looked out. She was wearing some of Grandpa's pyjamas, as usually, even though the arms and legs are miles too long. She saw me, and waved and smiled, and then she made tremendous beckoning gestures.

I mouthed, "Do you want me to come up?"

She nodded violently. Perhaps she'd got something for me or perhaps she just wanted some early morning tea. They drink tea all the time, Grandpa and Cara, despite all Grandpa's published papers on the adverse effects of too much caffeine.

I whistled to the dogs, who came at once, as Duncan's dogs always do, and went back in to the kitchen. Ma was making tea. She wore a blue denim shirtwaister with a long, full skirt, and a cowboy belt, and her hair tied back with a spotted scarf. When I came in, she stopped pouring boiling water and came haring across the kitchen and said, "Oh Carly, darling, oh happy birthday, darling Carly, oh happy, happy day!" and we had a tremendous hug. I can hug her easily, it's just saying loving things that's difficult. Then Duncan came in, in the clothes that he has worn all my life, greenish heathery, tweedy kind of clothes and he hugged me and congratulated me, and then I said that Cara seemed to want some tea.

"Be a darling and take it up, then," Ma said, "while I bake the brioche. Birthday brioche."

Needless to say, Ma is a brilliant cook. When I was six or seven, she went away to France to work in some terribly admired French chef's kitchen, and then she sent Jimmie Blair, who is now our head chef, and she's never looked back. She tried to teach me, but I seem to be learning-resistant to cooking. As she has pointed out on several occasions, however, I don't seem learning-resistant to eating.

I put the teapot and two mugs — Cara and Grandpa like mugs but Ma always wants them to have cups and saucers — and a jug of milk on a tray, and went out of the kitchen, leaving Ma singing over her brioche and Duncan pretending to read the *Oban Times* but really watching her, which is his favorite occupation.

I went up the stairs past all the antlered heads which the boys used to have names for — Stalin, I remember, was one and Ted Heath and Elvis and Mickey Mouse — and along the first floor landing, banging on the boys' doors as I went by and shouting "Time!" which was one of our private jokes because Jamie said that's what madams do in brothels when you've had your money's worth. Then I came to the spare room door, and knocked.

"Come in," Cara said.

She was sitting up in bed in her idiotic pyjamas with her glasses on reading a horrible report about child sex abuse. Grandpa was lying on his back in the other twin bed staring at the ceiling and thinking.

"Darling!" Cara said. "Happy birthday!"

Grandpa said, "Whose birthday?"

Cara said, "Oh Stephen, you are the most exasperating man I've ever met," and threw a pillow at him, which missed and went sailing past him and knocked over a glass of water.

"That might have had my teeth in it," Grandpa said reproachfully.

"Except that they're in your mouth."

He sat up and held out his long, thin, striped cotton arms to me.

"Happy birthday, Charlotte Emily."

Cara said, "It's nearly fifty years since I was twenty-one. Extraordinary."

When I had hugged them both and poured out their tea and found Grandpa's glasses, Cara said, "I've got something for you."

"Oh," I said, "I'm afraid I was hoping you had."

She patted the bed. "Come here."

I went and sat on the edge of the bed, and she put an oblong, heavy parcel into my hand, very badly done up in old Christmas paper. Cara never wastes anything. Inside was a small fat old book, bound in red morocco leather. There was no title, nothing on the spine at all. I looked up at Cara.

"It's Emily's diary," Cara said. "It's the one Emily kept in 1841 when she and Charlotte went to Afghanistan. It's the story of Charlotte's love affair with Alexander. It's for you now."

I was so pleased I couldn't speak. I opened the book and looked at the beautiful schoolroom handwriting and then I shut it and stroked the covers, the covers that all those generations of Charlottes and Alexandras had touched. I thought I was going to cry. I leaned forward towards Cara and put my face against hers and she put her arms round me and said, "Oh, I'm so pleased you're so pleased."

I said, "I think it's the best present I ever had since Dog on Wheels. I really do."

"Read it when you've got lots of time. It ought to be read at a sitting. It makes our lives seem very humdrum."

I went downstairs, clutching my diary in a sort of daze. It was like being given a holy relic.

"Look," I said to Ma.

She nodded. "You are absolutely the best person to have it."

Then she gave me her present, a gold chain to wear round my neck, like a Victorian Albert, with a T-bar. I knew she had been going to give me her pearls, which Cara had given her and Alexandra had given Cara, but I asked her not to. I'm not a pearls sort of person, really, and she wears them all the time and they are part of her. She looked sad when I asked her not to give them to me, but relieved too. The chain was lovely, in any case, just my kind of thing, very simple.

Then the boys came down and beat me up a bit and Duncan said there seemed to be a vehicle in the yard for my inspection, he couldn't think where it had come from, and we had a wonderful breakfast, a real, slap-up, huge breakfast with new-laid eggs and new-baked brioche and new-brewed coffee. I felt utterly happy. I went on feeling happy all day, trying out my delicious new birthday car, going for a picnic up to the very top of Archadoon, going down to the hotel to be congratulated by all the staff, most of whom I've known since I was a baby, having an amazing dinner, cooked by Ma, with just the family, which was what I had chosen.

But then it blew. I can't really remember how it started, but I do recall feeling that I must confess now, before I took one more step into my new grown-up life, that I wasn't going to join Ma and Duncan in running the hotel. So I think I just said it, blurted it out.

Ma gazed at me as if I had hit her.

"But, Carly, you've always said that was what you wanted. Why else do that hotel management course? Why spend the last three years learning to do something you don't want to do?"

I tried to explain. I said I had thought I wanted

to go into the business, but as the three years at college in Edinburgh went on, I had realized that I didn't want to, more and more I didn't want to, and what was more even than that, was that I knew I had to get away from Bewick.

That was when the row really blew. My mother accused me of being spoiled and selfish and immature and I screamed at her that she was materialistic and narrow-minded and possessive. We went on and on screaming, louder and louder. It was horrible, and it might have gone on all night if Duncan hadn't suddenly said to me, quite calmly, like someone throwing a bucket of water over two fighting dogs, "Well, if you don't want to work here, what do you want to do?"

I said sulkily, and on a defiant impulse, "I want to be a journalist."

"A journalist!" Ma said in horror. "A journalist! Where?"

"In London."

"In *London!*" she said, and then she stopped. There was a small, disagreeable pause and then she said, in a cold, hard voice, "I see. You want to go to London and live with your father."

Chapter Two

I didn't want to live with my father. I didn't, actually, want to live with anyone (except of course, with some perfectly wonderful man I hadn't met yet), I wanted to be free and by myself. I wasn't quite sure what form this freedom would take but I was very sure of how it would feel, how I wouldn't have to keep taking other people's reactions and feelings into account before I made even the tiniest decision.

To be fair to me, I had tried living with my father. I used to go and stay with him and my stepmother and my other half brother every school holidays, first in a very nasty villa in the Midlands and then in a lovely cottage in Essex and then in a comfortable Edwardian house in south London, depending upon my father's ever-changing jobs. I quite like my father, he's clever and amusing, but I don't really trust him because he's such a fidget, and he's also exactly like Mr. Micawber in *David Copperfield* and always thinks his great good fortune is just around the corner as long as he stops what he's doing at the moment and immediately starts doing something else.

My stepmother, who is called Susie, says that he has had six jobs in twenty years, not counting several false starts. Living with Martin (I call him

Martin not Dad because he doesn't feel a very fatherly kind of father) has worn Susie out. She's really rather pathetic now, very anxious-looking and always sighing and being exhausted, but you can still see very plainly how pretty she once was. There are photographs around of Susie in the sixties and she really was delicious. She told me once that she broke off her relationship with Martin to get engaged to a very wealthy man with vast prospects, but that she couldn't seem to stay away from Martin, who had no money and no prospects. She won't ever discuss Martin's leaving my mother to live with her. I think she feels guilty.

I don't know if Martin feels guilty or not. He's one of those slightly cocky people who would never let you know he felt remorse even if he did. What he plainly does feel about my mother is envy. He's eaten up with it. She has succeeded precisely where he has failed. He was going to be a Harley Street consultant making millions out of Arabs, and he's ended up as sales manager for a small drugs company. My mother was going to be just a good little wife and mother, and she has ended up as something of a hotel-keeping phenomenon. And she married Duncan who has money (though I know she'd have married him anyway) and Martin married Susie who has nothing.

Susie told me that Martin was once absolutely obsessed by her. Looking at them now, not exactly bickering but not exactly companionable either, it's a bit difficult to imagine. They don't have rows, they just needle and have meaningful silences. Ma and Duncan have rows. Not often but they sure have them. The boys and I used to keep a tally of who we thought had won, in chalk marks on the back of the door up to the attic at Inverbrae. It began to come out pretty even, so it got boring and we stopped doing it.

My other half brother — Martin and Susie's son — is called Jake. I feel I must be perfectly honest and confess that I can't stand Jake. He's slightly older than me, and very good looking in a vain, male-modelish way, and he is only interested in his social life. He's the most boring company you can imagine. He buys all those glossy magazines for men — not the pornographic ones because all his fancying energy is taken up by fancying himself — and pores over the articles on clothes and style. He thinks about nothing but style.

If I went down to London to live with my father, I'd have to live with Jake as well which would be a fate worse than death. Jake is supposed to be doing a business studies course at the local polytechnic in south London, but he plays hookey all the time. I tried to explain to my mother that I had neither the intention nor the desire to live with Martin, but she wouldn't listen. She is completely unreasonable when it comes to anything to do with Martin, and always has been. When I was very small, and he came to see me, Duncan always stayed with me, otherwise Ma got hysterical. She calmed down a bit as I grew older and better able to take care of myself, but she has never been able to be normal about my seeing Martin.

"The thing is," she said, "I can't bear to think that you are at all his, that he has any right at all to any part of you."

Without knowing it, she went right to the heart of the matter when she said that. She doesn't want anyone else to have me, but she wants to have me all right herself, and that's what I had to get away from. She wanted all of us to live together in our beautiful, happy, successful little Scottish world where nothing nasty could touch us, and she was appalled to think that one of us wanted to leave the paradise. Well, I did. I wanted to do so very badly and I said so. Then I did it.

I took a train south to London in early July. Only Jamie and Xan came to see me off, at my request. It wasn't at all easy, leaving, although I pretended to be very cool and excited about going away to keep my own spirits up. I don't think the loch had ever looked so beautiful, or all the animals so dear or Ma more in need of reassurance. Jamie drove my new car — I was going to leave it in Scotland until I was settled — and I sat in the passenger seat and craned to see out of the back window as we went down the drive, and there was Ma standing in the circle of Duncan's arm and looking about sixteen and quite forlorn.

"Dad'll cope," Xan said. "He said they've got a VAT inspection which will take her mind off everything, poor thing."

"I didn't mean it to be such a big deal," I said, "I really didn't. I'd no idea she would take it to heart so."

"She takes everything to heart," Jamie said. "It's why the hotel's so good. She minds about everything and everybody."

I turned my head away as we went along the lochside because I didn't want to see the castle. I wasn't at all sure I could stand it. I told myself not to be melodramatic, that I could be back here from London in eight hours any time I wanted, but I still felt that deep down some really enormous parting was taking place.

Xan said, "Mind you get a flat big enough for us to doss down in."

"Look here," I said, "I'm leaving Bewick precisely to get away from you. I don't want you and Jamie and your smelly friends all over my nice new life, thank you very much. Get it?"

"Charming," Xan said, and gave my head a light cuff from behind.

I began to feel better. It was easier to be teased than to be sympathized with or mourned over. Jamie started singing. He can't sing, but that doesn't stop him, and Xan and I joined in and we went over the pass and down towards Loch Lomond singing our heads off, and I quite forgot to cry.

When we got to Glasgow Central Station, the boys bought me a whole lot of chocolate and some dreadful comics — on the principle that that is what *they* like on train journeys — and found my seat and said watch out for the old lady in the corner, she's really a white slaver, and then they gave me a couple of rough, doggy hugs and went loping off down the platform. It was horrible seeing them go. I even had a moment of thinking I'd just seize my bags and rush shrieking after them, but luckily I managed to sit quite still until the moment had passed. Then I put all the comics on an empty seat across the aisle so that any passenger with similar depraved tastes to Jamie and Xan could have the benefit of them, and settled myself in my corner with the treat I had been saving up for myself for this moment — the treat of reading Emily's journal.

I had packed it in my grey canvas holdall in a padded envelope. I took it out now, and held it on my lap while the train filled up with other passengers. I wanted to think about it before I started it, to form some sort of image in my mind's eye of the girl who wrote it and the girls it was about, Emily and Charlotte Brent. In 1840 they would have been about my age, and they had been brought up very primly in Richmond by their widowed mother. Cara told me that. She said their little house in Richmond is still standing, although it has been much added to, and I had already determined, when I was in London, that I would go and see it. I shut my eyes. I wanted to picture Charlotte and Emily in 1840, in their tight-waisted, full-skirted dresses, with their hair (Charlotte's dark red, Emily's lighter, like mine) neatly braided up under straw bonnets. Two good little early Victorian misses.

"Except," Cara had said, "that Charlotte wasn't good at all. As you will see."

The train started with an apologetic little jolt and then slid smoothly out of the station. I made myself wait until we were well clear of the heart of the city before I opened the padded envelope and slid the fat little red book out into my hand. I opened it. It felt like lifting the lid on a treasure chest.

" 'Praise the Lord,' " said the first line, " 'Praise the Lord,' Charlotte said, 'George is coming tomorrow,' and she threw the letter so that it whirled about the room like a seagull and then came to rest in the log basket."

I didn't notice time passing on that train journey. I didn't notice my fellow passengers either and it never struck me to go staggering along to the buffet car for even a cup of coffee. I just read. I don't think I have ever read anything with such total absorption in my life. Emily's handwriting was very clear and easy, and I read it as if it were print. I followed the girls from Richmond all the way to India, and then all the way through the Khyber Pass to Kabul, and then all the hideous frightening way back through the pass to the prison fort at Budeabad. I met Charlotte's poor first husband, Hugh, and then the devastating Alexander and I met kind, steady Richard Talbot who was to become Emily's husband. I shuddered at Hugh's sending away the little leper child, and at the menace of Kabul, and at Charlotte's astonishing risk taking and the cold and the savagery and the truly terrible slaughter in the Khyber Pass. I could imagine myself wherever Emily was, I could see the harsh mountains ringing Kabul, against the blue sky, and Charlotte's exotic house, furnished from the bazaar, that the English regimental ladies so disapproved of, and the hopeful little garden that Richard Talbot made inside their fortress prison. I could smell things too, and touch them and hear them, and, above all, I could feel the passion of the relationship between Charlotte and Alexander. It was incredibly romantic. They were both, quite literally, prepared to risk anything for one another, and often they did. They were like a pair of beautiful panthers somehow, untamed and unordinary. I was completely captivated.

When the train finally drew into King's Cross, I could hardly remember where I was. I looked out of the carriage window and expected to see wild mountainsides and yelling Afghan tribesmen, but there were only the usual sort of people you see everywhere, dressed in grey and navy blue and fawn, as if they hope their clothes will make them invisible.

I got up, feeling as if I'd been asleep, and fumbled Emily's diary into its envelope, then stuffed that into my holdall and heaved everything else off the rack, and almost fell off the train onto the platform. This arrival in London should have been a great moment, but because of Emily's diary, I couldn't think straight, and I must have looked as if I was drunk.

I got myself somehow to the taxi rank. I was going to stay for a few nights with a school friend, a girl called Sasha Wallace, who had a flat in Redcliffe Gardens. She had won a talent contest, and was working for an extremely luxurious magazine, and she said I could stay with her for a few days while I sorted myself out. Of course, I could have gone to Culver Square and stayed with Cara and Grandpa, but Cara had the tact not even to suggest it. As Ma often said, she was as good at handling me as she'd been bad at handling her. Cara knew that when I said I wanted to be free, I meant it.

I sat in the taxi, and looked rather dazedly at London. I don't think I'll ever learn to love London. Poor London, so taken over by foreigners it doesn't even feel English any more in the way that Glasgow and Edinburgh still feel distinctly Scottish. I've no idea where the taxi went, and it seemed to take ages, and I suddenly realized that I was starving hungry. I also realized that I felt a bit small and nervous.

Sasha's flat was in a huge house with a vast porch on pillars. There was a whole line of bells beside the front door with labels next to them. Sasha's said "Wallace, Preston and Thoroughgood." They sounded like a firm of solicitors. I pressed the bell, and almost at once Sasha's voice said loudly out of the grille by my ear, "Hello?"

"It's me," I said to the grille. "It's Carly."

"Great," she said, "push the door and come on up. Third floor."

I bumped and dragged my bags up a gloomy stairwell carpeted in the kind of carpet my mother despises, all swirly and whirly with a lot of orange and brown in it. When I finally got to the third floor, the front door of one of the flats was open, and in the doorway Sasha was standing wearing skintight jeans and a sleeveless black T-shirt and dark red lipstick.

I dropped everything in a great heap. Sasha kissed me.

"Great to see you," she said, "simply great. Come on in. Meet Lally. And Simon. Have a drink, have some wine."

There was a tall, thin, fair girl in the little sitting room, in jeans and a silk shirt and pearls. Very Sloaney. She said, "Hi. Lalage Thoroughgood."

I said rather feebly, "I'm Carly."

Then a very nice looking dark boy in a green polo shirt said, "And I'm Simon. Are you all right?"

"Actually," I said, "I'm starving. I forgot to eat on the train."

"Poor you," Sasha said, "I'll find some bread. Hang on."

Simon went out on to the landing and hauled in all my bags. Thoroughgood looked at them as if they were dustbin bags.

"Heavens. I don't know where we're going to put all that —"

"Behind the sofa!" Sasha shouted from the kitchen.

"I thought she was going to *sleep* behind the sofa —"

"I'll sleep wherever you like," I said hastily.

"No, you won't," said Simon. "Why should you?"

Sasha came out of the kitchen licking her fingers with a plateful of oozing rye bread sandwiches.

"Tuna. Will that do? What d'you think of the flat?"

I looked round. After years and years of my mother's comfortable, pretty taste, it looked bare and bleak.

"Minimalist," Sasha said. "Cool."

She sat down on the floor, cross-legged, and lit a cigarette.

"Welcome to London," Simon said. He winked at me.

A car honked in the street outside, imperiously. Lally ran to the window.

"Oh," she said, "what a bore. Gustav." But she went out of the flat at a rate of knots, all the same.

Chapter Three

Independence is, quite frankly, easier said than done. I stayed four nights with Sasha and Lally and Simon, sleeping on the sofa — Simon wanted to lend me his bed but I wouldn't have it — but four nights was quite enough. There wasn't really enough room for three people in the flat, let alone four, and, however nice they were, I couldn't help feeling in the way. I tried to keep all my belongings crammed behind the sofa, but bits kept seeping out, sweater arms and jeans legs and odd socks and paperbacks, and Lally had a strong line in sarcastic sighing when she fell over one of my shoes, or I left all my washing things less than regimented in the bathroom.

During the day, I went to seven separate agencies and looked at a total of nineteen flats and they were all, for various reasons, no good: too big, too expensive, too utterly sordid or depressing. I had stupidly visualized myself in a charming attic flat with sloping ceilings and a view of treetops in a London square and a balcony or windowsill on which I would grow herbs and feed the birds. I only saw one attic flat and it was pitch dark and had skylight windows and just looking at it plunged me in gloom. None of the others exactly cheered me up either, and I got very tired, not just physically, but of being fed all that awful estate agent's jargon, where spacious turns out to mean slightly bigger than a cupboard and quaint is only another word for creepy.

On the third afternoon, I was sitting irritably in a café in the Fulham Road having a cappuccino, and reflecting in exasperation that I had got, in three days, precisely nowhere, when it struck me that I was being a bit obstinate about this freedom thing, and that there really was no shame in asking people for help if you thought they could give you some at not too much cost to themselves. Having thought this, and felt better, and ordered a second cappuccino, I then remembered Amanda.

Amanda is a very unlikely friend of Ma's. She's unlikely because she is the complete opposite to Ma, highly, slickly urban and appearing to take nothing seriously, but she has been a wonderful friend to Ma ever since Ma went to work for her, fresh out of school and, as Amanda said, "all smudged mascara and panic." Amanda has been to stay at Castle Bewick every year since it opened, and Ma won't let her pay now. We used to love her coming up to Bewick because she was like some enamelled, burnished, exotic bird to us, very sharp-tongued and funny. Sometimes she came with a man called Victor, whom she was hopelessly in love with. We didn't like him much, because he seemed very dull to us and also we thought he ought to leave his wife and marry Amanda. But he never did, and then he died of cancer, and Amanda came up to Bewick looking like a broken bird, all the gloss and glamour gone, and Ma had to almost nurse her for weeks. When she didn't bring Victor, Amanda brought Felicity, who used to be her business partner, but who left to marry an Austrian. Amanda said Felicity's Austrian was an arms dealer. Felicity, who is quite different from Amanda and what you might describe as a pure party animal, always said she didn't care what he was as long as he gave her heaps of money and didn't expect her to be wifely. Sometimes, I have to say, I was rather shocked by Felicity, but I expect that's because I'm not a child of the swinging sixties.

Anyway, I drank my second cappuccino — it was very good: the café owner was extremely generous with the grated chocolate on top — and went out into the Fulham Road, and wondered how to get to Amanda. It wasn't a blazing hot day, just one of those rather dreary medium English summer days where there's more cloud than sun, but I really didn't feel I could walk all the way to Knightsbridge, where Amanda now lived, after all the depressing trailing round the wrong flats I'd already done. So I hailed a taxi. Ma was brought up never to take them, on moral grounds, and although she could now afford taxis every minute of the day, she still hesitates before getting into one. I got into mine, and said "Lowndes Square, please," and sat back and felt very relieved and, I'm afraid, not at all guilty.

Amanda's business, which started, Ma says, in a damp basement with old shoeboxes instead of filing cabinets, has boomed. It's now called The Chelsea Curtain Company and it has a showroom in the King's Road with workrooms above it. I simply can't imagine being able to bear spending a quarter of a century making curtains, and Amanda said quite frankly nor can she but look at what it's brought her — a mews house in London and a farmhouse in Tuscany. But not Victor. Whatever she says, she'd have given the whole lot up to have had Victor.

As it was after five-thirty by the time the taxi crawled into the Brompton Road through the traffic, I thought I'd chance finding Amanda at home. If she wasn't I would just sit on her door-step until she was. She has a little white doll's house — Ma says it's just like the little pink doll's house she used to share with Felicity, where Ma went to work — with burgeoning window boxes and a lipstick-red front door. Inside this conventional and pretty exterior is a great surprise — black and white marble floors and astonishing modern Italian furniture and no curtains, only severe black blinds. I suppose twenty-five years of making frilly chintz pelmets and tie-backs are bound to cause a reaction.

I paid the taxi off and got out. I wondered if I looked rather scruffy for Amanda, so I peered into her dining room window to see my reflection. Nobody, not even if they were besotted with me, could call me pretty, but at least my face isn't dull. My nose is too big and my mouth is too wide, but I do have dark eyelashes despite this ginger mop which does what it wants to do no matter how much I, or a hairdresser, tries to persuade or threaten it to do otherwise. Peering at my reflection, I ruffled my hair up a bit and tucked my T-shirt in neatly. Then I rang the bell.

Amanda opened the door. She was wearing a black linen jump suit and she didn't look at all surprised.

"Ah," she said.

"Were you expecting me?"

"Of course," she said. "You haven't got anywhere to live and you haven't got a job. Right? It's very odd how like your mother you can be when you aren't really like her at all. Come in."

I went in and sat on one of her white leather chairs. It was like a deck chair, only made of white leather and chrome.

"Are you hungry?"

"I'm afraid so," I said. I was always hungry.

She went out into her tiny kitchen, which was hardly a kitchen really but just a gleaming white and chrome alcove where she opened champagne and oysters, and came back with an unopened packet of Chelsea buns.

"All for you. They've been sitting in the fridge waiting for you ever since Alexia rang me in tears to say you'd gone and I knew you'd turn up here sooner or later."

I had a pang at the thought of Ma.

"In tears?"

"Your darling mamma," Amanda said, "cries at the flick of a switch. Do you?"

"No," I said, "I get cross instead."

Amanda lit a cigarette.

"Eat those buns. Now then, tell me what you've been doing."

Jeannie Blair, who was my nanny while I was little and Ma was working, used to fly into a rage if I talked when my mouth was full, so I tried to talk to Amanda with it only half full.

"I've trailed round nineteen of the dreariest flats you can possibly imagine and I'm staying with an old school friend and her two flatmates and they are being very nice but I'm in the way and I feel I get more in the way every day and that I ought to move out, I *want* to move out, I just can't find anywhere to go."

Amanda blew out a cloud of smoke. "I see."

"So I came to ask if you could suggest anywhere I might turn to, other agencies, or friends with coal holes they're not using."

"You could turn to me."

"I couldn't stay here!"

"No, you certainly couldn't. But you could stay above the shop."

I put my bun down on my knee and stared at her.

"There are a couple of empty rooms on the top floor, above the workrooms. You could use the staff loos and I've put in a shower for them too. And we could rig up something for you to cook on."

"Amanda?"

"But —"

"What but?"

"You have got to get yourself a job. I won't have you up there if you aren't working. Ma said you wanted to be a journalist."

I went scarlet. That had been an invention on the spur of the moment. All I knew was that I didn't want to run a hotel; I didn't have the first clue as to what I wanted to do instead.

"I see," said Amanda. "As I thought. You haven't a clue."

I said, stammering a little, "I want to do something constructive, a bit helpful —"

"Helpful? What on earth do you mean? Soup kitchens?"

"I don't know," I said. "The thing is —"

"What is the thing?"

I was very doubtful about explaining my heartfelt but hazy ambitions to Amanda, but I'd got myself into a corner and I clearly had to attempt it.

"I feel . . . I feel I've been so privileged all my life, so sheltered, that things have been so easy and interesting that I'd like, I'd like —"

I stopped because Amanda had lowered her dark glasses for a minute to look at me, and I always found that unnerving.

She said, "Carly treasure, that's your age. It's like spots. You'll soon grow out of it."

"I rather mean it —"

"I don't doubt it. And I mean what I said too. You can live above the shop as long as you're employed. If it's making coffee in a newspaper office or soup for Cardboard City, I don't care. I just can't stand people who don't *work*."

"I will," I said, "I want to. I'm going to."

"Then bring the remaining buns," Amanda said, "and we'll go and look at the rooms."

I couldn't believe it. There, high above the King's Road with a glimpse, even, of some trees in Chelsea Hospital Gardens, were two sloping ceilinged rooms with windows, with windowsills. I had been expecting dusty attic rooms full of boxes and clutter and the usual things people put in attics because they can't think of what else to do with them, and they can't quite bear to throw them away either, but these rooms had cream-washed walls and lovely seagrass matting on the floor, woven in flat plaits.

"I was going to have my office up here," Amanda said. "I thought I'd get a bit of peace and quiet, but it was hopeless. The staff interrupted me just as much and spent hours gossiping on the telephone when I wasn't down there to snarl at them, so I went down again to the shop floor to everyone's disappointment."

"I *love* it!" I said.

I did. My mind was already whirling with images of how the rooms would look with furniture in them, and my books, and a big squashy cushion on the floor to lie on for reading, and the sunset coming in all rosy and glowing from the west. I saw myself coming in from work — perhaps in a suit? I'd never owned a suit — with my supper in a supermarket bag, and turning on lamps and some music and . . .

"Won't you be lonely?"

I'd never thought about it. I said, "Why should I be?"

"Because you have lived in a perfect dog basket of people all your life and London is very lonely."

I looked round the room we were standing in. It couldn't have looked more welcoming if it had tried, even though it contained nothing but a night storage heater and, for some reason, a blue plastic bucket.

"I think I'll just feel private."

Amanda shrugged. "I want a hundred pounds

346

a month and the loos and shower left sparkling."

"I promise."

"And I want you to find a job in three weeks."

"I'll try —"

She looked at me again with her glasses lowered.

"You'll *do* it."

I slept there the next night on a blowup mattress lent to me by Simon Preston. He was extremely kind in other matters too, and took me to an electrical discount place to buy a kettle and a toaster and two lamps, and then helped me to settle in. He toiled up and down the two flights of stairs most uncomplainingly with all my stuff, and then said he was taking me out for a pizza.

I sat opposite him in the pizza place and thought I had almost never seen anyone so clean looking. His dark hair shone and his teeth gleamed and his hands and nails were a reproach to mine. He was peaceful company because he was openly friendly without being flirtatious and I don't really like being flirted with. Other people think it's a lovely game, and it certainly looks like that from the outside, but I don't seem to know how to play and I don't much want to. Jamie and Xan always used to tease me and say I was Little Miss Lonelyheart Waiting for the Big One, and the awful thing is that they are right and it's true. It seems to run in the family, this kind of singlemindedness in matters of the heart. All very well, but sometimes, in the middle of the night, I have wondered what will happen if I don't ever meet The Big One? Or I do and he's already married to someone else?

I asked Simon if it was easy living with Sasha and Lally.

"Of course it is. Why shouldn't it be?"

"I just wondered. I mean, suppose you began to fancy one of them —"

Simon grinned at me. "No problem, Carly. I don't go out with girls."

The light broke. I grinned back.

"Nor do I," I said.

He laughed and poured me a glass of wine.

"Have you got a fellow?"

"I did have. I had one for two years at college in Edinburgh, but then I noticed that he was looking in real estate agents' windows a lot and talking about state versus private education, and so I thought it had better stop before I found myself in a suburban semidetached worrying about how clean my windows were."

Simon said, "Didn't you love him?"

"Oh yes, I did. But it had turned into a rather cosy kind of love."

"What do you want then?"

Our pizzas came. They looked wonderful, huge and crisp and sizzling.

I said, "I'd like something more exciting."

"Do you like olives?"

"Love them."

"You'd better have mine, then," Simon said, and carefully picked the olives off his pizza with the blade of his knife and transferred them to my plate. Then he said, "You'd better meet my friend Tom Pasco."

"Is he —"

"Gay? No. Just exciting."

"I've got to get a job next," I said, wolfing pizza. I was starving hungry. "I can't think about anything exciting until I've found a job."

"I'll talk to the features editor on my magazine," Simon said. "She's quite nice as journalists go."

"Oh thank you! You're being so kind —"

He said simply, "That's all right. I like helping people."

When I got back to my rooms, I thought I would feel very happy and contented, but I didn't seem to. I felt restless and unsettled, and fidgeted about wondering what I could do rather than go to bed, which didn't seem a very appetizing prospect. In the end, having moved my mattress from one corner to all the others, and back to the first one, I made a cup of coffee with water boiled in my new kettle — I'd forgotten to buy any milk — and lay on the mattress with Emily's journal, thinking I would distract myself with a little re-reading.

But reading about Charlotte only made the mental restlessness worse. What was the matter with me? I had left home, been given charming rooms to live in within a week of getting to London, and had a kind new friend who said he would help me find a job. Wasn't that exactly what I had wanted?

Then it dawned on me. It wasn't what I wanted at all. I didn't, in my heart of hearts, want a cosy domestic nest in the King's Road to which I returned each evening, wearing the suit I also didn't want, to cook a sensible supper for one. I didn't want to work shut up in an office and — dreadful to admit this after all the fuss I'd caused — I didn't want to be in London either. I lifted the precious red book above my head in both hands and looked at it fixedly. What I wanted, I realized, like that long-ago Charlotte had wanted, was adventure.

Chapter Four

I had a dream that night that people were ringing and ringing at the shop door, all longing to come in and order curtains, and I wasn't sure if I should let them in because it was the middle of the night. In the end, I thought I had better go down and explain that Amanda would be very pleased to see them all at nine thirty, but not before, and as I roused myself to do this, it dawned on me that it was not the middle of the night, but early in the morning, and the shop bell was actually the telephone on the floor below.

It had been ringing for so long I thought the person at the other end would be bound to give up any second, so I simply flew downstairs in a panic and fell gasping on the receiver.

"Hello? Hello? Are you still there?"

"Oh Carly," Ma said, "I'm so relieved. Did I wake you?"

"It doesn't matter, I was just afraid you'd give up. Are you all right?"

"Not terribly," Ma said. Her voice shook a bit. I panicked at once.

"Is Duncan okay? And the boys?"

"Oh yes. They're fine. They're here with me. It's Mary. Your great-aunt Mary. She died last night. She —"

"Oh Ma," I said.

"It was a heart attack, very sudden and quick. She wouldn't have known anything. But it's James, really, poor James —"

"And you," I said.

Ma had loved Aunt Mary. Aunt Mary had, during her childhood, been all the cosy, sweet, motherly things that Cara could never be. Aunt Mary couldn't have a baby of her own and so Ma became that baby, and when Ma found she was pregnant, she went home, as she felt it was, to Uncle James and Aunt Mary's farm at Bishopstow in Cornwall. I was born there, in the room Cara was born in. I would have liked best, of course, to have been born at Bewick, but if I couldn't have that, then Bishopstow was a very good second best.

I remembered Aunt Mary as very sweet in a trembling sort of way. She was very nervous, and prone to breakdowns, but she was incapable of thinking or doing anything unkind, and she had great gifts; she was extremely clever and very musical. She wasn't really a natural farmer's wife at all, but she had adapted herself to it wonderfully, and did the farm accounts, and kept the books for Uncle James's clotted cream business, which wasn't doing quite so well now, what with everyone being in such a panic about cholesterol.

Ma said, "I'm coming down to London on Wednesday, darling. I'll stay the night with Amanda, and then I thought we could drive to Cornwall together for the funeral."

"Of course," I said. I wanted to go with her, and I knew I ought to, but I also knew I ought to get on with sorting out my life. That would just have to wait a week, I reflected.

"Duncan will stay here and keep an eye on things."

"So it'll just be you. Does Cara know?"

"It was Cara who rang me. Do you realize that the house Cara rescued Mary from in 1943 is only fifty yards from where you're living now? Cara said she feels as if she's lost a child, in a way."

And you, I thought, feel as if you'd lost a mother, in a way.

"I'll see you on Wednesday, Ma," I said. "Try not to be too sad. Love to the others."

I went back upstairs and dressed and then I went down to the early summer morning. It was lovely then, the air felt cool and clean, and the King's Road looked all sleepy and shuttered. I wandered down to the supermarket that never seemed to shut, and bought myself a croissant and an apple, and then I went on south — how Jeannie would have fumed to see me eating in the street — to the turning where the once bombed house stood that had trapped Mary.

Of course, it had been mended long ago, and now looked very expensive and Chelsea, with a dark green front door and a lot of brass knobs and numbers and Amanda's kind of ruched and ruffled curtains at the windows. But in 1943, it had been owned by someone called Mrs. Violet Pink, who had let out rooms to single girls working in London. Mary had actually been in her room when the house was hit, prostrated with grief after my great-uncle Alex, to whom she had been engaged, was killed. It was difficult to imagine, looking at the calm, prosperous white front of the house now, that it had ever seen such dramas.

I stood there for quite a long time, licking the last delicious buttery flakes of croissant off my fingers, and gazing at the house. It occurred to me that however illogical it might seem to envy anyone who had been involved in anything as terrible as the Second World War, I *did* envy Mary and Cara. I envied them the tension and the excitement of those times, even though I knew it had brought agonizing loss and grief too. Quite simply, seeing it from the peacetime safety of 1988, I envied them the adventure. Standing there on the early morning pavement, biting into my apple, I longed and longed to know, as they had known, the true value of the preciousness of life.

Ma and I took it in turns to drive all the way to Cornwall. During the journey, she told me a great deal about her childhood holidays at Bishopstow, and how she loved being there so much that she used to cry like a waterfall every time she had to go back to London.

"Of course James and Mary spoiled me terribly, and made me feel I was very clever and pretty special, but I also think I learned about the importance of home comforts there and how people love being looked after and well fed. Are you eating properly?"

"I'm eating heaps," I said truthfully. It is an amazing stroke of luck that I seem to stay the same shape when you consider what I stuff in.

"But properly. *Well*. I hope you aren't just eating junk."

I said, "I'll make up for it in Cornwall, I'll eat only the purest things for three days."

"I see," Ma said. "So you are existing on burgers and buns."

"And apples."

"And what about a job?"

"Ma," I said, changing gear to overtake a lorry, "you are as bad as Amanda."

"I don't want you to squander —" she stopped.

"Squander what?"

She gave a little self-conscious laugh.

"I caught myself sounding just like Cara talking to me twenty years ago. When I vowed I never would."

"Happens to us all."

"Yes," Ma said, and then she looked very sad. As I said, she has Charlotte's lovely face, but I can't imagine Charlotte's looking sad. Grief-stricken perhaps, or wildly happy, but not just sad. "Like dying," Ma said. "That happens to us all too."

Bishopstow felt quite different without Mary. Since Lyddy and June, the two stalwart retainers of the household, had died within three months of each other ten years before, Mary's had been the only female presence in the house except for someone who came up from Bishopstow village twice weekly to help clean. I remembered Lyddy as a very old woman in an armchair in the kitchen, who used to tell me I was the spitting image of my great-grandmother, Alexandra, carroty hair and temper and all, and June as a tiny, bent figure, always in dungarees who took me to find eggs in the hay and let me watch a litter of piglets being born. Lyddy died first, in hospital, which she hated, and June died soon after because the two of them had been together for so long that there wasn't any point to life if they couldn't be together any more. I know that when they had gone, both Ma and Cara found it quite difficult to go down to Bishopstow for a while.

"You don't realize," Cara said, "what huge chunks of your landscape people occupy until they die."

The same was true of Aunt Mary. Poor Uncle James had done his best, but Aunt Mary had loved flowers and filled the house with them, and now there weren't any except for a single depressing pot of shop chrysanthemums in the hall. Uncle James was a big, round, fresh-faced man, the epitome of a West Country farmer, but he seemed to have shrunk, and his flesh hung on him as if it were clothes that were far too big for him. He was pathetically pleased to see Ma, and wanted her with him all the time. He was, she always said, the one person besides Duncan and Amanda who knew the extent of her professional achievement, because he knew she wasn't naturally a confident person at all. She kept close to Uncle James all those three days, not saying much, but just being there, holding his hand or simply sitting beside him while he talked about Aunt Mary.

I ought to have learned a great deal about love from listening to Uncle James talking about Aunt Mary, but I'm ashamed to say, I didn't learn it until much later when I had to find it out for myself. I ought to have learned then about tenderness, and about caring for someone else's vulnerable side, and about mutual respect and about appreciating what it is to be loved by someone else. Uncle James knew about all these things. Aunt Mary had been very fragile in many ways and he had loved protecting her.

"Who am I going to look after now?" he said to Ma.

The funeral was in Bishopstow church which is lovely, tiny and grey and half sunk in a hillside. It was absolutely crammed with flowers, because that is what Uncle James said Aunt Mary would have wished, and also with people because she had been much loved locally on account of being so gentle and kind. There was us three and Cara and Grandpa, and my fat, red-faced, great-uncle Alan, and a whole crowd of cousins from my grandfather's side who are not at all like him or Aunt Mary, but rather hearty and jolly. They sang the hymns in huge, booming voices and I wished they wouldn't. There ought, really, to have been just children singing. That would have been much more appropriate to Aunt Mary.

After the service, we all went back to Bishopstow to eat the wonderful tea that Ma had thought of and organized and I had helped her make. The tables looked like a schoolboy's fantasy, plates and plates of delicious, imaginative things like brandy snaps no bigger than my little finger and baby quiches the size of a fifty-pence piece. As usual, food cheered everyone up a good deal, and then Uncle James produced some bottles of old Madeira and I began to think that all the Langley cousins would never go away but just stand there stuffing themselves and bellowing stories until we all went mad. But Ma suddenly got very firm, like she does when there is staff trouble at the hotel.

"James has had quite enough for one day," she said clearly and definitely to each little group of people, "and the kindest thing you can all now do for him is to go away at once."

When they had gone, and several kind people from the village had helped us to clear up, and Grandpa and Cara had said they would just go back to the church for a quiet time there together, the three of us went into the drawing room and sat round the fireplace over which the most famous portrait in the family hangs. It's of my great-grandmother, Alexandra, and it was painted by Michael Swinton, who was very celebrated in his day, and whom she later married. It shows her in an Edwardian blouse, and a voluminous tweed skirt and, amazingly for those days, bare feet, sitting on a rock at the sea's edge, lost in a dream. It's a lovely portrait, very romantic without being sentimental, but it doesn't stir me and fire me up like Charlotte's portrait does. I can't resist Charlotte's hint of wildness, and Alexandra, for all her daring bare feet, does look just a tiny bit tame.

Even though it was July, it wasn't a very warm evening, and poor Uncle James looked so sad and shrivelled, that I offered to light a fire. Ma said that would be an excellent idea, so I went off to collect kindling and newspaper and an armful of logs. I have to say that lighting fires is one of my few practical talents, I really am brilliant at it, and in ten minutes there was a bright fire to comfort Uncle James.

He held his old hands out to it.

"Ought I to move?"

"Move?" Ma said. "From here?"

"It's so big —"

"But it's *home*. We'll find you a housekeeper and you can stay."

"I'd like to stay as long as I can. I'll be the last of the line here, you know, the last of the direct line. Or as direct as it can be. Just think, Richard Talbot's father built this house for his bride in 1810 and then Richard brought Emily here, as his bride, just over thirty years later. Then it was Alexandra's, and now mine. I'll leave it to all those Langleys, you know. They're a boisterous lot, but good-hearted. I'd like to leave it to you, my darling," he reached out and squeezed Ma's hand, "but I think I oughtn't to give you any more after Bewick. I think it would look like favoritism. Which it would be."

"Yes, it would," said Ma. She looked round the room. I could see her struggling with herself because she loved that house.

"As for you, you baggage," Uncle James said to me, "where are you going to live?"

"In a tent," I said. "Or on a boat. Or up a tree."

He grinned at me.

"I've got something for you," he said.

He got up with difficulty and hobbled out to his study. When he came back, he was holding a little picture, which he put on my lap as he went by.

"Mary wanted you to have it."

I looked down at my lap. The picture, in a heavy, old-fashioned dull gold frame, was a charcoal drawing of a lovely, lively girl in some kind of exotic drapery. It was very freely done, slightly impressionistic and simply bursting with life and energy. The girl was Charlotte.

"Oh, Uncle James —"

"My father drew it. It's rather good, don't you think? Mary —" he hesitated a little over saying her name, and then he went on, "Mary and I thought you ought to have it to go with Emily's journal. Emily always said to Alexandra that this drawing was far more like Charlotte than that fashionable portrait Alexander had done of her. Emily had it by her bed, for the rest of her life."

I found I very much wanted to cry. It wasn't just the nature of the gift, or the generosity, or the connection with Charlotte, it was the assumption that I was the right person to have this precious thing. I got up and went over to kiss Uncle James.

"Don't you cry now," he said.

"Don't worry. I almost never do. I can't thank you enough."

He looked up at me. He had the family's blue eyes, pale in his case, faded by the years. He said, "What's going to become of you, Carly? What are you going to do with your life? What is your heart's desire?"

I looked back at him for a moment, and then I looked at the drawing in my hand, and then I said, quite without intending to, "I want to go to Afghanistan. Like Charlotte."

Chapter Five

When I got back to London, I found that Simon Preston had very kindly arranged for me to have an interview with the magazine where Sasha worked for the fashion department, and he worked for features. I didn't really want this interview at all, but I felt it would be churlish, to say the least, to turn it down just because I was now all fired up with this mad idea of going to Afghanistan.

At least Ma said it was mad. She said a great deal more besides, like who was going to pay for it and that she really despised all these spoiled young people trailing about the world with backpacks, paid for by their parents, as a way of putting off getting down to anything. She also said, quite sarcastically for her, that had I noticed that there was a war on in Afghanistan? I said the Russians were pulling out, and she said well they hadn't done so yet, and she forbade me to go.

Then Uncle James said, most unexpectedly, "You can't forbid her, darling. She's twenty-one."

Ma gasped. "But I thought you'd be on my side!"

"When you were twenty-one," Uncle James said, "I sent you all alone to Bewick with two hundred pounds spending money, as far as I can remember, and told you to get on with it. This isn't so very different."

"There wasn't a war on at Bewick!"

"She won't get mixed up in the war," Uncle James said firmly. "It's much more difficult to get mixed up in wars than you think. I should know."

Later, I tried to thank him for standing up for me, but he waved me away.

"One of the few things I've learned in a long life is that it's wisest and best to give the women of this family their heads. Mind you, don't go and lose yours, that's all."

He had no idea how much he encouraged me. He had encouraged me enough to get me through a very difficult car journey back to London with Ma, and through what turned out to be a very surprising interview at Simon's magazine.

The magazine was in a huge white thirties building just off Oxford Street. The offices were on the fifth and sixth floors, open plan with black desks, and black slatted screens dividing the more important people from the lesser mortals, and a lot of plants and spotlights. Instead of the sandwich crumbs and full ashtrays and squashed paper coffee cups you expect to find in most offices, this one was strewn with French mineral water bottles and plates with mango peel and pumpernickel crusts on them. All the girls who were flitting about with files seemed to be extremely thin, dressed in black with earrings the size of saucers, and the men were very pretty indeed, much prettier than me. I asked a very sweet-looking one in a yellow shirt and a Red Army belt if he could tell me where to find

Simon. He said he'd do more than that, he'd show me.

He led me between the black desks and the grey and white filing cabinets to a corner where, lounging gracefully under a weeping fig, Simon was saying into the telephone, in a very affected way, "Well, I don't really care *how* upset he is, I really *only* care if I don't get this interview."

The sweet boy in the yellow shirt gave me a black canvas chair to sit in and found me a cup of coffee, and Simon made faces at me to say that he wouldn't be a minute. He was in fact several minutes, and I sipped my coffee and looked round me and thought how miserable I would be, working in such a place, with such people. When Simon finally put the telephone down, I said, "D'you know, I think I'd better say straight out that I don't think I could work here and I'd better not waste the features editor's time. I'm so sorry, when you've taken all this trouble."

Simon dropped his telephone voice and said in his normal, kind, steady one, "Don't be so impulsive, Carly. You've got to have a job and this is probably the most highly regarded women's magazine in the world. Certainly in England."

I indicated my clothes. I was wearing jeans — clean, but not, I'm afraid, ironed — and a denim shirt — ditto — and my beloved American loafers which I had polished specially for the occasion. I was also wearing one brass earring of a pair Jamie had given me, shaped like a parrot perched in a hoop, and one silver star stud earring that had been a present from Xan. I liked wearing odd earrings.

I said, "Well, look at me."

"You look great. Anyway, that's not the point. The point is that you are literate, original, and articulate and that you need a job."

"But I don't want one."

"What do you want then? To go on the dole?"

"I want to go to Afghanistan."

"There's a war on in Afghanistan."

"You sound just like my mother."

Simon leaned forward. "Why do you want to go to Afghanistan?"

I squirmed a bit. I said, "It may sound silly to you, but I want to go because my great-great-great-grandmother went there a hundred and fifty years ago, and also because I want to have an adventure."

Simon stood up.

"Then you'd better meet the travel editor. He's very fierce and *very* adventurous."

"But, Simon, I don't want to work here!"

He said patiently, "You have to work somewhere, Carly, if you are going to make enough money to get to Afghanistan. Or did you intend walking?"

I went scarlet. "I'm afraid I didn't really think," I said. I stood up too and looked at Simon. He wore the half-patient, half-exasperated expression that Duncan used to wear when I'd got into yet another teenage scrape and Ma was worn out with disciplining me. I felt suddenly very half-baked and very silly. "Sorry," I said.

He gave my cheek a brisk little pat, and then he led me back across the office to a desk by a window, where a grizzle-haired man was sitting with his back to us talking into the telephone.

"No," he was saying, "that's the whole point. I intend to cycle from California to Tierra del Fuego on a pound a day, or rather I intend to find someone who is prepared to do it for me. I know it's seventeen thousand miles. I know Peru is dangerous. I know, I know, I *know*, that's why I'm asking you. Okay then, think it over and ring me back. You can spend up to six hundred pounds on a mountain bike. Ciao."

He banged the telephone down and swiveled round and glared at us. He was about fifty and he had a broken nose and very small, very bright eyes.

"Well?" he said to me. "D'you want to spend fifteen months on a bike?"

Simon said, "Matthew, this is Carly Angus. Matthew Mott is our travel editor."

I liked the look of Matthew. I said, "I wouldn't mind the bike, but I don't want to go to Peru, thank you all the same. I want to go to Afghanistan."

"There's a —"

"I know there's a war on. But it's stopping."

"It's very uncool to go to places where wars are stopping."

"But *I* want to go because an ancestor of mine was involved in the Siege of Kabul in 1841. My great-great-great-grandmother."

Matthew Mott looked at Simon. "Where did you find this person?"

"She was at school with Sasha. You know, fashion Sasha I share a flat with."

Matthew looked back at me.

366

"Are you any good at anything at all?"

"I did a hotel management course and I'm brilliant at lighting fires. Oh, and I've got three A-levels and I can ride and I got a life-saving badge when I was fifteen."

"I see," said Matthew. "In other words, you're no bloody use for anything to anyone."

"I suppose not —"

"Can you type?"

"Yes," I said not quite truthfully. I had been the worst in the class.

"Liar," Matthew said. "And use a word processor?"

I opened my mouth to say I had done computer studies at school, and then shut it again because I had been banished from the classes for playing games with the machines. I shook my head.

"And you think, and so does soft-hearted, simple Simon here, that I'm going to give you a job to help you make enough money to go to Afghanistan and get riddled with bullets from a Kalashnikov carried by a jumpy mujahideen who thinks you're a Russian spy?"

"No," I said.

"Well, you're wrong. You can have a hard-working, ill-paid job here for six months. You can't go to Afghanistan in the winter anyhow. And you will take a night school course in photography and do absolutely everything I tell you, however inconvenient or disagreeable."

I put my hands to my face. I really liked him very much and he was clearly, according to his peculiar lights, being very kind, but I had to be honest.

"But I don't want a job here! I can't work with all these glossy girls —"

"You won't be," Matthew said, "I have my own microclimate over here, and you'll share that. I need a dogsbody and you'll do, as long as you don't argue. You'll start at a hundred pounds a week — I said don't argue — and at the end of a month, I'll either fire you or double it. Now go away and come back in the morning with matching earrings. I can't stand adolescent affectation." Then he picked the telephone up again and swiveled his chair away from us. The interview was over.

I looked at Simon.

He said, "He liked you."

"*Did* he?"

"He'll work you terribly hard. You'll spend your life in geographical libraries checking things, or booking impossible trips and then having to cancel them, or sitting in third world embassies for days on end for visas they won't give you."

He put a hand under my elbow, and began to steer me away, back towards the lift.

"Simon, please don't think I'm ungrateful, because I'm really deeply, truly, but I do feel a bit stunned —"

"That's Matthew. Now I'm going to do one more thing for you, and then I think I can let you off the lead. I'm going to introduce you to Tom Pasco."

"Who's Tom Pasco?"

"He's a friend of mine. I told you the other night. I've known him since we were six, at nursery school."

"Why should I meet him?"

Simon halted me in front of the lift doors, and pressed the "descend" button.

"Because you wanted to meet someone exciting, and he is, and because I think you'll discover you have a lot of aims in common and because — well, you'll see."

I still felt a bit dazed after Matthew Mott. I said, "Okay," rather faintly and not properly taking in what he was saying. Then the lift came and I kissed Simon gratefully, and sailed downwards to the street and went home to my funny little rooms, and sat on the seagrass matting, and wished and wished that my spaniel was there, for me to talk to and take comfort from.

After a bit, I shook myself resolutely and got up and went downstairs to wash and brush my hair and teeth. I found I wanted to do this a great deal in London, which made me feel permanently grimy. I looked at myself in the mirror for a long time after all this brushing and I gave myself a very stern talking to. I told myself that I had said — or, more accurately, shouted — to Ma and Duncan that I wanted to be free and independent and make my own life and my own way without being propped up or influenced by them or by the hotel. I had then announced that I was going to Afghanistan and upset Ma still further. I had come to London, all full of how I was going to do this and do that and how nobody was going to stop me or help me, and what had actually happened was that I had wetly allowed myself to be assisted by both Amanda and

Simon, without whom I should probably be living in a depressing hostel or even a cardboard box. I told myself that I had behaved hypocritically and like a coward, and that I was spoiled and extremely childish. I then said firmly that I had to take my life into my own hands now, make a proper plan for Afghanistan — if that was ever going to become more than just a symbol of elderly teenage rebelliousness — and make a real go of working for Matthew Mott.

I then went upstairs and took the brass parrot out of my ear, and replaced it with the matching silver star. Then I put on some mascara and lipgloss, collected the Greek orange basket I used as a handbag, some money, and my new *London A–Z*, and went down to the showroom floor.

Amanda was sitting at her desk in a black linen suit with huge white buttons, reading her horoscope out of the *Daily Mail*. I said, very casually, as I went by, "Oh, by the way, I've got a job."

She said, equally casually, and not looking up, "What sort of job?"

"Dogsbody and general assistant to Matthew Mott, the travel editor for *Marshalls* magazine."

"Well done," she said.

"A hundred pounds a week, doubling if I'm any good."

"That wasn't very difficult, was it? First try, bingo. Lucky little Carly."

I didn't like her tone of voice. It echoed exactly my own feelings that I wasn't standing sufficiently on my own feet, after all the fuss I'd made. She looked up briefly.

"Your horoscope says it's a good day for impul-

370

sive decisions, so there you are. Where are you going now?"

"I'm going to Richmond," I said. "To look for Charlotte's house. And then I'm going round to Sasha and Simon's flat to meet a friend of Simon's."

She looked a bit teasing. "And then to Afghanistan?"

I tried to appear dignified. I lifted my chin a little. I said, "Going to Richmond, Amanda, is the first step on the road to Kabul," and then I went out very quickly so as not to hear her shrieks of laughter.

It was difficult, getting out of the train at Richmond Station in 1988, to imagine the place in 1840. I really had to picture the place in my mind's eye, and think about Emily's journal, rather than about what I was now seeing. Richmond was, of course, still very rural in 1840, but with lots of newly built villas and terraces of houses in the Regency style. It was famous for its hill, from which there were celebrated views down across the Thames — the only thing, as far as I could see, which still remained as it had been — and for its huge and beautiful park where Charlotte and Emily went riding and Charlotte's hat blew off, and her hair came down and she was spotted, in this unseemly state, by the rector's wife and daughters who thought she was an unprincipled hoyden.

Charlotte and Emily and their widowed mother had lived in a little house between the river and the Richmond Gate to the Park. Their house backed onto Petersham Common, where cows once used to graze, and it has narrowly escaped being flattened under the huge main road that now runs down south towards Kingston. Cara had told me exactly how to find the house, so it wasn't difficult, not as difficult as visualizing Charlotte and Emily coming out of the front door tying their hats on, when I got there. You could see, in this neat suburban house almost deafened by traffic, the shadow of an eighteenth-century cottage. The front door had a graceful pediment, and the sash windows were arranged neatly either side of it and above it. But an imitation eighteenth-century modern wing in hard red brick had been added to one side — definitely stockbroker's Georgian — and a garage with a flat above it on the other side, and the old garden, the little outdoor rooms formed by hedges and the plum tree and the forsythia, had quite vanished under a horrible blanket of crazy paving with the occasional flowerbed filled with some very neat little orange flowers I didn't know the name of. I couldn't picture Charlotte and Emily there at all, pressed in on by the later surrounding houses, with litter blowing about on the dusty pavements and no nice cows peering interestedly over the garden hedges to see what they were doing. There seemed to me almost no echo at all of two significant Regency girlhoods, except for one curious little lingering piece of evidence. Screwed to the wall beside the front door was a varnished oval of wood, with the name of the house chiselled into it very blackly, and the name was "Brent Villa." So Charlotte and Emily

Brent were still living on in this distorted house in a way, like a faint but unmistakable breath of the past that nobody could ever quite blow away.

I sat on the train going back into London, and thought hard about Charlotte. I thought of how confined Richmond had made her feel, with its refined, genteel ways, just as the fashions of the day had made her feel physically confined. I understood how she felt, because I too, although I had grown up in a place that looked much wilder and more open than Richmond, found life confined me, because of the little, sheltered world created by Bewick and Inverbrae. Our circumstances were different simply because we were children of our own times, a century and a half apart, but our feelings weren't very different. It was, I discovered, both consoling and inspiring to think of this affinity between us, even if we didn't look the same or live in the same way. It was as if some powerful genes that she had inherited from her traveling father had lain dormant and peaceful all down the years, through Iskandara and Alexandra and Cara and Ma, and then woken up again, at last, in me.

I got out of the train at South Kensington and walked round to Redcliffe Gardens, stopping on the way to buy a bottle of wine for Simon as a very small thank you for taking such trouble with me. I think, like Ma, he thought my desire to go to Afghanistan was pretty insane, but then, he wasn't at all interested in his own family's history, so he couldn't really understand what was firing me.

I toiled up the stairs of the building to the third floor and knocked on the flat door. Sasha opened it. She was wearing a black towel swathed round her head like a turban, and a white bathrobe. She said, "Wow, Carly, and who just walked in and picked a job off Matthew then?"

I said, "Simon did it for me."

"Nonsense," Sasha said. "Actually you'll only last ten minutes. Matthew eats his assistants for lunch. The last one left in tears on Friday, and she'd been on Operation Raleigh and everything and was a real toughie. Is that nice Chardonnay for me?"

"No," I said, "it's for Simon."

She stood back. "Come in and give it to him then. He's in there with Tom."

She waved a hand towards the sitting room door. "Must dash or my henna'll go purple." She vanished into the bathroom.

I pushed the sitting room door open. Simon was sitting on one of the cream sofas, and there was a man standing with his back to me, looking out of the window. Simon got up and came to kiss me. I held the wine out.

"This is for you. You really deserve a case of it."

He said, "No, I don't and Chardonnay is my favorite. Come and meet Tom. He thought he saw a hawk a minute ago and he's trying to see it again. He's mad on birds. Tom! Come and meet Carly."

The man at the window turned round and came toward me, holding out his hand. He said something to me, but I couldn't hear him, I couldn't hear anything above the hammering of my heart. I took his hand, and stared up at him, and that, quite simply, was it. The Big One.

Chapter Six

When I met Tom Pasco, he was exactly six years, two months and fifteen days older than me. I know that because I worked it out on a calculator the minute I discovered his birthday. He was taller than me, too, and I'm quite tall for a girl and certainly taller than Ma, and he had that lean look of someone who is fit, and rather self-denying. His hair was brown, light brown, but bleached blond by the sun in front, and it was very thick and straight, and fell over his eyes when he bent forward to concentrate on something. He had pronounced features, and very direct clear grey eyes and beautiful hands, very strong and flexible. He was also very brown. I noticed all this, quite distinctly, while I stood there in Simon and Sasha's sitting room, with my hand in Tom's and my ears simply buzzing with excitement.

He said, "I don't think you're listening to me."

I swallowed. Or rather I gulped. But I couldn't utter.

Simon said kindly, "I expect she's hungry. She's always hungry."

I felt a slow unbecoming tide of scarlet flood hotly up my neck and face to the roots of my gingery hair. What a color combination — I couldn't bear to think what I must look like.

"Are you?" said Tom Pasco.

I gaped. "What?"

"Are you hungry?"

I said, "No, not specially," in as offhand a voice as I could manage, and took my hand away from his, although it was the last thing I wanted to do. Then I went and sat down beside Simon and felt miserable and foolish. Tom Pasco sat down opposite me and looked graceful and amused.

"Simon says you are going to work for the terrible Matthew Mott."

I nodded.

"I've known him for years. He's a magnificent editor. He has the temperament of a nineteenth-century explorer really."

Simon said, "I'm going to open this wine," and got up and took the bottle out to the kitchen to find a corkscrew. I stayed where I was, longing to gaze and gaze at Tom Pasco and, instead, gazing fixedly at the floor. I had never felt like this in my life before, not remotely like this, and it was rather frightening because, after all, I didn't *know* this man at all, I knew nothing about him except that he was a friend of Simon's.

Tom leaned back into his chair. He seemed perfectly at ease, his hands and forearms, below the rolled-up sleeves of a pale khaki shirt, lying loosely along the chair arms. I couldn't take my eyes off his hands. I wanted them to be . . .

"Do you hate London as much as I do?" he said suddenly.

I managed to look him directly in the face.

"I don't like it at all —"

"Were you walking this afternoon? Did you

have to find a space, a park or something and walk?"

I said, "I went to Richmond, actually, to find the house where an ancestor used to live —"

"What kind of ancestor?"

"My great-great-great-grandmother."

"Who went to Afghanistan?"

I sat bolt upright.

"How did you know?"

Simon said, coming back in with the opened bottle and a fistful of wineglasses, "I told him."

I pretended to be indignant. "And what else did you tell him when you didn't tell *me* anything about him?"

"You wouldn't listen," Simon said truthfully. He poured the wine carefully into three glasses. "I told you that you ought to meet, didn't I?"

I couldn't look at Tom. I muttered, "Why ought we?"

Tom said, "Because of going to Afghanistan."

I felt completely bewildered. It was disconcerting enough to be introduced to this devastating man without having what I thought was my private adventure thrown into the meeting almost before I'd recovered my breath. I took the wineglass Simon offered me, but I was shaking so badly that some of the wine splashed out onto my hand.

"Here," Tom said. He leaned forward and held out a big, clean red spotted handkerchief. I think he was smiling, but I couldn't look.

He said gently, "I'm a filmmaker. I'm making, at the moment, a series of films for television about refugees. I've already made one about Palestinian refugees, and one about refugees from Red China, and now I want to go to the North West Frontier of India and make one about the refugees from the Russian occupation of Afghanistan."

"See?" Simon said. He looked very smug and triumphant, like someone who's finished a crossword in record time.

"No," I said. I sat there, holding my wineglass and Tom's spotted handkerchief, feeling unsteady and foolish.

"Simon says you want to go to Afghanistan, in the footsteps of your great-grandmother."

I felt myself going scarlet again. It sounded such an adolescent ambition, put that way.

"I think it's a fascinating thing to want to do," Tom said.

"Do you?"

"Yes, I do. When was she there?"

"During the siege of Kabul."

"1841."

"Yes."

"I don't know that one can get to Kabul itself. Even by next year."

I said hesitatingly, "I . . . I just wanted to . . . see the place, what kind of place —"

"Of course," Tom said, "we don't know each other at all well yet, and a lot depends on that, naturally, but the point of us meeting like this, is for me to put a tentative proposition to you —"

My heart leaped into my mouth. It was all I could do not to say that he could put any proposition of any kind he liked to me.

"If you spend this winter working for Matthew, and learn a bit about cameras, and about Afghanistan, I wonder what you would think about joining my crew when we fly out next year? We plan to be away about ten weeks. If you can find the money for your flight, I'm sure I can find a way to keep you while you're there. It would be so useful to have a woman with us, particularly when it comes to trying to talk to refugee women and children. Would you mind growing your hair a bit by next summer and of course it would be a huge help if you could learn a little Farsi —"

I was staring at him.

"Is this a joke?"

"Carly," Simon said, almost in exasperation, "it's to *help* you. I wanted you to meet Tom to *help* you."

I put my wineglass down rather unsteadily on a little table beside the sofa. I said, "Look, I don't want to be ungrateful, but everything's happening so fast that it doesn't feel quite real. There's Matthew this morning, and now you —"

"That's *how* things happen," Tom said. "The best things. The most worthwhile things." He stood up, graceful and easy. "I've got to go, I'm afraid," he said. He looked down at me. "Could we meet sometime? We ought to get to know each other better in any case, and I would love to hear about your great-grandmother."

"Yes," I said stupidly.

He said patiently, "Could I have your telephone number?"

I fished about in my orange basket and found a

pen, and wrote the King's Road number on a deposit slip torn from the back of my check book.

"Thanks," Tom said, "I'll call you. I'd really like to stay now, but I'm afraid I'm supposed to be somewhere else by six-thirty."

Simon grinned. "Still Laura?"

"Still Laura," Tom said shortly and then he said, "Bye, Carly. I'll see you very soon," and then he went out of the room and seconds later, we heard the front door of the flat slam shut behind him.

I said, "Who's Laura?"

Simon picked up the wine bottle and offered me a refill. I shook my head.

"She and Tom have been together for about four years. She's pretty formidable. She's a lawyer, terribly bright, and she hates all his traveling and filming."

I wanted desperately to know if she was good-looking, but luckily pride prevented me from asking. Instead I said, "So she doesn't go on these film trips?"

"Heavens no," Simon said. He looked at me. "Did you like him?"

I nodded.

"I'm so glad. He's one of the most interesting people I know. Very brave and, I'm told, very good to work for." He lay back on the sofa and patted his chest. "All in all, I feel very pleased with myself, putting you two together. Perfect, really perfect pairing."

"Yes," I said. My voice didn't sound anything like as enthusiastic as it should have done. "I'm so grateful. Thank you."

He turned his head. "What's the matter?"

I couldn't possibly confess. I couldn't possibly say that I had apparently fallen in love at first sight with a man who had suggested I go with him to the one place in the world I was bent upon going to but unfortunately he was in love with someone else, and that the combination of all these things happening in the space of half an hour on top of everything else that had happened that day, had made me feel as if I'd been hit on the head, hard, several times with a brick. I opened and shut my mouth once or twice, like a fish, trying to think of a way to sound enthusiastic without giving my true feelings away, and failed completely.

Simon sat up and leaned forward.

"Carly, what *is* the matter? Aren't you pleased with me?"

I nodded. I nodded violently, and then, to my horror, because I so disapprove of sobbing maidens, I burst into tears. But this turned out to be the perfect thing to do, because Simon thought I was overcome with pleasure and excitement and he was highly gratified. So he came over to my sofa, and patted me and said there there, and what a wonderful reaction, and that he, Simon, hadn't done anything really, while I howled for Tom Pasco into Tom Pasco's handkerchief which he had given me to mop up the wine with, and which I had forgotten to give back. If Sasha hadn't come in, soon after, with astounding, gleaming purple-chestnut hair, and thought we were having a row, I think I might, out of tension and longing and disappointment and agitation, simply have wept and wailed all evening, and might easily have given way, and spilled all the beans.

I hardly slept at all that night. I lay in bed and thought, with a considerable amount of shame, that I had overreacted disgracefully that evening, in imagining that I could possibly fall for someone just by looking at them. I told myself that that didn't happen in real life, only in fairy stories, and I reminded myself that when I was little, and Ma used to read me the tale of *The Sleeping Beauty* (which she loved) I used to get terribly cross with the silly princess for opening her eyes after a hundred years and saying "I love you and of course I'll marry you," to a perfectly strange prince who might, for all she knew, have had a really nasty character. But here I was, behaving exactly the same way, and wanting to fling myself into Tom's arms the minute he turned round from the window. It was the behavior of a complete and utter airhead. Then I remembered something; I remembered Emily's journal. I got out of bed and found the padded envelope in which I carefully kept it, and slipped it out, and turned quickly to a bit I loved and had read over and over again because it thrilled me.

It was the description of the first time Alexander Bewick saw Charlotte. She knew about him, from his wicked reputation, but he knew very little about her except the intriguing fact that her keeping a Pathan servant and then furnishing her house in the Afghan way had caused raised eyebrows in the English community in

Kabul, and if there was one thing Alexander Bewick loved to do, it was to shock the stuffy English. So he came to Charlotte's house, out of curiosity, and when he saw Charlotte "dressed in her black robes," says Emily, "but with no jewelry because she had been riding, no ornament at all except those long wine-coloured plaits," he went down on one knee in the dust, struck dumb and entirely captivated.

Well, that had happened to me, too, now. Not so romantically of course, being in a Kensington flat and not in a Kabul compound, and Tom and I being dressed in banal twentieth-century drill and denim, and not in exotic Asian robes, but I had felt just like Alexander, awestruck and speechless. Of course it was partly the way Tom looked, his being spare and hard and tanned by the wind and sun, but it was also how the room had felt when he was in it, full of an extra electricity and power, and how dull and flat it was when he had gone.

Would it, however, I thought, sitting on the floor clutching the precious journal, also turn out to be dull and flat to go on an expedition with a man who wasn't looking my way at all? Would I simply die of misery and frustration? Would I be able to concentrate on nothing because I would be consumed with wondering how much he was thinking about and missing the clever and strong-minded legal Laura? At least Alexander had been buoyed up by the arrogant feeling that he could have any woman he wanted — even the beautiful Mrs. Charlotte Connell — if he really put his mind to it, but I didn't have one thousandth of his self-confidence. Alexander had determined to possess Charlotte. All I could do, a hundred and fifty years later, was just hope and hope, and quite frankly, sitting on the floor there at three in the morning, hoping seemed a pretty pathetic thing to do.

When the dawn chorus began about an hour later, I felt a little stronger. I made myself a mug of tea, and I put the journal carefully away, and had a good long look at my great-grandfather's drawing of Charlotte, which I had put up on the wall by my bed, to be like Emily. I looked very carefully at Charlotte's face, and decided that whatever else she was, and whatever of her I had inherited, she had not been fatally introspective as I was, and that if I wasn't careful, I could very easily simply talk myself out of doing anything worthwhile, all my life.

So I made a resolution. I would, I decided, accept Tom Pasco's kind offer and make a go of it, just as I had resolved to accept Matthew Mott's offer and make a go of that. I was being offered a golden chance to follow Charlotte to Afghanistan, and I mustn't muck that up by having attacks of the vapors. I should learn a great deal, and be given wonderful opportunities and perhaps, in the course of the next exciting eighteen months, I would find out what it was I really wanted to do. I might also, I told myself firmly, find out when I next met Tom Pasco that he was a perfectly ordinary man after all, and that my reaction on first meeting him had been a mere aberration, like a sort of emotional migraine.

Chapter Seven

I worked harder that autumn and winter than I had ever worked before in my life. Matthew Mott turned out to be a relentless taskmaster with no idea of the convention of keeping to office hours, and I found myself on most days staggering back to the Kings Road in a daze of fatigue, and eating bread and marmalade — Ma would have been horrified — because it was quick and filling and I was too tired to think about even the simplest kind of cooking.

The travel section of *Marshalls* magazine occupied fifteen glossy pages which had, each month, to be filled with the highest caliber and greatest variety of material that Matthew could find. Almost no contributor, however famous and spoiled, seemed to turn down Matthew's suggestion that they should go and count how many of the lovely ancient painted churches were still standing in Romania, or travel rough the road to Damascus in the footsteps of St. Paul. Matthew's corner of the office hummed with life, which he directed, in his brusque way, from behind his desk, while I scurried about breathlessly trying to carry out his shouted orders. I was typist, secretary, copy editor, subeditor, courier, travel agent, sandwich getter and general errand runner. In one day in November, I made a note that I had typed fifteen letters, redrafted two thousand words of copy on Haiti whose tone Matthew didn't like ("too bloody arch"), spent an hour and a half in the visa section of the Turkish Embassy, collected, for Matthew, two rounds of prawn sandwiches, some razor blades and a pair of shoes from the mender, planned an itinerary for someone wanting to retrace Robert Louis Stevenson's *Travels with a Donkey*, answered the telephone nonstop, and sat in on a meeting — or rather, a row — between *Marshalls'* editor and Matthew, in order to take notes, but really, I suspect, because Matthew wanted me to see him win. Such a day wasn't at all untypical. On Tuesdays, I went to evening classes on photography, and on Thursdays, in slavish obedience to Tom's suggestion, I started elementary classes in Farsi. I only started them, however. Our teacher was a thin, passionate Afghan, and the rest of the class were tremendously politically motivated students of every race and hue, all violently opposed to the Russian occupation of Afghanistan, and the classes degenerated, after ten minutes or so, into screaming political harangues and diatribes. So I gave up. Learning how to ask for food or mosquito repellent was one thing but having half-digested, incomprehensible, political theories shrieked at me was quite another.

I explained this, rather shyly, to Tom. He said he quite understood. One of the most agonizing aspects of my life was discovering that Tom understood most things, that he wasn't just wonderful looking, but imaginative, sensitive, interesting, and marvelous company. I saw a lot of him, I couldn't help it, he was so often in touch, making plans, asking my opinion, giving me scraps of information, and I grew terrified that he would notice how I felt about him, which on some days, I thought must be as obvious as if I'd got it stamped on my forehead in scarlet letters.

He wanted to know all about Charlotte. He understood, without my having to explain, how very precious Emily's journal was, and he introduced me to a friend of his, who worked in the British Museum, who photocopied it for me most beautifully, on an ultrasophisticated and sensitive copier, so that it came out looking like a facsimile.

Tom said, very diffidently for him, when it was done, "Would it be very impertinent to ask to read it?"

I felt a little shy about it, because the diary was my most precious possession and I felt very possessive about it, in consequence, as well as identifying so strongly with Charlotte's feelings. He saw my hesitation. He said, "I shouldn't have asked, Carly. I'm so sorry. It was clumsy and insensitive."

I held out the thick buff envelope with the photocopy in it.

"No. I'm being silly. Of course, read it. But you must read it in one go."

He gave it back to me the next day. He put it into my hands and said simply, "No wonder you want to go."

I just nodded.

"It's one of the most romantic, in the widest sense, stories I've ever read. Are you like her?"

I shook my head. "Not at all. My mother is. My mother is lovely."

Tom looked at me with a queer, cool look. He said, "I really meant temperamentally, you know."

"I don't know about that. I haven't tested myself out. I suppose I won't know the answer, either, until I'm there."

He said, "I really do appreciate your letting me read the journal. It's given me a lot to think about."

Shortly after that he introduced me to Laura. I had built up such an intricate and precise picture of her in my mind that it was quite a shock to meet her, and find that she was not tall and dark as I'd imagined, but small and fair. However, I had been right to imagine her as forceful. She was very neat, with smooth hair, an immaculate suit and well-kept hands, and she was very, very decided. She was also charming and good company and she smiled a lot, but you could see, behind the smile, her efficient brain keeping watch all the time, ready to pounce. She was kind to me because, beside her, I was young and scruffy and unprofessional and therefore no kind of competition. I couldn't help noticing Tom watching her with pride and satisfaction, smiling at her intelligent well-finished sentences with no "ums" and "ers" in them. It was, all in all, an awful evening; worse, in a way, than I'd even imagined it because she and Tom seemed to complement each other so well, he so enthusiastic and idealistic, she so practical and controlled. I went to bed fully determined to cancel going to Afghanistan altogether, and woke in the morning knowing that I couldn't do any such thing. I am a hopeless liar and how could I possibly have told Tom the truth? "I'm afraid I can't come on your expedition any more because I can't bear you being in love with Laura, who is everything I'm not, and not with me instead." How would that have sounded?

I got up and dressed and trailed into work, looking very downhearted and trying to hide this from Matthew who always made a huge thing of despising emotions. So it was a great surprise to me when he brought me a cup of coffee about half past ten — he had never done such a thing before — and plonked it down on the copy I was trying to edit, and said, "Want to know something?"

"Not much," I said.

"Listen." He bent down so that his little bright eyes were only inches from my face. "When you want something desperately badly in life, Carly, you either get it in the end — or you stop wanting it."

I stared. I said, "What's that supposed to mean?"

He gave me a light cuff on the ear and said, "Tom Pasco, you daft ha'p'orth."

"Oh Matthew —"

He held up both hands in self-defense. "No confessions, Carly. Can't stand them."

"But . . . but if you've guessed, do you think he has?"

"Nope," Matthew said. "He has no vanity."

"Are you sure?"

"Look," Matthew said, raising his voice to his usual half-shout, "d'you want the boot, or don't you? You're not being paid to sit around whining, Miss Angus, so get on with what I've told you to do or you're fired on Friday."

In November, Ma started asking me when I was coming back home for Christmas. Christmas at Bewick is perfectly wonderful, and guests who spend it at the hotel write rapturous letters afterwards saying that they will remember it all their lives and will certainly be booking again in the future. Ma turns both her hotel and Inverbrae into a sort of magical Highland Forest, all green garlands and sparkling lights and tartan ribbons, with banks of moss holding up arrangements of branches and berries and gilded fir cones, and the air is perfumed with scented candles. All the guests in the hotel get Christmas stockings and she puts miles and miles of tiny white glittering lights in the trees around the castle, and the effect is more magical than I can possibly tell you. It's the best of traditional Christmases — roaring fires, mince pies, carols, frosty walks — and the best of glamorous modern Christmas — marvelous presents and champagne and comfort. As children, Jamie and Xan and I used to start getting worked up about Christmas before we'd even had Halloween or Guy Fawkes Night, and of course, in Scotland, Hogmanay is even more important than Christmas, so there was really a nonstop party for us, from Christmas Eve until everybody went back to work with hangovers in the first week in January.

We never spent Christmas anywhere but Bewick. I'd never spent one with my father, although he'd asked me to, because I just couldn't bear the thought of being away from Scotland. But this year, when you would expect, after five months of being worked to death by Matthew and living in London and the strain of being hopelessly in love with Tom, that I'd have been simply counting the days to going home, I found, to my own amazement, that I wasn't. I thought of home often, and with love and even with longing, but I also had a strong instinct that I mustn't go home just yet. If I was going to stay free, I must stay away. This became quite clear to me, though it was difficult to explain to Ma.

"What do you mean, you might not come home?"

I held the telephone receiver very tightly.

"Just that, Ma."

"Not come home for Christmas! Not *come*, Carly?"

"Ma —"

"Darling, what's the matter, are you ill?"

"No, not at all, I'm fine, but —"

"But what, Carly? What possible 'but' can there be for not coming home at Christmas?"

I shut my eyes and prayed for inspiration, and tried not to visualize how dreary Christmas might well be if I stuck to my guns and didn't go home.

"Carly? Carly darling, are you there?"

I opened my mouth and said, quite easily, to my own utter and complete amazement, "I thought I'd go down to Cornwall and keep Uncle James company."

Ma gave a long, long sigh, like the air slowly escaping out of a balloon.

"Ah."

"He must be so lonely —"

I could picture her so well, on the rush-seated stool by the telephone in the kitchen at Inverbrae, still in her tidy jersey and skirt and pearls from a day at the hotel, forcing herself to acknowledge that Uncle James's need was really so much greater than her own.

"Carly — that's truly kind."

I said truthfully, "It was an inspiration."

"Have you asked him?"

"Not yet."

"He's got a new housekeeper."

"Oh —"

"Perhaps you could plan Christmas between you," Ma said bravely. I could see she was already plotting a hamper she could send down from Bewick, full of delicious things.

I said, "I'm sure we'll manage."

"Carly," she said suddenly, "Carly, are you all right?"

I had a bad few seconds. During them, I was severely tempted to break down and tell her all about Tom, but if I did that, it would be opening the whole Afghanistan can of worms again, with several new worms thrown in. I took a deep breath and said, "I'm fine. I'm just a bit tired."

"You're doing so well," Ma said proudly. *Marshalls* magazine lay, I knew, in the hotel drawing room often open at the travel section

393

even though my name was far too lowly to feature anywhere in it. "When you've rung James, let me know what he says."

I rang him at once, before I had time to regret my impulse.

He said, "You're a kind child, Carly dear, but I wouldn't hear of it."

"Why not? Don't you want me to come?"

"I wouldn't be so selfish. Think how dreary it would be for you after all the fun and games you usually have. I'll be fine."

"But I *want* to come."

"No, you feel you ought to. I'll be all right with whatsername —"

"What *is* her name?"

He lowered his voice to a whisper. "She's called Pamela Merryweather."

"Is she awful?"

"Not entirely. Just relentlessly cheerful."

"Uncle James," I said, "I need to come to Bishopstow. I *want* to come. Please, please let me come and then Pamela Merryweather can go and be merry somewhere else."

There was a long, long pause, so long I wondered if he had fainted or gone to sleep, and then Uncle James said, "How soon can you come?"

I went down to Cornwall by train. I felt rather guilty about my almost unused birthday car sitting in Scotland, but Duncan said Ma was finding it very handy and he didn't seem at all put out or to think me ungrateful. He said a present was a present, and shouldn't have any strings attached to it, and he was sure a car was an awful nuisance in London. I told him he was a brick, and I meant it.

Uncle James came to meet me at Bodmin Road station. He wore the huge stiff old British Warm overcoat which had been part of his demobilization kit at the end of the war and it made him look rather fragile, as if he no longer had the strength to carry such a weight. We hugged each other with great enthusiasm, and I was suddenly very glad I'd come, thankful to be out of London and away from the strain of various things.

Uncle James said, "I've bought a whole Stilton and a bottle of port and a box of Carlsbad plums. And I've ordered a goose. Shall we know how to cook it?"

"I haven't a clue, I'm afraid. I'm a hopeless cook."

He opened the car door. "There's always cook books. I suppose any fool can follow a recipe."

The back seat of the car was full of parcels and clinking with bottles.

"What about Pamela Merryweather?"

"Oh, she's a good sort, but very tiring. Will call me Major Swinton. I keep explaining to her that it was a wartime rank only but she won't listen. Very keen on doing things her way."

"What is her way?"

He gave me a sidelong look.

"Only one whisky before dinner and no dogs on beds."

"Oh dear. And is she going away for Christmas?"

"You bet," Uncle James said. "I packed her off

395

in her Mini Metro this morning to stay with her daughter in Tenterden. And then —" he gave a little chuckle, "then the dogs went straight upstairs and made themselves comfortable."

It was a very different Christmas from any I had ever known, but I loved it. Uncle James put me to sleep in the room where I was born, and where everything was deliciously faded and tattered because of being ninety years old. I was very happy in that room. It was full of echoes of the family and felt safe and contented, and I felt as if I belonged there.

Uncle James was very easy to look after. Aunt Mary had never been much of a cook, so that since Lyddy died, he had grown accustomed to eating undistinguished food, and was perfectly amenable about eating whatever I put in front of him. I discovered that recipe books are actually very kindly written as if most people who use them are half-witted, which suited me fine, and I managed to make a chicken casserole and to roast the goose — that was very alarming — without too much mishap. Apart from that, we ate cheese and tangerines and mince pies beside Uncle James's study fire, and he told me about his and Cara's childhood, and about his fierce, funny father and mother, and about being a prisoner of war, and we were very happy together.

During the days, I did quite a lot of exploring. I went all over the house, poking about in cupboards and attics, because I now felt quite differently about Bishopstow, having learned so much about Emily from studying her journal. Her bedroom had been the one that was now Uncle James's, with its huge, wide, sunny bay window facing west to the estuary, and inside a wall cupboard I could still see the remains of the wallpaper she had chosen for the room, bunches of fat, pink cabbage roses in garlands of duck-egg blue ribbon. I walked along the passages and climbed the stairways, and visualized her swishing along them in her wide Victorian skirts, perhaps overseeing the maids preparing a bedroom for Charlotte and Alexander who were coming to stay, or later, when she was an old woman, creeping into Alexandra's room, while Alexandra was out at some dinner party she hadn't wanted to go to, to make sure that Lyddy had made up the fire and warmed the bed.

I pictured Emily outside, too, in the rose garden she had made with Richard Talbot, or gazing at the old fig tree her father-in-law had planted, and thinking of that other faraway fig in the compound in Kabul. And I felt that Alexandra was there too, materializing out of the stories Uncle James told me during our evenings by the fire, hating being a drawing room lady and happy only with her hens and her cows.

"I'm not a drawing room lady, either," I said.

He looked at me, and grinned.

"No, you're not."

"I love it here," I said, "I never thought I'd love anywhere but Bewick, but I love it. Perhaps it's all these layers of family living collecting here over the decades, generation after generation."

He said sadly, "And I'll be the last."

"The Langleys are still family," I said, trying to cheer him up.

He gave me a faint smile. "They aren't the same, are they? Not the same as all you red-headed girls."

On Christmas Day, we went to church together. He held my arm very tightly, and on the way home, we went to look in silence at Aunt Mary's grave. "Mary Swinton" it said simply, above her dates, "Beloved by all."

"She was too," Uncle James said. He gave my arm a little shake, as if to pull himself together.

"What about you, Carly?"

"What about me?"

"You're a dear child," he said. "When you were born, I told your mother you looked like a little orangutan. Well, you've grown up into a very kind and characterful big orangutan. Are you a happy one, too?"

I said, as truthfully as I could, "Nearly."

"Hm," he said. "Love? Is that the trouble?"

"Yes," I said, "what else?"

"A loves B and B loves C?"

"Exactly."

"It couldn't be the chap you're going to Afghanistan with, could it?"

I said, "I'm afraid it could."

Uncle James stopped by the lych-gate and turned and took me in his stiff overcoated arms.

"Poor little monkey. What rotten luck."

"I'll get over it —"

"In my experience," Uncle James said, "you don't get over things, but you do get used to them."

We looked at each other very solemnly for a minute, then Uncle James aimed a kiss roughly at the end of my nose.

"I won't forget this Christmas, Carly dear. I promise you that. I won't forget it."

Chapter Eight

By the spring of 1989, I felt ready to go home. I mean, I felt that I was independent enough to go home for a short holiday without getting sucked back in to the seductive, easy life at Bewick. It had been a terribly hard winter in many ways, but I couldn't help feeling rather proud of all the skills and experience I had acquired, not to mention saving up enough money to go to Afghanistan so that I didn't feel beholden to anybody. Matthew also said to me, in a very disagreeable voice, that he supposed he'd have to keep my job open for me while I went and fooled about in the Hindu Kush, which was his way of saying he was pleased with the way I'd worked for him and would I go on doing it. I hugged him and said I'd love to go on working for him. He pretended to be revolted by both the hug and the gratitude.

"Geroff, Carly," he said, shoving me away. "I can't stand hypocrisy and melodrama, as well you know."

Just before Christmas, as promised, he had doubled my salary. It was still a very small salary for living on in London, but I was resolute about not buying clothes, and perfectly happy to live on baked potatoes. In the New Year, I even launched out on my own and left my attic rooms in the

King's Road for a scruffy little studio room in Fulham which cost over twice as much. Everybody said I was barking mad to abandon all the comforts Amanda was offering me at a bargain price for a battered room with a dripping shower off it, at the market rate. I suppose in economic terms, it was mad, but in personal terms it wasn't. I was quite free in Fulham. I was starting to live as I meant to go on, relying only on myself and not on my parents or my parents' friends or my expectations.

Needless to say, Tom understood my motives completely. He and Laura came to Fulham and looked at the room, and Laura sniffed and said, "Is that drains or curry?"

I said, "Both."

I took her over to the huge west-facing window — the room's one great asset — and pointed at the marvelous cluttered skyline view of trees and gable ends and crazy chimney pots and said, "Look. Isn't it lovely?"

She did look; then she said, "But you'll only get sun in the summer, because in winter, it'll be too low to reach you in the afternoon."

Tom said quietly, "It's a great room."

I thought he was being kind, to cheer me up, and that he thought it was as dreary as Laura did. But the next day he telephoned and asked if I would like him to help me paint it.

"Paint it!"

"Yes. Laura's going to Brussels this weekend and I'd be so happy to help you, if you'd like me to."

It was one of the best weekends of my life. We

bought two huge tins of something called Blush White Matt Emulsion, which I think was really just dear old magnolia by another name, and painted the whole room in two days. And while we painted, we talked. We talked about our childhoods and our ambitions and our hopes and fears and we discussed books and food and music and people, and it was so natural and easy and interesting that I could hardly bear to think that when the room was finished, the talk would have to stop. By Sunday afternoon, the room was indeed finished. It was transformed. It looked bigger and lighter and I felt a growing affection for it and a real excitement about living in it.

"Of course you do," Tom said. "It's yours. That's why."

Amanda, who was, I think, secretly quite impressed, gave me a pair of enormous russet linen curtains she had made for someone eight years ago, that they had never collected, and two Indian cotton rugs to cover, at least partly, the wildly swirly carpet the room had already and which I had to learn to live with. Ma, once she had got used to the idea that I was not going to live at the kind of address she would have liked, hired a van and sent some furniture down from Scotland, driven by Jamie, who nearly died of envy when he saw my room, and that was wonderful. He and Tom carried the furniture up from the street for me, and we played a lovely game of arranging it, and then Tom stopped the shower dripping and Jamie went out for a celebratory bottle, and we drank it sitting in a little circle on one of Amanda's rugs, and I just wanted the moment never to end. I looked at Tom and Jamie, getting on as if they had known each other all their lives, and I looked at Tom's brown, paint-splashed hands, and I looked at my transformed new home, so characterful and cluttered and already feeling like mine, and I just wanted to stop the clock of my life right there, because it couldn't be better than this, and was bound to get worse.

When Tom had finished his wine, he said he'd got to be at the airport by eight, so he'd better get going.

"Why?" Jamie said.

Tom got up and stretched, like a big, graceful cat.

"I'm meeting Laura back from Brussels. She's been at some Euro legal conference."

Jamie nodded, in a man-to-man way, as if he knew all about Laura and European law. "Don't want to keep her waiting —"

"No," Tom said. He bent and ruffled my hair. "See you soon, Carly."

I looked up at him. I said, in a slightly strangled voice, "I can't thank you enough for this weekend, and all the help you've given me."

He said, "I enjoyed myself. It looks wonderful. I'm quite envious."

I looked at the floor, so that I wouldn't actually have to see him go.

"Nice bloke," Jamie said.

"Yes —"

"Great. Ma wants to meet him."

"I don't think —"

"That's what I told her. I said, 'Ma, you can't

go through life vetting every person Carly says hi to.' She wants to make sure he's capable of looking after you in Afghanistan. I'll tell her. I'll tell her he's a great bloke." He looked at me. "I'm dead jealous, Carly."

I turned away and scrambled to my feet. I said, "Independence will be miles easier for you. You're a boy and I'll have softened Ma up a bit by the time you launch out."

"Can't leave poor old Xan —"

"Then you'll have to leave together."

We looked at each other, visualizing it.

"Jesus," Jamie said.

Then we went out to find something to eat, and I thought, with some pride, that this was the first time in my life that I had had one of my relations to stay, as my own responsibility.

Oddly enough, going home to Bewick felt as if I was staying, not living there any more. I had a wonderful reunion with Ma and Duncan, and with my spaniel and my bedroom and the loch, but I didn't feel, as I used to feel when I came home from school in the holidays, that I was the last piece of a jigsaw fitting finally and smoothly into place to make a whole picture. I felt like a very happy observer, pleased to be there but not belonging.

Ma's first remark was, "Oh darling, you look lovely, and you've grown your hair!"

I had, for obvious reasons. I had never had other than quite short hair, all my life, because the theory was that it was such thick hair that if it was allowed to grow, it would just grow out, and not down. But to my amazement, it not only liked being grown, but it seemed to become more docile as it grew. The curls turned into curves, and were soft and manageable. The only trouble was that having got the idea of growing into its head, it couldn't stop, and in the eight months since I had told it that it could, it had shot well past my shoulders and was a thick, shining mane. Secretly I was rather proud of it though I had to admit to myself the sad fact that Tom didn't even seem to have noticed. In fact, I don't think he actually noticed that I was a girl. To him I was just a nice friendly someone called Carly.

I said to Ma, "Do you like it?"

She looked at it for a long time. It was loose on my shoulders, with an Indian silk scarf tied loosely round my head, like an Alice band. She said, "Yes. Yes, I like it very much. You look quite different."

"Do I? What sort of different?"

"Lovely," she said.

Jamie and Xan yelped and snorted and fell about with laughter.

"She looks exactly the same, except that she now looks like an orange floor mop instead of an orange dish mop —"

"Take no notice," Ma said.

"When have I ever?"

"Come and see," she said, leading me over to the little mirror she kept in the kitchen, so that she could check to see if she had lipstick on her teeth or flour on her nose before she opened the back door to anyone.

"See?"

I looked. I did have a mirror in London, but I wasn't overkeen on looking in it. In the Inverbrae mirror, to my surprise, I saw someone quite — well, presentable. All the same, I said, "My nose is too big and my mouth is too wide and I hate my chin."

"Hear, hear," Xan said.

"You've grown to all of them," Ma said. "Perhaps it's your hair. It balances everything. Why did you grow it?"

I said carefully, "To look as feminine as possible for talking to and not frightening refugee women and children."

"Oh dear," Ma said, "I wish you didn't want to go to Afghanistan."

"Well, I do."

"And I haven't even met this Pasco man —"

"I *told* her," James said, "I told her he was ace."

I said, "He's *frightfully* responsible."

Ma said suddenly, "You won't go and do anything silly like fall in love with him, will you?"

I gulped. "Heavens no —"

"It's just that you're so carried away with this Charlotte thing, I thought you might feel impelled to have an affair too —"

Jamie said helpfully, "He's got a woman, Ma. She's called Laura."

"Anyway," Xan said, "I expect she'll get raped. By an Afghan."

"Or a leftover Russian —"

"Shut *up*," Ma said. She was watching me.

I said, "I am not going to fall in love with anyone until I am at least thirty."

"It doesn't work like that."

I opened my eyes wide. "Doesn't it?"

"No," Ma said seriously. "It happens when you aren't looking and you don't intend it to."

"What does?" said Duncan, coming in with the dogs.

"Falling in love."

"Ah," he said. He kissed Ma and then me. "You career girls haven't time for love, have you?"

"Not a minute."

He gave me a quick look, and then he said to Ma, "You leave her alone, Alexia. Her heart's no more your business than yours was Cara's."

I had a very happy week. I went down to the hotel and saw Jimmie and Gregor and all the staff, and I admired the new summer dining room that had been made out of a rather gloomy arched loggia that ran along the house facing the loch, and the new award for a "European Hotel with National Character." I went to see Elsie in her cottage — she was now retired officially but nothing seemed to have escaped her, including every detail of my trip to Afghanistan — and the keepers, and the head keeper's new puppy, and I walked and walked in the lovely, familiar hills in order, as Jamie said, to give my legs some idea of what they were in for. Everyone told me that I looked very well, considering that I lived in London, and that I seemed very positive, and I agreed with them. I felt positive. I also felt, the night before I was due to go south again, taking my car, that it wasn't going to break my heart this time to leave Scotland. I knew that as I drove away over the pass — a journey that had meant misery all my childhood and growing up — I was going to feel a great affection and admiration for everything I was leaving behind, but I wasn't going to feel that I'd sell my soul to stay.

On the last night, we had a very peculiar conversation. I had been telling Ma about my Christmas with Uncle James and how much I had liked being with him, and how much I had liked the house now that I knew so much more of its human history, and she said, "I used to feel that my heart was breaking every time I had to leave Bishopstow. I went on feeling that until I fell in love with Bewick. Isn't it odd? And my grandmother, your great-grandmother, Alexandra, felt exactly the opposite. Bewick was a prison to her, almost a literal prison in those days, and it was Bishopstow that turned out to be her release and her refuge."

I opened my mouth to say that my own feelings weren't so different, and I was just beginning to feel free of my clinging adoration of Bewick, when some instinct told me to shut it again.

Ma went on, "I wish the whole estate was going to be easier to divide up. It must have struck you and the boys that there are two great houses and the three of you. Perhaps the boys will go into partnership or something —"

"Or I won't want to be left anything so enormous," I said and the moment the words were out of my mouth, I regretted them bitterly. I watched Ma, and waited for her to spin round and rage and say she hadn't worked all these years just to have all she'd worked for thrown back in her teeth by a spoiled brat like me. But she didn't. She came over to where I was sitting at the kitchen table and said, in a very calm voice, "Explain."

I said clumsily, in a rush, "It isn't that I'm not awfully grateful for a wonderful upbringing in a wonderful place because I am, but I've got to feel that I've earned things in life, that I haven't just been given them and that's one of the reasons for going to Afghanistan, not just the romantic idea of following Charlotte, but I want to see the refugees, I want to see what it is like, to feel what it is like, not to be privileged and sheltered and safe, like I've been. Do you see?"

She said, "You sound just like Duncan."

"Duncan?"

"He described your feelings to me, more or less as you have done. He said I was to get off your back."

"Did he?"

Ma said suddenly, "Carly, what would have become of me if I hadn't met Duncan?"

"Don't think about it. You did, didn't you? So don't think about it."

She leaned forward and took my hand. "Oh Carly darling, it's *so* important!"

"What is?" I said, acting dumb but knowing perfectly well what she meant.

"Falling in love. Finding the right partner."

"Yes," I said. "I expect it is."

She gave me a searching look. "Have you fallen in love yet?"

I put my chin up. "I thought I had in Edinburgh. Remember? Guy Barnes."

"Oh," she said, making a dismissive gesture.

"Ma, I'm trying very hard not to think about love just now. I'm trying to think about Afghanistan and work instead."

She nodded, like an obedient child. Duncan must have given her a really terrific ticking-off about not prying, about leaving me alone. Not for the first time, I thought gratefully of him. I said, "Ma, I do promise that if and when I get my love act together, you'll be the first to know."

She smiled at me. She said, "I expect I'll know without being told. The only advice I'd dare to give you is not to allow yourself to be other than absolutely honest with yourself."

"What do you mean?"

"When I came up here," Ma said, "there was a young man, left over from the school at the castle, who wanted to stay and help create the hotel, partly because he was in love with the place, but mostly because he fell in love with me. I let him stay and I let him fall further and further in love, and get fond of you, because it was easy and cosy and flattering. But then there was a horrible ending, which was all my fault, when he wanted to marry me and I had to tell him that I didn't love him and I never had. I don't think my conscience will ever be quite comfortable about it, even though he went off to be an architect, which was what he'd always wanted, and got married and has two daughters of his own. He was called Peter Burton."

Something about the earnest way she spoke made me want to smile, just a little. I leaned forward. I said, "Ma darling, why are you telling me this?"

She said very seriously, "Because you are exactly the kind of girl that men do fall in love with. That's why."

I couldn't help smiling then. I leaned all the way across the table and kissed her and said, "You are a very dear Ma, and hopelessly biased, but I'm afraid you couldn't be more wrong."

Chapter Nine

Getting ready to leave for Afghanistan was a major enterprise. I reread the part of Emily's journal where she described getting ready to go to India, and although there were awful complications about furniture for their cabins on the boat out, and about needing dozens of pairs of kid gloves, and flasks of raspberry vinegar, and buckets for drawing water up out of the ocean, there were no bureaucratic complications at all. Charlotte's fiancé, Hugh Connell, simply booked their passages and that was it; no visas or air tickets or inoculations or insurance or currency regulations. There were several days when I felt the whole thing was quite beyond me, and that I would be quite happy to go back to being a good conventional girl with a nice job on *Marshalls* magazine. There were also, inevitably, other days when I wished with all my heart that I had never met Tom Pasco.

Being in love with someone who is perfectly charming to you but is not in the least in love back, is a state I wouldn't wish on my worst enemy. I strove, all the time, to hide my feelings — I suppose out of pride — and I don't know how much Sasha and Simon guessed. They were certainly very tactful to me, and as for Matthew, having made it plain just once that he knew, he never mentioned the matter to me again. But I felt as if I had toothache, all the time, or that part of me was paralyzed. I tried very hard not to let it obsess me because I do think that lovelorn people who go on and on about their broken hearts are very boring indeed, but I couldn't ignore the fact that wanting something so badly that I couldn't have did, at times, make me very miserable.

In April, Tom introduced me to the rest of the film crew. We went, appropriately, to an Afghan restaurant called The Great Khan and sat on cushions on the floor and ate palao, which I thought was wonderful. I asked Tom what was in it, and he asked our waiter, who grinned and put his hands together as if in prayer and then recited at great speed. "Basmati rice, lamb, pigeon, chicken, onion, cardamom, coriander, clove, aniseed, salt, sugar, almond, vinegar, lemon juice, saffron, sultana, pistachio, and —" he held up one finger.

"And what?"

He grinned again. "Hot water."

It was obviously his party piece. We all applauded. I said happily, looking at my piled plate, "I'm not going to go hungry, am I?"

Abdul, an old university friend of Tom's, who was coming with us as an interpreter, leaned over and said, "In Afghanistan, all plates must be heaped, all food must be in profusion. Small helping is big insult."

"Suits me," I said.

I also thought the film crew was going to suit me. There was Joe Blunt, the sound recordist, a small square man with a strong Northern accent and a quick smile, and Andy Parsons, the cameraman. Andy was tall and agile and fair, with a thin, funny face, like a jester. He had worked with Tom before, in Palestine. He said to me, "What are you coming along for then?"

"Oh, just the ride —"

Joe said, "I'll bet it's to make Laura jealous. What do you reckon?"

Tom laughed easily. I couldn't bear to see him laugh quite so easily. He said, "Carly has a private mission. She might tell you if she thinks you deserve it."

"What do I have to do to deserve it?" Andy said.

"Andy, you're not to *start* by teasing her."

Andy winked at me. "She looks like someone who could take a little teasing."

I said, "Actually, I want to see the country where my great-great-great-grandmother went in 1841."

"She never!"

"She did. She bought the freedom of a Pathan slave, and she was an excellent horsewoman and a splendid shot, and she had a scandalous affair with the British Resident in Kabul."

"Wow," Andy said. "You going to do the same, Carly?"

"Have a scandalous affair with me," Joe suggested.

Abdul said seriously, "No Pathan is slave now. Is not called Pathan. Is called Pashtun. Pathan English Empire name. No Pashtun slave to English now, or to anyone."

"No, of course not —"

"What are you looking for?" Andy said.

I shook my head. "I don't really know —"

"Leave her alone," Tom said sharply. "That's her business."

Andy held up his hands in mock defence. "Sorry, sorry, I never meant —"

"It's all right," I said. "It doesn't matter."

Andy gave me a crooked grin and raised his glass of green tea.

"Let's just hope you find it!"

There seemed to be a lot of people to say goodbye to. I was only going to be away a few months, but all the same, the journey had a momentous feel about it, and I thought I couldn't just push off casually as if I were going to Spain for two weeks in the sun.

The first person I went to see was my father. He wanted to take me out for a meal on my own, but I had a feeling that if he did that, the conversation would inevitably get round to Ma, and how brilliantly she had done and that would in turn lead to a self-pitying session on how badly he had done, by comparison, and I knew I couldn't stand that. So I said I'd come for supper, even though that would probably mean having to put up with Jake.

I got in from the office late, as usual, and showered, and found a clean shirt, and a very nice short white drill skirt that Sasha had given me after a photographic session on the magazine, because someone had spilled coffee on it, so it couldn't go back to the shop. I managed to get the stain out, and I wore it a great deal. I was just zipping it up over my dark blue shirt when my doorbell rang. Thinking it was probably the very annoying man from the floor below who was perfectly sure that English girls who said "no" usually said "yes" if you went on at them long enough, I pressed the intercom and snapped, "Yes?" into it.

"It's Andy," a voice said.

"Andy?"

"Andy Parsons. Andy the camera. Can I come up?"

"Yes," I said, terribly pleased. "I mean no, I'm going out, you see —"

"Two minutes," he said.

He was carrying flowers. I nearly fainted. I had never been given flowers in my life before, except once, by Guy in Edinburgh, who gave me a single red rose on St. Valentine's Day and I rather unkindly told him I'd never heard of anything so corny, so he didn't, somewhat understandably, do it again.

These were freesias, little pale scented trumpets of white and yellow.

"But they're lovely! Why do I get flowers?"

"To make you think you'd like to come out and have supper with me."

I groaned. I said, "I've got to have supper with my father."

"You're too old to have one of those. I lost mine years ago."

"Andy, I do have to. But I'd love to have had supper with you, and please, may I another time?"

416

He sucked his teeth. "Oo," he said. "Depends."

"I'll keep the freesias anyway," I said, "just in case you never ask me out again."

"I'll drive you to your father's."

"I've got to drive myself, so that I can get back, you see —"

He came and leaned against the edge of the tiny shower room where I was filling a jug with water for the freesias. He was much taller than me, very tall in fact, with just the lean spare quality I like in men. He said, "Did I annoy you the other night?"

"No," I said, "it was only teasing."

"I don't want to annoy you —"

I stepped past him and put the flowers on the table I had painted black, and used as a desk.

"Look. Aren't they lovely? They sort of light things up."

"I don't know anything about flowers," Andy said. "Tom's the one for that. Flowers and birds."

I picked up my hairbrush and began to brush vigorously.

"Look, I've got to go. I'm really sorry, but I've got to."

"I know," Andy said, "I'll be off."

He stood watching me for a few seconds, while I shook out my hair and put on my parrot earrings. Then he said, "See you, Carly," and let himself out of the flat. I collected a jacket and my car keys and door keys, and the latest copy of *Marshalls* magazine for Susie and raced down to the street. It was most peculiar, but I suddenly felt rather happy, certainly happier in a light-hearted, excited way, than I'd felt for ages. Andy

417

Parsons's brief, unexpected visit seemed to have made a difference.

Supper with Martin and Susie was perfectly all right. Susie had made a great effort with food, knowing my enthusiasm for it, and we had a proper chicken curry, with all the trimmings, and fruit salad. Jake wasn't there, being out at the opening of a club featured in his favorite magazine, which certainly improved the atmosphere, and Susie was in good spirits having managed to lose five pounds and join a local women's group which she said was teaching her not to undervalue herself. Martin sighed heavily while she was telling me this, and I guessed he had been very dismissive and cutting about it privately to her, so I was ultraenthusiastic and told her it was a brilliant idea.

Martin said, "Well, seeing a few Muslim women will certainly give *you* something to think about."

"What do you mean?"

"About how lucky you are."

I glared at him. "I know that already, thank you very much."

Martin got up and went out of the room.

"Oh Lord," I said, "is he sulking?"

"No, no," Susie said, smiling at me. She was still really pretty when she smiled. "I'm afraid he's jealous again, that's all."

"Jealous? Of whom?"

"You."

"Me!"

"Yes," Susie said, spreading out her left hand and

thoughtfully twisting her wedding ring. "It's suddenly struck him that you are young and free and about to launch out on life and adventure, and it's made him feel old and stuck, all over again."

"Poor you," I said. "Don't you get absolutely sick of him sometimes?"

She bent her head. "It doesn't do to think about that too much. That's why I'm going out to find other things to think about. Have some more fruit."

I looked regretfully at the bowl. I said, "Do you know, I haven't an inch more space, to my great disappointment."

The door opened and Martin came back into the room, holding a parcel done up in blue paper spangled with little gold stars. It was a neat, solid parcel. He put it down in front of me.

"For you."

"For me!"

"Yes," he said. "I'm not much of a father on the whole am I, but I think this is something that you'll want to have as much as I'd like to give it to you."

I never know what to do when people who are usually impossible are suddenly generous and sweet instead. I ducked my head and looked at the parcel.

"Open it," Martin said.

I did, very slowly. Inside was a perfectly marvelous camera, a Canon Supershot, compact and brilliantly versatile.

"Now that you know how to use one," Martin said, "I thought you'd better have something to practice on."

I got up and put my arms round his neck. I had spent my childhood enthusiastically hugging Ma and Duncan and Xan and Jamie, but I had never felt very easy about hugging Martin. But now I did, because he had plainly given me a present which was not only perfect for me, but which was something he would have *loved* for himself.

"Oh, thank you!" I said.

"Like it?"

"Oh, so much. It's wonderful. It's exactly what I needed and wanted."

He gave my bottom a brisk fatherly pat, half a slap.

"Well, Carly my love, you just go on getting what you need and want, that's all."

I didn't know what to say to this, and felt rather shy, but then Susie saved the situation by bursting into tears because, she said, it was so lovely to see us being fond of one another, so we had to stop and rush round the table and mop her up instead.

When I got back that night, very full of curry and affection, and clutching my beautiful camera, I found someone had left a note for me. It was a folded over piece of paper, torn out of a reporter's notebook, with my name written on the outside, and on the inside it said, "Good night. Sleep tight. Andy the Camera." That was all. I put it between my teeth, so that I had enough free hands to unlock the door to the flat as well as to hold my camera, and then I carried it over to my table, and switched on the lamp, and put the note down beside the little jug of freesias.

Then I looked at it. I looked at the note, and I looked at the freesias which were even more lovely by lamplight, and which were filling the room with scent. The sight of the note and flowers made me want to smile, partly because there was something very zany and attractive about Andy, and partly because it was heavenly to feel so complimented. He had wanted to take me out, he had brought me flowers, and he had gone on thinking about me enough all evening to come back and leave a little good-night message. It was the most purely happy thing that had happened to me for ages, and I found I wanted to sing. I can't really sing, any more than Jamie can, but that hasn't ever stopped me trying either, so I danced round my room singing "Love Is a Many Splendored Thing" (a song I despise) until the Australian next door, with whom I got on really well, came and shouted through the door that if I didn't shut myself up, he'd come in and do it for me. So I did shut up, or sort of. I lay on my bed, clutching my camera, and had a really happy fit of the giggles.

Two days later, I went to Culver Square to see Cara and Grandpa. It's quite amazing to think that they have lived in that house, and no other, for over forty years and, as Ma points out, they haven't done anything to it at all *except* live in it. It's almost a museum piece, everything's so antiquated. It isn't charming antiquated like Bishopstow, with lovely old furniture and silver and pictures, or magical antiquated like Bewick or even solid old-fashioned antiquated like Inverbrae. It's just absolutely, utterly shabby. If you gave Cara ten thousand pounds and said, "Paint Culver Square from top to toe," she would be utterly shocked and would probably point out that the front door was painted only yesterday, when Ma and Martin were married in 1966.

Culver Square is a rather smart square now, full of expensive young families and Volvo estate cars to put them in when they go off to their country cottages for weekends. Cara doesn't seem to have noticed this change, and Grandpa just thinks it's very nice to have lots of little boys playing conkers and cricket in the square when he goes out for his daily constitutional. Cara and Grandpa are genuinely the least snobbish people I have ever come across, and probably the least materialistic too. I once asked Cara if she didn't miss the great portraits of Charlotte and Alexander when she sent them back to Bewick, and she looked amazed and said, "Why should I? I never looked at them anyway and they never belonged here. I often can't see the point of pictures. I'd much rather have a lovely view."

I went to have tea with them, as Cara is such a dreadful cook that it's the one meal she can't really ruin. She had made, as Susie did, a great effort for me, with some rather uneven cucumber sandwiches, and a big, black gloomy cake which the help, Edna, had made. Cara said the cake was called a Black Stirling Gingerbread. Edna was getting on a bit, and had never been much of a cook either, so I looked at the cake with a certain apprehension.

Grandpa had to be reminded of where I was going and why and who with several times, and then he looked at me intently and said, "Good heavens, Carly dear. Just like Charlotte."

I gave him a kiss and said, "Well done. Ten out of ten," and he looked very pleased, and then went back to reading the *Guardian* which is the only newspaper he can stand because, he says, all the others are so right wing.

Cara said, "You're looking particularly pleased with yourself, Carly. Are you excited about this trip?"

"Yes," I said. It was perfectly true, I was excited, but there was also, in my pocket, another note from Andy. This one said, "Will you come out with me even if I don't give you freesias?" I had written one back which said, "Certainly not. No freesias, no date."

Cara held out the plate of sandwiches.

"I expect you're sick of people telling you how envious of you they are, but I'm afraid I'm joining the queue."

I said, taking a bite of sandwich, "But you had the adventure of the war!"

She looked at me. She said, shaking her head, "There was only that one tiny little adventure of rescuing Mary, at the end. The rest was more monotonous than you can imagine, and cold and full of drudgery and the long, long tension of waiting, always waiting."

"But I thought —"

"I know you did," Cara said. "It's become a family myth that I had an amazing war. But I didn't. I was the only one of my contemporaries who couldn't leave home in the war, and I nearly went mad."

"I'd no idea," I said. I put my sandwich down. Cara had forgotten to put salt in them and had drowned the cucumber with pepper.

"And all the time," Cara said, speaking in her normal voice without a trace of self-pity or melodrama, "I was, or thought I was, madly in love."

"With Grandpa?"

"No," she said. She gave a little smile. "No. Would you believe it, with your Uncle Alan?"

I remembered Uncle Alan at Aunt Mary's funeral, huge and red and bursting out of a very expensive overcoat with a velvet collar. "I don't *believe* it!"

"It's true," Cara said. "He was frightfully attractive then, and I was wild about him. Looking back, I think it was just sex."

I gulped. She looked at me. She said, "Carly, do your level best not to confuse love and sex, won't you?"

I nodded. I was quite speechless. I almost fell off my chair when Grandpa emerged over the edge of the *Guardian* and said, "I think what she means, Carly, is don't think mere sexual attraction, however strong, is automatically love as well."

I stared at them both, and then I managed to say, "Is this . . . is this advice for Afghanistan?"

"Of course," said Grandpa. "Of course it is. After all, look what happened to Charlotte."

Chapter Ten

When I got back from Culver Square, Andy
was perched on a litter bin in my street, waiting
for me. He had a single freesia in his hand, a
mauvey-pink one, and he held it out to me.

"A compromise," he said.

I laughed. I couldn't help it. I said, "I haven't
got room for supper. I'm full of cake."

"Then we'll go roller-skating first."

"Roller-skating!"

"Yes," he said, "why not? Can't you roller-
skate?"

"No."

"Can you ice-skate?"

I thought suddenly of Bewick, of the frozen
lake in the castle grounds where the boys and I
had learned to skate pushing kitchen chairs
around the ice to hold us up.

" 'Course I can —"

"Then you can roller-skate."

"But *why*, Andy?"

"Because it's energetic and thus energy con-
suming and more fun than sitting in a litter bin
arguing with you."

I smiled at him. "Okay then. But not in this
skirt."

He eyed me in a speculative way.

"I don't see how you can even get upstairs in

that skirt. If you take it off for skating, will you promise to put it back on afterwards, for supper?"

"Promise," I said.

I took him upstairs and made him look out of the window while I exchanged my skirt for jeans, and my shirt for a sweatshirt. It was brilliant green and Xan had given it to me because it said on the front, "Expensive, but worthless" in huge yellow letters.

"You can turn round," I said to Andy.

He spun round and read the slogan. He said, "Somebody really fond of you gave you that."

"My brother."

"As long as it was *only* your brother."

Roller-skating was the most wonderful fun. It was deafeningly noisy and terrifyingly fast, and Andy turned out to be an expert, noisier and faster than anyone else. At first, I insisted he go off and burn round the rink on his own while I crept and tottered round the edge and said, "Whoops" and "Sorry" to everyone, but then he came back for me and insisted I skate with him. I said I couldn't, I was far too scared and feeble, and he said pack it in, would you, and laced our arms together firmly across each others' backs, and we were off. It was quite scary, but when I felt how strong and experienced Andy was, and how thrilling the speed and movement were, I stopped squeaking like a jittery mouse, and began to relax into the rhythm. In the end, of course, I adored it and didn't want to stop.

"You'd better," Andy said, "or you'll be so stiff

in the morning we'll have to break you up with a hammer."

We had hot showers and a coke at the rink, and then, glowing and grinning, we went off for supper, to a little Thai restaurant Andy knew, run by the brother of someone he had once met on an assignment to Thailand. It had been a pretty dangerous assignment, he said, because a lot of the filming had to be done secretly, on the edges of the Golden Triangle, where the opium poppies grew. It was exciting to listen to him, and delicious to eat the delicate, spicy food and luxurious to feel myself so alive and tingling after the skating.

"Carly," Andy said.

"Yes?"

"You know what I think, don't you?"

I pretended not to understand. I picked a frond of lemon grass out of my rice and said, "About what? The Green Movement? God?"

"Don't muck about," Andy said. "About you."

I said nothing. I didn't want this happy, carefree, fooling-about stage we were at to go any further.

"Look," Andy said, "don't get me wrong. I don't want anything heavy. I just think you're great and I didn't want us to fly off next Sunday without my telling you."

I smiled at him. "You're great too," I said.

His funny thin face was suddenly very serious.

"There can't be any big deal on a trip like this," he said. "It doesn't work, when we've got a job to do. But I'd just like you to know that I'm there if you need me, that I've got a special eye out for you."

I put my hand on his. "Thank you. I mean that. Thank you."

"I've never met anyone like you," he said. "Not a girl, that is. You seem . . . you seem to have so much your own character somehow."

I thought we'd been serious long enough. I said, "Well, I certainly haven't got anyone else's. Andy, that was a lovely evening, but I have to go to work tomorrow, and I have to be in by eight-thirty because Matthew is being quite manic this week to punish me for going away for three months."

Andy leaned across the table and kissed my cheek.

"Message received and understood. Come on. I'll take you home."

Despite being so well exercised, and well fed, it wasn't easy to get to sleep that night, for the most obvious reason. My mind, so long full of Tom, was now full of Andy too, as well as a great deal of puzzlement. Why should it be that I yearned for Tom and he didn't yearn for me and that situation made me very unhappy, yet at the same time strangely satisfied some part of me, while simultaneously I really liked Andy, and he plainly more than liked me, and that *that* situation should make me happy, yet oddly unsatisfied. It was all most confusing, but one thing was plain and simple, and that was that Andy definitely made me feel better about Tom. I lay awake, wondering about this until three in the morning, and finally came to the conclusion that Cara was right. When it came to Tom, I had merely confused sex with love. Yes, I told myself firmly, turning over for the hundredth time, that was what I had done. Otherwise, why should I, every time I saw Tom, not just long for his approval and affection, but also long and long to be in bed with him?

The remainder of the week was one mad rush. I had a goodbye drink with Amanda, and a goodbye lunch with Sasha — who was only, I think, interested in what I planned to wear while up the Khyber — and two goodbye suppers with Simon because, in a kind Simonish way, he said he hadn't been very good company during the first one, on account of being very sleepy, so he wanted to make it up to me on the next night. I tried to have a goodbye something, at least, with Matthew, but he said I was the most repellently sentimental assistant he had ever had and he couldn't wait for me to be gone. The day after he said this, he dropped into my lap the most invaluable-looking guide book to Afghanistan and West Pakistan, saying "I suppose you'd better have this," and I said, playing his game, "I suppose I better had," and he winked at me.

In between all these farewell meals, I had my final injections, collected my malaria pills, and packed and unpacked my bag about a hundred times on account of not being able to decide what was, or wasn't, absolutely essential. I could be sure I didn't need a party frock, but could I be equally sure I mightn't need my sailing oilskins (well tried on Loch Bewick) or tidy shoes? Tom had said, "You need Outward Bound kind of clothes, but the absolute minimum." Was an absolute minimum for three months two T-shirts or six? Did Outward Bound include a bathing suit and climbing boots? All I knew I had to take, without question, was my new camera, and the photocopy of Emily's journal, and my parrot and star earrings for luck. The real journal, and the drawing of Charlotte, I made into a neat parcel and took to the bank for safekeeping.

The night before we actually flew off, I had refused all invitations because I wanted to pack for the hundred and first time, wash my hair and go to bed early. I felt very calm and organized. All the clothes and kit I had finally decided on were in piles on the floor, all my documents and my passport were in another, smaller pile on the table, and beside the second pile lay a very efficient list I had made for Jamie. Jamie was going to borrow my flat and my car for the summer, to celebrate having left school, and I was going to leave the keys for him with the Australian next door, the one who couldn't stand my singing.

My plan was to wash my hair, and while it dried, to pack and lay out my clothes for the morning, like we used to have to do at boarding school. I considered having supper, but surprisingly for someone as keen about food as I am, I didn't feel very enthusiastic about eating. I supposed it was excitement, or nervousness, though I couldn't honestly say I felt either; I just wasn't quite myself at all.

I washed my hair in the shower, and wound it up in a towel, and then knelt down on the floor and looked at the neat, un-Carly-like squares of clean T-shirts and clean jeans and clean jerseys.

Then I checked it again. Then I sat back on my heels and checked all the people I knew to make sure I had either seen or spoken to everyone — Ma, Duncan, the boys, the grandparents, Amanda, Matthew, Simon, Sasha! — I stopped. Uncle James. I had completely forgotten Uncle James! I felt full of sudden panic. How *could* I have forgotten him after our Christmas together, after he had supported me against Ma about this trip, after he had given me the precious drawing of Charlotte?

I jumped up, and pulled the towel off my head, and shook out my hair. I would ring him, I would ring him at once. But the moment I had had that idea, I had another one, a much more urgent one. I would get into the car, and drive down to Cornwall, now, and *see* him.

I looked at my watch. It was seven o'clock. If I drove almost without stopping, I'd get to Bishopstow at one in the morning. Then I'd be there just to see him and have a couple hours sleep, and then I'd drive back to London, and be in the flat by ten and out at the airport by midday to catch the two o'clock flight. I was suddenly filled with energy and pleasure. I felt that it was the absolutely right thing to do. I considered telephoning Bishopstow and decided against it because Uncle James would only tell me I wasn't to come, and I *wanted* to come, I had to, because . . . because I was afraid, in my heart of hearts, that I might not see him again.

I brushed out my wet hair, seized a jersey from one of my piles and my keys and some money and rushed down into the street. Doing something active seemed to have woken my appetite up again, so I paused at the ever-open little newsagent's to buy some chocolate, and then I went along the street to find my car. I had filled it up with petrol, the day before, as a present for Jamie to start on his first taste of independence, so all I had to do was to get in it, and go.

I don't remember much about that journey. I was so buoyed up by feeling I was doing the right thing in dashing down to Bishopstow, that I didn't really stop to calculate whether I had enough time or whether I should in fact have telephoned or whether it would have made sense to pack before I left. I just thought, "I have to see him because I have this awful feeling he might die while I'm away," and that thought kept me going, mile after mile after mile, while the sun sank in the west ahead of me and the light faded and faded until other people's headlamps were like stars in the darkness all around me.

It was, luckily, a lovely night. As the hours wore on, and the roads gradually emptied, I could see how bright the moon was, almost bright enough to drive by without lights. I thought of all the eighteenth-century people in Wiltshire and Somerset and Devon, as I drove through them, being so pleased when there was a full moon because that meant they could see well enough to get out their carriages and go to have dinner with each other, or to the local assembly rooms for dancing, like characters in a Jane Austen novel. The moon seemed to swell and swell as I got further westward and when I turned right in Wadebridge towards the coast and Bishopstow, it was so big and brilliant that I began to feel it was a special beacon, guiding me kindly on my mission.

Bishopstow was, of course, in complete darkness when I crunched the car as softly as I could to a halt on the gravel. It was a solid black silhouette, guarded by fretted black silhouetted trees, against the moonlit sky that hung over the silvery waters of the estuary. It looked indescribably beautiful, and settled, and timeless. I opened the car door very softly, and crept out onto the drive. My plan was to tiptoe round to Uncle James's bedroom window, and throw pebbles up against the glass until he heard me.

But I had forgotten about the dogs, now banished from Uncle James's bed to downstairs, and about Pamela Merryweather. I hadn't taken three steps across the gravel before the dogs started barking madly inside the house, and a few seconds later, a sash window was thrown up on the first floor and a commanding female voice called, "Who's there?"

"Me," I said idiotically.

"Who's me?" said the voice.

"It's Carly. I'm Uncle James's niece, I've come to say goodbye."

The voice went from command to outrage. "To say goodbye? Do you realize, young lady, that it is one o'clock in the morning?"

"But I'm leaving tomorrow," I said pleadingly. "I've only come for three hours. I've come all the way from London —"

The voice gave a kind of exasperated snort, and the window was thumped down. There was a short interval, during which I felt suddenly very tired and deflated, and then lights began to come on, one after another, as Pamela Merryweather made her way downstairs. The light above the front door flashed out and then the door was opened and the dogs dashed out at full cry and flung themselves on me with licks and squeals.

Pamela Merryweather stood in the lit doorway wearing a full-length quilted dressing gown, which made her the shape of an upholstered telephone box. She also wore furry slippers and a very unwelcoming expression. She said, "This is highly inconsiderate. Why couldn't you have telephoned? Major Swinton is neither young nor fit and it is the height of thoughtlessness to disturb him like this."

I came forward, holding the wriggling dogs by their collars.

"Please don't be cross. I know it seems a mad thing to do, but it was a really urgent impulse and I just obeyed it. To come and say goodbye to him in person, I mean."

She looked a tiny bit mollified. She shut the door behind us all and said, "And where are you going?"

"To Afghanistan. Tomorrow."

She goggled at me. I was plainly, to her, a perfect example of irresponsible, selfish, mad modern youth.

"Well, what do you expect me to do? I'm not waking Major Swinton —"

"No, you're not," I said firmly, "I'm doing that."

She opened her mouth to forbid me, so I

434

simply slid past her, and dashed up the stairs with the dogs at my heels. She called after me, "I won't be held responsible for this, you know! I won't be held responsible for the consequences!" but she didn't try to follow me.

There was a light on, on the landing. Uncle James's bedroom door was shut. I felt awful about waking him, but it was what I had come for, so I had to do it. I tapped softly, expecting silence, but he said, to my surprise, "Come in!"

I opened the door. The room was not, as I'd expected, in complete darkness. Uncle James was half-propped up on his pillows, with his bifocals on, and a book lying open on the bedclothes, upside down. His face completely lit up when he saw me. I thought I was going to cry.

"Carly!"

I tiptoed in. The dogs rushed past me and leaped on to the bed, wagging furiously.

"I'm so sorry to come like this, all unannounced, and so late, but I had to see you, I had to come and say goodbye properly and I only realized that, at the last minute —"

He held out his arms to me. I sat down on the edge of the bed and hugged him. He felt like a frail old bird, all bones and feathers, and no good solid flesh, like he always used to have.

He said, "I thought you were a prowler. I wondered if I ought to get up and see, and then I thought that if *I* were a prowler, I wouldn't prowl much further once I'd seen Pamela Merryweather, so I left it to her."

I began to giggle. "She's so cross with me —"

"Of course she is. You're very naughty, interrupting her beauty sleep." He gave my face a little pat. "What a dear monkey to come like this."

"I just drove and drove and drove. I thought that if I telephoned you'd tell me not to come."

"Quite right. I would have. How long can you stay?"

"Three hours."

He twinkled at me. "You're mad. Quite mad. And I expect you're hungry too."

"Terribly."

He leaned forward and whispered conspiratorially, "Tell you what. Go downstairs and make yourself a sandwich or whatever you'd like and then, while you're at it, go into the study and look in the bottom drawer of the filing cabinet, and bring me a thumping measure of what you find hidden there."

Pamela Merryweather had left the lights on, and had retired to bed in dudgeon. I could hear the civilized tones of the BBC's World Service on the radio as I went past her bedroom door. The kitchen was beautifully warm and welcoming, because of the Aga, and in the larder beyond it — a really wonderful old-fashioned larder with slate shelves and hooks for hams which Ma always says gave her her first taste of the importance of good food — I found a new brown loaf, and a huge crumbly piece of farmhouse cheese. I cut myself wedges of both, and found an apple and a couple of tomatoes and a glass of milk — real Bishopstow milk from Uncle James's herd — and put it all on a tray. Then I went across the hall to the study, where I remembered Aunt Mary sitting, doing farm accounts to deafening Wagner on her ancient record player, and opened the bottom drawer of the filing cabinet. It contained two box files, one marked "National Farmers Union" and one marked "Miscellaneous." "National Farmers Union" turned out to be full of papers, but "Miscellaneous" contained only a bottle of whisky, a very good malt whisky at that, which I recognized, being the child of a sound Scots upbringing.

I poured a hefty measure of the whisky into the spare glass on my tray, and then carried the midnight feast back upstairs to Uncle James. He had propped himself more upright in bed, and brushed his hair, and looked quite ready for a party. So we had one, just the two of us, and the dogs had a piece of cheese each so that they didn't feel left out, and with every second I grew more glad that I had come.

We didn't talk about anything very significant. I can't look back on that brief lamplit hour and say that we had one of those conversations that one remembers all one's life, because it wasn't like that. It was just cosy and happy and fun, eating and drinking and telling each other silly things and at two o'clock, I yawned, quite by mistake, and Uncle James said, "Now, you're going into my dressing room to sleep for two hours, and I shall set the alarm and wake you at four."

"But you won't want to wake again —"

"Rubbish," he said. "At my age, you don't need much sleep, and what you do need, you need at daft times, like eleven in the morning. Go on, now, shoo. Off with you."

I rinsed out the whisky glass so that the smell wouldn't be detected, and then I put the tray outside, on a chest on the landing. I went back to Uncle James, and kissed him, and patted the dogs, and then I went through to his little dressing room, which smelled of tweed and polish and old-fashioned lemony men's hair-dressing, and rolled myself up in the quilt on the bed, and fell into sleep like a stone being dropped off a cliff.

It was agony to be woken. Uncle James shuffled in, shrunken in the huge old camel-hair dressing gown he had once comfortably filled, and gently shook me and shook me until I had struggled, miserable and drugged-feeling, to consciousness. He had been downstairs and made me a flask of coffee, which he gave to me with a paper bag of bread and cheese and bananas. I was deeply touched. I washed my face at the basin in his dressing room and rubbed my teeth vigorously with some of his toothpaste on the end of my finger, and felt marginally more wakeful.

Then we went downstairs together, very slowly, not saying anything, just arm in arm with the dogs accompanying us in respectful silence. I slid back the bolts on the front door, and opened it to the most beautiful dawn in the world, clear and dewy and full of sleepy twitterings. I turned to put my arms round Uncle James, and we just stood there together for a moment, and then I went slowly across the drive and got into my car, and started the engine. As I drove away, I kept glancing back, in the driving mirror, and my last sight of Bishopstow was the soft grey façade of the house lit pink by the growing light, and Uncle James and the dogs, waving and wagging together under the pedimented porch.

Chapter Eleven

The first part of the journey was glorious. There was nothing on the roads but me and the occasional rabbit — and, once, a fox, streaking across in front of me in a flash of russet fur — and I felt strangely awake for someone who had had only two hours' sleep. The light grew and strengthened and the dew began to rise from the verges in vaporous plumes as I passed. I felt full of contentment on the one hand, and excited anticipation on the other. I had fulfilled one very important mission and now I was going to fulfill another, that of following Charlotte to Afghanistan.

By the time I got to Devon, there were more cars about, but they were peaceful Sunday morning cars, very easy to overtake. I settled myself into the driver's seat and prepared to cruise comfortably and speedily all the way to London. I rehearsed my plan when I got there, including the order I would pack things in. I decided that I would take out one pair of jeans and substitute for them a long, full skirt of fine Indian cotton that I had, very dark green with a band of embroidery round the hem. If I needed more feminine clothes like that when I got there, I was sure I could buy them in a bazaar. The book Matthew had given me said that most tailors in the Pakistani bazaars would make made-to-measure clothes for a few pounds. I wasn't even sure what my measurements were, except that I would have liked more of some parts of me, like my bosom, and less of others, like my nose.

I drove on, deep in thought, the way one tends to get on a long, steady journey. I thought about Bishopstow and Uncle James, about Tom and Andy, about the way Pamela Merryweather had looked, full of affront, in her padded dressing gown, and I was just beginning to think about how nice one of those bananas Uncle James had given me would be when there was a dull bang somewhere just behind me, and the steering wheel whipped itself out of my hands and the road and hedges went spinning past my gaze in a crazy kaleidoscope. I remember shouting out, and trying to control the car, but I don't really remember anything else until I found that I had stopped somehow and that a large bramble bush appeared to have climbed onto the bonnet, in order to try to get in with me.

I was completely unhurt, but stupid with shock and surprise. I got out of the car, and looked up and down the empty road. What un-believable luck that it was eight o'clock on a Sunday morning and not a weekday rush hour when I'd have been bound to hit something. I peered at the car. It looked absolutely innocent and untouched at first, but then I noticed one of the back tires, which seemed to have exploded and vanished leaving the rim of the wheel sitting on the verge in a sea of strips of black rubber and coils of sprung wire. I had had, I believe they call it, a blowout.

I suddenly felt rather peculiar. I went behind the car and sat down on the verge and put my head in my hands. It was, I soon realized, no good just sitting there thinking, "Gosh, I feel peculiar," because I had to be in London in two hours. I had just come through somewhere called Zeals, in Wiltshire, I had a burst tire, and I had to admit, to my shame, that I had never changed a tire in my life. I looked up and down the road again, hoping that a lorry containing a nice, efficient driver would materialize and come swiftly to my aid, but there was nobody. It was quite a big road, but it was still early and it was after all a Sunday.

I crawled back to the car and got out all the handbooks and looked in a very hopeless, uncomprehending way at the diagrams. The first thing to do, which even I could understand, was to find the tools and the spare tire which the manufacturers had concealed in a special compartment in the boot. That bit was quite easy. I got all the tools out, and spread them on the grass, and looked at them. Apart from the jack, which I didn't know how to use, I couldn't even have put a name to one of the others.

I was just beginning to feel a real fury of frustration coming on when I heard the blessed sound of an approaching car. I dashed out into the middle of the road, and leaped up and down like a mad thing, and a very neat, old Morris puttered to a stop at my feet. The driver wound down his window. He had a dear old country face like an apple, and not very many teeth.

"Now," he said cosily, "what've *you* been and gone and done?"

I said, "I've had a blowout on my back tire and I've never changed a wheel before and I've got to catch a plane to Afghanistan in six hours and I haven't even packed and I've got to get to London first —"

He clicked his teeth. He said, "Wait there."

He wound his window up again very slowly, then he reversed the car very slowly into a gateway on the opposite side of the road and then he got out very slowly and walked, very slowly, across the road and stooped down to examine my car.

"You've had a blowout," he said.

I said, "I know. I know, but the thing is, I've got to get to London in a terrible hurry."

He stood up. He took off his cap and scratched his head and put it back again and eyed the car and after what seemed like ten minutes, he said, "Soon fix that."

I wanted to fall on his neck and embrace him. Fifty minutes later, I wanted to fall on the same neck and strangle him. I have never known anybody take so long to do anything. He was quite oblivious of my urgings and pleadings and agitations, and went through the business of changing my tire with the most maddening deliberateness you can imagine. Nothing would hurry him. Other cars began to go by, each one containing, I was quite sure, a swift, competent changer of tires, but I was stuck with my original rescuer who would have made a snail look jet-propelled.

At ten past nine, almost beside myself with

443

frustration and anxiety I pressed far too much money into his hand, leaped into the car, reversed it really carelessly back into the road and almost into an oncoming car towing a caravan, and shot off towards London. I had lost well over an hour, and by now the holiday traffic either going to or coming from the West Country had built up and settled into a steady crawl in both directions. Then, to crown it all, I noticed that I was very low on petrol, and would have to stop at the next garage and thus lose yet more time.

I really can't bear to recount that last part of the journey back to London. I felt quite sick and to say I felt frustrated would be an understatement. All the way, crouched over the wheel as if leaning forward would somehow make the car go faster, I became increasingly, agonizingly aware that I was going to miss the plane. I was not only going to miss it, I was going to have to explain to everybody involved that I had missed it just because I had obeyed an impulse to drive to Cornwall during the night before the most important journey of my life.

I reached the flat at five minutes to midday, five minutes before I was supposed to be checking in at Heathrow. I was almost sobbing in my panic. I hurled everything pell-mell into my rucksack and canvas grip that I was taking, stuffed my documents into my money belt, and fled out again, throwing my keys through the Australian's letterbox without a word of explanation. James would have to do that, later in the day.

Needless to say, once out on the street I

couldn't see a single taxi. Car after car went by, full of smug people in no hurry at all, but no beloved black taxi. I didn't find one for nearly fifteen minutes, and when I did, it was driven by someone who must have been the brother of the man who had changed my tire in Wiltshire. We drove at a stately thirty-five miles all the way to Heathrow, which we reached at twenty minutes to two.

I fell on the check-in desk incoherent with panic. The British Airways girl, cool and immaculate, looked at me as if I was something very unpleasant that the cat had brought in, and said, "The flight to Islamabad closed three minutes ago."

I went bananas. I screamed and shrieked at her and told her the whole awful saga of the last ten hours and then what I thought of her and then I burst into tears. I'm ashamed to say that they were tears of pure temper.

She listened to me without a flicker of reaction of any kind, then she stretched out a perfectly manicured hand and picked up a telephone and said something very quietly into it. Then she actually took my ticket, and tied labels on to my bags and told me to wait where I was.

I gaped at her. "You mean I can go? That I'm not too late?"

She nodded, turning to the next passenger.

I went from agony to ecstasy. I said she was wonderful and beautiful and kind and clever and that I adored British Airways and would never, ever fly with anybody else. She took, hardly surprisingly, absolutely no notice of me, and then another official, a man, came up and said, "Miss Charlotte Angus?"

I nodded. I wanted to fall on the floor and kiss his shoes. He gave me a quick searching glance, which was quite enough to remind me of how awful I looked by then, crumpled and unbrushed and haggard with lack of sleep and tension, and said crisply, "Follow me."

I trotted obediently behind him, like a happy dog that's been reprieved from a punishment it knows it richly deserves. I followed his immaculately uniformed back at terrific speed through customs control and the security check and then down those miles and miles of sinister carpeted passages that are such a grim feature of modern airports, and found myself, quite suddenly, at the open door of an aeroplane. My aeroplane. My dear, darling, kind, beloved aeroplane that had actually waited for me. I turned to the official.

"I can't thank you enough —"

He said, "I'd get on board if I were you, and not waste any more time," and then he said to the stewardess in the doorway, "Your missing passenger," and strode off.

I began to apologize to the stewardess, but she was clearly used to incompetent passengers like me, and merely gave me a bored smile. She led me down the huge plane, between the packed rows of people, and indicated my seat. Then she left me, and it was only then, with the immediate frenzy of missing the plane over, that I remembered the others. I remembered Abdul and Joe and Andy and Andy's assistant cameraman, Philip — and Tom.

446

I looked down at my empty seat. Then I looked beyond it. Beyond it was Tom, and I don't think I have ever in my life seen anyone look so cold with fury. All my excited relief at catching the plane drained out of me in an instant. I put my hand luggage under the seat in front of me, slipped into my own, fastened my safety belt, and bowed my head.

"Sorry," I muttered.

Tom said nothing.

I drew a deep breath. I said, without looking at him, "I really am sorry. I had a series of mishaps —"

"I see."

"I really couldn't help it —"

"Carly," he said, interrupting, and turning on me eyes like grey ice, "Carly, I'm not interested in your mishaps, or what you couldn't help. I was in my flat until eleven this morning, and I imagine that whatever mishaps there were, they had made themselves manifest by then and you could have telephoned?"

I couldn't speak.

"May I remind you," Tom said, "that we are on a professional assignment, paid for by a television corporation which is, in turn, financed by the public's money? This puts us under a great obligation, not just to bring home the goods in terms of a really excellent program, but to behave with absolute responsibility and professionalism. I talked you onto our team because I thought nine months of working for Matthew would mean I need have no qualms about your sense of serious commitment and about your competence

447

and reliability. I now find, at the absolute outset, that you are behaving like an irresponsible teenager. I dread to think what comes next."

If I had felt awful in the car, struggling back to London, I felt a hundred times worse now. I felt I was all the things he said I was, and on top of that, I felt a burning sense of shame. I couldn't possibly tell him what I had been doing, as that would only confirm, at a single stroke, his evident belief that he had made a terrible mistake in taking me on. I simply sat there, and wondered if it would indeed have been better if I had just missed the flight after all.

The plane began its slow lumbering reversings and turnings before taxiing out towards the runway. I sat staring at my lap, so that my hair hung forward and provided a protective curtain, and Tom got out some very erudite-looking paperback. I wondered if I could endure him next to me all the way to Islamabad knowing how angry he was, but I also knew that I couldn't possibly open my mouth and say a single word to him.

We took off, and creaked upwards into the clear English summer sky. The seat belt signs went off, and the cabin crew went through their routine about not smoking in the lavatories and wearing seat belts whenever sitting down, and I suddenly became aware that Tom was speaking to me. His voice was just a fraction less furious.

"I'm sure the last person you want next to you for the next nine hours is me, so I'm going to swap places with Andy."

I nodded. I heard the click of his seat belt being undone, and then there was a bit of agile scrambling, and then Andy said in my ear, "You all right?"

"I feel so awful —"

"What happened?"

I glanced at him. He looked really concerned.

I said, "I obeyed an impulse to go to Cornwall last night."

"To Cornwall! Are you mad?"

"I wanted to say goodbye to Uncle James," I said. "I told you. It was an impulse."

Andy put a hand on mine. "If you want my advice, you won't have any more of those."

"I won't."

"Tom —"

I said quickly, "Don't talk about him."

"You look shattered."

"I am —"

"Tell you what," Andy said, "I'll put my sweater on my shoulder to make it less bony, and you just get your head down."

"Don't be kind to me," I said. "Please don't. I deserved every word of what Tom said, I know I did."

"Okay," Andy said, and he was grinning. "I'll leave my shoulder where it is, and you can use it when you decide to take your hair shirt off."

So of course I put my head down on the pillow of his sweater at once, and slept gratefully until we touched down to refuel.

Chapter Twelve

I don't quite know what I had expected of Islamabad in precise terms, but I know I had hoped for somewhere at least exotic as my gateway to Afghanistan. Islamabad isn't remotely exotic. It's modern and dull, and built on a grid system, which makes it even duller. Trailing tiredly out of the airport just after dawn behind the others and our mountains of bags and cameras, I reflected rather sourly that my arrival couldn't have been more of a contrast to Charlotte's arrival in Bombay, which seemed, from Emily's description of it and, even taking into account her apprehension about the whole enterprise, full of light and color and movement and brilliance.

My arrival was flat and dun-colored. The sleepy customs men just waved us through, hardly even looking at the cameras, and we emerged to a pale colorless sky, no view, and a row of elderly Morris Minor taxis, which reminded me uncomfortably of my tire-changing friend in Wiltshire. I had expected to feel some kind of thrill, but I felt nothing, just weary and dirty and as if I had made a mistake.

"We'll need at least three taxis with all this," Tom said.

I could hardly bear to look at him still, especially as he seemed to have emerged from the aeroplane looking fresh and uncrumpled and purposeful.

"I will bargain," Abdul said. He went forward, shouting to the taxi drivers. They went jabber, jabber, jabber at each other and then Abdul said "Bus" and stamped off.

I said, "What's 'bus'?"

"It means, that's enough," Tom said shortly.

Sure enough, three of the taxi drivers went scuttling after Abdul and after a bit, he came back to us and said, with a satisfied smile, "Done. A hundred and fifty rupees."

"Heavens," Tom said, "that's only about six quid —"

"Yes."

"That doesn't seem anything like enough."

"It's plenty!" Abdul said, eyes flashing. He was clearly enjoying himself. He strode back to the drivers and began to order them about, which bits of luggage should go on the roof racks of their endearing, ancient cars, and which in the boot, and then he ordered us all in after the luggage, two of us into each taxi.

I found myself with Joe. He gave my knee a brotherly pat and waved his other hand at the view.

"Looks a right dump, doesn't it?"

I nodded. "It's not at all what I was expecting."

"Work with Tom," Joe said, "you learn never to expect anything. When he's good and ready to tell you things, you get the plan, the whole plan, in every detail. But until then, you just trot about behind him."

I put my head back on the padded seat-back behind me. The taxi smelled of dust and bruised jasmine flowers.

"Where are we going?" I said, not really caring.

"F2."

"F2? Is that a mountain?"

"No. That's K2. F2 is the district of this delightful city where most of the foreigners live. We're going to stay with friends of Tom's."

"Oh."

"Tom's got friends everywhere. I've never known such a bloke for friends. Put Tom down the middle of the Sahara and he'd have a mate at the next oasis." He turned and looked at me. "Did he tear you off a strip?"

"Yes. I deserved it but it was pretty awful."

"What were you up to?"

I turned my head away. I said, "I'm sorry, Joe, but I really can't tell you," and he gave a great guffaw of laughter, and I realized, miserably, that he thought I'd been with a boyfriend. I opened my mouth to explain, and then shut it again. Joe would never understand in the first place, and, in the second, the thought of Uncle James suddenly seemed very private.

We set off, in a swirl of dust, for the city. Our taxi was the last in the line, behind the precious one carrying all the cameras with Andy and Philip keeping an anxious eye on them. We seemed to drive and drive and drive down endless dust-colored streets, whose monotony was only occasionally relieved by the glow of a little cooking fire and a draped figure bent over, making — what?

"I dunno," Joe said, "chapattis, most likely."

We stopped at a high bare wall, like a garden wall, with ugly modern iron gates set in it. Tom got out of the first taxi, and went up to the gates and pressed the bell in the wall beside them. One gate opened cautiously, and a figure emerged. Tom stooped to speak to it. It bowed several times, like a Chinese doll, and then made a sweeping gesture to welcome us all in.

Inside the gates and the wall was a quite big compound with a strange, stiff-looking lawn, and a tree or two I didn't recognize and several square, whitewashed buildings. In the biggest of these, a light came on upstairs, and then down-stairs, and then on a kind of outside veranda, and then a door opened and a woman's voice called, in English, "Tom? Is that you? Tom?"

He went forward across the compound, and a dark-haired woman in a flowered cotton dressing gown came running out of the door, followed by a man in shirt and trousers, and flung herself into Tom's arms. The rest of us hung back, rather shyly.

"Patsy," Tom was saying with warm enthu-siasm, "oh Patsy, how lovely! And Christopher. This is so generous of you —"

Patsy broke away from him and turned to the rest of us. She was very pretty in a gamine way, with huge eyes in a little face with a pointed chin, and dark curls. She said, "You poor things, you must be exhausted and filthy," and then she came a little nearer in the growing light and exclaimed, "Tom darling, you never said you were bringing a real live girl with you!"

Tom said, a little stiffly, "This is Carly Angus, Patsy."

Patsy took my hand. "I do think you're brave. It's horrible traveling with Tom. He's quite ruthless. I did it once and never again."

"Perhaps this'll be my once, then —"

The man, having finished greeting Tom, came over to us all and shook our hands.

"I'm Christopher Tindall. I work for Chemical International. You're all most welcome. Come in and have breakfast and baths."

We trooped obediently after him and Tom and Patsy, while several dark figures flitted about behind us, gathering up all the luggage that the taxi drivers had unloaded into the compound. Patsy hung chattering on Tom's arm and he seemed to love it. Thinking of Laura, I reflected unhappily that he clearly preferred small women, small, self-possessed women of well over twenty-five.

The Tindalls had made their house — a dull, modern four-square building — very charming. Patsy clearly had, as Ma did, an eye for interesting and pretty things, and the room we were led into was furnished with a mix of dark rattan furniture and blue and white porcelain from the Far East, and wonderful rugs and rich embroideries from Afghanistan and Pakistan. On the table in the center of the room was laid a completely English breakfast, orange juice and cornflakes and a big blue teapot. I gaped at it.

Patsy said, "Were you expecting curry?"

"Well, I suppose I must have been —"

"We can get everything English here. You could live on a diet of shepherd's pie and spotted

Dick if you wanted to." She gave me a quick look. "Would you like a wash first?"

I nodded gratefully. "I'm afraid I look simply awful —"

"No, you don't," she said. "Nobody with that amazing hair could ever look awful. I just thought you might feel as I always feel after that wretched flight. Bring your bag up and then you can change too. I can't ever face the world in the clothes I've traveled in."

We left the men beginning to relax and talk over food, and Patsy led me out of the dining room and up a tiled stairway to a wide, white landing furnished, most dramatically, with nothing but a series of wonderful panel paintings on the walls, writhing figures and beasts in soft rich colors.

"We found those in the bazaar. I'm afraid they'd been ransacked from a temple somewhere, because they're on plaster so they would have been wall paintings."

I went a little closer to the nearest one. It was a picture of a pleasure garden, with a fountain leaping out of a tank of water full of goldfish, surrounded by trees garlanded with flowers. In the foreground was a richly dressed couple. She was leaning back on a pile of pillows in an attitude of ecstasy, and he, turbaned and moustached, was leaning over her and opening her bodice. I thought at once of Charlotte finding the erotic carvings in the temple in the mango groves, and being so enchanted with them because they seemed to her so full of love and life, and of poor Hugh, shocked to his conventional English backbone by her reaction.

"Christopher calls them our dirty postcards," Patsy said.

"I think they're lovely. Really lovely. So unself-conscious."

Patsy opened a door next to the painting of the lovers in the pleasure garden. "Here's the bathroom. Use anything you want to."

"You're so kind —"

"No I'm not, I'm thankful to see you all. It gets frantically boring here, I can tell you. Carly —"

I turned to her reluctantly. The sight of the bathroom, tiled and shining, made me almost drool with excitement and I longed to get in there and get clean.

"Yes?"

"Carly, are you . . . are you Tom's girl?"

I went completely scarlet all over in a single second.

"No," I said, almost rudely.

"I'm sorry to ask. I suppose it's a bit tactless, but I've known Laura and Tom since we were all students together, and he's never taken a girl on any work trip before, so I just wondered —"

"You needn't. Laura and he are still very much a number. Tom just said I could come along because I wanted to see Afghanistan for personal reasons, family reasons."

"So he's doing you a kindness, really."

"I suppose so —"

"That would be so like him," Patsy said with warmth, "he's the most imaginative man I know. He's —" She stopped and gave me a quick glance. "You get clean, Carly, and I'll go down and preside over the cornflakes. Don't hurry and there's gallons of hot water. Solar power is one of the very few pluses to this dreadful place. The other is servants. Just leave your dirty clothes here and Hamid Khan will deal with them."

"But I can't do that!"

"Yes you can," Patsy said. "And you'd offend him very much if you did it yourself. He doesn't mind me ironing, but he gets in a terrible state if I wash so much as a sock. Now help yourself. Shampoo is in the cupboard."

I locked the door firmly behind her and took off all my disgusting clothes, clothes that I had been wearing for two and a half days and which felt as if I had worn them for two and a half weeks. Then I ran a huge, deep bath and got into it with little shivers of rapture, and washed every inch of myself and shampooed my hair twice, and then I got out of the bath and brushed my teeth until my gums were tingling. Then I rummaged about in the shameful muddle of packing in my grip, and found some clean underclothes, and a white T-shirt and a pair of dark blue cotton trousers. I decided, in this cool, clean house, to leave my feet bare.

Mindful of Hamid Khan, whom I felt very guilty about allowing to clear up after me, I left the bathroom scrupulously tidy, with my dirty clothes in a neat heap, and padded downstairs with my damp hair down my back, and my parrot earrings firmly in place, to give me courage. Breakfast seemed to have heartened everybody, and they were all poring over maps and talking nineteen to the dozen. Andy looked up as I came in and gave me a pleased and approving nod, and Christopher Tindall gallantly got up to offer me a chair, but Tom didn't raise his eyes from an alarming-looking map which was entirely brown and purple, indicating mountains, with no comforting lowland green anywhere.

I slipped into the chair Christopher offered me, and gratefully accepted the toast and tea that Patsy pushed in my direction. She had exchanged her dressing gown for a soft heather-colored T-shirt and full muslin skirt in which she looked deliciously graceful and feminine.

She said, "I'm going to take you to the bazaar while they argue about routes and which camps and so on. It'll be awfully cold at night up where you're going, at Chitral. Did you bring some sweaters?"

"Several," I said.

"And the days will be hot and dusty. Tom says you'll have to do some bits on horseback. Can you ride?"

"Oh yes —"

Andy said teasingly from across the table, "She can roller-skate too. Can't you, Carly?"

I looked at him with gratitude. He had simply left me alone on the flight, while making it plain that he was there if I needed him. He said, "You look amazingly clean."

"It's a contrast, isn't it?"

Patsy said, "Your turn next. It'll be your last shave for weeks, so you'd better make the most of it."

I looked round the table, at the five faces which would, over the next few months, become as familiar to me as my own, all of them, except

458

Andy's, bent over the maps.

"I think this camp is one I'm aiming for," Tom said, putting his finger down on a brown space below a huge purple one, "and this, because that apparently contains the women and children from an entire village where the men were wiped out by the Russians. And then I want to trace their route back," his finger moved left-handedly across the purple space, "to the village they left, so that we can see the journey they had to make and the place they had to leave."

I put my toast down. I was suddenly conscious, as I had never, stupidly, been before, of what I was undertaking. I was actually going into this high, wild, still dangerous country; I, Carly Angus, was going to travel as primitively and excitingly as Charlotte Brent had done before me. A thrill of apprehension and delight ran through me in a sharp cold stream. I looked towards Tom, as if seeing him for the first time in a different light, seeing him not just as the man I was hopelessly mad about, but as the man on whom I had to depend, to look to, in the coming weeks.

As if he felt my gaze, Tom looked up from the map, and across the table, straight at me. He looked at me for several seconds, with a kind of surprise, as if he didn't quite recognize me, and then he said, in a voice which did my self-control no good at all, "Carly, Carly, I'm sorry I've been such a beast."

I nodded. I tried to say several things, but only succeeded in muttering "That's okay," like some gauche fourteen year old. He didn't add to his apology, but he went on looking at me, and I grew more and more self-conscious and bent my head over my plate until he couldn't see my face. I despaired of myself, I really did. There I was, eating my heart out for a serious look from him, and when I got one what did I do but bury my nose in my toast and marmalade.

Patsy said, "While you lot talk guides and routes and bivouacs, I'm going to take Carly shopping. Anybody want anything from the bazaar?"

"No thanks. All we want is a bath."

Patsy stood up. "Then let's go."

I said, "I forgot to bring a single skirt. I packed in a bit of a rush —"

There was a tiny silence. I got up and began to pile up my cup and plate and saucer to cover my confusion.

"Leave that, Carly, Ali Khan will clear the table."

"Ali Khan?"

"Hamid's nephew. Don't look so shocked. There is a great natural dignity here as you will see. And you will also see that you really can't do without help from someone."

She held her hand out to me as if I were a child.

"Come on. We'll buy you a whole wardrobe for ten pounds."

Tom stood up as we left the room, and as we passed him he put out a hand and just touched Patsy's face, in a fond, easy gesture.

"Thanks so much," he said, as if thanking her for taking a problem child off his hands.

She laughed. She said, "Don't thank me. It's me who ought to do the thanking. You've brought me someone to play with."

Chapter Thirteen

We stayed with Patsy and Christopher Tindall for three days. Tom tried to move us into a hotel, because he felt we were exploiting their hospitality, but Patsy wouldn't hear of it. So we stayed in their comfortable house, waited on by the Khan uncle and nephew, while Tom made plans and Andy and Philip played with their cameras, and I read an extraordinary book called *My Khyber Marriage* by a Scotswoman who had married an Afghan chief in the 1920s. It was a very romantic book written by someone unconquerably optimistic. I wasn't feeling optimistic at all. To tell the truth, despite Patsy's kindness and the air of anticipation in the house over our forthcoming travels, I could not get out of my mind the belief that I had made a terrible mistake in coming at all.

To start with, it was plainly a mistake to be so near, and yet so far from Tom on a daily basis. It wasn't just that his physical presence tormented me, but also the power and charm of his personality. Mix admiration and love with sex appeal, and then hang a notice up saying "Don't touch" and perhaps you will get some idea of my situation.

Tom, however, was only one of my problems. The other was Charlotte. Now that I had made all this fuss and got within striking distance of my pilgrimage in search of Charlotte, I could see, with miserable clarity, that it had been a daft thing to try to do. A hundred and fifty years had passed between us, a hundred and fifty years of violent change, not least the psychological change caused by Charlotte being a pre-Freudian, and me a post-Freudian creature. I was going on a fruitless search for something that had absolutely vanished; I was like the poor, silly White Knight in *Alice in Wonderland,* or Don Quixote tilting pointlessly at windmills. Charlotte's Afghanistan was no more; the soldiers of the past few years had been the conscripted, khaki-clad, resentful young Russians, not the scarlet-coated imperial might of the long ago Army of the Indus. I was behaving like someone who expected to find Camelot still standing with its towers and turrets, or Atlantis, pinnacled and perfect, safe beneath the waves.

All this made me very downcast, because I felt I had misjudged everything and was behaving like a child who insists something is true merely because it wants it to be. At the same time, I realized that I couldn't go back. I had managed, painfully, to be honest with myself, but I couldn't possibly face the humiliation of being honest with the Tindalls, and with Tom and Andy and Abdul and Joe and Philip. If I couldn't face confessing to them, then I couldn't do what I wanted to do which was to admit that I had made an awful mistake and that I wanted to go straight home. So — I had to stay. I had to stay with the crew, and go through with the expedition and somehow, without letting it show, channel my futile enthusiasm for "finding" Charlotte into a more constructive one for the project Tom had set his heart on. And while I was at it, I told myself sternly, I was to stop crying for the moon, and I was to appreciate what it was to have a steady, loving friend like Andy.

I'm afraid all these somber reflections made me a disappointing companion for Patsy, who was one of those delightful people who seem to carry a party atmosphere around with them. I think she suspected how I felt about Tom, and as she knew the situation with Laura, she was very tactful and kind with me, treating me as if I were some kind of mild invalid. I suppose I could have talked to her, but I'm not really a very confiding kind of person by nature, except with a very few people I feel extremely close to. So the three days in Islamabad passed — or rather were wasted — in gloomy reflection, unrelieved by the fact that I now possessed, thanks to Patsy, some wonderful embroidered clothes, long skirts and trousers, which were easily the most glamorous things I'd ever possessed.

We left Islamabad on a July morning, before dawn, in two hired jeeps, with fifteen hours of driving ahead of us to Chitral. The first two hundred miles were mostly up the Great Trunk Road, which the British built up the whole length of India to the Afghan border, and the last two hundred were among the mountains where, said Abdul, the roads were bad.

"The snows melted late and there have been

464

floods and landslides." He looked at me appraisingly. You couldn't fault his politeness to me but on the other hand, you couldn't help but notice that he thought I ought to have been at home in a kitchen with babies like a proper woman. He helped me into the first jeep, to a seat behind the driver. "Good view, less dust," he said. I felt grateful and self-conscious.

I also felt, to my relief, in better spirits. I'm not used to being cast down, and it scares me. But when I looked round at our little procession, at the rest of the crew in their old army fatigues and boots, with soft checked Pakistani cotton scarves wound loosely round their necks, ready to be dust shields later, I felt an unmistakable twinge of excitement. I also determined, as the official recorder of the trip, that I was going to do my job properly.

Tom came up and saluted me. He was smiling broadly.

"All shipshape and Bristol fashion?"

I saluted back. "Aye, aye, sir."

He leaned into the jeep. "Carly. Don't worry."

I said, "Oh, I'm not scared if that's what you mean —"

"No. I don't. I know you're not scared. I meant, don't worry about Charlotte."

I looked at him with wonder. How did he know?

He said, "You'll find her, Carly. But she just may not be where you expect. And she mayn't be what you expect."

I gulped slightly. "Thank you —"

He put his hand on mine for a second.

"Don't bottle things up," he said. "Tell me things," and then he was gone.

We drove out of Islamabad just before sunrise, leaving Patsy and Christopher waving rather wistfully from the gates of their compound and promising to send mail periodically after us. The air was delicious still, and the choking dust that I already felt to be horribly familiar was lying quietly and damply in the roadway. In front of me were the driver and Abdul, beside me Joe and Tom, and under my feet was tucked the satchel, like a fishing bag, made of khaki canvas that I had bought in the bazaar to carry my notebooks, my camera, and the photocopy of the journal. In the first notebook I had already written the date and time of starting. It felt a bit like being on a school expedition, with a project to hand in at the end. "Carly Angus (Form IIIB). Journey to Afghanistan."

At the beginning, everybody was very jolly and talkative, the way people are at the beginning of long journeys. Joe and Tom were reminiscing about past expeditions, and Abdul and the driver were shouting companionably at each other above the roar and clatter of the engine. When the sun rose, it seemed to do so with an explosion of light and heat, and by that time we had left the dust-colored suburbs of Islamabad behind and were heading northeast, towards the mountains.

Tom leaned across Joe and patted my knee.

"You all right?"

I nodded. I was. With each mile from Islamabad I felt more all right. The jeep was noisy and the view so far was nothing special and the other vehicles on the road were rowdy Pakistani lorries, not romantic camel caravans, but all the same I felt, for the first time since arrival, pleased to be where I was.

We stopped for lunch at a place called Attock, which had a bridge over the Indus river. In the sixteenth century, Shah Jehan, who built the Taj Mahal as a mausoleum for his beloved, dead wife, also built a fort at Attock, an amazing fort of glowing pinkish stone with walls like cliffs plunging down into the river, and battlements and crenellations. It was an extraordinary sight, the bright blue sky behind the rosy walls and the pale blue river below them. Abdul turned, seized my arm and pointed.

"Look."

I looked obediently. Some way to our right, I could see, as if divided by an invisible line, the blue waters of the Indus turn brown.

"Kabul River," Abdul said, "Kabul River brown. Meets Indus River blue. Never mingle."

A metaphor, I thought sadly, for Tom and me.

The drivers parked the jeeps under a row of dusty trees beyond the fort, and we all scrambled out, stiff and thirsty. It was terribly hot. Several small misshapen children, their navels inverted like acorns, came up very close to us and stared and stared.

"May I give them something?" I said to Abdul. Two of them were quite naked, and the others wore only scraps of loincloth, or parts of a T-shirt.

"When we go."

"Why not now?"

"If you give now," Abdul said, "is bother, bother, bother all lunchtime and the mothers coming too and the fathers and aunts and uncles. Give for goodbye."

I felt guilty. "Later," I said to the children.

One of them, a squint-eyed boy, held a hand up to me, palm upwards, opening his mouth wide as if to indicate that he was hungry.

"Bus," Abdul said firmly, taking my arm. He marched me away from the children, across the main street towards a dilapidated wooden shack, its front open like a windowless shop. "Christianity is kind religion," Abdul said to me, "but also very foolish. Mixes up good and bad."

"But the children can't be bad!"

He rolled his eyes heavenward. "Is exactly what I mean. Christians so foolish."

Inside, the shack proved to be a kind of restaurant of a truly primitive kind, furnished with several low rickety tables and stools set about on an earthen floor.

"Wow," Joe said, following us in. "The Café Royal."

"Food is excellent," Abdul said firmly.

A man appeared in the curtained opening at the back of the shack and clapped his hands at the sight of Abdul. The others all came in and we stood watching Abdul and the man greeting each other with a series of bows and claps and incomprehensible remarks. Abdul came bustling back to us, and ushered us all onto stools.

"Is most good lunch coming. Chicken, rice, dal, maybe omelette. You like omelette? Then mulberry. Fresh mulberry picked this morning."

He was full of hostly pride. I crouched on my stool, and looked past the others into the street. It was almost empty, but for the sad little band of potbellied children, and an old man who had come to join them, wearing a cap of striped cotton and a long dirty robe down to his feet. His feet were bare. The children's feet were bare. I looked down at my own feet, my clean, Western feet comfortably shod in new socks and dark blue canvas baseball boots. I looked at my clean hands and then at my shirt and my trousers, both without holes. I wailed, "Oh Abdul, I can't sit here and eat in front of them and not give them something!"

"Carly," Tom said gently, "there's worse to come, I'm afraid."

I nodded. I knew that, really. I also knew that I couldn't give money to every sad case along the road for three months, much as I would wish to. I thought briefly of Bewick, of the comforts of the hotel and of Inverbrae which seemed at this moment, sitting on a splintery stool in a dirty shack in Attock, to be so far away as to be utterly fantastic and not even possible.

"We are going to help," Tom said, still watching me, "but on a broader scale. That's why we've come. But I do understand how you feel."

A huge oval dish of rice with a pile of chicken in the middle was dumped down in front of us. Andy dug me in the ribs.

"How d'you feel about that?"

The smell wafting up from the dish was delicious, but I could see a chicken's foot sticking up among all the other bits. Joe saw it too and pounced on it, picking it up and brandishing it at me, dripping cooking juices.

"A delicacy for the lady?"

I gave a faint squawk. Abdul was watching me, laughing, his eyes appraising. I leaned forward.

"How kind, Joe. My absolutely favorite thing."

The foot felt just as you would expect, scaly and stiff. I laid it down on the edge of the dish with, I hoped, no sign of revulsion. No good relying on feminine vapors here, I thought, resolving to take the foot with me after lunch, and tuck it affectionately into Joe's sleeping bag on a later occasion.

The chicken and rice were as good as they looked, delicately spicy with all those lovely fragrant things like cumin and coriander. When we had eaten them, a huge omelette arrived in a great, flat, blackened pan, and we broke pieces off and it, too, tasted wonderful and not at all like any omelette I'd ever eaten before. Then came the mulberries. I knew about mulberries from the grotesquely bent old tree in the garden at Bishopstow, which Ma had always panicked about us going anywhere near in late summer because it seethed with possessive wasps, but I had hardly ever eaten any. These Attock mulberries were small, so dark a red they were almost black and amazingly sweet. They tasted both fruity and perfumed, unbelievably exotic, and had the same effect on me that the scent of jasmine always has, heady and unreal.

Then we had tea. It didn't taste like any tea I had ever encountered before and it was given to me in a tin mug so full of dents that it must have had a long history of being the kitchen football. While we drank our tea, several faces appeared around the edge of the ragged curtain at the back of the shack, and the band of children began to seep back towards us, like a tide coming slowly and inevitably up the beach.

Abdul put a handful of tiny coins into my hand, tiny little coins like the pretend ones in a child's post office.

"Only throw when the jeep moves off."

"Throw?"

"Yes. Throw. If you give, one by one, you will be torn in pieces. Is not cruel, Carly, is *sense*. You must learn some sense."

He led me to the second jeep where I was to ride for the afternoon with Andy and Philip.

"We stop later, for bathroom," he said delicately. "Mountains better bathroom than Attock."

Looking round, I rather agreed with him. Patsy's shining Islamabad bathroom, kept immaculate by Hamid Khan, seemed as far away already as did Bewick and Inverbrae, even though I had only left it that morning. I hoped fervently that the mountain bathroom would not be too far ahead.

Andy swung himself in beside me.

"You sit in the middle, so we can keep you upright."

"What did you think of lunch?"

He grinned. "It was all right at the time. The test is whether it's all right four hours later."

He was ominously accurate. Even as we drew away from Attock and I made a bungling muddle

471

of trying to throw the coins for the children so that half of them fell all over our own driver, I felt those distinct ominous sensations of internal unease that mean you can't think about anything else at all. As we drove on, they grew worse, and I was so preoccupied that I could hardly spare a thought for the vast brown mountains we had begun to climb up into, or the wonderful cedar trees that clung so dramatically to some of the lower slopes above the river. Andy put his arm around me.

"You okay?"

"Not very —"

He leaned across me and put his hand on the steering wheel.

"Got to stop!"

The driver glanced at me. He was a thin-faced, hook-nosed man in a loose robe over cotton trousers, and on his head, an American baseball cap. He leaned on the horn three times to signal to the jeep ahead of us that we were stopping, and crashed to a halt.

It was only just in time. I was out of the jeep, bursting and desperate, and behind a rock, in a second. Andy tried to come with me but I yelled at him to stay away. Never, ever has a bathroom, mountain or otherwise, been more welcome. I could have wept with relief.

When I emerged, they were all standing waiting for me. Joe, needless to say, was grinning. Andy came over and took my arm.

"Poor kid."

I shook my head. "Over now —"

Tom was holding out a capsule to me. "Poor

472

Carly. Swallow this. Loperamide hydrochloride. Brilliant stuff."

I took the capsule gratefully. Philip offered me some bottled water. They were all being so kind that I was embarrassed.

"Welcome to North East Frontier!" Abdul said, and then laughed loudly, in order to show that it was a joke.

Chapter Fourteen

It seemed like an eternity before we got to Chitral. I felt weak and disorientated, and Philip and Andy made me lie down on the back seat of the jeep, my head pillowed on a pile of sweatshirts. It was appallingly bumpy and noisy, but it was better than sitting up, and I lay there either with my eyes open watching snatches of blue sky or brown mountain lurch by, or with them shut, thinking of Emily, also laid low by some fever as she approached Afghanistan, and having to be carried in a litter. I suppose, if you really stretched your imagination, you could say that a thirty-year-old jeep grinding over the Loweiri Pass was the twentieth-century equivalent of a curtained litter swaying up the Khyber, but my imagination wasn't up to much stretching that afternoon. Like everything else about me, it just wanted the journey to be over.

Which, as the light began to fade, it finally was. Andy turned in his seat and said, "Carly. We're nearly there."

I raised myself gingerly, no longer sick but very wobbly. Below us lay a wide valley floor, with a swirling green river rushing across it, and, in an untidy straggle along its banks, some kind of town.

"Chitral?"

Philip nodded. "Chitral."

I peered between their heads at the town rambling beneath us. It looked, to European eyes like mine used to towers and spires and the height of office blocks, very low and sprawling, as if it were crouching there like a cowering animal beside the river. Beyond it, I knew, lay the camps Tom wanted to visit, particularly the camp called Kerala, where five thousand women and children lived, refugees from a village where almost every man had been killed by the Russians. That village had been called Kerala, and the camp was named after it as a mournful memorial. I shivered a little, despite the lingering heat, looking down into that valley in the fading light, and thinking of all the suffering there.

We were to stay with a cousin of Abdul's, a dealer in lapis lazuli who had a house in Chitral. Abdul had explained proudly that his family were Pashtuns, the renowned warrior people of the North East Frontier. He had said this in London, and it had, to be honest, sounded very melodramatic there, and a bit stagy, but here, jolting down this wild mountain road to a wild border town below the Hindu Kush, it didn't seem theatrical at all, but very natural and proper. How could such a landscape, so huge and untamed, produce docile, peaceable people? How could you think of living a gentle domestic life in a place where the very foothills of the mountains seemed to prowl like wild beasts? I shivered again, but for a different reason.

Abdul's cousin, a tall, strong-looking man called Nasir, welcomed us in the courtyard of his house. It was built on the same principle as the Tindalls' house in Islamabad but it was old and whitewashed and the high walls that guarded it were as thick as those of a small fortress. As the huge wooden doors that shut the compound from the street closed behind us, I felt a sudden thrill that everything western had been closed out too, that I was really now living in a place where I would have to start, as it were, with a blank sheet of paper; no preconceptions, no expectations, no settled opinions, just a mind as open as the huge sky arching above the compound, blue fading to apricot and turquoise, with grape-colored streaks of cloud and tiny emerging sparkles of stars.

I took my satchel over to a great wellhead in the center of the courtyard, and sat on its broad whitewashed rim. My lurching tummy, thanks to Tom's magic capsule and the end of the journey, was now much calmer and I was full of that grateful relief that always comes with feeling better. As the light from the sky dimmed, oil lamps were lit round the courtyard, and the most wonderful scents began to fill the air, burning charcoal and crushed flowers and other nameless smells I couldn't recognize with my ignorant Western nose.

Some kind person came up, soft-footed, and put a lamp down beside me, on the wall of the wellhead. I peered up at shining eyes in a dark face.

"Thank you —"

"Not at all," a voice said in English, a girl's voice. "Is Selima."

"You are Selima?"

"Yes."

"I'm Carly. You speak wonderful English."

"Of course," she said, laughing, "I went to school in London," and then she drifted off into the dusk, and I got out my notebook, determined to write up the day with professional accuracy. But I found I didn't want to. I gazed round me, at the shadowy figures moving in and out of the lamp-lit circles, at the fretted dark patterns cast on the rough white walls, and I thought, quite suddenly, that what I wanted to do was to write to Uncle James. I wanted to write and tell him all my feelings, all my myriad impressions, to describe to him the way my mood kept going up and down, from sunshine to shadow and back again . . .

"Carly."

"Yes," I said.

Andy sat down beside me on the wellhead wall, very close so that our shoulders and thighs were touching.

"You must be worn out —"

"Funnily enough, I feel better now. Tom's magic capsule. It's rather wonderful here, isn't it?"

He put an arm round me in the soft darkness, and laid his face against my hair.

"We're going to sleep outside."

I was enchanted. "Are we?"

"On charpoys. Wait till you see them."

I turned my face so that our cheeks touched.

"You've been so kind all day. I'm sorry to have been such a broken reed."

"You couldn't help it. I was worried about you. It'll be someone else's turn next."

"Andy —"

"Yes?"

"I've been a bit of a wet blanket the last few days. I've felt so muddled, afraid I was doing the wrong thing, or a silly thing and I'm afraid I got a bit introverted."

He took his face away from mine and brushed my cheek with his free hand.

"I know."

"That's very perceptive of you."

"No it isn't. Tom told us all to get off your back."

I drew away a little. "He did?"

"He's a bit fatherly about you."

"I see —"

"He's over there," Andy said comfortably, not hearing my tone of voice, "writing to Laura. He's always writing to Laura. I remember him sitting in the middle of a Palestinian camp, writing to Laura. Only hope the bloody woman reads them."

I turned back to look at him in the upflung light from the oil lamp, which made his face exaggeratedly beaky and thin, like a clever, funny bird.

"Don't you like her?"

"Nope," Andy said shortly. "Not my type."

"What is your type?" I said unwisely.

"Mixed-up redheads," Andy said, and bent to kiss me.

"I'm not mixed up!" I said indignantly, averting my mouth.

"Aren't you? I reckon we all are, I reckon everyone's mixed up except rare people like Tom who know what they want. Do you know what you want?"

"No," I said untruthfully. I don't like being untruthful ever, but evasions of truth are sometimes necessary to defend precious and vulnerable secrets.

"There you are then. Come on, Carly, get off whichever high horse you've climbed on, and give us a kiss."

I couldn't not. I turned to him in the sweet dim light, and kissed him and, I have to admit it, felt better for it. And when I had kissed him, I leaned back, supporting myself on my hands, and gazed up into that huge vaulted Asian sky and wondered if, when you couldn't have what you wanted, you could learn to want what you had?

We had dinner in a wonderful room. Or, at least, the men did, and Selima and I, and her mother and sisters and aunts and cousins had it in an adjoining room which was very similar. Tom was anxious that I might feel full of outraged Western feminism when I saw that I should have to eat alone with the women, but I didn't mind at all, in fact it seemed both natural and easy. It also seemed much more interesting, more truly Pashtun. After all, I said to Selima, I could eat with men any old day.

She laughed. She took me into the room where we were to eat, and it was whitewashed and square, with a blackly beamed ceiling, and low furniture, dark and carved. The only decoration was rugs, and they were marvelous. I'd never taken much notice of rugs before, being too busy walking on them, but these rugs were different, somehow, glowing and lustrous, with octagons and medallions of black and cream and gold on a deep red ground.

"All Afghan carpets," Selima said.

I knelt down and touched one that was spread over a low stool. It felt thick and silky.

"All woven by women. Hours and hours and hours. This pattern is called Filpai. It means Elephant's Foot. And this one is bleached and is called Golden Afghan."

"They're so lovely —"

They were. They were also oddly familiar, as was the lantern hanging overhead and the dark, brass-hinged furniture. I said to Selima, "An ancestor of mine went to Afghanistan a hundred and fifty years ago. She had a little house in the British cantonment in Kabul, and she furnished it from the bazaar."

"Did she?" Selima's voice was eager. "What did she buy?"

I closed my eyes. I said, quoting Emily, "Assisted by Sayid, Charlotte plundered the bazaar in Kabul and came home with carpets and quilts patterned in russet and black and ocher, Chinese jars, pierced brass lamps to swing from the black beams of the ceiling and strange marvellous chests and stools stained dull red and finished with greenish brass —"

Selima clapped her hands delightedly. "Open your eyes! Only Chinese jars missing! What were you reciting from?"

"My ancestor's sister's journal."

"Today, yesterday," Selima said, "all the same. British soldiers, Russian soldiers, what does it matter?"

"But not," I said, "in the camps."

Her face grew serious.

"No. Not in the camps. Tomorrow we go to Kerala. I take you to Kerala before the men go there. I returned from London because of the refugees."

"And what would you have done if you'd stayed in London?"

She looked at me very solemnly.

"I wished to work at Institute for Cultural Research."

"Yes," I said, duly impressed.

"And you?"

"I . . . I worked for a magazine."

"A woman's magazine?"

"Yes."

"Clothes, hair, makeup, sex appeal, that sort of magazine?"

I felt rather abashed. "Only partly —"

"Better for you at Kerala," Selima said gravely. "More useful at Kerala."

"Oh, I know —"

"Do you have husband?"

"No!" I said, startled.

"You have seen one you like?"

I said nothing. I didn't want to say I hadn't, and even less did I want to say that I had and that he was actually sitting ten feet away from us through the latticed wooden doors that divided the men's dining room from ours, politely listening to a very long story Nasir was telling him in Persian with Abdul trying to translate at the same time.

"I see," said Selima, "you have seen but has not seen you. Now my mother will come and we will eat."

"I'm afraid I can't —"

"Rice, you can. Rice good for stomachs. And mint. And paste from the prickly pear. My mother will give you paste from the prickly pear."

Selima's mother appeared in an inner doorway. Like her daughter, she wore a full robe of thick, richly colored cotton, billowing out from a small embroidered bodice, and her head was wound in a black scarf scattered all over with sequins and coins. I felt awkward and discourteously dressed in my shirt and trousers, and began to bless Patsy for the clothes she had made me buy in Islamabad.

Selima's mother held out brown arms to me, clanking with heavy silver bracelets, and said something very loud and very complicated.

"My mother bids you welcome —"

"Tell her I'm so grateful for her hospitality."

"She says she will bring you rice and lamb and then a stewed yellow orange from Jalalabad which is a speciality and a cure for all ills."

"Could you tell her —"

"And she would like to tell you that the lamb is her special palao with the meat dusted in powdered ginger and the rice soaked in pomegranate juice and with it the salan which is a hot sauce and the kofta which is spiced meatballs and the ashak which is —"

"Please," I said. "Please. Your mother is so kind but just rice tonight, just —"

"My mother says you are too thin," Selima said severely.

"Not in England —"

"You are not in England. You are in Chitral. My mother has ordered yoghurt and cucumbers and green tea and nan bread and omelette because you are guest and when she was a child in my grandfather's house, sometimes the guests numbered four thousand and *all* were fed to abundance."

I gave in. I supposed I could always appeal to Tom for one of his magic unpronounceable capsules again. The room began to fill with the ladies of Nasir's household, ladies of all ages and sizes with dark faces and handsome noses, some in the full embroidered smock-shaped robes that Selima and her mother wore, and some in baggy trousers under flowered shirts and veils, and every one of them simply clanking with jewelery.

Selima drew me to sit down by her, on the rug-covered floor, around the low central table. She indicated two young women opposite in trousers and veils.

"Are my cousins from Nuristan." She shook her head pityingly. "They do not read or write."

"Does it matter?"

Selima looked shocked. "Of course it matters!"

I looked round the rest of the table. There were fifteen of us altogether and I was the only one with a bare head. I was also the only one who looked at the immense steaming palao that was put down on the table in front of us with anything other than the wildest enthusiasm. Selima's mother flung her arms out towards me again with a wide smile and a stream of Persian.

"My mother says eat first. My mother says you are to take the choicest pieces. My mother says —"

The glistening dish of meat and rice and sauce seemed to quiver before my eyes. I said, "Selima, I'm so very sorry to seem rude, but I'm afraid I can't eat tonight, I simply can't —"

The chattering round the table stopped abruptly. Everyone looked at me.

"Selima," I said, "would you explain that I'm not very well? I hate to disappoint your mother, but I ate something at lunch, at Attock —"

"Attock!" exclaimed Selima, as if nobody in their right minds could ever even consider eating there.

"Attock!" cried all the ladies of Nasir's household in horror.

I suddenly felt very peculiar, sick and sweating, and the strange, wonderful room appeared to heave around me with buckling walls and rippling ceiling. I said, very politely, in a voice that seemed to come from miles away, "I'm so sorry to be such a difficult guest but I think I'm going to faint." And then I did.

I came to lying in a sort of hammock under a beautiful deep blue ceiling painted with brilliant silver stars, which turned out, after I had examined it carefully for some time, to be the sky. After a bit, I remembered that it was an Asian sky, the sky that hung over Chitral, and then I remembered, in slow sequence, the generously prepared dinner party at which I had rudely fainted. I turned my head to see where my hammock had been hung, and found that it wasn't a hammock after all, but a kind of string bed in a wooden frame, and on one side of it was the white wall of the compound and a dark-leaved tree which smelled beautifully of something citrus, and on the other side of it was Tom.

He was sitting on a low stool beside my charpoy, watching me. I said, rather foolishly, "Hello."

"Poor Carly. I'm so sorry. I should never have subjected you to that, not after lunchtime."

"That's quite all right," I said, in a polite voice I had used to say I was going to faint. "I am quite recovered, thank you."

I turned my head away. I didn't want him looking at me so intently after a day's traveling and being sick and fainting. I didn't want him seeing my tangled hair and my green face when he, even by moonlight, looked so beautiful, his sun-bleached hair slightly ruffled and his brown neck rising strongly out of his faded khaki shirt collar.

"Please take these," Tom said. "They'll make you feel so much better."

I sat up grudgingly, and took the capsules and the proffered cup of water.

"I want you to rest tomorrow," Tom said. "Kerala can wait until another day and I've told Selima so. Tomorrow is a day off. We'll find you somewhere comfortable in the shade. Perhaps a wicker chair, like Emily had."

I swallowed the pills and handed back the cup. "Please don't bother with me."

"But I want to bother —"

"Tom," I said suddenly desperate, "please leave me alone. Please stop fussing over me. Please, please stop being so bloody *kind*."

I lay down again on my charpoy and turned my back to him. There was a small silence, then he said, "Carly, I was going to sleep here, next to you, in case you felt lousy in the night, but perhaps you'd rather I didn't?"

"Right," I said rudely.

"I see. Is there anyone else you'd rather have next to you? I'd be happier to think there was someone —"

"Andy," I said.

"Andy —"

"Yes," I said, "send Andy. He doesn't fuss."

I heard Tom stand up. It was all I could do not to hurl myself over and fling my arms around him and beg him to sleep next to me, that night and for ever. Instead I lay rigid, staring at the wall.

"Of course," Tom said, his voice quite neutral. "Of course. Whatever you like. I'll find Andy at once and send him over."

Chapter Fifteen

Kerala Camp, they told me, was only one of three hundred refugee camps in the north of Pakistan, but for all that, it was special. It was special not just because it was small — only about five thousand women and children — but because it was the population of a whole village, and therefore had a kind of social unity. It had become Selima's particular concern because she, despite the sophistication acquired by her time in London, understood how it felt to be a displaced Afghan woman from a tiny, enclosed, Muslim village world.

She made me dress very carefully for my first visit. I had had two days of sitting about in the shade of two huge old fig trees while the women of the household fussed over me with herbal potions, and also went through the contents of my backpack with cackles of delight. My underclothes were particularly amazing and funny. They spread all the long, flowing, embroidered things that Patsy had so rightly said I would need, out on the sun-warmed stones of the courtyard, and clucked disapprovingly over the workmanship.

"They say is cheap Pakistani sewing machine made," Selima said. "Will not last. Cloth poor. In the villages of our country, the women weave their own cloth. I am setting up looms for cloth and carpets at Kerala. You will see."

She surveyed my wardrobe with the faintly resigned air of one who has to put up with what they are offered, poor though it is, and then she made a selection. She chose dark blue muslin trousers, their tight ankle bands embroidered in peach and gold, a long loose peach-colored shirt like a tunic and a huge wonderful scarf that I had needed no persuading to buy, made of deep blue crinkled cotton embroidered all over with spangles and tiny starlike flowers.

She dressed me in all this with great solemnity, arranging the scarf decorously over my hair, and lending me a pair of soft leather sandals. Then, to my great embarrassment, she took me to show me to the crew.

"Is suitable," she said to Tom.

He was crouched over a map, working out our route back to the original Kerala, a route we were to travel on horseback. He looked up. He was wearing sunglasses so I couldn't see the expression in his eyes, but it was a long, long time before he spoke. He just got to his feet, very slowly, and stared.

"Is suitable for Muslim women," Selima said again, more insistently. "If you wish the women of Kerala camp to speak to Carly, they will do so more freely if she is dressed like Muslim women."

Tom said slowly, "I see."

Joe came over. "Give us a twirl, darling," he said. "Dance of the Seven Veils —"

"Shut up," I said amicably.

"You look great," Andy said. "Great."

"We go now," Selima said. "We go for first visit."

I said to Tom, in as businesslike a voice as I could manage, "What are my instructions?"

He seemed to give himself a little shake as if coming out of a daydream. He said, "Just first impressions, Carly. Who are the women who seem likely to talk, a few initial stories, what their life is like. Have you got your camera?"

"Yes —"

"I leave it to you," Tom said. He took a step away from me. "You know what I'm after."

Joe let out a rude guffaw and to our collective amazement, Tom spun round and cuffed him.

"Shut up."

Joe gawped at him.

"Hey Tom," Andy said, "don't get heavy. It was only fun —"

Joe spread his hands out. "What did I say, skipper? Come on, now. Tell me. What did I say?"

"Is heat," Selima said. "Always like this with people from the West. Heat inflames tempers."

Tom put his hand out to Joe. "It wasn't the heat. I don't know what it was. But I'm sorry."

"That's okay —"

"We go now," Selima said to me firmly. "We leave the men and we go among the women."

I nodded. I looked at the crew and smiled goodbye.

"You look lovely," Andy said. He'd been the perfect companion while I wasn't well, kind without smothering and I felt a huge affection for him. "Really lovely," he said.

We went out to the camp in a new Japanese jeep belonging to Nasir and driven by one of his servants. There must be, I reflected, a good deal of money in lapis lazuli trading or, as Joe had suggested, in arms dealing under cover of lapis lazuli trading. Selima and I sat in the back, with our heads and faces completely muffled except for our eyes, and the canvas satchel containing my notebooks and camera wedged between my feet.

The drive took about half an hour, and although the distant landscape was magnificent, with rearing mountains snowcapped against a brilliant sky, the road itself ran through something altogether more depressing. The land close to the road was rough and dusty and dun-colored, and it was strewn all over with what could only be described as hovels, huts and shelters and lean-tos built of anything to hand, so that the effect was like looking at a giant rubbish dump. These had been built, Selima said, by displaced persons, not as absolutely destitute as the refugees from the interior of Afghanistan who were utterly dependent upon the camps, but who had still suffered bitterly from the Russian occupation.

"Some Pakistani, some Afghan, all Muslim," Selima said, "Islam is great bond." She glanced at me, as if checking to see that I still looked suitable and hadn't reverted to my shameful Western appearance when she wasn't watching. "Islam has many, many rules for women."

I set my teeth. "I know," I said.

490

"The laws of veiling and modesty are very strong for the women of villages such as Kerala. They are accustomed to men as their protectors and now their men are dead. They think it deep shame to be seen by a man who is not their relation, so we have great problem with doctors, because doctors in camps such as Kerala almost always men. I try to start clinic run by women at Kerala but that too is not easy because I need Muslim women doctors for such a clinic."

I looked out at the view, at the sad contrast between the squalor of the hovels and the majesty of the mountains.

"I wish I'd brought them something," I said. "Just some little things. Aspirins for the women, toys for the children —"

Selima snorted. "The children won't touch toys."

"Won't touch toys?"

"No. The Russians used to drop explosives from aircraft hidden in dolls and model cars. Many children blinded. Now they refuse toys, and their mothers also."

This silenced me. A huge rage and a huge accompanying sorrow began to rise in me like a choking tide. Selima said, "You are not going to hear happy things, Carly."

Abruptly, the jeep swung off the main dirt road and began to climb the slopes to the north over a rugged track through which boulders stuck like mammoth teeth. The driver didn't slacken his pace at all, and we were flung about like corks. The effort of hanging on was actually a relief to my jagged feelings, but the jolting was so terrific

491

that it was difficult to see where we were going except that the hovels began to fall away, and the brown mountainside seemed to engulf us all around like a hilly ocean.

Then the jeep stopped dead, and being unprepared for anything so sudden, I was flung on to the floor.

"Kerala," Selima said calmly. "We walk from here. Driver may not come."

She opened the jeep door and got out gracefully, with me scrambling most ungracefully after her. It was tremendously hot, the heat intensified by a fierce hot wind, like the blast from an open oven door. I looked about me. We were in a cup in the mountain foothills, a small, shallow valley, and ahead of us, beyond the rough wooden palisade that had stopped our driver, was my first sight of a refugee camp. It wasn't like the hovels on the roadside, and it wasn't like the corrugated iron huts in the photographs of Boer War camps in a book Duncan had and it wasn't like the only camp I had ever been to in my life, for pony-mad little girls in a wet field outside Craigmuir; and yet it was partly like all three.

As far as the eye could see stretched higgledy-piggledy lines of what appeared to be tents, dust-colored against the dusty earth. Occasionally there were huts of some kind, and also a few square prefabricated-looking buildings, but there seemed to be no pattern to the place, and no space to it on account of the pressing in of the steep hillsides all around and what was worst of all to my Scottish educated eye, nothing green at all.

"But where do the children play?"

Selima snorted.

"Play? Where they can. You will see. The children in this camp are lucky, they are still with their mothers. The Russians took tens of thousands of other Afghan children back to Russia with them, to educate them as communists. Come. Put on your scarf properly and follow me."

I followed. I followed Selima on the most moving and eye-opening walk of my whole life, stumbling in the glaring heat down the stifling alleys between the makeshift dwellings of these women and children trying to recreate their broken lives in this inhospitable, infertile dustbowl. There were people everywhere, swarming, chattering people, cooking and sewing and gesturing and, in many poignant cases, simply sitting and staring, too disorientated still, even after several years of this camp life, to do more than simply exist.

We came at last to a kind of square, a roughly rectangular space around a primitive-looking tap whose dripping had made a small muddy quagmire around its base in which several tiny naked children were happily playing. I was so relieved to see a sign of normal, healthy, carefree life, that I reached into my satchel for my camera and held it up to my eye. I was stopped by a thin high scream of pure terror, and felt Selima's hand pushing the camera down.

"Do not. Do not take pictures."

"But you said it would be all right and I only wanted to take the children —"

"No camera in front of Safia. Look at her."

I looked where Selima pointed. A woman in deep mulberry-colored robes was pressing herself back against a hut wall opposite, her face twisted with screams and tears.

"But what have I done?"

"I should have warned you," Selima said. "Safia had a gun fired point-blank at her. The camera always reminds her."

Several other women had come running up now to the hysterical Safia, but the children round the tap were playing on quite unconcerned. I felt simply awful, guilty and insensitive. Selima put a hand on my arm.

"Come. You could not help and she will recover. I will take you to meet Halima. She is, with some others, like the mother to all Kerala. We will talk to her."

We skirted round the playing children. I paused by the group of women clustered together with poor shaking Safia at their center. I said, even though I knew they couldn't understand me, "I am so terribly sorry. I had no idea. I have so much to learn."

One of the women detached herself from the group and came over to me. She had a merry, sparkling look and she put up a hand, and pushed my scarf back a little from my forehead to display my hair, and then she burst out laughing. She said something to Selima.

"What is she saying?"

"I am afraid she is saying you are bleached like a carpet —"

"I don't mind. I don't mind at all. Will you tell

her how sorry I am to have upset Safia?"

Selima translated and they all turned and looked at me, a dozen pairs of dark Afghan eyes that had witnessed things I would never know even in my worst nightmares. I held my hands out to Safia, but she turned away, gabbling, and hid her face against the wall. Selima took my arm, her bracelets clanking.

"Come. Come and see Halima."

"Selima," I said, "where is their jewelry? Why aren't they wearing jewelry like yours?"

"Sold," she said shortly.

"To buy things for their children?"

"No. To buy guns. Sold long ago to buy arms and ammunition for their men, for the men of Kerala, the men the Russians killed."

She began to walk briskly ahead of me. I followed, desperately wishing I had done more homework, before I came, at least enough to have bought a truckload of bangles in Islamabad for the women of Kerala. I thought suddenly that I would tell Tom about it, that he would understand about the jewelry and what it had meant to them, and perhaps he would arrange that as a thank you to the camp for their cooperation, we would send in anklets and bracelets and earrings and necklaces, a treasure trove of silver and garnets and turquoises . . . And then I thought in despair, oh Carly, you stupid romantic fool, what these poor people need is teachers and medicines and food, not *trinkets*.

"In here," Selima said, and stopped under a tent flap that looked, to me, like all the other tent flaps either side of it in the long meandering

495

alley. I bent too, and ducked inside.

It was very dark and smoky and there was a curious strong smell, partly human, partly cooking, partly dust and charcoal. My eyes began to water, and it was some time before they cleared enough for me to make out, sitting on a rust-red piece of cloth on the earthen floor, the figures of three women, two of them holding distaffs, like those you can see in medieval woodcuts in English museums.

Selima pressed me down on to the floor, and squatted beside me.

"This is Halima, and her sister and her niece. Halima's husband was one of the chiefs of Kerala village. He was shot by the Russians when he protested about the napalming of their fields."

I gazed at Halima, and then I bowed my head towards her with my hands together as if in prayer, as the servants in Nasir's household were inclined to do to us. Selima began to explain me to the three women in rapid Persian, and they all watched me intently, bright dark eyes in hawk-nosed dark faces, shawled and scarfed.

"I am telling them that you wish the Western world to know of the plight of the women of Kerala. I tell them that the film you will make will help raise money for the education of their children. Education for their children is the dearest wish of the women of the camp. Halima wants to know if you have children. I am telling her not yet. Like my mother, she says you are too thin."

I smiled at Halima. She had a face of great distinction, strong and handsome. She leaned forward and began to speak to me.

"She says she has seen some Western journalists but she has seen no good come from what she told them. She says she must have some kind of promise and then she will consider helping. She says you must understand that there are great psychological difficulties in this camp not just because of the atrocities of the Russians but because this place is a desert, and Kerala was fertile and lovely —"

"Tell her," I said, interrupting, "tell her that we are going to Kerala. We are going to see her village, because we are very serious about wishing to help."

Selima translated. A strange, emotional quiet fell upon the three women. They looked at one another and Halima and her sister clasped each other's hands. Then the niece spoke, urgently, looking straight at me.

"She says will you tell them if the Russians have gone and they may go back —"

"The Russians are going, but I don't think anywhere is yet safe to go back."

"That is true," Selima said. "But it is hard to explain to people who have lived a semifeudal life. They do not understand a devastated landscape, the danger of minefields."

Halima stretched her free hand out to me. Her wrists were also empty of bracelets. I took her hand; it was warm and hard and strong. She began to talk rapidly.

"She says that to go back to Kerala is a dream, the dream they all have. But they cannot live this dream today and today is important first. The women need help in carrying on their traditional tasks, their tasks of weaving and cooking. They need clothes and medicines. They need help from other women and above all, they need help for the future of their children. If you can promise this with your English film, she will assist you to make it."

I gulped. It felt a very solemn, almost sacred moment. I looked Halima straight in the eye.

"I promise," I said.

We drove back to Chitral almost in silence. I was at once all stirred up emotionally and completely exhausted. I was also terribly thirsty, but Selima would not allow me to accept even a cup of water in the camp because she said they needed every scarce drop for themselves.

"The hygiene and washing standards in the camp are well below what they are used to and the water supply is very poor. Water is gold to them."

By the time we reached Nasir's house, my tongue was almost glued to the roof of my mouth. The courtyard was empty in the noonday sun, and the doorkeeper told Selima that all the Englishmen had gone off with their machines to make pictures.

I was rather glad of this, in order to have a little time to myself to sort out my thoughts. I went over to my favorite fig tree, and squatted in its deep, delicious shade and one of the servants, ordered by Salima, brought me a pitcher of water and a plate of nuts and fruit and slices of lemon. I drank like a mad thing, on and on until the jug was empty. It was a heavenly relief.

"Carly?"

I looked up. Tom was squatting at the edge of the shade.

"Are you all right?"

I said, "I thought you'd all gone filming —"

"The others have. I wanted to wait for you. Are you too tired to talk?"

"No," I said.

He crawled in under the tree beside me and sat with his back to the trunk so that, I couldn't help noticing, our shoulders were touching. I felt suddenly sick with relief that he was there, that he was the very person I wanted to unburden myself to.

"Tom," I said. "Tom, I've got so much to tell you!"

He turned to look at me. His eyes were warm with approval.

"I knew you would have," he said.

Chapter Sixteen

For the next two weeks, I spent every day at Kerala Camp. Selima would wake me early, while it was still cool, and supervise my dressing — I think she was afraid I would lazily revert to impropriety if she didn't watch me like a hawk — and then we would breakfast off nan bread and green tea and dried apricots, and afterwards go jolting off in the Japanese jeep as the sun rose burning in the heavens.

The aim of my coming so regularly, Selima said, was to make me a familiar and trustworthy figure to the women of the camp. If I dressed modestly, behaved discreetly and showed a true sympathy, she informed me severely, then I would stand some chance of winning enough confidence for Halima and the other influential women in the camp to allow filming. Being with Selima was like spending one's days with a kind of pernickety governess; she was genuinely anxious to help me, but she was equally anxious to see that I behaved like a properly brought up child and didn't do anything to disgrace her.

She certainly had enormous energy. Sometimes, after a long, hard morning in the relentless sun, I began to crave even a brief nap in the shade, but she went determinedly on with the steadiness of a traction engine. Some of the women noticed this, and the sparkling-eyed one who had teased me about my hair, and whose name was Amina, used to beckon me into her tent to hide from Selima.

Amina had three children, all boys. The eldest one had a scar on his forehead, caused by a thrust from a Russian bayonet, and he touched his finger to the scar all day in a sad little anxious, remembering movement. The boys had all seen their father killed.

"I cried," the eldest one would say, over and over again, "I cried and I lay on the floor because I was sad when they killed my father."

"That was three years ago," Selima told me, "but to him it is yesterday."

For Selima, there was only tomorrow. Tomorrow she would achieve a loom for every woman in this camp, a school, and a proper clinic, not just the present rudimentary dispensary. As the days wore on, I began to see that I and Tom and the crew were a vital part of that tomorrow. Our film, if Selima had anything to do with it, was going to change the face and the future of the camp at Kerala, and I was her chief instrument.

My prime task, apart from the slow winning of trust, was to build up a careful, detailed picture of what had happened at Kerala when the Russians came, and what life in the camp was like now. The latter was easy because it lay all around me, the boredom and the frustration and the difficulties and the tremendous sense of unity and religious fervor which had arisen, Selima said, as a binding force and inspiration against the Russians. I quickly saw that my greatest problem was going to lie in persuading these devout Muslim women to be filmed by Western men, even distant Western men using zoom lenses and wearing dark glasses so that the direction of their offending gaze couldn't be seen.

This meant hours and hours in Halima's tent, with long, slow, convoluted conversations passing through Selima in an endless ebb and flow of English and Persian. I was, to be honest, amazed at my own patience because I'd never had much or troubled to exercise what little I did have. But this was too important for self-indulgence, and it had become plain, after my first visit, that I was a vital link in the chain between these five thousand desperately needy people in a Pakistani mountain camp and the millions in the West with the power to help them.

Joe teased me about it all the time. He called me Flo, after Florence Nightingale, or the Kerala Kid or The Secret Weapon. He was actually rather a relief because I'd never, in all my life, done anything as absolutely *serious* as I was doing now, and however serious anything is, it's fatal to lose your sense of humor about it entirely. Coming back to Chitral after a long, hot day, as tiring emotionally as it was physically, it would have been alarmingly easy just to have sat about all evening brooding on the ills of the world and getting into a deeper and deeper gloom, so it was refreshing to have Joe mopping me up and playing the banjo he had discovered in the Chitral bazaar and generally reminding me that there was another world outside the tiny one I

502

had suddenly got obsessed with.

While I was at the camp, slowly talking my way into some kind of agreement, the rest of the crew were making arrangements for our trip into the interior including confirmation of our permits to travel and film which was, Tom said, like trying to get blood out of a stone. Our original jeeps and their drivers had long since gone back to Islamabad, and we were going to hire a truck and drive up beyond a place called Garam Chasma, where there were supposed to be thermal baths, to a spot in the mountains where we would be met by horses and tents and local guides. We were to be escorted over the border by two Chitrali scouts in order that there wouldn't be any trouble with our permits.

I think the only way you can cope with the prospect of a huge, unfamiliar adventure in your life, is not to try to imagine beforehand what it's going to be like. I'd grown rather fond of my string bed by the orange tree in Nasir's compound, and discovered that I didn't much like the thought of relinquishing its familiarity, and the cosy, busy domesticity of his house for a whole lot of wild men and wild mountains. I had, despite my fatigue, a couple of bad nights anticipating all sorts of horrors that might befall me, which I didn't dare confide to anyone in case I was remorselessly teased about it. They all seemed, by contrast, not only calm but looking forward to it.

"This place is choking me," Andy said one night. "All these jabbering women and these damn walls. And this hanging about. If there's one thing I can't stand, it's hanging about."

Tom had been to a money changer, and had exchanged what I thought was an enormous sum of Pakistani rupees for huge tattered wads of the local currency. They were notes called Afghanis and they looked as if they too had been deep in the wars, dirty and dog-eared and worth about two pence each. We packed them up in plastic bags, and stowed them away in some saddlebags Tom had bought. I wondered what Charlotte had used for money. Gold? Indian rupees? Or the ancestors of these grubby, near-worthless pieces of paper, battered silver Afghan coins that the men of the hills had used to buy swords and slaves?

The day before we left, I paid my last visit to Halima. On Selima's advice, I took a bag of Basmati rice, another of sesame seeds, another of Herat walnuts and a small sack of lemons whose peel, Selima said, the women would use to cure sores and skin infections on their children.

Halima accepted my presents gravely and I put them down beside her pathetic little collection of earthenware cooking jars. Then I sat down in front of her — I'd got quite good at sitting cross-legged for hours by now — and, through Selima, I put my proposition.

I said that in order to help the camp properly, we should have to film inside it. We would need to film some of the inmates while they told their stories and we should need to show what some of the tents and huts were like inside.

There was a pause and then Halima said the whole thing was out of the question because of the laws of modesty. I got to my feet. I bowed to Halima and to her sister and her niece and said how sorry I was that after all we could not help Kerala Camp, and then I went out of the tent and began to walk down the alley outside, and Amina's poor, pointing son came up to me and began to tell me his story all over again in his flat singsong monotone.

I hadn't gone more than twenty paces, when Halima's niece came running after me and plucked at the sleeve of my tunic. She said something urgent, and pointed back the way she had come. I wanted to smile, but I didn't dare, so I simply said, "I see," and went back very slowly, not hurrying, in order to show that the whole matter was of supreme indifference to me.

"Will be bargain, bargain, bargain," Selima had said. "Will be like buying carpets. They want something, you want something. Cannot be hurry."

Clearly there could not be hurry. I sat down in front of Halima again and she said she hadn't at all changed her mind, but that she'd like to hear my proposal again. I made it and she said, no men in the camp. So I got up and went out into the alley and the niece came after me and I went back and Halima said there could perhaps be filming but no men filming. I said no men, no filming. Halima said no men, so out I went again.

This time the sister came after me, and several other women began to gather out of neighboring huts, holding babies and cooking pots. Halima said men could come into the camp but must not film any women. I said if they couldn't film a few women, they wouldn't come. Halima said no women under any circumstances so for the fourth time, I got to my feet and went out into the dust and heat and began to think, with nostalgic affection, of dealing with the tax authorities back in England, who seemed, by comparison, to be a helpful pushover.

Both the sister and the niece came pattering after me, so I went back yet again, trying terribly hard not to look as exasperated as I felt, and Halima said that the men could come into the camp and film the boy children. I saw Selima fixing me with a bright, hard gaze and realized that we had actually won the first tiny round in this tedious battle. I held out my hand to Halima and smiled.

"Done," I said. "The men may enter the camp with their film cameras and film the boy children and the camp."

"Not the camp," said Halima, "only the boy children."

It took five hours. By the end of it, I was as ready to strangle Halima as I had been to strangle the old countryman in Wiltshire who had so kindly and maddeningly changed my wheel. I could scarcely croak for fatigue, let alone croak politely. I simply couldn't believe that someone who needed my help as badly as Halima did could raise quite so many impossible objections to being helped. She ceded her ground millimeter by millimeter and at the end looked as fresh as a daisy.

I crawled out of the camp and collapsed in the back of the jeep.

"Now you see," Selima said, "difference between Christian mind and Muslim mind, between Western and Eastern."

"I nearly murdered her —"

"You have no patience," Selima said reprovingly. "What is five hours to get most of what you want?"

"It was five hours on top of two solid weeks, may I remind you."

"Bah! Is nothing. Is blink of eye."

"It was jolly nearly black of eye," I said, and shut my eyes to indicate I didn't want to talk any more.

That, however, didn't stop Selima talking. She seemed as turned on by that interminable haggling as Halima had been, and chattered on, all the way to Chitral, about how she would carry on the good work all the time I was away in the interior, and find a few women who would consent (heavily veiled — Halima had insisted on that) to be filmed on our return. Then she started on all the things I must beware of on our trek, and how I must take some of her mother's hollyhock leaves to make a paste in case any of us cut ourselves, and eat coriander to prevent insects from biting us, and how I must not reveal my face to any man at any time and what we must eat and what we would say to strangers. She went on and on and on, like some dreadful noisy machine you can't turn off, and by the time we got back to Chitral, I was almost beside myself with rage and despair.

I limped into the courtyard, rudely not even waiting for her. The men were all sitting under my fig tree busy with charts and maps. I flopped down next to Andy.

"You look happy."

"I have slowly been driven round the bend today, bargaining with Halima. You can't imagine what it was like. I wanted to murder her by the end. How on earth do real charity workers stay charitable?"

Joe grinned at me. "They aren't red-headed firecrackers like you."

"You shut up," I said. "You'll owe your precious film to me."

"Will we? Did she agree?"

"In the end, she agreed about eighty percent. Selima says she'll concede most of the remaining twenty percent once we get started."

Andy leaned sideways and kissed my cheek.

"You're a star. Tom'll be thrilled."

"Where is he?"

"Having the same sort of day as you've had, with the chief of police, about our permits."

Philip looked across at me. He was a quiet, private man who was happier alone with a camera than at any other time. He said, "We're still starting tomorrow, you know. At daybreak." He smiled. "Up into the mountains. Think of the air up there."

I did. I leaned against Andy and closed my eyes and thought of mountain air and great wild, untamed spaces, and the contrast that would be to the dust and the heat and the crowds and the squabbling of the last two weeks, and suddenly all my fears about going were replaced by a longing to be there.

Chapter Seventeen

We were, in a suppressed kind of way, terribly excited when we set off the next morning. Nasir had got up himself to see us off — and, as Joe pointed out, no doubt to make sure he was paid for putting us up — and he supervised our breakfast in a lordly way, and then ushered us graciously into the old army truck that was taking us up to the mountains. Then he and Abdul embraced each other fervently and Abdul climbed into the truck, and sat down on one of our rolls of bedding.

"Most sophisticated man, my cousin Nasir," Abdul said proudly. "Much power, and knowledge."

We nodded politely. The truck, driven by an Afghan beside whom sat the two Chitrali scouts in their grey and red uniforms, lurched forward, and we watched over the tailgate as the white walls of Nasir's house faded away from our view in the glimmering dawn.

As we ground out of Chitral — the truck was even noisier than our original jeeps — there was a tremendous honking of a horn, and some vehicle, its headlights blazing, came charging up behind us, swerved past and then braked violently in front, forcing us to stop.

"Bloody hell," Tom said, "the police —"

A figure jumped out of the jeep and came rushing back towards the truck, waving some object and shouting. One of the scouts got down into the road and began to shout back. The waving figure started to explain something energetically, and the scout seized his arm and frog-marched him round to the back of the truck. They both then said a great deal at the tops of their voices to Abdul.

"This man," Abdul said to Tom, "is come from Mr. Tindall in Islamabad. Is driving all night. Is bringing letters."

We all leaped up.

"Letters!"

"God bless Christopher —"

"Fantastic —"

"Will you thank him, Abdul? What should I give him?"

"Oh, hundred rupees —"

"No. He's driven all night."

"Two hundred —"

Tom dived into his rucksack and pulled out his remaining wad of Pakistani rupees. He peeled off several notes and pressed them into our courier's hand, thanking him warmly.

"Christian fool," Abdul said sourly.

Luckily, there were letters for everybody. Tom had the most, and two of them, addressed in Laura's confident, feminine handwriting, I saw him button up into a shirt pocket of his bush shirt with a care I could hardly bear to watch. He was plainly saving them for later. I decided to do the same, largely because the light wasn't yet strong enough to read by properly. Mine — both of them — were from Ma. I suddenly felt very fond of her and very far away. She might drive me mad with her possessiveness and her determination that we should all live our lives as she thought fit, but she was as loyal as a rock. I could be in the middle of the Gobi Desert, and not see another human for days, but the first one I did see I could bet would be carrying a letter from Ma.

The letters cheered us up still further. Andy's was from his sister, Joe's from his wife, and Philip, reading intently by the light of the torch, declined to reveal who his was from. There were also several communications from our television company, a rude postcard from Matthew, a nice one from Simon and a jolly one from my brothers, showing two identical cartoons, side by side, of a gloomy sheep standing in the rain. Under the left-hand sheep it said "Winter in Scotland" and under the right-hand one it said "Summer in Scotland." On the back the boys had written, "Your flat is brilliant which is more than can be said for the fishing at Bewick. Everybody fine. Take care and don't get sold into slavery."

We got to Garam Chasma at midday. It was a disgusting place, dirty and crowded, the narrow streets crammed with shoving, pushing, shouting Afghans and lined with terrifying-looking eating houses. Abdul led us firmly into one, and ordered a meal for us in his usual authoritative way. When it came — a steaming pile of rice, dotted with bits of grilled sheep's liver — I was painfully reminded of my last lunch on the road, at Attock, and stuck firmly to rice only, despite Abdul losing his temper with me and shouting that I was insulting his country.

"No, I'm not," I said crossly. "Your country insulted my stomach last time. I don't want to have to be carried into Afghanistan."

Abdul speared a piece of liver on a stick provided for the purpose, and thrust it at me.

"Eat! Eat! Is excellent!"

Tom looked up. He hadn't unbuttoned the pocket in which Laura's letters lay. "Leave her alone," he said sharply to Abdul.

"She is fool not to eat —"

"Leave her, I said. She has worked harder these last two weeks than any of us, and she may eat what she wants."

Abdul subsided, muttering. I looked gratefully at Tom, and then as quickly I looked away because I couldn't help seeing that in a clearly unconscious gesture he had laid his left hand — the one he wasn't eating with — across his shirt pocket as if to reassure himself that his precious letters were still there. I swallowed hard and felt for my own letters. I had an idea I might read them while the others ate the disgusting food, but then I decided to save them until we were away from this sordid place and I could have both privacy and beauty of scenery.

After lunch, everything changed. The truck took us on, about another hour, away from the squalor and racket of Garam Chasma, up the most beautiful valley. We were now only a mountain pass away from Afghanistan, and I had never, even in beloved Scotland, seen scenery so thrilling.

Huge brown mountains, still blotched with dazzling patches of snow, heaved all around us, as far as the eye could see, the distant ranges purple and gun-metal gray against the brilliant blue sky. The track we were on was edged on one side by the rough slope of the valley side, and on the other by a kind of drystone wall beyond which the mountain wall fell away steeply, down and down to a wonderful racing green and white river, swirling and roaring below us. The sun was hot, but the air was clear and fresh despite the dust that the truck wheels churned up. I felt extremely happy and full of energy.

Gradually, the track began to dip down, towards the wild lovely river, and the mountainsides opened up and we found ourselves crossing a water meadow, green and fresh, dotted with some wonderful little yellow hopping birds, as bright as buttercups.

"Yellow wagtails," Tom said, following my gaze. "Not to be confused with gray wagtails, which are yellow and gray."

The truck stopped suddenly and we clambered out. We were on a grassy platform, just above the river — it was the loudest river I'd ever met — and on the platform was a little stone mill, with a huge wooden wheel turning and creaking in the rushing water. Beside the mill stood a group straight out of an illustration in *The Arabian Nights* — a small herd of fine-headed, long-tailed ponies, and six bandits. At least, they looked as I had always supposed bandits to look, swarthy and scarred, dressed in loose trousers and soft boots and waistcoats and sashes, with rifles slung across their backs.

"Our horsemen," Abdul said. "The leader is Atik. He distinguished himself in the war against the Russians. The others are mujahideen."

We looked at each other, sizing each other up. I thought how like these men Charlotte's Sayid would have looked, narrow-faced, hawk-nosed, dark-eyed, except that Sayid would have worn a turban, and these men wore the soft, round Chitrali wool caps with padded, rolled brims that we had begun to believe were a fixture on every Afghan head.

Atik came forward to greet us. He looked very astonished to see me, and distinctly disapproving.

"Back to the kitchen with you," Joe said.

"Too late —"

"Telling me. Where has bloody Thomas got us this time, I ask you? Middle of nowhere, with six cutthroats for company."

The cutthroats were put to work at once, unloading the truck while Philip and Andy danced round them yelling instructions while their precious cameras were taken off. Film equipment, I learned very quickly, is the absolutely worst luggage you can take anywhere, being awkward, fragile, sensitive to heat, damp, and sudden movements, and so vital that it turns anyone trying to look after it into an instant neurotic.

When we were unloaded, the truck went screeching off back up the valley towards Chitral, and the muja built an instant bonfire and made tea. Then Atik said they would kill a sheep in our honor, and I thought I really couldn't bear to watch this, and that also I had at last reached a place that was right for the reading of Ma's letters, so I left them all to the horrible slaughter, and went across the lovely meadow among the yellow birds and some little bright blue flowers I thought might be speedwell, and climbed up the shingly foothills of the nearest hillside until I found a perfect, private rocky outcrop, facing towards the river, but away from the camp.

I sat down and leaned my back gratefully against the sunwarmed rock. For a moment, I didn't open the letters, but simply sat and drank in the air and the wonderful view and the sound of that energetic river whirling below me and tried to convince myself that I really was sitting in the middle of the extraordinary landmass that literally rolls away to Europe in the West and China in the East. After ten minutes of wonderment at this, I took out Ma's letters and smoothed them — they were on that crackly, flimsy blue airmail paper — and looked at the dates.

One had been written almost the day I left, the other two days later. Dear Ma — was she really going to write to me every forty-eight hours for almost three months? I opened the first letter. It was all you could wish for as a letter from home, full of news of people and animals, and funny stories of disasters at the hotel, and a touching description of a long telephone call she'd had from Uncle James, and how he'd loved our midnight feast and defying Pamela Merryweather. I felt very choked at the thought of him, and of

Scotland and Bishopstow. At the bottom, Ma had scrawled "I'll write again very soon. I know you can't write so I will just assume that no news is good news."

I found a crumpled tissue in my pocket and blew my nose hard. Then I opened the second letter. It was much shorter, just a single sheet and the writing was less firm, and the lines ran away downhill as if it had been written in a terrible hurry.

Darling Carly,

I'm so sorry to have to send you bad news when you're so far away, but having agonized all night about whether it was kinder to tell you now, or to leave it until you came home, I've decided to opt for the former.

Uncle James died last night. He died very peacefully in his sleep. It was his heart, it just gave out. I just wish someone else had been with him, except Pamela Merryweather, although I know she's very competent.

I'm so glad you made your mad dash to see him and I'm only sorry I'm not there to comfort you when you get this. I shall go down to Bishopstow to pick up the mementoes he's left us — including the Swinton portrait of Alexandra — and to say goodbye to the house, because of course it's the Langleys' house now. That won't be easy. I wish you were coming with me.

Don't cry for him, Carly darling. He had a happy life after the war, a happy and tranquil one. We were so lucky to have him.

Lots and lots of love,
Ma

The "lots and lots" was smudged. Ma had been crying while she wrote. Poor Ma, to whom Uncle James had been both an extra father and a fairy godfather too. I thought about Ma, and I thought about Uncle James and our funny, happy Christmas together, and his vast, quiet kindness to us, and his protecting love for poor Aunt Mary, and suddenly, in a rush of pain I was quite unprepared for, I absolutely could not bear the thought that he was dead, gone, finished, and that I would never see him again. I crumpled Ma's letter up in my fist, and put my head down on my knees, and wept and wept and wept.

I don't think I've ever cried so painfully before, but then, in my sheltered, easy life, I don't think I'd ever had to face loss before. And now I'd lost someone I not only valued, but someone I'd only learned to value too late, and who I'd hardly begun to talk to properly or to tell how much I loved them. It was an added agony to think I couldn't go to Bishopstow again either, or at least not in the old easy way. If I went in the future, it would be as these Langley cousins' guest, and I didn't know them very well, and wasn't at all sure that I wanted to know them from what I'd seen at the funeral. They were bound to want to change Bishopstow, they would never be imaginative enough to leave it in all its warm, sweet, old-fashioned, faded charm.

When the most violent sobbing was over, I did what I could to mop myself up with the only tissue I had, and I smoothed out Ma's letter and folded it up, intending to put it away in my pocket until I was calm enough to read it again. Then I heard footsteps. I froze. They were below my perch, on the tumble of rocks that led out of the water meadow and up the mountainside.

A voice called "Carly?"

It was Andy. I relaxed at once. Andy was the perfect person for my present state, a person I didn't in the least mind finding me blotched with crying and badly in need of comfort.

"I'm up here!" I called.

I heard his feet slip on the scree and then his hands appeared over the rock beside me, followed by his head, except that it wasn't his head, it was Tom's.

"Tom —"

He heaved himself up the last of the rocks and landed gracefully beside me, like a big, supple cat. Then he turned to look at me.

"Carly," he said. His voice was so gentle it nearly dissolved me again. "I heard you. I heard you crying. I was down there, below you, looking, like you were, for somewhere to be alone for a moment and I heard you. Do you want to tell me what's happened?"

I sniffed. I turned my head so that he wouldn't see my swollen eyes.

"Someone special died, that's all. It was in a letter from my mother."

He said nothing. We sat there for some time, side by side, me looking away to the river and then I felt him take my hand in his warm, strong grasp.

"I'm so truly sorry."

"It was my great-uncle," I said. "Most people don't know their great-uncles very well, but Uncle James was different. He was a tremendously fatherly man who never had any children, so all his nieces and nephews became his children instead. He was the most trustworthy person I've ever known."

"What a compliment," Tom said seriously.

I turned to look at him, feeling suddenly that my appearance didn't matter a stuff.

"That's why I nearly missed the plane," I said. "I had an awful premonition that I might never see him again, and we'd just got to know each other properly and he was so wonderful, and I just *had* to go and say goodbye to him, I had to. I know it was awfully irresponsible, but I didn't feel I had any choice and now —" I paused and swallowed. "Now, to tell the truth, I'm absolutely thankful that I did."

Tom put his other hand over mine so that mine was enfolded in his grasp.

"Of course you are. I'd no idea. I feel dreadful that I bawled you out the way I did."

"But you couldn't know —"

"No," he said, "I couldn't know, but I might have used my imagination and guessed. You see, I thought —" He stopped.

"What did you think?"

"That you were with a boyfriend, saying

goodbye, something you could have done for days before we left."

I pulled my hand free.

"I haven't got a boyfriend. I went to see Uncle James. We had a midnight feast and I gave him a huge slug of whisky which he loved and which he wasn't allowed and then I flew away — and then he died."

I bent my head. Tears were threatening again.

"Where did he live?"

"North Cornwall."

"You drove to *Cornwall?*"

"Yes."

"You're amazing. Every day I'm with you, there's something happens that makes me think you're amazing."

My heart was thudding. I daren't look at him, but stared steadily out at the valley and the river.

He said abruptly, "I love Cornwall."

I turned my head. "Do you?"

"My mother was Cornish. From the north coast too, near Newquay. We used to go to Cornwall every summer, until I was fourteen."

"Why did you stop?"

"Because she died," Tom said simply. "She died of cancer and then my father couldn't settle anywhere and couldn't bear to go back to Cornwall so it's become, in my mind, the nearest to roots I've ever had."

"Oh *Tom*," I said, "I'm so sorry."

He gazed at me.

"I know you are," he said. "You're so sweet," and he put out his hand and pushed my tangled hair back from my face, and then he laid his hand lengthwise down my cheek. I turned my head so that my face was almost hidden in his palm and I felt at once both at peace and tingling with excitement. Then, very gently, he took his hand away and said, "Come on, Carly love. We'd better go down and join the others."

Chapter Eighteen

"As fate would have it," Emily wrote in her long ago journal, "my coming into Afghanistan was just as much like a dream as my sleepy brain had foretold." Mine, a hundred and fifty years later, was strangely dreamlike too, and, although several very alarming things happened, a very happy dream at that.

After the miraculous little episode among the rocks, Tom was wonderful to me, sweet, attentive, considerate and fiercely protective of my feelings. When Abdul told him that Atik and the horsemen didn't like a woman in the company because they felt it was improper, Tom grew really angry, coldly, dangerously angry as he had with me in the plane, and told Abdul that if Atik's principles stood in the way of his job as our guide, he should leave at once, without pay. Abdul said that the men of the hills were proud men who believed in protecting women.

"In that case," Tom said furiously, "they have a splendid chance to put all these principles of theirs into practice. You can tell them from me that if one hair of Carly's head is harmed I shall hold them personally responsible and take pleasure in cutting every one of their intolerant throats."

Joe sidled up to me. "What've you been and

gone and done then, to get the boss behaving like Sir Galahad?"

I felt myself growing pink.

"Oh, just blubbing all over him —"

"Hm," Joe said looking sceptical. "It's making poor old Andy look a bit pea-green."

"Andy and I are just friends, Joe."

"That's what they always say."

I couldn't help noticing, however, that Andy was sticking pretty close to me, or at least as close to me as his anxiety about the cameras would allow. These were loaded onto three ponies, on peculiar wooden pack saddles, precariously strapped on with Afghan girths, which don't have buckles, but are just strips of cloth pulled through rings, yanked tight and then knotted. Philip, who wasn't a very accomplished horseman, rode one side of the camera ponies, and Andy rode the other, when the path was wide enough, dropping back whenever he could to where I rode peacefully at the back of the caravan, filled with a gentle melancholy about Uncle James, but also with a growing happiness which was opening slowly up inside me like a huge bright bud coming into flower.

The long valley track up to the high pass which would bring us up into Afghanistan was marvelous. The path was stony, but the ponies were sure-footed and we could safely gaze about us at the magical mountainous distances or, close at hand, at the profusion of wild flowers, deep pink dog roses and pale pink clover and the tiny blue stars of speedwell that I had noticed in the water meadow where we had camped. As we got higher, the little fields of maize and wheat beside the track began to give way to huge, smooth, dazzling fields of snow, so white it hurt to look at them. The sun shone warm, the air was like wine, and we weren't yet high enough for it to be difficult to breathe.

Our long caravan of horses looked wonderful, winding up the long pass to the summit. At the head rode Atik, and behind him the two Chitrali scouts, who were stiff, unfriendly men, very much on their dignity. Then came several pack animals, pairs of them led by the mujahideen, and then the ponies with the cameras and Philip and Andy and me, followed by Tom and Joe, the remaining pack horses and Abdul in the rear, like a teacher keeping an eye on a school crocodile.

We rode all the long morning, stopping only once for the horsemen to brew tea, and Joe to share out a packet of English ginger nuts he had bought in Islamabad, and been hoarding. They tasted unbelievably delicious, and the crunchy texture was a real treat after days of rice and nan. The whole way, we passed only one other human being, a brown, wrinkle-faced man with eyes like bright little currants, dressed in red and blue woollen leggings and jacket, trudging along with a slab of wood slung on his back with a rope.

"What is he doing?" I shouted back to Abdul.

"Is toboggan," Abdul called. "Is carrying toboggan. Walk up hills, slide down. Very clever."

A little rough village had grown up at the border post itself, the houses built of logs laid lengthwise and filled in between with pale creamy mud. It had a slightly Alpine look and a fierce goaty smell. The checkpoint itself was housed in what Abdul said was a *koffi,* or hotel, a prefabricated concrete block-shaped building, as ugly and out of place as the striped wood and mud houses were pretty and suitable.

Inside, in a bleak and dirty reception area, a border policeman sat picking his teeth on a chair with a broken back, and a crowd of locals lined the walls, spitting and chattering and clicking their strings of worry beads. The place smelled disgusting and was somehow rather menacing. The two scouts strode in, in a very official and overbearing manner and presented our permission documents from the police in Chitral. The border policeman took them without getting up, yawned, flicked through them, yawned again and then summoned several henchmen by snapping his fingers. He gave them a short command, and they trudged across the squalid room, and before we realized what was happening, herded us all, Tom and Abdul and Joe and Philip and Andy and me, into a corner and stood in front of us in a human barrier.

Abdul shouted something. The border policeman called back idly.

"He insults me!" Abdul said furiously. "He say, 'Prove you are an Afghan.' To me! When I am an Afghan and he is not an Afghan! Look at him! He has Arab blood —"

"Sh," Tom said, putting a soothing hand on his arm. "Wait."

The border policeman looked up at the two Chitrali scouts and spoke to them, and they nodded and came over to our corner and said something to Abdul.

"They said is rubber stamp only of documents and we can go over border. They say will be ten minutes. They are returning to Garam Chasma now."

"No," Tom said. "Not till we are out of here."

"Cannot stop," Abdul said despairingly, indicating both the retreating scouts, and the half-dozen cartridge-belt-slung backs dividing us from freedom.

"Bloody hell —"

"Abdul, look here, you said —"

"I've got to get out of here, all those cameras are out there guarded only by bandits —"

"What a bunch of —"

"Shh —"

The border policeman at last got up. He sauntered over to us and looked at us in our human cage with some amusement. Then he spoke to Abdul.

Abdul said, "He wants baksheesh."

"What!"

"He wants fifteen hundred rupees for himself and three hundred for each of his men here."

"Well, tell him he's not bloody getting *one* rupee —"

"Then he will detain us."

"Detain us? Where?"

"In cells here."

I saw Philip grow pale, and even Joe's grin faded.

"He has no right to detain us," Tom said angrily. "We have permission from Chitral."

"He says he is not returning our permission without baksheesh —"

"Tell him I shall report him to the district commissioner."

Abdul translated this, and the border policeman laughed, displaying a set of disgusting, broken teeth. I don't know if it was his teeth or his laughter or his greed that did it, but I was suddenly so filled with rage, I couldn't control it. I ripped off the scarf I had modestly worn all the way from Chitral as Selima had instructed me to, shook out my hair, and literally barged my way, screaming like a banshee, between the two men directly in front of me.

At the sight of me, and even more of my mane of hair, a hubbub rose in the room. The border policeman stopped laughing and stared at me, his mouth hanging open.

"You are a greedy, thieving dishonest pig!" I yelled at him. "You are a disgrace to humanity and in particular a disgrace to your country and your police force! We aren't giving you a single penny and we are going over that border as we have every right to do! No wonder people from the West have to come and help your refugees if all the poor things have to help them otherwise are dishonest thugs like you. Give me our permits this minute and let us go!"

And then I leaned forward and twitched the tattered sheaf of papers out of his hand. He made no resistance, but just went on staring at me as if I had two heads and his henchmen began to look at one another and mutter.

"There you are!" I said triumphantly. "Bully

equals coward. Come on everyone!" and waving the permits, I stalked out of the *koffi* and out into the sunshine where our caravan was patiently waiting. The rest of the crew pushed past their now unresisting captors and followed me.

"*Carly!*" everybody said.

I looked down and shuffled my feet a bit in the dust and the stones.

"You were amazing —"

"What a heroine!"

Tom took my arm. "What would we do without you?"

"Oh, it's nothing, anybody could —"

"It gave them fright to see a woman," Abdul said. He didn't look very pleased. I could see that he would have preferred to be the hero of the hour himself. "I tell you, men of the hills proud men and protect women. No man in there would lay hand on woman."

Tom said teasingly, "You grudging old sod. She was fantastic."

"Is hair," Abdul said, glaring at it. "They never see orange hair."

"It's not orange!"

"No, of course it isn't, it's like . . . like —"

"Barley sugar —"

"Marmalade —"

"Oranges —"

"I'll kill you, Joe," I said, but I was so elated I didn't care what he said.

We went back to our respective ponies and the policeman and his cronies came out and watched us mount. I didn't like the way the policeman was looking at me now, a look without an atom of anything pleasant in it, so I rode my pony round to the far side of Andy's, so that I was obscured from view. We clattered out of the village, and the little knots of people who had gathered instantly at the prospect of a row, fell back as we passed and stood gazing up at us with their expressionless brown faces.

I was so happy, I wanted to sing. The others kept urging their ponies up beside me so that they could, in turn, tell me how wonderful and brave I was. Even Joe paid me a compliment that wasn't a tease and Tom — well, Tom made one of those remarks that one treasures. He came right up close to me, took my nearest hand, kissed it and said, "Carly, I look at you with new and wondering eyes every day," and I felt like a blissful cat stretching itself in the sun.

Andy rode beside me all the afternoon. We got to the summit about four, having dismounted and led our ponies for the last hour. It was a strange and wonderful moment, to be fifteen thousand feet up towards the heavens, even though the air was thinner so high up and my lungs heaved and wheezed as if they were full of holes. We looked out on an amazing snow world at our own height, and below us, at a series of magnificent valleys, greenish blue with cedar trees and laced with foaming waterfalls and racing rivers. Andy and Joe and Philip unstrapped the cameras and the sound equipment, and made us repeat the last half mile, so that they could film us, and then the extraordinary panorama of eastern Afghanistan that we were about to tumble down into.

"Where's your sweater?" Tom said solicitously, coming up to me. "It's going to get really cold."

"I don't care," I said, laughing. "I'm not cold —"

"Well, I care," he said.

My heart lurched. I said, "It's in my saddlebag."

"I'll get it out for you."

I watched his beautiful, strong hands deftly unbuckling my saddlebag and pulling out the huge navy blue jersey that had seen so many fishing seasons in Bewick. He held it out to me, smiling.

"Put it on."

I pulled the sweater over my head and thrust my arms into the sleeves.

"I'm not risking you catching cold, you see," Tom said. "In fact, I'm not risking you in any way. You're far too precious."

The ride down the other side passed in a happy daze. Andy and Joe and Philip had gone ahead to film us coming, so I led Andy's pony which was luckily, unlike several others in our caravan, not a stallion and therefore reasonably docile. We picked our way across a rather alarming snowfield littered with boulders and huge cracks, and then zigzagged down a long, stony path while the landscape around us grew lovelier and lovelier, and the ground beneath the horses' hooves changed from pebbles and dust to the most magical meadows, straight out of *Heidi*, thick with flowering clover and hovering with brilliant yellow butterflies.

We finally came down to the banks of one of the delicious, energetic mountain rivers, and found the others waiting for us, picturesquely under a huge wild rose bush. I looked at the water, clear and pale green, racing among its boulders.

"I want to swim."

Abdul was horrified. "Is out of the question! Would not be modest."

"You could all look the other way."

"No," Abdul said, wagging his finger at me. "I forbid. It breaks laws of Muslim country."

I opened my mouth to argue and then thought, what did I care? It was such a heavenly day, that I wasn't going to spoil it by arguing with Abdul. The muja were, as usual, brewing up the green tea they seemed addicted to, so we sat on the river bank and drank it and I said a silent prayer to whoever might be listening, asking that this day should simply go on and on forever.

When the sun slipped behind the peaks above us, we climbed, wearily by now, into our saddles and rode along the riverbank to the little village where Atik said we should spend the night. The air was quite sharp now, and the light was more beautiful than I can describe, clear and soft and almost turquoise, and strange birds — hoopoes, Tom said — began to whoop and call from the wooded slopes. Then Tom began to sing. I had no idea he could sing, but he had a lovely voice, a clear, strong tenor, and he started on all the nostalgic melodious songs of my childhood, like "The Skye Boat Song" and "The Snows of Glencoe" and "Mhairi's Wedding," and soon we were all singing too as we rode along that perfect valley in the fading light towards the little carved wooden village with a mosque at its center where we were to sleep for our first Afghan night. As we approached the village, we could see, here and there, the golden glow of lamps and the rosy glow of cooking fires, and Andy rode up beside me and took my hand and I squeezed his hard, out of sheer pleasure and gratitude.

"Happy?" he said.

I looked at him. I know my face was as luminous with happiness as the great white moon which had swung into the darkening sky above the mountains.

"Oh," I said. "Oh Andy. Happier than I've ever been."

Chapter Nineteen

We were offered beds that night in the village *koffi*, but Tom took one look at it, and asked if we might instead sleep on a small turfy cliff above the river, and just outside the village. The headman seemed disappointed — he was a grinning old man with no teeth and an embroidered woollen cap — but he agreed, and forgave us sufficiently to bring us his best cups to drink tea out of. They were white china, surprisingly fine, patterned in russet and green, and they were shaped like stumpy wineglasses, on thick stems, with little domed lids of silvery metal, to keep the tea hot.

Our muja had so far forgiven me for being a mere woman after the episode at the border, that they wanted Abdul to buy a goat from the village to be slaughtered in my honor. I said I utterly refused, flattered though I was, but they took no notice, and sure enough, the inevitable great tray of rice finally appeared, garnished with bits of the poor goat.

"I'm so sorry," I said to Tom, "but I can't possibly eat it."

He smiled, "Just pretend to eat a bit, for manners. I've got a tin of sardines in my saddlebag. Would you like those?"

I closed my eyes in rapture. Sardines sounded

like caviar. "Oh I *would* —"

"Then you shall have them."

"If you aren't careful, Tom, I shall get terribly spoiled."

"I like spoiling you," he said.

I hadn't slept in the open since I was a child. I was really tired after all those long hours in the saddle but my mind was like a firework, fizzing and sparkling and exploding into colored stars every time I tried to tell it to go to sleep. I lay there in my bivvy bag on my grassy bed and looked up into the exquisite Afghan night, all deep blue and brilliant silver, and thought of Charlotte and Emily, and of the day we had just had, and of every, precious, wonderful thing Tom had said to me during the course of it. I drifted off to sleep finally, lulled by the river, and woke to a day as perfect as the night that had preceded it.

The headman of the village told us that our journey to Kerala would be all the way through country as spectacularly beautiful as this valley. Tom and Andy were thrilled to hear this, because this ravishing landscape which the refugees had been forced to leave, would provide such a heartbreaking and powerful contrast to the wretched, arid dustbowl of the camp at Chitral. We spent the day in the village while the camera crew filmed the processions of village women carrying firewood, and some boys playing a strange game, rather like golf, and a group of girls, charming in small versions of their mothers' wonderful embroidered dresses, knocking the branches of the old mulberry trees that grew along the river, so that the dark, sweet fruit — *"Shah tut,"* Abdul said, "the most rich and juicy" — fell onto the sheets that had been spread on the ground underneath.

I wandered about happily, from group to group, looking at things and thinking how very different this primitive, fertile, beautiful place was from the bony, threatening chasms of the Khyber Pass which Emily had described so vividly in her journal. I was seeing a very different face of Afghanistan, and I was seeing it as Charlotte would have loved to do, unfettered either by English notions of what was respectable, or by the heavy protective force of the British army. At one point, a girl came up to me and shyly offered me a posy of wild flowers, tied with a blade of grass like a ribbon, and it was as bright as a paintbox. I took it over to the camera, and Tom was fascinated.

"Look at that. Orchid, gentian, geranium, harebells, wild lupin, dog roses, celandines, primula, even buttercups. Oh what a place!"

It was hard to leave it. Tom said we must push on, otherwise we should become like the lotus-eaters who were unable to tear themselves away from their enchanted island. So we all, in turn, went down to the river to bathe — I went a long way upstream so as not to offend the villagers — and put on clean shirts and trousers, while the muja loaded the horses and made a parting brew of green tea. The men were already acquiring shadowy stubbled chins. As Tom had warned us, there would be no hot water again until we were back in Chitral.

The ride that day was very different from the day before. We all set off in great spirits, expecting, as the headman had told us, that we'd be riding through these fairy tale Alpine meadows, day after day, but after an hour or two the path suddenly turned steeply upwards and we found ourselves with our noses almost pressed to the mountains.

Atik came riding back down the caravan, shouting at us.

"Must dismount," Abdul said, "Atik says take horse tail and horse will pull you up mountain."

"But it'll kick my bloody teeth in —"

"Not likely!"

"Do as say," Abdul thundered.

Meekly we dismounted and went gingerly round to the backs of our horses. Mine eyed me with a distinctly unfriendly expression and raised her upper lip to show me her long yellow teeth. Then she laid her ears flat back.

"Grasp!" Abdul shouted to me.

"I can't —"

"*Do* it, Carly!"

I put out a tentative hand, waiting for the mare's back hooves to come lashing out at me, but weirdly enough, the moment I had her tail in my grip, she looked at me with quite a different expression, one of quiet tolerance, and set off up the steep, shaly path with me scuffling behind her, and my eyes almost shut to avoid flying flakes of rock she kicked up as she scrambled. Halfway up, two of the other horses, both stallions, remembered that they were deadly enemies and there was a terrible fight, all hooves and teeth and screaming. I noticed, to my admiring amazement, that Andy had got a camera off a packhorse and was filming the scene, precariously balanced on a chimney of rock some fifty feet above us.

The whole day was like that, up and down treacherous mountainsides with the horses quarreling and the muja yelling and the air full of flying chips of slate and stone. It was absolutely exhausting and when we finally struggled into the village where we were to camp, another village straggling along a river, but this time full of suspicious, unfriendly people with a headman only interested in our money, I was too tired and sore and nerve-racked to care much where we were. We stayed in the village *chaikana,* a primitive tea house hopping with fleas, and after three hours of lying scratching on a charpoy, I got up and lugged my bivvy bag outside to try to sleep in the open, whereupon it promptly rained on me.

I finally fell asleep just before dawn and woke to broad daylight to find that the others had already been off filming because Tom was tremendously excited by the birds.

"I knew it was a birdwatcher's paradise, but I never believed it would be this good. I've seen two kinds of linnet already, and, would you believe it, a black redstart!"

"Fancy," I said grumpily, crumpled from lack of sleep and stiff from lying on the ground.

Tom knelt down beside me.

"Don't be cross."

"I'm bitten *all* over —"

"And I've got magical insect-bite cream. Smile

537

for me, Carly, come on, smile."

I looked at him. He was wearing a crumpled blue denim shirt tucked into army fatigues, and his hair was ruffled and his eyes were brilliant gray, almost like mirrors, in his glamorously stubble-shadowed face. I could no more have denied him a smile than I could have stopped breathing.

"Good girl," he said, and kissed me on the cheek.

The villagers relented towards us in the matter of breakfast and brought a huge shallow wooden bowl full of rough dark honey, all speckled with bits of bee, and a pile of soft, warm, newly made nan, tasting deliciously of charcoal. After breakfast, I washed myself rigorously in the icy water, even my hair, thinking how strange it was seeing the foam of sophisticated, synthetic Western shampoo swirling away on a pure, wild Afghan river. Then I went back to the caravan, and found my mare, whom I was beginning to grow very fond of despite the way she lifted her lip and sneered at me, and mounted and took my place in the column behind the horses with the cameras.

It was a lovely morning, washed clean by the night's rain, and a lovely ride to match. We came across a herd of goats and the two silent shepherds who looked after them and who lived, Abdul said, strange lonely lives with their goats on these empty uplands, making butter and cheese.

"This area," Abdul said, swinging his arm in a wide circle to embrace the whole stupendous landscape, "once famous for butter carriers!

They walked all the way from these mountains to Chitral, carrying butter, and back again."

Gradually, the harshness of the high mountains gave way to another delicious valley with a gentle river flowing placidly along it, fringed with willows and silver birches and walnut trees, and there was a moment of huge excitement when Tom saw a golden eagle circling the pine-clad crags above us. We stopped at another *chaikana*, where the owner brought us maize bread, which I thought disgusting, and cups of sharp, clean-tasting yogurt, called *dugh*. Then we rode on and the sun grew fiercely hot and Tom began to sing again, to keep us going, and I started to feel a strong sense of unreality, that I wasn't really here and that this long, clattering, jingling ride across what felt like the roof of the world, wasn't happening.

We stopped for a late lunch, and Atik boiled us up some noodles, and we opened various tins from our packs — I was so pleased to see some corned beef that I vowed I would never speak disrespectfully of it again — and then Tom announced that we were spending the afternoon here, as the next village was only an hour's ride onwards.

It felt oddly like being given a half holiday from school. We all scattered along the riverbank, to film or birdwatch or draw or think, and the muja drew themselves into a circle in the shade and squatted there playing some game with counters that looked a bit like backgammon. I walked up the river bank with my dirty washing and a bar of precious soap, until I came to a lovely little pool formed by a ring of rocks, under a willow tree, where I did some laundry that I reckoned even Ma, who was a perfectionist, wouldn't have been ashamed of. I wrung everything out, and then clambered up the bank and spread my shirts and knickers out flat on several rocks to dry in the hot sun. There was a walnut tree nearby, with lovely dappled shade, so I lay down in that and watched the bright green leaves moving gently against the bright blue sky until I fell asleep.

"Carly," someone said.

I opened my eyes.

"Hello," said Andy. "You've been asleep for ages and I got tired of waiting for you to wake."

I sat up slowly. Andy's camera lay beside us, in the shade of a rock, tenderly wrapped in a sweat-shirt. I yawned.

"You been filming?"

"Wonderful," Andy said. "I went back to film those shepherds and found a couple of blokes threshing wheat with four oxen yoked together. Amazing. Can't have changed for hundreds of years."

He moved until he was sitting beside me on the turf, and put his arm comfortably around my shoulders.

"Happy?"

"Yes," I said, "isn't it odd, but I feel so free —"

"Anything else?"

I turned to look at him. His face was already brown after only three days riding in the sun, and he was growing a red-gold beard, much redder than his tousled fair hair.

"What do you mean?"

"Just this," Andy said and, pulling me gently closer, bent his head to kiss me on the mouth.

It was a soft kiss, very sweet and unbullying, and I didn't pull away. After a second or two, Andy pushed me back on to the grass and bent over me to kiss me more firmly. I still didn't pull away, partly because I didn't want to, being full of mountain air and contentment and affection for Andy, and partly because I was still drowsy and not feeling like taking the initiative. But then things changed. Andy put his hand to the front of my shirt, feeling for the buttons, and began to kiss me more fiercely, pushing his tongue deep into my mouth.

I twisted my head sharply sideways.

"Don't," I said.

He didn't move, but his hands stopped their exploring.

"Carly?"

"Yes —"

"I've got it wrong, haven't I? It isn't . . . it isn't love, is it? —"

I rolled free of him on to my side and lay very still. I wanted very much to be truthful to him. After a bit I said as steadily as I could, "No, Andy, it isn't love, but it's an awful lot of like."

He gave a short laugh, like a little bark.

"Fair enough," he said. "You've never pretended otherwise. I just hoped, as time went on —"

"Sorry," I said. I rolled back and lay looking up at him. "You can't love to order somehow, however much you want to."

He nodded. He said, "It's Tom, isn't it?"

"Yes," I said simply. "Always has been."

Andy sat up and began to pick twigs and pebbles out of the grass and chuck them down at the river.

I said, "I really am sorry but equally I can't help it."

"I know that —"

"It's hopeless anyway. I mean, he's being very kind to me but —"

Andy looked down at me again.

"He's gone on you," Andy said. "That's why I thought I'd try my luck today. I reckoned there was just an outside chance for me, depending on how you were feeling. But if you want Tom, I'm not going to kid myself otherwise."

I sat up very slowly and peered at him.

"Andy? Are you sure?"

"Sure of what?"

"That Tom . . . that I . . . that he —"

"Is keen on you? 'Course he is. Can't keep his eyes off you and only keeps his hands off because we're all watching him like hawks."

I looked away from him. The landscape, lovely before, seemed to have blossomed into the Garden of Eden. Never was water so clear, sky so blue, grass so green.

"I . . . I thought he was just being kind and grateful, after the incident on the border and persuading Halima to let us film in the camp when we got back —"

"Not likely," Andy said. "Joe and I've been taking bets to see how long he can hold off."

I bent my head so that my hair would swing

forward and form a curtain behind which I could have a little private rapture. I suddenly felt full of elation, wanting to laugh and cry and sing all at once. I was like Charlotte after all, I was! Afghanistan was going to give to me, as it had given to her, the great, glorious romance of my life. I was not mistaken at all; Tom's solicitous sweetness to me recently was not just Tom being Tom but Tom being loving. It was almost beyond bearing, it was so wonderful.

"What are you going to do now?" Andy said.

I pushed my hair back and looked at him.

"Do?"

"Yeah. Do. Are you just going to hang about until Tom falls down on bended knee?"

"Well," I said, "I can hardly —"

"Yes, you can."

"What, *tell* him?"

"Why not?" Andy said. "Why not just come straight out and tell him? I won't stand in your way."

I put my hand out and took his.

"You're a nice bloke."

He grinned. "Yeah, maybe. But I've been nice enough for long enough this afternoon." He took his hand away and got to his feet, stooping for his camera. "I'm going to find a vulture to film, to relieve my feelings. Carly —"

"Yes?" I said, squinting up at him against the sun.

"Good luck."

Chapter Twenty

I spent that night in a silent daze of happiness. We rode on to the next village where the tea house had several tents, donated by a refugee organization, pitched outside it for visitors. I started the night inside a tent, but then felt a huge longing to be out under the sky, so I pulled on all the jerseys and socks I could find and took my bivvy bag out into the sharp, clear night. I didn't sleep, but then I didn't really want to. When you're as happy and full of excited anticipation as I was, you don't want to waste a second of it being unconscious. I lay and listened to some funny little night frogs croaking away in the nearby reeds and just grinned and grinned to myself like an idiot.

In the morning, I wanted to swim, but the water was so icy it scared me, so I just splashed my face and hands, gasping at the cold, and climbed into some of yesterday's newly done laundry, crisply dried by the sun. The owner of the tea house brought us bowls of *dugh*, which I had come to love, and some honey, and great hunks of awful tasteless maize bread. We ate it washed down with green tea, and I thought that whenever I drank green tea anywhere else in my later life, I should remember this brilliant Afghan morning, with the muja moving about muttering and loading up the horses, and my whole world simply exploding with the promise of the day ahead.

As if by silent consent, the pattern of the caravan changed, and I found myself riding at the back, with Tom, in Abdul's old place. I was burning to confess, but knew I had to wait until the right moment, and the ride was so extravagantly beautiful that I was, in a way, in no hurry to break the spell of my perfect mood. We rode through the meadows bright with flowers, through little fields green with new maize, past a sheepfold loud with fat-tailed sheep, and, most heartbreakingly, past a little Afghan graveyard, scraps of green and white cloth fluttering on poles thrust into the hillside, to mark where Russian jets had dive-bombed a helpless column of refugees, making for the border with Pakistan. There were even bones in the grass. I couldn't look, my eyes were filled with boiling tears of rage and pity.

"Carly," Tom said. I felt his hand closing, warm and firm, on mine as I gripped my bridle.

"It . . . it makes you want to *kill* them —"

"I know. It's why we're making the film. Remember?"

I nodded, brushing away the tears with my free hand.

"You're so sweet," Tom said. "So sweet and so fierce, all at once."

I took a deep breath.

"Tom —" I said.

There was a yell from the cavalcade ahead of us. We looked up. The track on which we were wound downward to cross a river, not a wide river but, like almost all Afghan rivers, a racing one, swollen and pale green with melted snow. Atik and the front horsemen had successfully forded it but the next two horses, the one carrying all the film, and the one carrying Joe's sound equipment, seemed to be stuck in the middle, screaming and plunging and refusing to be coaxed onwards. Philip and Andy and Joe were racing down the slope towards the river, yelling like banshees.

"Tell me later," Tom said, dropping my hand and charging after them in a hail of stones. I followed him, slithering down the track in his wake, and arriving at the bank in time to see one of the horsemen take off his scarf and bind it over one of the ponies' eyes so that the poor thing couldn't see to be terrified about where it was going. Someone else did the same to the second pony, and gradually they were both urged gently through the boiling water onto the far bank, where they stood shaking and blowing, looking perfectly miserable and hanging their heads.

Once I was in the river, I could understand their feelings. I'd ridden through scores of Scottish rivers — when Duncan's keeper wasn't looking — but I'd never had to persuade a horse through water so violent. If I hadn't felt so buoyant, I probably would have chickened out altogether, and have had to be towed across, but this morning I felt I could rule the world, and the brave little mare responded.

Abdul said we must now pause.

"The horses have cut their legs and must be medicined."

"I want to check the film," Andy said. "I taped all those bags up but I want to make sure they didn't get damp."

"Teabreak then," Tom said. He shouted at Atik, "*Chai!* One hour."

Atik bellowed back his agreement. I climbed off my pony and inspected her; she had only one small cut which I smeared with antiseptic cream from a tube I kept hidden from the horsemen on Abdul's advice.

"They take and use all on wrong thing. Do not understand Western medicine, only herbs. Think all Western medicine cure everything."

When I had finished with the mare's leg, I led her over to graze with the others, and then climbed away from the cavalcade up some big, smooth gray rocks close by, certain that Tom would follow me. At the top of the rocks, before the steep mountainside began, was a little grassy platform, no bigger than a wide bench. The view, as all views had been since we left Pakistan, was stunning.

I sat down with my back against the warm rock wall behind me, and hugged my knees. I couldn't quite see our caravan, but I could hear them quite clearly and knew what they would be doing. Andy, Philip, and Joe would be meticulously checking all their equipment, the horsemen and Atik would be doctoring the ponies' legs and building a fire for tea, and Abdul would be shuttling between the two issuing instructions that nobody took any notice of and asking questions that nobody answered. The only person who wouldn't be busy would be Tom, and that would be because he was climbing the rocks to my platform, to sit beside me as I was willing him to.

"Carly."

I looked down, over the edge of the little platform. Nobody.

"No, up here, come up here!"

I swiveled round, like a dog out on a walk trying to identify where a shouted command has come from. Thirty feet above me, on another ledge, Tom was standing and waving.

"It's an easy climb, and an even better view —"

I scrambled up beside him. He was right. It was glorious.

"I feel I can see all the way to India —"

"And China —"

"And Tibet —"

"Oh, Carly," Tom said, "despite all the sadness and cruelty, isn't it wonderful too?"

I turned and looked at him, outlined against that clear, clean, blazing blue sky, tousled and bearded and smiling at me with his whole wonderful face illumined. I took a deep breath.

"I love you," I said.

There was a tiny pause. His smile didn't diminish, but it changed from being exhilarated, to being kind. I hardly noticed.

"I've loved you for months," I said, rushing on, "from the moment I first saw you — crash, bang, into love, just like that. I didn't think I had a chance, I didn't dare because of Laura and because, well, I'm not exactly a raving beauty, but Andy said . . . he said yesterday that you —"

I stopped. Tom had his arms open. I flung myself into them, and as they closed about me,
something in their embrace — the embrace of a
loving friend — told me that I'd made a terrible,
awful, humiliating mistake.

"Oh my dear Carly," Tom said, and his voice
was hoarse with pity. "Oh Carly, I'm so sorry,
I'm so sorry, I'd no idea —"

I wrenched myself free, appalled at my
misjudgement and at my behavior. Tom tried to
take my hands but I snatched them away.

"Please don't. Please don't touch me. I just
made a huge mistake, didn't I? I just misread all
the signals."

"Carly," Tom said pleadingly. "Look at me."

I couldn't. I turned away from him and leaned
against the rock face, chipping out little flakes of
it with my fingernail.

"You are a wonderful person," Tom said to my
back. "I've never met anyone I like or admire
more. If I ever had any reservations about you,
they've all vanished in the last few weeks because
you get more bloody marvelous every day. I feel
terrible that I seem to have led you on. Of all
people, you're the last one I'd want to deceive."

He put a hand on my shoulder. I shook it off.

"Carly, I'm committed to Laura. I always have
been. I suppose that . . . that I'm pretty single-
minded. Please turn round."

I debated whether to, or not. I was furious with
myself, and burning with shame, but I couldn't
honestly be angry with him. I turned, very slowly.
He was looking terribly serious.

"I can't bear to give you pain, Carly. Am I at

fault? Have I flirted with you?"

I sighed. "No," I said, "you just said some very affectionate things —"

"I meant them. I still do."

"— and I built them up in my mind to mean what I wanted them to mean."

"And Andy?"

"He told me that they all thought you . . . you were . . . you were keen on me and were just waiting for me to tell you so."

Tom swore. He said, "I'm afraid Laura isn't very popular with them. She's so competent, she makes them feel inadequate."

I bit back saying she was also extremely superior and patronizing and violently opposed to all this foreign filming. Instead I said, in a bright, hard voice, "Well, that's that then. Story over, start a new one."

"You'll fall in love again," Tom said with a kind of longing, as if he wanted it to happen right there and then. "You're so lovely and so young. Andy thinks you're great, for a start."

I put my chin up. Kindness was hard enough to bear, but being even mildly patronized was unbearable.

"I'm not like that," I said furiously, "I'm not like any old girl moving from man to man, anyone who'll have her. The women in my family happen to be truly loyal. I'm not a child, Tom, I know the difference between love and a stupid crush."

"Yes," he said and his voice was rough. "Yes, I know you do. That's why I'm so sorry."

"Well, don't be," I snapped. "Spare me your

pity at least. I've made a fool of myself, and I'll have to live with that, but that's my business."

I went over to the edge of the platform on which we stood, and began to lower myself down towards the ledge below. I looked back at Tom just once. He was gazing at me with a peculiar, wild look, as if he was suddenly furious with me for being so ungracious about his being genuinely sorry for me. I didn't care. I was in such fierce and awful pain that I didn't care what he thought. As I slithered out of view, I yelled childishly, "And I hope you and darling Laura will be blissfully, utterly happy for ever and bloody ever!"

Try as I might to hide it, my face told everybody everything. Andy came over and began apologizing for having led me up the garden path and Abdul said that his mother's cure for a broken heart was a concoction of honey and saffron stewed in green tea, and even Philip whispered shyly that he was sorry and that he'd tell me about his own problems one day. I'm afraid I wasn't very nice to any of them. I hadn't the energy to comfort Andy or humor Philip and I certainly didn't want Abdul dosing me with his mother's potions. I snarled and snapped — it seemed, at the time, the only alternative to bursting into tears, and that I was determined not to do — and said I was absolutely fine and accused them all of exaggerating. Joe, needless to say, kept his distance while I hissed like a cornered cat but I could see that he was grinning. I was thankful when all the tea drinking was over, and the fire stamped out, and we could all mount our ponies and resume the ride. I rode firmly alone, behind Atik and the first few pack ponies. Behind me, the rest of the caravan was uncharacteristically silent, and Tom, also riding alone at the rear, looked as if someone had hit him. I tried to keep the fuel of my temper banked high, because I was terrified of breaking down, but everything seemed stacked against me. The countryside we were riding through was no longer lush and lovely, but bleaker and more mountainous, streaked with snow patches, and the bright, warm sun became engulfed in tearing, purple clouds, and a harsh wind sprang up and we had to muffle ourselves in jerseys. Despite my best efforts, my spirits dropped lower and lower, and the bitter pain that the anger had briefly kept at bay began to twist in me like a knife being slowly turned.

I realized that someone was riding beside me, in silence. It was Joe. He held something out.

"Have a barley sugar."

"No thanks —"

"Do as you're told —"

I took the sweet and unwrapped it with shaking fingers.

"Don't you go wasting energy ticking yourself off," Joe said, "You didn't make a mistake."

"Oh Joe, how can you say such a thing? Of *course* I did!"

"Then we all did. I'd got twenty-five quid on you, with Philip. He's such a miserable gloomy guts, he never thinks there'll be a happy ending."

"Well, in this case, he's right."

Joe said, "If you want my opinion, Tom's a bloody nut case."

"Don't —"

"Tina and I've been married four years. She's great. Keeps me sane. But I can tell you, if it wasn't for her, I'd have had a go myself." He grinned at me.

I tried to grin back. "The trouble with me, Joe," I said, "is that I'm afraid I'm horribly faithful."

He pulled a face. "You'll learn."

I tried a second grin, but I knew in my heart of hearts that I didn't really want to learn.

I said, "I'll be okay, Joe. I'll just think about work now."

"Plenty of that ahead. We're nearly there."

"To Kerala?"

"Yup. Two days."

I looked up at the racing, inhospitable sky. Guilt at briefly forgetting why I was in Afghanistan in the first place surged into my feelings and joined the boiling misery already churning away there.

"Great cure-all, work," Joe said.

"Yes. Yes, I expect it is." I thought of all those frantic months tearing about trying to achieve the impossible for Matthew. Matthew! He seemed as far away as if he inhabited another planet, an incomprehensible planet which appeared at this moment to be as remote as the moon.

Joe looked back down the long straggle of our cavalcade.

"He's miles behind the others," Joe said.

I didn't need to ask who he meant.

"Bloody fool," Joe said cheerfully.

"He's not," I said. "He just utterly, painfully straight. That's why I —"

"Don't say it."

"No," I said, "I won't." I raised my head and looked at the horizon above us, where Atik was already silhouetted against the fading light. "Don't worry, Joe. I won't ever say it again."

Chapter Twenty-one

Even if I had had the emotional energy to try to imagine it beforehand, I don't think anything could have prepared me for Kerala. It had been a big village, almost a small town, built most picturesquely into the steep cliffs above a river, tier upon tier of wooden houses with carved eaves and balconies looking out over a beautiful valley to the rearing mountain range beyond. I say had been, because it was now a ruin, a blackened, burnt out, savagely wrecked ruin. Up those cliffs, where the peaceful people of Kerala had climbed on centuries-old paths after their innocent days farming in the valley below, we saw only devastation; splintered beams sticking up out of gaping holes in walls, avalanches of rubble and ash, grotesque lumps of charred masonry and timber. And higher up, where the village proper had stopped because of the steepness of the mountainside, the rocks were scarred blinding white, the result of being strafed by Russian bombers.

We were all completely horrified. We sat, the whole cavalcade, silent and motionless on our ponies, and looked at the evidence of a brutality that didn't bear thinking about. Andy had his arm flung up against his face, and when I glanced sideways at Tom — not an easy thing to do these days — I saw that tears were streaming down his cheeks and he was doing nothing to stop them. Despite everything, I longed and longed to go over and comfort him, and be comforted — and I couldn't. I had to sit there, on my little mare, and suffer alone as everyone else was suffering.

It wasn't really much better when you looked away from the ruined village either, across the valley floor. Little brave patches of emerald green here and there showed where cultivated fields had once been, but their pattern was crudely interrupted by great hideous bomb craters, and the orchards of cherry and walnut trees were no more than clumps of splintered stumps out of which a few courageous new little branches were struggling. It had clearly been a paradise, a simple, primitive, fertile paradise in a landscape as lovely as Switzerland, and it had been utterly vandalized by everything that is most horrible and savage and cruel in modern life.

I heard Tom beginning to give orders, the professional producer taking over from the shocked human being. Atik and the horsemen were sent down to the edge of the river on the far side, over an alarmingly basic bridge made of young tree trunks lashed together, to pitch camp for us by a group of willow trees. The rest of us were sent to explore, alone or in pairs, as we chose.

"Carly?" Tom said, coming up to me. "What would you like to do? Go with Joe or be alone?"

He was as kind as ever. It was, to be honest, a hair's breadth away from unbearable that he should continue to be so courteous and considerate. But then, what else did I expect from him? Why did I love him if it wasn't for this particular quality in him that made him so sensitive to other people? Even when he was making it plain that Laura was the love of his life, he hadn't rubbed it in, he hadn't gone on and on elaborating his feelings; he'd simply said, "I'm committed and always have been," as if I knew that to say a word more would have hurt me even harder.

I said now, "I think I'll be alone."

He looked worried. "Are you sure? Will you promise not to go clambering about in all that rubble because it's lethal —"

"I promise. I'll stay right out in the open."

He hesitated a moment, and then he said, pointing down across the river, away from the spot where Atik and his gang were yelling and swearing their way across the river, "Okay. But not over there."

"Not over where?"

"Not by that sheepfold."

"Why not?"

"It's where the Russians lined up the men of the village and shot them. Against that wall. Abdul told me. I don't want you going down there alone."

I swallowed. "Don't worry. I won't go."

He smiled at me. How could he, despite everything, be so *easy* with me? Answer — because he felt nothing for me beyond what he told me he felt, brotherly affection and pride.

I said, pointing upwards, "I want to circle the village and go up to that fortress. Or what's left of it."

We both looked up the mountainside. At the very top of the village stood the great broken walls, pale honey-colored on account of being plastered with the local mud, of the Q'ala, the huge fortified house where the chief family of Kerala would once have lived.

"Perhaps, you see, it was Halima's house —"

"Of course. But no climbing about in it, promise me."

I rode my pony down to the river bank, and handed her reins to one of the horsemen, who grinned at me, with blinding white teeth, as they all now did. Then I tugged my canvas satchel out of a saddlebag, slung it across me, and began the climb, half scramble, half walk, up the rocky hillside beside the village.

The fact that Nature was doing her best to cover the scars of the bombardment was as heartbreaking as it was consoling. Little spires of wild lupin, and clumps of fat pink clover pushed their way up optimistically through the rubble, and various merry-looking little birds — I still could only identify the really distinctive-looking ones — hopped and cheeped about among the rocks. It was a long, hot climb, despite quite a stiff wind, and as I clambered on, I began to wish I'd brought my water bottle, which was now, uselessly, several hundred feet below me.

The Q'ala, when I finally, breathlessly, reached it, stood alone, above the village, rather like a Royal Box in an English theater. Like Nasir's house in Chitral, it had a high wall, roughly crenellated at the top, all round it, and huge wooden entrance gates, one wrenched off and lying half burned outside, and the other lurching drunkenly off a single, massive, twisted hinge. I peered through the opening. A bomb had fallen plumb in the middle of the courtyard where, I sadly imagined, the wellhead had once stood, and it had reduced most of the dwelling rooms round the edge to rubble, but the courtyard walls, two feet thick, had largely withstood it, except for a few spots, one overlooking the valley, where jagged holes had been blown out.

I looked cautiously round. None of the building in the Q'ala had been high, so that there were no dangling beams and balconies to crash on my head. The devastation was all under foot, piles and heaps of broken mud bricks and charred timbers, and that great hideous hole in the middle. I didn't like to think who might have been innocently drawing up water when the bomb fell; a cousin of Halima's perhaps, a niece, even a daughter. I stepped inside the courtyard, and felt myself step out of the wind into sudden, complete stillness.

I picked my way carefully through the chaos, thinking as I did so of Cara and Aunt Mary picking their long-ago, stumbling way through the debris of bomb-blasted wartime Chelsea. At least I had to be grateful that the Afghans had had no glass to be blown out of their windows, shattered into wicked splinters. When I came to the gap in the wall looking over the valley, I found a convenient lump of brickwork — it could have been anything, an archway, a chunk of wall, part of the poor wellhead — and rolled it into the space so that I could sit down and take in the view.

From so high up, it was quite spectacular. Far away below me, Atik and his men and the ponies were as tiny as toys, busy putting up tents no bigger than candle snuffers. If I half closed my eyes, I could almost pretend that the tumble of cream and terracotta and charcoal gray below me was a charming confusion of roofs and terraces, not a chaos of destruction, and that the reddish-brown bomb craters in the valley were only innocent patches of plough.

I unbuckled my satchel and took out my now tattered photocopy of Emily's journal. I knew exactly what I was looking for in it and, equally exactly, why I had wanted to be alone in this ruined building while I read. It seemed to me the perfect place to read about Charlotte's anguish, the anguish she had felt when Alexander had vanished after the slaughter in the Khyber Pass, and she had come to believe that he no longer loved her.

Akbar, the Afghan leader, had locked up all the British women and children in a fort at Budeabad, a fort probably not unlike this broken building where I now sat.

"We were crammed," wrote Emily, "into five icy, cell-like rooms."

They slept on straw mattresses, there was no sanitation, they existed on revolting meals of boiled rice and shredded mutton and the guards screamed and howled at them for the smallest stepping out of line. It was horrible, Emily said, and more than horrible, but only she knew that for Charlotte there was a worse pain to be borne than the physical and mental one of their terrible imprisonment. Charlotte was afraid that she had now lost the one thing she valued — the love of Alexander Bewick.

"I knew," Emily wrote, "I knew she wondered if, now Hugh was dead and she might be Alexander's in a perfectly orthodox way, he didn't want her. He mightn't care for a widow that society would sanction him having, but only the wild, romantic, unlawful pursuit of someone else's wife. That was, in her blackest moments, Charlotte's nightmare."

Mine wasn't, in essence, so very different. I knew I wasn't wanted; Charlotte dreaded to discover that she wasn't. I folded up the photocopy again and pushed it back into my satchel, and then I put my elbows on my knees and cupped my chin in my hands and stared outwards into the ruined valley of Kerala.

I knew that everything, all my life, had been very easy for me. Unlike Ma, I'd had a secure and happy childhood and enough confidence — or brass neck to be honest — to refuse to do things I didn't like, even to the point of running away from school. I'd made friends easily, I'd never been afraid to misbehave, and I'd found allies wherever I'd turned — look at how Duncan had supported me in my refusal to follow Ma into her beloved hotel. When I'd gone to London, Amanda had given me somewhere to live, and Simon had found me a job, and been the instrument, by introducing me to Tom, of my fulfilling this dream to follow Charlotte to Afghanistan. I had to admit to myself, sitting there on that ruined mountainside, that I, Carly Angus, had so far had everything in life I wanted, handed to me on a plate.

Until now. Now there was this — there was love, and it was far and away the hardest thing to bear that I'd ever known, and easily the most powerful. I'd never felt so close to Charlotte as I did that day, never understood so keenly that however much fashions and customs and moral attitudes change over the years, the needs and desires of the human heart haven't altered one iota. I wanted someone I couldn't have, just as she had — or thought she had. I didn't think it, I knew it. I couldn't have Tom, now or ever, and that was that.

I stood up. It was perfectly plain to me that a bit of instant growing up had to be done, starting right now. I was to stop wailing and keening like a spoiled child not allowed to go to a party, and I was to get on with the rest of my life. As Joe said, there was always work. There was also, on a very private level, something else to be done.

I picked my way back round the courtyard wall to a sunny corner at the back where there was a sandy space on the floor between piles of debris. In the middle of this space grew a little rose bush, the deep pink-flowered wild rose that we had seen all along the way, and which only gave out its delicious scent after rain. I collected, from the rubble round about, a pile of smallish stones, the same sort of size, and arranged them in a neat square about a foot from the rose bush, like a frame. Then I found a twig, and in the sand I wrote, inside the border of stones, "James Swinton, Beloved Uncle and Friend, from Carly."

We camped at Kerala for three days. Nobody actually put it into words, but we all seemed to feel fired by a kind of missionary zeal, as if the sight of what the Russians had done had finally brought home to us how truly important it was to help the women in the camp at Chitral. We worked all daylight hours, almost feverishly, filming and recording hours of descriptive dialogue, some written by Tom and some by me, of what had happened in the village that hideous week when their world blew apart.

We got terribly tired. I think the emotional strain was quite severe in the first place, but we had now been a long time without hot water or really clean clothes or anything but the most basic things to eat, and that produced another and different kind of weariness. We began to play a game, imagining wonderful meals in tremendously civilized surroundings, or boiling hot baths with huge fluffy towels to dry ourselves on afterwards, or whole piles of newly ironed crisp clothes, smelling of soap and English wind, not of Afghan river water. Living the sad history of Kerala wasn't very conducive to peaceful nights either, and often, from my own private tent which I had been gallantly given, I could hear the coughs and stumbles round me as one of the others, unable to sleep, paced about restlessly in the moonlight.

Before we left, we had a little ceremony in memory of the men of Kerala. Abdul and Atik and the horsemen, being Muslim, couldn't fathom what we were doing, but they understood it was something deeply respectful to Afghanistan, and stood in a quiet semicircle watching us. We built a little memorial, a cairn of stones, and planted in the top of it a small flowering shrub with yellow plumes, which Tom said was a relation of a buddleia, and which all the nearby butterflies, tortoiseshells, and hairstreaks, immediately fluttered over, like tiny healing spirits. When the cairn was finished we all stood round it, in a ring, for two minutes' silence, a silence broken only by the wind and the sound of the horses, saddled and bridled ready to go, clinking their bits. It was terribly moving, and nobody wanted to break the silence when the two minutes were up.

We rode away at last, in our now familiar caravan, turning the horses' heads southeast back down the long track to Chitral. I couldn't look back as we left. It was rather like the time I left Bewick for London, as if I was afraid to look at something I loved and had to leave. But in leaving Bewick, I always knew I could come back. Leaving Kerala, I not only knew that I wouldn't — and shouldn't — come back, but also that I had left something irrevocably there, part of myself, part of my deepest, most hopeful self, that I would simply now have to learn to live without.

Chapter Twenty-two

The return journey was much quicker than the outward one. Tom, fired by everything he had seen at Kerala, was now eager to get back to the camp and film, as it were, the other half. Andy and Philip had filmed so much of the way the women had walked, fleeing to safety and Pakistan, on our outward journey, that there was little to do on the way back except for odd little incidents, like meeting a boy leading his old grandfather, blinded by a mortar explosion, or a little caravan of lapis merchants who showed us their wares, queer lifeless lumps of bluish stone; nothing, to my eyes, before they were cut and polished.

Atik and his horsemen were also now eager to get shot of us, and be paid, and were as sick as we were of nursing the camera equipment up rough tracks and across whirling rivers. As if they sensed our impatience, all the stallions in our little troop began to fight at every opportunity and we wasted hours, and precious tubes of antiseptic ointment that I had planned to give Selima for the camp dispensary, in doctoring their legs where they had slashed each other open in great gashes. With every mile, we grew more impatient, more fed up with the endless repetition of green tea, maize bread, *dugh,* rice, and stringy chicken and more restive inside our worn, unironed clothes. Andy said even his beard was beginning to hurt.

"A beard can't *hurt* —"

"It can if you don't want the bloody thing any more."

Atik offered to shave all the men and produced a cutthroat razor which had them all fleeing in terror.

"I bet it's what he uses on all those poor goats —"

I rode mostly with Joe. He was easy company, talking about his childhood and his ambitions and was not requiring any response from me. He'd been born in Bradford, and his one aim was to make enough money to buy a cottage in one of the Yorkshire Dales, Wharfedale maybe. He wasn't a poetic man at all, but hearing him talk about the dales even in the simplest way, filled me with a great, urgent longing for home, for beautiful Bewick and, most perversely, for Bishopstow, with its green fields running up to the tamarisks and the silvery dunes that divided the land from the sea. I knew it wasn't any good thinking about Bishopstow, because Bishopstow was gone, but I couldn't stop myself feeling that if only Bishopstow were still there to go to, Uncle James would in some mysterious, benevolent way, still be there too.

We slept each night in the villages we had slept in on the way up, knowing which tea houses to avoid because of the fleas, or filth, or the greed of the owner, and which camping spots to make for. It was odd how familiar the track seemed, after only one previous journey on it, and how this curious, slow, traveling life had become so natural that I could hardly remember the flavor of the other one, full of cars and planes and television. And noise. We had, for weeks now, known no noise except that made by wind and water and hooves.

Our last night in Afghanistan, I couldn't sleep at all. I'd got quite good at sleeping anywhere, and felt that I could probably now sleep, like any self-respecting Indian, on a railway platform but this last night we spent on the flower-speckled turfy cliff outside the very first magical village we had come to after the pass from Pakistan. I suppose, despite my resolution only to look forward, I was haunted by memories. I had last lain in this place, looking at the star-spangled sky, believing that Tom was beginning to love me. "I like spoiling you," he'd said, and I had taken that to mean what I wanted it to mean — the romantic indulgence of a man towards a girl he hopes will be his. Well, I'd been wrong about that. I'd been wrong about a lot of things besides, but that had been the most painful mistake. Perhaps, I thought, shifting slightly to avoid a lump in my grassy mattress, it would all be easier to bear when Tom wasn't within sight and sound of me all day, and sleeping peacefully six feet from me at night. On the other hand, however stern I was with myself, the thought of *not* seeing him every day filled me with something close to panic.

We all got up the next morning feeling a little subdued at the thought of leaving Afghanistan — all that is, except our horsemen, who now felt

Garam Chasma was within sight, and with it, payday. The village women came out to bid us farewell, and gave us handfuls of dried mulberries as a parting present, and we rode away up the valley towards the pass, looking back at them from time to time, and they waved and waved, their dresses and scarves bright against the silvery weathered wood of their pretty carved houses. I'm not very religious, but I couldn't help praying that someone, somewhere would keep those villagers safe, and allow them to go on living their timeless, simple, sheltered lives in their heavenly valley.

"Carly," Andy said, "stop sniveling."

"I'm not —"

"Yes, you are. You're a sentimental twit." He gave a loud sniff.

"Look at you!"

Andy pointed ahead.

"And him."

Tom was riding with his head bent, and his face buried in his shirt sleeve on an upflung arm.

"I'm not looking at him any more," I said slowly.

"Sorry," Andy said. "Sorry," and urged his pony on ahead of mine.

It was a long, hard day, toiling up to the summit, leaving the green valley behind and crossing that huge treacherous, patchy snowfield which I had ridden down before in such elation. We came to the border post in the early afternoon, and the policeman who had tried to extort a bribe from us came out of the *koffi*, and lounged on the steps, picking his teeth with a matchstick and endeavoring to indicate that as far as he was concerned, our departure from Afghanistan was good riddance to bad rubbish. We stopped for tea on the far side of the border village, and ate a sort of lunch, memorable only because it was composed of the last of our rations, including Joe's last packet of fruit gums, some queer-tasting Afghan butter bought in the last village, the final tin of sardines, a handful of lifeboat biscuits Philip had been hoarding, and a poor little roasted bird on a stick, no bigger than a thrush, which Atik presented to me, with great ceremony, as a tribute from him and his men. I had grown quite ingenious about dealing with these gruesome little niceties of Afghan etiquette, so I thanked him profusely, took the pathetic little object away behind a bush as if I were going to eat it modestly out of the sight of male eyes, buried it, and returned with the empty stick, smacking my lips.

After lunch, we rode on. We rode all down the valley into Pakistan, past the place where we had met the man with the sled, and across the lovely water meadow with its little stone mill and the rocks among which I had read Ma's letter about Uncle James. It felt like a lifetime ago, not just in time, but in experience, as if the Carly who had ridden up that pass wasn't really at all the same person as the Carly who was riding back down it. Whatever had happened to me, good and bad, joyful and sad, had made me in some curious way, stronger. I had set out into Afghanistan to find Charlotte, but in a sense, and perhaps because I hadn't been looking for it, I felt I had found myself.

As dusk was falling, we toiled, weary and dusty, into Garam Chasma. After the beauties of Afghanistan, it looked even more squalid and scruffy, and the noise in the narrow streets was perfectly awful. We clattered on obediently, behind Atik, to a strange dusty kind of square on the eastern edge of the town, where the local boys plainly played football, and probably war games too, and there, parked in the middle, looking as sleek and shining and out of place as a spaceship, stood Nasir's Japanese jeep, all ready and waiting to take us back to Chitral.

Nasir's courtyard felt like a five-star hotel. "Feel that," Joe said reverently, laying his hand on his charpoy, as if it was a goose feather bed. "Bloody paradise."

Selima and her mother and aunts and cousins had prepared a celebration dinner for us, a dinner worthy of great conquerors, not just a weary, grimy film crew, and had, even better, boiled up huge pots of water for washing in with even a special, private one for me which they carried behind screens in a corner of the courtyard. Never in my whole life will any bath, however opulent and scented with exotic oils, be as luxurious as that copper pot of hot water in the open air, balanced on three bricks. I didn't wash, I scrubbed. I scrubbed so violently that the bits of me that weren't pale golden from the sun went bright scarlet and tingled. Then Selma brought me more water for my hair, and cold water for my teeth and — oh wonder of wonders — some of the clothes I had left in her keeping, smooth and soft and light, and best of all, really *clean*. When I had finished, I not only felt revived to the point of exhilaration, but like a princess, a barefoot princess with red hair, a pale brown face, neck and hands, white everything else, clothed in a tunic and trousers of pale green cotton made by a bazaar tailor in Islamabad for sixty rupees and which couldn't, in my eyes, have been exceeded that night by the finest couturier in Paris. The crowning touch was Selima coming behind my screens to tell me that I looked quite suitable, and that, as a special favor for all I was doing for the women of Kerala, I should be allowed that night to eat Western fashion, with the rest of the crew.

Selima's mother had exceeded herself and we had the whole culinary works, palao and meatballs and coriander-flavored rice and roast lamb and yogurt and spiced cucumbers and omelettes and something called *ashak*, which were like pockets of ravioli, stuffed with leeks. We ate and ate, and when we had got to the stage of wanting to lie about on the floor and groan, we were given sweetmeats flavored with walnuts and rosewater, and pistachio nuts, and cherries, and sultanas soaked in pomegranate juice, and almonds — and green tea.

"*Chai-i-Sabz,*" cried Selima's mother, plonking down the tea urn, "*Chai-i-Sabz!*"

The Nasir came in, with all our mail from England that the faithful Christopher Tindall had sent up from Islamabad, and there were four letters from Ma, and one from Simon and one from Matthew in which he asked me, in the baldest way possible, to become his permanent assistant at a salary of thirteen and a half thousand a year.

"Your absence," he wrote, "has made me realize I could do worse than hang on to you."

I wanted to laugh and to cry. I felt so full of well-being, and so touched by his brusque compliment, and so thrilled and relieved to have some kind of future to go home to. I looked up, wanting to catch one of the others' eye, to communicate my elation — and I saw Tom. He was sitting where he had sat all dinner, cross-legged on the floor opposite me across the low table, dressed in clean, faded jeans, and a soft blue shirt, the sleeves rolled up to the elbow as was his habit. In his hand, he held a little packet of letters, perhaps half a dozen of them, all in the same square white airmail envelopes. I recognized the envelopes, and the clear writing on the top one. Tom was holding his letters from Laura, and he was gazing down at them in awe, as if they were a kind of miracle.

The next few weeks were grueling. Selima had capitalized on all I had said to Halima before I left, and a variety of grudging and complicated permissions had been given for our filming in Kerala Camp. The only thing she was adamant about was the filming of women — the Muslim laws of modesty would never permit it.

Tom had a brainwave. He got several rolls of the still film that Philip and Andy had taken in Kerala, developed and printed in Chitral —

needless to say, Nasir had a cousin with a dark-room which he would rent to Andy for a few hours at a very competitive rate — and he gave these to me to show to Halima.

I wasn't at all prepared for her reaction. She sat, cross-legged in her tent as I had left her, peering in the gloom at these pictures of the place that had been her world, and as she looked at them, she quietly dissolved, like a candle melting, until she was lying on the ground completely racked with grief. I was desperately sorry for her, but I was equally desperate to gain my point.

"If you help us, we can help you in return. If the West sees what you have lost, there is at least a chance of your getting it back again. Let us film your women, and your sons can rebuild Kerala."

She agreed in the end. A few women, the younger ones less steeped in a lifetime of veiling, might show themselves to the camera from a distance, but never with their faces bare. It was a triumph. I went racing back to Chitral and we celebrated with Panther Beer from the local brewery which gave us all headaches.

Then the filming began. It was unbearably hot, and dusty, and the crew were appalled at the conditions in the camp.

"And this is *good* camp," Selima said.

At first, no one would come near us, not even near me whom I hoped they felt they now knew, but then the odd child, like an inquisitive kitten, began to stray towards the men and the cameras. The first one was a little boy, perhaps six or seven, wearing a ragged khaki shirt and a Chitrali cap too big for him, and an expression at once merry and watchful. He came within ten feet and then stopped.

Tom went down on his hunkers in the dust, so that he was more at the boy's level. He didn't move, or speak, he just waited. The boy came a little further, his eyes darting from Tom's watch to his belt buckle to his sunglasses. Tom took off his glasses and held them out. The boy snatched them, put them on and began to caper about, giggling.

"You're the camp clown," Tom said, "aren't you?"

The boy came right up to him and peered at his face cheekily through the too-big black lenses. Tom put his arm round the thin, swollen-bellied little body, and for a few seconds the boy leaned against him, trusting and innocent, and I caught a glimpse of Tom's expression and had to look away hastily before the jagged lump in my throat exploded into tears.

That child was the beginning. He was called Khalili and he had two brothers and a sister, and a thin, exhausted mother who looked old enough to be their grandmother. Khalili's oldest brother had been dragged down the village paths by the Russians to watch his father and his grandfather and his uncles being shot, and he told his story straight to camera, Selima softly interpreting. After Khalili's family, they all came, even some of the women, shyly holding their scarves and shawls across their mouths, and at the end, like some kind of crowning glory, Halima emerged from her tent and from behind her veil described, at great and eloquent length, how life had once been in Kerala, the happy, natural, unsophisticated life of that mountain-locked village among its fields and orchards and flocks of sheep and goats.

"We gave money," Halima said. "We sold our jewelry and our household things for money to buy guns to help the mujahideen, and so, of course, we were doomed. I do not regret what we did, and I will never forgive what they did."

We stood round her in silence afterwards, Joe still holding out the microphone in a kind of trance, even though we didn't understand exactly what she had said. But we understood the spirit of it all right.

"And we won't forget," Tom said, for all of us, motioning to Selima to translate. "We won't forget either."

Chapter Twenty-three

"You're so thin!" Patsy Tindall wailed. She twirled me round as if I were a stand of birthday cards in a news agent's. "Look at you! Nothing of you —"

"I've been eating," I said truthfully, "I ate all the time. I always do."

"Well, it's simply not fair, in that case. You look absolutely stunning. Your hair's bleached and you've got the best kind of tan like a pale cornflake, and you're as slender as a wand. *And* you've been a heroine, I gather."

"I haven't —"

"Yes, you have. Tom said so. What's the matter with Tom?"

I looked across at her, startled. We were in her little upstairs sitting room in Isamabad — "my boudoir," she called it — whose prettiness and comfort looked quite breathtaking to me after all those weeks of tents and bivvy bags. On the low table between two cushioned cane armchairs was a tray bearing cups and a pot of coffee, and the smell of coffee, after all those weeks of green tea, was enough to make me almost faint with longing.

"I don't think anything's the matter. In fact, he was the only one who didn't succumb to Afghan tummy —"

"Oh, I don't mean that, he's got a constitution

like iron. I mean his mood. He's frightfully subdued, almost depressed."

I said carefully, "The sight of Kerala was pretty
upsetting."

Patsy went over to the table and filled our
coffee cups. She was wearing a little short shift of
coral-colored cotton spotted in white and she
looked as new and neat as a doll.

"That was weeks ago. *I* think —" she stopped.

"What do you think?"

"I think you and Tom have had a run-in."

If I have any say over the characteristics I have
or don't have in my next life, one thing I'll do
without is blushing. I'm a simply hopeless, instant blusher and I hate it. Nobody with red hair
should have to be so prone to blushing — I end
up looking like a blood orange. I could feel myself, now, flaming with color all up my face and
neck in a horrible, hot tide.

"Oh God," Patsy said, staring at me. "You
didn't go and make a pass at him, did you? I *told*
you how it was with him and Laura."

"He told me too," I mumbled, dropping my
head so that my hair would swing concealingly
forward.

"That's what's the matter then," Patsy said triumphantly. "He's in an agony of remorse. He's
got the world's most neurotic conscience. What
were you playing at?"

"I wasn't playing!" I said crossly.

"But you knew —"

"Did you mean to fall in love with Christopher? Did you *intend* to?"

"No, of course not, but he —"

"Well, then," I said furiously, "it was just jolly lucky for you, wasn't it, that he didn't have a Laura in tow when you fell for him."

Patsy said stiffly, "Laura's a splendid person."

Forgetting all the rules of good manners due to one's host, I said sarcastically, "Oh I'm *so* glad."

"You *have* got it badly, haven't you —"

I marched to the door. I was simmering with rage, not just with Patsy's making love sound like an attack of the measles, but also for her insinuation that the little smug quartet of herself and Christopher and Tom and Laura was completely impervious and indifferent to anyone outside their charmed circle.

"You need a bad fright, Patsy Tindall," I said. "You need to suffer a bit and then you might have a little more tolerance for people outside your gilded cage."

Then I went out and, I'm ashamed to say, I slammed the door. I stamped down the beautifully polished staircase and out into the courtyard, which was full of eye-aching midday sunlight. The only person there was Joe, whistling tunelessly while he blew dust out of all his precious equipment before packing it up for the flight home.

I flopped down beside him in the shade of a tree.

"It's time I went home. I've just been very rude to our hostess."

"Tut tut," Joe said, going on blowing and polishing.

"Tom will be furious, he's such a stickler for manners."

"Shouldn't think he'll notice. Seems in some kind of daze —"

"Dreaming of Laura —"

Joe shot me a look. "You reckon?"

"I do. So does Patsy."

"She thinks she owns him."

I gave a little snort. "He seems to have that sort of effect on women."

"One day," Joe said, "he'll learn. He'll learn where he's best off, where he's got room to breathe. But maybe that'll be too late. Just keep your hair on, Carly. Nine hours and we'll be out of here."

"I know," I said soberly. "I want it and I dread it."

"It's the transition. It's never easy."

"And it's so *fast*. At least in Charlotte's day you did things at a human pace, in ships or on foot or horseback, now we just hurtle from one kind of life to another and we have to change gear in a second. It *must* have been easier for her."

"Don't you believe it," Joe said. He did up the last neat buckle. "Life never was easy. Not for anyone." He leaned forward and gave me an un-expected peck on the cheek. "I shouldn't think it's easy for Patsy, either, even if she does look as if she's got everything. You go and say sorry."

"Joe!"

"Go on," he said, "You're a great girl but that doesn't mean you don't need your bottom smacked sometimes. Do what Uncle Joe says and then we can all fly away with a clear conscience."

We boarded our plane late that night. The

Tindalls came to see us off, and when I saw the undisguised envy on Patsy's face at seeing us returning to England, I felt a sharp pang of remorse that I'd flown off the handle at her. I'd done as Joe said, and apologized, and to my surprise, Patsy had only replied, "That's okay, Carly. It's just that nothing's as secure as it looks, everything's so fragile," but when I asked her to explain she wouldn't say any more, simply shook her head and changed the subject.

We were all rather quiet, getting on to the plane. It was completely full, one of those huge wide-bodied jets crammed with people, none of whom seemed to be taking any notice of the cabin crew or the lights instructing them to sit down and belt up. I found myself next to Philip, which was something of a relief because I knew he wouldn't expect to be talked to all the way home and indeed would object if I tried.

It was a horrible flight, noisy, hot and cramped. We were all scattered about the plane for some reason, so there was no chance of an end of trip party, and sleep was out of the question because of the ceaseless chattering of all the other passengers and the running about of all their endless children. I like children usually, but I didn't like them on that aeroplane. I tried to sit back, breathe deeply and count my blessings (my health, my family, my future on *Marshalls* magazine, my flat, my car) and all I felt was a terrible restlessness and a sensation that all my nerves were screaming like a badly tuned violin. The calm I had felt only recently as we left Afghanistan seemed to have quite deserted me. I could only think that the adventure was now over, that I had gained nothing from it, and that I was in grave danger of seizing the next little Pakistani child who ran yelling down the aisle, and throttling it.

The face that greeted me the next day in the huge mirror of the ladies' at Heathrow was a pretty discouraging sight. I was pale green with fatigue, there were dark shadows under my eyes and my hair, which I had washed in Patsy's wonderful bathroom just before we left, hadn't liked the flight any more than I had, and hung lank and lifeless-looking. I splashed my face with cold water and brushed my teeth, and tied my hair back with a scarf, but I still looked like someone who'd spent the night in an opium den.

I pushed my way back through the milling crowds to the carousel where our luggage was supposed to be appearing. Anticlimax was making everyone snappish, and they were all standing about, slightly hunched, as if resisting the transition back to the real world. Tom was talking about editing the film and how we should have to have a lot of meetings and the others were grunting and making noncommittal noises. I suspected that they were all, like me, trying not to long to be back on a mountain track in Afghanistan, where there were no crowds and no pressures, but only those wild, wonderful distances that man could never tame.

It took almost an hour for all our luggage to appear, and there were panics that a bag of microphones had gone missing and then, even worse, a taped-up box containing over a hundred reels of film. Finally, for the last time, we loaded all our unwieldy bags and cases on to a whole caravan of trolleys, and set off into the outside world. Needless to say, we were stopped in customs, and every single piece of our baggage was searched, and they even went over our passports again as if we had somehow fooled passport control into thinking we were innocent when we weren't. When they gave our passports back, they handed them all to me, as if I was Wendy to all the Lost Boys, and then stood watching while we crammed all our jumble-sale-looking possessions back into bags that suddenly seemed far too small for them.

At last we were outside, in English September air, in an English queue, waiting for an English taxi. I handed everyone's passport back.

"Hang onto it a sec," Tom said, wrestling with his luggage. "I haven't got a hand —"

"Shall we share a cab?" Andy asked me. I nodded gratefully, stuffing Tom's passport and mine into my pocket so that I had both hands free to combine my luggage with Andy's.

"I'd love to. I'd hate to go alone."

"It's always like this, the end of a trip. You think you're longing for home, but it's never like you think it's going to be."

Saying goodbye was extremely hard. As each taxi came up, one or two of us got in and we all hugged each other and said goodbye and good luck and it was a real wrench. When it came to my turn to kiss Tom, I could hardly look at him in case I saw the happiness in his face at the prospect of being reunited with Laura. I just bumped my cheek against his.

"Bye, Tom. It's been great, it really has. Thank you so much for making it possible for me to come —"

"Couldn't have done it without you —"

"Come on, Carly, get in —"

"I'll ring you."

"Yes," I said. "Thanks."

"Give my best to Matthew —"

I nodded. Andy gave me a shove into the cab and I nearly missed the seat for the floor.

"Honestly," Andy said, "you don't half pile on the agony." He leaned forward, giving the driver my address, and then his own in Battersea. Then he sat back beside me and took my hand. "We could always go roller-skating again, you know."

I glanced at him. His funny thin face was dark brown, except for his nose, which was peeling.

"I'd like that."

"What are you going to do tonight?"

"I'll have supper with my brother. He's been using my flat. And then I'll sleep —"

"Tomorrow, maybe?"

"Andy," I said, "I'd love to go roller-skating, if you see what I mean, but I'm not back where I was."

There was a little pause and then he dropped my hand and said, "I guess not. I'm just a hopeful kind of guy —"

"And a really nice one."

He pulled a face, and then began to talk resolutely of other things, of how the process of editing the film still lay ahead, and about the crucial question of getting it scheduled for the right television slot and how much I could do, via the magazine, to publicize it. I was too tired and disoriented to take in much of what he said, so I just sat and listened and watched the oddly orderly lines of traffic on the M4 swish by us, and in what could have been either minutes or hours, we seemed to be in Fulham and there was my front door, black and battered, with, I could have sworn it, exactly the same hamburger cartons lying on the pavement in front of it as I had seen lying there in June.

Andy heaved all my luggage out onto the pavement.

"I'll come up with you."

"No," I said, "it's sweet of you but I can manage. Jamie'll be there."

"Sure?"

"Quite sure."

I turned and put my key in the lock. Andy put an arm around my shoulders and kissed my cheek.

"See you, Carly," he said. "See you on the cutting-room floor," and then he climbed back into the taxi and it bore him away into the traffic. It was all now, finally, over.

There was no Jamie in the flat. It was quite empty, and I could see that, according to his lights, Jamie had made a huge effort to tidy it. The bed was made, even if it did look as if a dog had tried to do it, and although the wastepaper basket was full, there was no rubbish on the floor, and no dirty mugs or glasses or socks. But it looked forlorn somehow, and neglected, and dust lay on every surface like a fine coating of gray flour. On the table, there was, very touchingly, a bunch of white lilies stuffed just anyhow into one of my Indian pots, a tall blue and turquoise vase from Jaipur. The sight of them made me feel a bit tearful; lilies were special in our family because of Duncan's habit of giving them to Ma on special days, those magnificent, glowing, copper-colored ones that matched her hair.

By the lilies was a note.

"Dear Carly," Jamie had written, "I'm really sorry not to be here to welcome you but I got asked to an ace party at home, so I've bunked off. Your car's parked outside Amanda's house, FULL OF PETROL, you'll be glad to hear, I thought it would be safer there. It's been AMAZING having your flat, I'm really grateful. I've left you some wine in the fridge and all your letters are in the Tesco carrier bag. Ma says to ring her. See you soon. Love and kisses, Jamie."

I read the note three times, then I found the Tesco carrier bag and looked, without much enthusiasm, through the contents, which all seemed to be bills or envelopes from banks and credit card companies. I dumped the pile on the table and decided not to look at it again before I'd had some sleep. I thought about ringing home, and decided I'd better not do that until I felt less gloomy or Ma would panic and think I'd brought back some Asian plague and was at death's door. Instead I roamed round the room which seemed at once familiar and unfamiliar, as if Jamie's personality had temporarily overlaid mine, and I would have to give the place time to remember that I was the rightful owner. I sat down on the sort-of-made bed and looked around me and gave way to the utmost depression.

After a while, I lay down, pulling the pillow round my neck for comfort. Perhaps if I just went to sleep for a bit, I would wake up more in my right mind and able to face the thought of unpacking and telephoning and generally picking up the threads of life again. I had vowed to myself at Kerala that I would not look back, only forward, that I would endeavor to behave in a positive, grown-up manner, but somehow that had been easier to do there than it was in what seemed a lonely, neglected, sad little room in London. I closed my eyes on it all, and waited for sleep.

It didn't come. I lay there for fully twenty minutes and felt no more drowsy at the end of them than at the beginning. I was just starting to tick myself off and tell myself that I must get up and shower and pull myself together, when the buzzer to the front door rang. I got up without much enthusiasm, and trailed across the room and leaned against the wall by the intercom button.

"Yes?" I said into the speaker.

"Carly? Carly, it's Tom —"

My hand went automatically to my pocket.

"Of course. I've still got your passport —"

"Yes —"

"Come on up," I said, and went tiredly across the room to open the door.

Chapter Twenty-four

I heard the street door slam; then I heard his feet on the stairs. I wondered whether to go out onto the landing to meet him, but discovered that I was oddly reluctant to move, so I simply stayed where I was, standing a few feet inside the open door.

He stopped for a moment when he saw me, and then he came in, rather hesitantly, and closed the door behind him.

"So sorry," he said. "Such a stupid thing to do, forgetting my passport —"

I pulled it out of my pocket and held it out to him.

"Doesn't matter," I said.

He held the passport for several seconds, looking down at it, then he slid it into the back pocket of his trousers, and said, "Carly —"

I didn't, for some reason, feel particularly helpful. I just said, "Yes?" and waited. Tom cleared his throat.

"I wanted . . . I wanted to say something to you. I felt I'd acted insensitively while we were away, and that I hadn't apologized properly and —" he stopped.

I said nothing. I could hardly believe myself, but I didn't feel my whole future hung on what he said next. I went over to the table and began to rearrange the poor lilies into a softer, more natural shape.

"I've never had a filming trip like that one," Tom began again. "I've had plenty of moving or terrible experiences, but none that were as poignant as that expedition, or as powerful. And I have to admit that it was you who made the difference, not just because of what you achieved in the camp, but because of your reaction to everything. I saw so much with a completely different dimension, through your eyes. I think I understood more about the human condition in all its needs and desires than I've ever done. I just wanted you to know how much I appreciated that, how much I value it."

For some reason, my right hand gave a little involuntary jerk, and broke off a lily head.

"Damn," I said, and then, politely, "Thank you."

Tom came across the room and stood the other side of the table from me, so that the lilies were between us.

"I don't think I'm saying what I'm trying to say very well."

I said, "Well, I can't help you, I'm afraid, because I don't know what it is you're *trying* to say."

He put his hands on the table and leaned towards me.

"Could you look at me?"

I raised my eyes from the flower head in my hand, and found to my amazement that I could, quite steadily.

"I hope," Tom said earnestly, "that you'll come with me on the next trip. I'm planning one to

Peru. I hope you'll allow me to think of you as the first person in my crew from now on because I really don't think I could do without you, now that I know what a huge contribution you make. What I want, I suppose, is a reassurance from you that you've . . . quite forgiven me for that scene on the way to Kerala, and that you'll consent to be my assistant but with far more input than I could allow you this time."

I caught my breath. I laid the lily flower down on the dusty table very carefully, and then I walked away at a measured pace, and stood for several seconds looking down at my rumpled bed. It was most extraordinary, but I felt quite calm, and more than that, I felt confident, almost resolute. Then I turned round and went back to the table.

Tom was still waiting there, his open face as open as ever. I looked at it for a few seconds, that face that had haunted my days and my dreams for so many months, and then I said, "You're a lovely man, Tom, and an interesting and kind and brave one. But you are also very unimaginative and a terrible prig."

He straightened up. His expression didn't exactly darken, but it grew extremely puzzled.

"Carly!"

"I did love you," I said, "I did, desperately. I still do in a way because you can't just switch off deep, true emotions, like lights, the moment they become inconvenient. I understand exactly what you feel for me — a huge amount of friendly affection but loving someone else — because that is precisely what I feel for Andy. But I also understand something that you don't seem to have a clue about, compassionate though you generally are. I understand about needing to keep one's dignity. I probably shan't see any more of Andy, because of his dignity, his self-esteem, and because I genuinely want him to recover. You must now do the same for me."

I felt rather exhilarated at the end of this speech. It was certainly the most high-minded utterance of my life, and I hoped I hadn't sounded as priggish as I'd accused Tom of being. He was looking at me very strangely. After a pause, while I tried to descend from my lofty moral pinnacle, he said, "You are wonderful."

Suddenly I was cross. I didn't like the reverence in his voice, and abruptly, I didn't want this kind of compliment to change the atmosphere between us.

"I'm certainly not," I snapped. "Almost nobody is."

"You are," he said. There was a queer excited look in his eye, which alarmed me.

I said, "Go home, Tom." I marched across to the door and held it open. "Home to Laura," I said, "quick march."

He looked at me.

"But what are you going to do?"

"I don't know."

"Back to work for Matthew, I suppose —"

Quite without meaning to I said, "Oh no."

"No? But Carly —"

"Tom," I said sharply, "will you please go home and leave me to unpack?"

"But will you be all right?"

"Not," I said, "unless you go away."

He came slowly towards me, and then he stopped in front of me and bent and kissed my cheek. His cheek was rough against mine, after the unshaven night on the plane. For a split second, I closed my eyes, and then I snapped them open again, put my free hand on his shoulder and gave him a brisk shove out on to the landing.

"Bye, Tom," I said. "Thanks for everything. And love to Laura."

Then I shut the door. I leaned there for some moments, feeling slightly stunned, and then I went across to my bed and sat on it and realized with a kind of wonder that the last few minutes with Tom had been balanced on a sharp emotional knife edge and then, with a leap of exhilaration, that it was *me* who had taken charge and pushed him out of the room, not the other way about. I hadn't been left; I had done the dismissing. I might not have wanted to, in the least, but I had known it was both the right, and the only thing to do, and I had done it.

I stooped down and unlaced my long-suffering and now very battered canvas boots. Then I took them off, and swung my feet on to the bed, and lay down with my hands behind my head. I considered myself. It was absolutely no good pretending that there wasn't an ache in my heart, the ache of loss and of dashed hopes, but it was an ache that I now knew that time and my future would gradually soothe away. I had supposed, in my rather childish way, that I was exactly like all the women of my extraordinary family, and destined to love one man, and one only, and that that man would form my life and my whole commitment. I had certainly thought that when I met Tom. I had even said "The Big One" to myself with a kind of excited awe and felt exhilarated and enslaved. But already, despite the pain in my heart, I could see that I was different. I was a different generation, for one thing, and I had very different chances. Tom was not the love of my life; he was my first love, and with a glimmer of a smile at the ceiling, I thought I could even congratulate myself on choosing such a man as the object of my first real passion.

The thing was, I realized, staring up at the graceful cobweb which swung gently in the draft below the center light, that I didn't, however much I thought I wanted Tom, want to lose myself in any man. I had thought I did, but the last strange, wonderful, eye-opening months had taught me to know better than that. I could feel a dawning certainty that one day I should fall in love again, and perhaps for good this time, but that I shouldn't, that second, better time, be such a slave to love. Instead, I should be its partner, its companion, I should find myself equal to it, not its victim.

In the meantime, I wanted something else. I had felt cross and restless coming home and had supposed, out of habit, that I was still miserably chafing against Tom's rejection of me. Now I began to feel that it wasn't Tom I was missing so keenly, and had been missing since we left Chitral, but rather Afghanistan. I was missing the mountains and the freedom and the adventure; I was missing those wonderful, exasperating women in Kerala Camp; I was missing, above all, that rich, marvelous sense of purpose which I had had there, the sense of achievement, the sense of being really, truly useful. Hundreds of girls could go and work on magazines, even for Matthew Mott, but perhaps not very many could cope productively with life in a refugee camp.

I sat up. I didn't feel excited, I simply felt full of a steady, pleased resolve, as if I'd come upon the answer to a crucial question, an answer which had been quietly waiting there, for a long time, for me to find. I swung my legs off the bed and looked round the room which I had felt so powerfully to be mine. I didn't feel that any more. It was a nice room, and it was my first independent home, but I didn't feel any more at home in it, or possessively about it, than I had about my charpoy by the orange tree in Nasir's whitewashed courtyard. Such things didn't seem to matter now. There would probably come a time in the future when the place where I lived, and my possessions, would matter very much, just as there would probably come a time when I met the real love of my life, but that time certainly wasn't now, and what's more, I wasn't in any hurry for it to come. I felt, for the first time in my whole life, released — released from all my frustrations and longings because I knew where I was going.

I was going back to Chitral. I was going back to find Selima, to offer myself to her to use in the camp in whatever way she thought best. I had, to my sorrow, no useful training like medicine, but I could at the very least teach English to the children, and thus offer them the chance of a passport out of the prison of being a refugee, into the world of being a citizen. There would be a lot to work out, to decide, to organize but nothing that would prove impossible. I could start by gently telling Duncan that I wanted to sell my car to raise some money — Duncan! Ma! I'd been home almost three hours and had got so engrossed in my self-revelation that I hadn't even telephoned.

I jumped up, and as if by telepathy, the telephone began to shrill. I dashed across the room and seized the receiver.

"Hello?"

"Darling!"

"Ma! Oh, Ma, how lovely to hear you, I was just going to ring —"

"Carly, darling Carly, how are you, how was it?"

I sat down on the floor and put the telephone on my lap.

"I'm brilliant. Never better. It was wonderful, the best thing I've ever done in my life."

"Were you ill?"

I grinned into the telephone. Ma never changed.

"The faintest tummy twinge. Nothing more. Honestly, you're hopeless —"

She was laughing, in spite of herself.

"And did you find Charlotte?"

"No," I said, "I found me."

"What do you mean?"

"Ma," I said, "are you sitting comfortably?"

"Of course I am. I'm sitting where I always sit, in the kitchen, on the stool so I can see out of the window while I talk. Why? Why do you ask?"

I felt my whole face illumined by a huge, helpless smile, a smile of hope, of love for Ma sitting there in Scotland, and of faith in my future.

"Because," I said, "I've got something very exciting to tell you."